ACKNOWLEDGMENTS

To my lovely wife, Lysa, for once again keeping things together. To my editor, Emily Bestler, who came up with some great ideas that made this novel better than it would have been without her. To Sarah Branham for all of her hard work. To Jack Romanos and Carolyn Reidy of Simon & Schuster for all of their support. To Paolo Pepe and the art department at Atria Books for coming up with a great cover. To Larry Norton and the Simon & Schuster sales force for all of their tireless work. To Judith Curr of Atria Books and Louise Burke of Pocket Books, and all of the other folks who fall under the S&S umbrella who helped put this book together and get it out the door.

To my agent, Sloan Harris, and Katherine Cluverius at ICM for all of your hard work and candid advice. To Carl Pohlad for all of your generosity and friendship, and for providing me with a quiet place to write. To Larry Johnson for once again being an endless source of information. To Sean Stone for backstopping me on a few ideas. To Bill Harlow, the director of public affairs for the CIA, for once again patiently answering an endless stream of questions. To Paul Evancoe, a retired SEAL commander, who was kind enough to offer me his wisdom. To FBI Special Agent Brad Garrett, who has devoted an entire career to locking up the bad guys. And as always to all of my sources who wish to remain anonymous. Any mistakes in this novel are mine and mine alone.

To Sloan Harris

VINCE FLYNN
EXECUTIVE POWER

**SIMON &
SCHUSTER**

London · New York · Sydney · Toronto · New Delhi

A CBS COMPANY

First published in Great Britain by Simon & Schuster UK Ltd, 2003
This edition first published by Simon & Schuster UK Ltd, 2011
A CBS COMPANY

1 3 5 7 9 10 8 6 4 2

Simon & Schuster UK Ltd
Africa House
64-78 Kingsway
London WC2B 6AH

Simon & Schuster Australia
Sydney

www.simonandschuster.co.uk

A CIP catalogue record for this book is available
from the British Library

ISBN: 978-1-84983-562-6

Printed in the UK by CPI Cox & Wyman, Reading, Berkshire RG1 8EX

Vince Flynn is an international No. 1 bestseller, published in 20 countries. He lives in Minneapolis with his wife and three children. Visit his website at www.vinceflynn.com.

Also by Vince Flynn

PRELUDE

The sleek gray craft sliced through the warm water and humid night air of the Philippine Sea at twenty-five knots, its twin engines rumbling toward its destination with a guttural moan. The boat was in violation of international law and at least one treaty, but the men on board didn't care. Technicalities, legalities and diplomacy were for other people to sort out, people who sat in comfortable leather chairs with Ivy League degrees matted and framed on their office walls. The men standing on the deck of the Mark V special operations craft were here to get a job done, and in their minds, it was a job that should have been taken care of months ago.

The low profile Mark V special operations craft was designed to sneak in under radar. It had been designed specifically for the United States Navy SEALs, and it was their choice of platform when running maritime insertions. It was eighty-two feet in length but the boat only drafted five feet when it was fully loaded and dead in the water. Instead of the standard screw it was propelled by two waterjets. All of this allowed the boat to maneuver very close to the beach with great precision.

Five men wearing black flight helmets and night vision

goggles manned four .50-caliber machine guns and a 40mm grenade launcher. Eight other men dressed in jungle BDUs and floppy hats sat on the gunwales of the rubber combat raiding craft they would soon launch off the Mark V and went over their equipment for at least the tenth time. Their faces were smeared with warlike green and black camouflage paint, but their expressions were calm.

Lieutenant Jim Devolis looked down at his SEAL squad and watched them go through their last check. He'd observed them doing it countless times before and for some reason it always reminded him of baboons picking bugs from each other at the zoo. They meticulously examined their H harnesses to make sure every snap was secure and all grenades taped. The communications gear was checked and rechecked. Fresh batteries had been placed in everyone's night vision goggles, and along with backup batteries the expensive optical devices were stowed in waterproof pouches attached to their H harnesses. Weapons were sandproofed with condoms secured over the muzzles and a bead of silicone sealant around the magazines and bolt covers. The only person wearing a rucksack tonight would be the squad's medical corpsman, and Devolis sincerely hoped they wouldn't be needing his expertise. The group was traveling light tonight. No MREs, only a couple of Power Bars for each man. The plan was to be in and out before the sun came up. Just the way the SEALs liked it.

The tension grew as they neared the demarcation point. Devolis was glad to see that the jaw-jacking had subsided. It was time to get serious. Turning his head to the right and down, his lips found the tube for his neoprene camel water pack and he sucked in a mouthful of fresh water. The men had been drinking all the water they could hold for two days. Hydration before an op in this part of the world was crucial. Even at night the temperature was still in the mid-eighties and the humidity wasn't far behind. The only thing that was keeping them from sweating through their BDUs was the breeze created by the boat as it cruised at twenty-plus knots. Once they hit the beach, though, that would change. They had a two-mile hike ahead of them through the thick tropical jungle. Even with all the water they'd drunk in the last two days, each man on the team would probably lose five to ten pounds just hiking in and out.

A firm hand fell on Devolis's shoulder. He turned to look at the captain of the boat.

"Two minutes out, Jim. Get your boys loaded up."

Devolis nodded once and blinked, his white eyes glowing bright against the dark camouflage paint spread across his face. "Thanks, Pat." The two men had practiced this drill hundreds of times back in Coronado, California, at the headquarters for Naval Special Warfare Group One.

"Don't go wandering off on me now," Devolis said with a wide grin.

The captain smiled in the manner of someone who's confident in his professional ability. "If you call, I'll be there guns a'blazin'."

"That's what I like to hear." Devolis nodded and then turned to his men. With his forefinger pointed straight up he made a circular motion and the SEALs instantly got to their feet. A moment later the boat slowed to just under five knots.

The Mark V, in addition to being extremely fast, also came with a slanted aft deck that allowed it to launch and receive small craft without stopping. Without a word the men grabbed the sides of their black CRRC with the forty-horsepower outboard leading and walked down the aft ramp. The men stopped at the end of the ramp just shy of the Mark V's frothy white wake and set the rubber boat on the nonskid deck, the lower unit of the outboard hanging in the water. A crew member from the Mark V held on to the rubber boat's bow line and looked for each man to give him a thumbs-up. All eight men were low in the boat clutching their handholds. One by one they returned the sign.

The call came over the headset that the launch was a go and the crewman tossed the bow line into the boat. A second crewman joined the first and together they shoved the black rubber boat down the ramp and into the relatively warm water. The small rubber boat slowed instantly, the SEALs hanging as far to the aft as possible to prevent the bow from submarining. The boat rocked gently in the wake of the Mark V and no one moved a muscle. The men lay perfectly still, listening to the ominous moan of the Mark V as it sped away. Not one of them had any desire for the boat to return until they needed it. They eagerly looked forward to carrying out their mission. Unfortunately, they were unaware that thousands of miles away they'd already been fatally compromised by someone from their own country.

ONE

$\mathbf{A}$nna Rielly drifted in and out of sleep, the warm sun enveloping her in a hazy dream. Her bronzed skin glistened with a mixture of sweat and sunscreen. A slight afternoon breeze floated in off the ocean. It had been the perfect week. Nothing but food, sun, sex and sleep. The ideal honeymoon. A small resort on a remote Caribbean island with their own secluded cabana, gravity pool and beach. Total privacy, no TV, no phones, no pagers, just the two of them.

She opened her eyes a touch and looked down at her wedding ring. She couldn't help but smile. She was like a schoolgirl again. It was a perfect diamond set in an elegant platinum Tiffany setting. Not too big, not too small, just right. Most important, though, it was from the right man. The man of her dreams.

She was now officially Mrs. Anna Rapp. He had been a little surprised that she'd taken his name without so much as a word of debate. She was a feminist, after all, with definite liberal leanings, but she could also be an old-fashioned romantic. She could think of no other man she respected more. It was an honor to share his name and she wanted the world to know that they were now a family.

In addition, she could also be pragmatic. She had no desire to one day see her grandchildren running around with four last names. Professionally though, she would keep her maiden name. As the White House correspondent for NBC she already had name recognition and a solid career. It was a good compromise and Mitch didn't object.

Amazingly, the entire wedding had gone off without a hitch. Rielly couldn't think of a friend who didn't have at least one big blowout with her fiancé, or mother, or mother-in-law while planning her wedding. For her part, Anna had always clung to the romantic notion that one day she'd fall in love and have a big wedding back at St. Ann's in Chicago. It was where her parents had been married, where she'd been baptized and confirmed and where she and her brothers had gone to grade school. But in the months after they got engaged she could see that this was an idea Mitch was less than enthusiastic about. It wasn't that he was uncooperative. He told her that if she wanted a big wedding back in Chicago, that is what they'd do, but she could feel his apprehension. He didn't have to state it.

Mitch Rapp did not like being the center of attention. He was a man who was used to working behind the scenes. The strange truth was that her husband had been a covert operative for the CIA since the age of twenty-two. And the harsh reality was that in some circles he was known as an assassin.

In the months before their wedding, during the confirmation hearing for Mitch's boss at the CIA, a member of the House Intelligence Committee had leaked Mitch's story to the press in an attempt to derail Irene Kennedy's nomination as the next director of the Central Intelligence Agency. The president had come to both Rapp and Kennedy's defense and a version of the truth was released to the media. The president told the story of how Rapp had led a team of commandos deep into Iraq to prevent Saddam Hussein from joining the nuclear club. The president called Rapp the single most important person in America's fight against terrorism and overnight the politicians lined up to shake his hand.

Rapp had been thrust into the spotlight, and he didn't do well. Having survived for years because of his ability to move from city to city, and country to country, without being noticed, he was now recognized virtually everywhere he went. There were photographers and reporters who hounded him. Rapp tried to reason with them at first. A few listened, but most didn't. Not one to let a problem fester, Rapp arranged to have a few noses smashed. The others took the hint and backed off.

There was something else, though, that worried Rapp a great deal. He was now a marked man. Virtually every terrorist from Jakarta to London knew who he was. Bounties had been placed on his head and fatwas, Islamic religious decrees, had been thrown down by dozens of fanatical Muslim clerics across Arabia, Asia and the Pacific Rim. Thousands if not millions of crazed Islamic zealots would gladly give their lives to take him down.

Rapp worried incessantly about Anna's safety and had even asked her if she was sure she still wanted to spend the rest of her life looking over her shoulder. Without hesitation she had said yes and told him not to insult her by bringing it up again. He had stoically honored her request, but it didn't stop his worrying. He'd also taken some serious precautions, having ordered her a customized BMW with bulletproof glass, Kevlar-lined body, and shredproof tires. They were also in the process of building a house on twenty acres outside D.C. in rural Virginia. Anna had asked more than once where the money came from to pay for all this, but Rapp had always deflected her questions with a joke or change of subject. She knew he was a man of many means, and in the end she reasoned that there were some things she was better off not knowing.

When they sat down to plan the wedding, Rapp brought up a laundry list of security concerns that would have to be addressed. As the weeks passed, Anna began to realize that he simply would not be able to enjoy the day if they held such a large wedding. She made the decision then to have a small private ceremony with their families and a few close friends. The news had been received well by Mitch.

The event was held where they'd met. At the White House. Anna's entire family, her mom and dad, brothers and sisters-in-law and seven nieces and nephews were there. Mitch's only surviving relative, his brother Steven, was best man while Anna's longtime friend Liz O'Rourke was the matron of honor. Dr. Irene Kennedy and a few of Rapp's friends from the CIA were present as well as a select group of Anna's media friends. Father Malone from St. Ann's was flown in to officiate and the president and the first lady were the perfect hosts. President Hayes also used his significant clout to make sure there wasn't a mention of the wedding in any of the papers or on TV. It was agreed by all that it would be wise to keep the identity of Mrs. Mitch Rapp off the front pages.

The guests all stayed at the Hay Adams Hotel, just a short walk across Lafayette Park from the White House. They celebrated well into the night and then the bride and groom were taken by the Secret Service to Reagan National Airport where they caught a private jet to their island. Courtesy of the CIA, they were traveling under the assumed identities of Troy and Betsy Harris.

Anna sat up and looked over the edge of the patio down at the beach. Her husband was coming out of the water after a swim. Naturally dark-skinned, after a week in the sun he looked like he'd gone native. The man was a prime physical specimen, and she wasn't just thinking that because she was married to him. In his twenties he'd been a world-class triathlete who competed in events around the world. He'd won the famous Iron Man competition in Hawaii twice. Now he was in his mid-thirties, and was still in great shape.

Rapp sported some other physical features that had taken Rielly a little getting used to. He had three visible bullet scars: one on his leg and two on his stomach. There was a fourth that was covered by a thick scar on his shoulder where the doctors had torn him open to get at the bullet and reconstruct his shoulder socket. There was an elongated knife scar on his right side, and one last scar that he was particularly proud of. It was a constant reminder of the man he had sworn he would kill when he started on his crazy journey into the world of counterterrorism. It ran along the left side of his face, from his ear down to his jawline. The plastic surgeons had minimized the scar to a thin line, but more important to Rapp, the man who had marked him was now dead.

Rapp stepped onto the patio, water dripping from his shorts, and smiled at his bride. "How ya' doin', honey?"

"Fine." She reached out her hand for him. "I was just dozing off a bit."

Rapp bent down and kissed her and then without saying another word he jumped into the small pool. He came up and rested his arms and chin on the edge. "Are you ready to go back tomorrow?"

She shook her head and pouted prettily for him.

Rapp smiled. She really made him happy. She was

smart, funny and drop-dead gorgeous. She could be a bit of a ballbuster at times, but he supposed any woman who was going to put up with him had to be able to assert herself or it'd be only a matter of years before he screwed everything up.

"Well, we'll just have to stay a little longer, then," he said.

She shook her head again and put the pouty lips back on.

Reaching across the patio for the bucket of iced Red Stripe, he laughed to himself. He'd called her bluff. She needed to get back to work or the network would have a complete shit fit. If Rapp had it his way she'd quit. The exposure was an ever increasing risk to her safety. But Anna had to come to that conclusion on her own. He didn't want to wake up ten years from now and have her go nuts on him for making her throw her career away. His only consolation was that her current assignment at the White House meant close proximity to more than a dozen well-armed and supremely trained Secret Service agents and officers.

"Would you like a beer, honey?"

"Sure."

Rapp opened one, handed the ice-cold bottle to Anna and then opened one for himself. Reaching out with his bottle he waited for his wife to do the same. The two bottles clinked together and Rapp said, "To us."

"To us," she replied with a blissful smile.

They both took a drink and Rapp added, "And lots of cute healthy babies."

Anna laughed and held up two fingers.

Rapp shook his head. "At least five."

She laughed even louder. "You're nuts."

"I never said I wasn't."

They sat there basking in the sun, talking about their future for the better part of an hour, teasing each other playfully about how many kids they were going to have, how they were going to be raised, what names they liked and what they would do if one of the kids was as stubborn as either of them. Rapp refrained from sharing his opinion as she talked about what she would do with her job after they had a baby. It was one of those new things he'd learned about relationships. He understood that she was talking it out, and not looking for him to throw in his own two cents.

For her part, Anna kept her promise that she would steer clear of digging for details on the goings-on at Langley. Rapp knew that if they were going to survive in the long run he would have to share certain aspects of his job with her, regardless of what Agency policy dictated. Anna was too curious to spend the rest of their lives never discussing what he spent the majority of the week doing. The general subjects of terrorism and national security were fair game, but anything involving specific intelligence or covert policy was off the table. Having been silent for so many years, Rapp actually found it satisfying to be able to share his opinions with someone who had a decent grasp of the issues.

They opened two more beers and Anna joined him in the water. They clung to the edge of the gravity pool and looked out at the ocean, their elbows and chins resting on the edge, their legs gently floating behind them. They laughed about the wedding and their week of seclusion and avoided mentioning that it was about to end. Rapp could tell that Anna was getting tipsy. She weighed only 115 pounds and the combination of beer, warm sun and a lazy breeze meant a siesta was in the cards.

After a little while she kissed him on the lips and swam

to the other end of the small pool. Climbing out, she stopped on the top step and pulled her hair into a loose ponytail. As she twisted it with both hands the water cascaded down her smooth back and over her tiny white bikini bottom. With a flirtatious glance over her shoulder she began to unhook her top. "I'm going to go take a nap. Would you like to join me?" Keeping her back to him, she slipped off her bikini top and draped it over the hammock hook to her right.

Needing no further encouragement, Rapp set his beer down and hoisted himself over the edge. He followed his wife into the bedroom, losing his swim trunks along the way. His eyes never left her body, and for a brief moment he found himself wishing they could stay on this tiny island forever.

When they got back to Washington it wouldn't be like this. There would be fires to be put out and plans to be put into action. He watched Anna slip out of her bikini bottom, and the problems awaiting him in Washington vanished. They could wait, at least for another day. Right now he had more important things on his mind.

TWO

The black boat lay still in the water while Devolis took a quick fix with his handheld GPS. They were right on the mark, two miles off the coast of Dinagat Island in the Philippines. The men retrieved their night vision goggles (NVGs) from their waterproof pouches and secured them tightly on their heads. Thick clouds obscured the moon and the stars. Without the NVGs they'd be blind. On Devolis's signal the boat moved out, the modified Mercury outboard engine no louder than a hum.

The powers that be in Washington had finally decided to make a move. Abu Sayyaf, a radical Muslim group operating in the Philippines, had kidnapped a family of Americans on vacation, the Andersons from Portland, Oregon. The family, Mike and Judy and their three children—Ava, nine, Charlie, seven, and Lola, six—had been plucked from their seaside resort on the Philippine island of Samar five months earlier.

Devolis and his men had followed the story closely, knowing that if the politicians ever got off their asses, it would most likely be their job to go in and rescue the Andersons. Devolis had spent a lot of nights thinking about the family, especially the kids. The twenty-eight-year-old officer wanted to rescue those kids more than anything else he'd wanted in his six years as a U.S. Navy SEAL. He'd stared at their pictures so often the edges were worn and brown, and read their files over and over until those innocent little faces visited him in his sleep. For better or worse this mission had become personal. He wanted to be their savior. With Devolis it was not false bravado but an honestly and fiercely held conviction that someone needed to show these fanatics what happened when they screwed with the United States of America.

Devolis was in no way sadistic, but he felt an unusual amount of hatred toward the men who were holding the Andersons. He couldn't grasp what type of person would kidnap innocent children, but whoever they were, Devolis felt confident that he would lose no sleep over whacking the whole lot of them. Tonight Abu Sayyef was going to feel the full force of the U.S. Navy and the terrorist group would deeply regret having locked horns with the world's lone superpower.

The USS *Belleau Wood* was lurking fifteen miles off the coast of Dinagat Island. The Tarawa-class amphibious and air assault ship could bring to bear an immense amount of firepower. One of five such ships in the U S. Navy's arsenal, the *Belleau Wood* was the air force, army and navy rolled into one. She was a hybrid aircraft carrier and amphibious assault ship with an 800-foot flight deck. She carried six AV-8B Harrier attack jets, four AH-1W Super Cobra attack helicopters, and for troop transport, twelve CH-46 Sea Knight helicopters and nine CH-53 Sea Stallion helicopters. The 250-foot well deck in the stern of the ship held the navy's superfast 135-foot, cushioned LCAC, capable of delivering heavy equipment, such as tanks and artillery, to the beach at forty-plus knots.

She carried a crew of 85 officers, 890 enlisted men

and women and a battalion of 2,000-plus marines. The *Belleau Wood* provided true tactical integrity. Rather than waiting for various air force and army units to come together to form an integrated fighting force, the *Belleau Wood* delivered a complete self-contained fighting unit to the hot spot with air power, muscle, and logistical support all at the same time. She was the culmination of everything the marines and navy had learned as they clawed their way across the Pacific during World War II.

Devolis's squad was the advance element of the operation. Their job was to go in and recon the camp. Once they'd verified what the intel guys had told them, they were to set up a blocking position between the main opposing force and the hostages and call in the doorkickers. Because of this they'd left their suppressed MP-5s back on the *Belleau Wood,* sacrificing stealth for firepower. Six of the eight men were carrying the M4 carbine, an undersize version of the venerable M16. With a shorter barrel and collapsible butt stock the weapon was much easier to maneuver through the thick jungle. The squad's machine gunner was carrying an M249 SAW and the sniper was carrying a customized silenced Special Purpose Rifle. When the shooting started it would be very noisy, but for tonight's mission, this would be a plus. The noise created by Devolis's squad would both shock and disorient the opposing force as the helicopters swooped in from above and disgorged the assault teams.

Three more squads of SEALs, twenty-four men total, would then fast-rope in from above and both secure the hostages and sweep the camp. From there the doorkickers would move the Andersons one click from the camp to a small clearing for a helicopter evacuation. The clearing would be secured by a platoon of Force Recon marines, and if things started to fall apart and they met more resis-

tance than they'd planned, the Harrier attack jets and
Super Cobra attack helicopters were on station for quick
deployment.

The squad would remain until the rescue element was
safely out, and then work their way back to the beach and
exfiltrate the same way they'd come in. A pretty straightforward plan, with one exception: they would be operating in the backyard of one of their allies and the Filipinos
weren't going to be involved in the operation. Not only
were they not going to be involved, they weren't even
going to be told it was going on. No one had told the
SEALs why, but they had their suspicions. The Philippine
army had been promising for months to rescue the Andersons and they hadn't done squat. There were rumors
working their way around the teams that our old Pacific
allies could no longer be trusted, so the United States was
going to take care of things on its own.

Devolis had learned early on in his career to steer clear
of diplomatic and political questions. They tended to cloud
the mission, which for a SEAL was a very bad thing. Mission clarity was crucial for a Special Forces officer. Besides,
all that stuff was way above his pay grade. It was for the
hoity-toity crowd with all their fancy titles and degrees.

Despite knowing better, Devolis couldn't help but
wonder how some of this might affect the mission. The
scuttlebutt was that some pretty heated debates had taken
place in Washington before they green-lighted the rescue
operation. A rivulet of sweat dropped from his left eyebrow and landed on his cheek. He pressed the sleeve of
his jungle BDU against his forehead and mopped his face.
Silently, he cursed the heat, knowing that if it was warm
out here on the water, it would be completely soupy in
the jungle.

As they neared the beach, the boat slowed and settled in

the calm water. There was only about fifty feet of sand between the waterline and the jungle. Every pair of eyes in the little rubber boat scanned the beach and the thick jungle in search of a sign that they weren't alone. Even with their night vision goggles there was nothing much to glean beyond the empty beach. The jungle was too thick. Insertions were always a tense part of the op, but for tonight, at least, the intel guys had told him that it was highly doubtful they would meet any resistance upon landing.

A large, mangled piece of driftwood sat at the water's edge. On Devolis's order the boat headed in its direction. Unless it had moved since this morning's satellite photographs, that was their spot. Just to the right of it, and in from the beach approximately a hundred yards, was a shallow stream they would use to work their way inland to the camp.

The boat nudged onto the sand beach, just to the right of the driftwood. The men moved with precision and speed. This was where they were most vulnerable, here on the beach out in the open. They spread out in a predetermined formation that they'd practiced with numbing repetition. The lead men in the front of the boat maintained firing positions while the others fanned out, creating a small secure beachhead that provided 180 degrees of fire.

Devolis lay in the prone position slightly ahead of the others, the muzzle of his rifle pointed at his sector of the jungle, his heart beating a bit faster but under control. The goggles turned the dark night into a glowing green, white and black landscape. Lying completely still, the lieutenant squinted his eyes in an attempt to pierce the wall of vegetation in front of him. After he'd given it a good look he took his right finger off the trigger and pointed toward the jungle twice. Ten feet to Devolis's right, Scooter Mason, his point man, popped up and scampered off toward the jungle in a low crouch, his weapon at his shoulder ready to fire. Devolis took a second to check their flanks and looked down the beach in both directions.

That was when it happened. A three-round burst that shattered the still night. Three loud distinctive cracks that Devolis instantly knew came from a weapon that didn't belong to any of his men. As Devolis swung his head around he saw Scooter falling to the ground and then the jungle in front of them erupted in a fusillade of gunfire. Bright muzzle flashes came from everywhere. A bullet whistled past the young lieutenant's head and the sand in front of him began to dance as rounds thudded into the beach. In return, the squad let loose with everything they had. Each man hosed down his sector, focusing on the bright muzzle flashes of the enemy.

Devolis unloaded his first thirty-round magazine and ejected it. While fishing for a fresh magazine, he yelled into his lip mike, "Victor Five, this is Romeo! I need an immediate evac!" Devolis rammed home the fresh magazine and chambered a round. A muzzle flash erupted at one o'clock and he sent a three-round burst right back down its throat.

"Say again, Romeo" came the reply back over Devolis's earpiece.

Devolis continued to fire and shouted, "We are taking heavy fire! We have at least one man down and we need an immediate evac! Bring it right in on the beach!"

An earnest voice crackled back over the radio, "We're on the way."

Devolis knew the rest of the team had heard his call for an evacuation over their headsets. They had covered it thoroughly in the premission briefing. The Mark V was to circle back after it dropped them off and take up station a mile and a half off the beach in case they were needed. It was a standard mission precaution, but one that no one thought they'd need tonight. As Devolis returned fire, he loudly cursed the people back in Washington. They'd walked right into an ambush and for the life of him he couldn't figure out how it had happened.

"Guys, give me a sit rep, by the numbers." Devolis continued to fire while his men sounded off one by one. Only five men checked in. Devolis knew Scooter was down and that left only one other. "Irv, talk to me." Devolis repeated the request, then looked to his left. He could see Irv's prone figure, but there was no movement. "Listen up!" His shout was interrupted by several loud explosions as one of his men fired his M203 40mm grenade launcher into the jungle. "Gooch, put some smoke into their position. The boat will be here any second. When the big fifties start to rake the jungle we move. I'll grab Irv. Gooch, can you get to Scooter?"

"Affirmative."

Devolis tore off his night vision goggles, reached for an M-18 smoke grenade and pulled the pin. Rolling onto one side, he lobbed the can of soup upwind from their position. The grenade rolled across the sand and began to hiss its white cover. Slowly the fog worked its way back down the beach. Devolis knew the boat had to be near and started his crawl toward Irv. He had to get to him. No one could be left behind. When he was just a few feet away from his friend a bullet found him. It slammed into his right leg. Through gritted teeth Devolis let out a muffled scream and a slew of profanities. The pain had been so complete he wondered briefly if his leg had been blown off. He looked over his shoulder to reassure himself that it was still attached.

He reached Irv just as the battle reached a new crescendo. The big .50-caliber machine guns of the Mark

V tore into the jungle with vicious force. Shredded leaves rained down, branches snapped free, trunks absorbed the big rounds with cracking moans and thuds and then the 40mm grenade launcher let loose with a salvo of explosions. The enemy's guns all but stopped as they dove for cover.

Devolis called out his friend's name and reached out for his shoulder. When he turned him over all he saw was a lifeless face staring blankly at the night sky, his jaw open and loose. A bullet had struck him in the forehead and a mixture of sand and blood covered one side of his face. Devolis froze briefly in sorrow as the finality of the moment hit home and then a line of bullets popped in the sand just in front of him. A voice inside told him to get to the water. Now was not the time to mourn his friend's death. Devolis grabbed Irv's H harness and began dragging him toward the safety of the sea. As he struggled with the lifeless body and only one good leg, he called for his team to report in.

While they did, he reached the warm salty water and looked over at the rubber raft. It was too shot up to bother recovering. He continued to move away from the shore, pulling his friend with him as the salt water began to bite at the bullet hole in his leg. He gave the team orders to abandon the raft and swim out for pickup. Devolis stopped in about five feet of water and waited for each team member to pass. The Mark V continued to rake the beach with its big .50-caliber machine guns until the enemy fire was reduced to a few sporadic shots. Devolis side-stroked with all his might, clutching his dead friend as they moved farther and farther away from the shore. As he neared the safety of the boat, he blocked out the agonizing pain and tried to understand how they could possibly have walked into an ambush.

THREE

The man sat on the backseat of a power launch, his oil-black hair blowing in the wind like a lion's mane as the boat sped away from the Monte Carlo dock. The sun was climbing into the bright blue Mediterranean sky. It looked to be another perfect day in the playland of the ultrarich. The passenger's dark skin was offset by a loose-fitting white shirt and a pair of black Ray•Ban sunglasses. He looked like something out of a travel magazine with his arms stretched across the back of the white leather seat and the sun shining down on his chiseled face, a postcard, if you will, for how to get away from the everyday grind of life. For the passenger sitting in the back of the launch, however, this little sojourn out to sea would be anything but relaxing. He was not getting away from the everyday grind, he was heading directly into it. He was on his way to pay a visit to a man he disliked intensely. And to make matters worse, the visit was not his idea. It was a command performance.

The handsome man went by the name of David. No last name, just David. It wasn't his real name, but one that he had adopted years ago, while he'd attended university in America. It was a name that suited him well in a profession that called for striking just the right balance between anonymity and panache. David was a survivor. He had grown up in an environment that bred violence and hatred, and had somehow managed to master both at an early age. Controlling his emotions instead of being driven by them was what allowed David to pick his way through the minefield of his youth and set a course for greatness. And now at the relatively young age of thirty-four he was poised to change the world. If only the man he was going to see would leave him alone, he could put the final pieces of his plan into place.

David looked over the windscreen of the launch at the massive yacht anchored out at the far environs of the harbor and sighed. In David's mind the yacht and its owner were almost indistinguishable. Both were huge, both demanded to be noticed by all who slipped into their sphere and both needed a crew of tireless workers to keep them afloat. There were days when David wondered if he could turn back the clock and start over, would he have chosen someone else to be his benefactor? He traveled a great deal, and in his line of work, if you could call it that, taking notes was a very bad idea, so he constantly mulled over his previous decisions and how they would affect his next move. Every flight and train ride was an endless scrolling through of what-ifs and whos.

At some point, though, it was all moot. He was too far into it now to change horses. Prince Omar was his partner, and at the end of the day David had to begrudgingly admit that the man had held up his end of the bargain, at least financially. As the ostentatious yacht loomed larger with each passing second, David once again had the uneasy sensation that he was being pulled into the prince's orbit against his wishes. The man was like an illicit drug. In small doses he was tempting and beguiling, but if not monitored, his excesses could rot your body and your soul to the core.

As the launch pulled up alongside the massive 315-foot yacht, the sun was blocked out, its warmth dissipating in the cool morning air. David glanced down and noticed goose bumps on his arm. He hoped this was merely a result of the change in temperature and not an omen of bad things to come. The prince had requested that David join him for lunch and drinks at two that afternoon, but David wasn't about to waste an entire day in Monaco. There was far too much to be done. The prince would not be happy, but at this point in the game there wasn't a lot he could do other than stamp his feet and protest.

Before the launch came to a stop, David shoved a hundred euros into the driver's shirt pocket and leapt onto the stern deck. He landed gracefully and immediately noticed five white garbage bags filled with the waste from last night's party. Even in the cool morning air he could smell wine and beer and God knows what else leaking from the bags. The prince would be in rough shape.

A voice sounded from somewhere above. "You're early."

David recognized the French-accented English of the prince's chief minion and said, "Sorry, Devon." Looking up, he saw the prince's assistant, Devon LeClair, and next to him, the prince's ever-present Chinese bodyguard, Chung.

Devon looked down at him with an irritated frown. "You're going to have to wait, you know."

David started up the ladder, keeping his eye on Devon. Dressed in a suit and holding his leather encased Palm Pilot he looked more like a cruise director than quite possibly the highest paid executive assistant in the world.

David smiled and said, "You're looking well this morning, Devon." He clapped the prince's assistant on the shoulder and added, "I trust you didn't take part in last nights activities."

With a dramatic roll of the eyes, Devon replied, "Never. Someone has to stay sober enough to make sure this enterprise stays afloat."

"True enough." David almost asked how the party went and then thought better of it. If he hung around long enough the prince would probably force him to sit through a private viewing of the debauchery that had most certainly been recorded for posterity.

"Will you be staying with us long?" The prince's assistant had his pen poised over his now open Palm Pilot, ready to go to work.

"No, I'm sorry." David always treated Devon with great respect and care. As the gatekeeper to the prince, he was someone you wanted on your side.

"Well, you're going to have to wait quite a while for His Highness to awake. The sun was starting to come up when he finally called it a night."

David pushed his sunglasses onto the top of his head and checked his Rolex. It was a quarter past nine. "Devon, I'm sorry, but I can't wait. He ordered me to show up today, and to be truthful, I didn't even have time for that." He leaned in and lowered his voice. "I really can't afford to sit around all day and wait for him to sleep off last night's hangover."

The thin Frenchman closed his Palm Pilot and looked at David pensively through his silver-rimmed oval spectacles. "He will not be happy."

"I know he won't, and you can blame it all on me." David could see Devon was on the fence. "If you would like, I will go wake him up, but I absolutely can't afford to waste the day away waiting for him." He watched as

Devon's eyes quickly scanned him from head to toe and then looked over at Chung, who shook his head. There was no way the man charged with keeping the prince alive was going to let this particular guest enter the prince's inner sanctum unannounced, for David was a man with many talents.

As he turned to go, the ever efficient assistant said, "I will see what I can do. In the meantime, are you hungry?"

"Yes."

Pointing up he said, "I will have breakfast prepared for you on the aft sundeck." With a curt nod the assistant turned and disappeared into the ship leaving David and Chung alone with one of their uncomfortable moments of silence; the assassin and the bodyguard.

FOUR

A small table lamp was the only illumination in the large corner office of the building. It was past ten in the evening and all but a few of the thousands of bureaucrats who toiled there had gone home. The black-clad security staff patrolled the hallways and the woods outside, as they did twenty-four hours a day every day of the year. There were no holidays in the business of protecting secrets.

For the woman charged with protecting those secrets, and stealing those of her adversaries, it was a never-ending circle of suspicion. On this particular night an unshakable sense of foreboding enveloped her as she looked out over the dark landscape that surrounded the massive office complex. Nightfall had crept across the countryside, bringing to a close another day and with it more worries. She sat in her office on the top floor of one of the world's most notorious organizations, and pondered a multitude of potential threats.

They were not imaginary, exaggerated or petty. Dr. Irene Kennedy knew better than anyone the lethal nature of her foe. She had seen it with her own eyes. She had watched the tide of fanaticism swell over the last thirty years, watched it roll toward America's shores like an increasingly ominous storm. She had been Churchillian in her warnings about the growing threat, but her dire predictions had fallen on deaf ears.

The people she answered to were infinitely more concerned with the issues that dominate the political discourse of a peacetime democracy. No one wanted to deal with, or even hear about, an apocalyptic threat. They were more concerned with triangulating issues and with weakening their opponents through real or imagined scandals. She was even called an alarmist by some, but through it all she stayed the course.

It was an irony that didn't sit well with her, that many of the same senators and congressmen who labeled her an alarmist were the same ones who were now calling for her resignation. Some had even suggested that the CIA should be put out to pasture like some old plow horse that had served its purpose, but was no longer capable of doing its job.

The storm that she had predicted, however, was upon them, and the professional politicians who had ignored her warnings, and frustrated her actions at every turn, were not about to take an ounce of the blame. This unique breed of human was utterly incapable of accepting responsibility for any past mistakes, unless they wrapped it first in a well-timed act of contrition that would gain them sympathy.

Fortunately for Kennedy there were a few honorable senators and congressmen on the Hill who shared her commitment and concern. These were men and women who had been with her every step of the way as she attempted to change policies and operational procedures in order to prepare for the coming threat. They and the president had come to her defense and stymied a plan to have her removed as the director of the CIA.

Now it was time to play catch-up. In the glow of the desk lamp Dr. Irene Kennedy looked down at the transcripts before her and was sickened by what she read. It wasn't in her personality to get angry; she had divorced intellect from emotion a long time ago. She was simply pained. Men had died. Good men with families and children and mothers and fathers, and they had died because people who should know better couldn't grasp the importance of operational security. Even worse, they couldn't even keep a simple secret for just twenty-four hours.

Even after September 11 they lacked the commitment to protect their country. People simply didn't understand how serious the task before them was. Intelligent, educated people put the politics of their various agencies before operational security and because of it two men were dead, an entire operation involving hundreds of soldiers, marines, aviators, airmen and sailors was called off and a family of innocent Americans were still trapped in a hell that no adult, let alone child, should have to suffer through.

The entire episode was a monumental security failure and Kennedy had decided enough was enough. She would not lose her cool and begin screaming for people's scalps. That was not the way she'd been taught to perform her duties. She had been trained by one of the best. Thomas Stansfield, the now deceased director of the CIA, was fond of saying that a master spy should be a closed book unless it wished to be opened. A day did not pass that his advice went unheeded.

Before her were two red folders. The one on her left consisted of e-mail intercepts between a high-ranking State Department official and an overseas ambassador. It also contained some transcripts of phone conversations and other intelligence data. The folder on the right was much thicker. It contained bank records from the last several years for a variety of accounts spread around the Pacific, an in-depth biography of the person in question, and satellite images and intercepts. Both folders held clear and convincing evidence that certain individuals, at home and abroad, were guilty of compromising the hostage rescue in the Philippines.

In years past, this was the type of information the CIA would have quietly disseminated to a few select individuals around Washington. Since no administration liked scandal, that's where it would have ended. A few wrists would have been slapped. Some people might have been reassigned to less desirable posts or asked to retire early or find a job in the private sector, but rarely was anyone really made an example of.

This time it would be different. Kennedy was adamant about what needed to be done. The file on her left was going to be handled very publicly. When the press found out, the two bureaucrats involved were going to get a nonlethal dose of what those SEALs faced when they hit the beach over in the Philippines. They would be met with a landslide of lights and cameras, and where the cameras were in Washington, you could always count on politicians to show up.

As Kennedy looked out the window she knew which senators and congressmen would take to the airwaves. There were a handful from each party that couldn't resist. Their vanity made it impossible for them to ever pass up an opportunity to show their faces to millions of potential voters. There were a few others who knew TV time meant increased campaign contributions, and increased contributions meant reelection. Within those two groups there were those who would try to blame the president, there were those who would try to blame the previous president, and there were those who would try to blame the State Department for being a bastion of lefties who cared more about the UN than the national security of America. There were also those who would demand justice, when justice was the furthest thing from what they wanted. And finally there were those who would demand justice and really mean it.

All of this would be a side show to the main event, though. What Kennedy really wanted to do was remind everyone in Washington with a security clearance that this was serious business. It was not up to any given individual to decide what secrets they could and couldn't discuss. These were not just bureaucratic rules, they were laws. And to break those laws would mean public embarrassment, prosecution, and if a judge and jury saw fit, jail time.

The other file was going to be handled more subtly, and in a much more final way. Kennedy knew just the man to take care of both problems. She had been tempted to recall him from his honeymoon, but decided it could wait another twenty-four hours. Things were about to change in Washington, and Mitch Rapp was going to play a crucial role.

Kennedy knew Rapp better than anyone. She had recruited him, she oversaw his training and she had been his handler through the most stressful of times and delicate of situations. Over the years she had grown to love him like a brother. His sense of commitment and honor was of the highest order. When he got back from his honeymoon and found out what had happened he would need no direction, no prodding, no explanation of the bigger picture. The only thing he might need was restraint, and Kennedy had yet to decide if she would even attempt to calm him when he heard the news. There would be those at the White House who would want to keep this entire mess out of the papers. They would want to sweep it under the rug and have the offenders in question transferred to different jobs. That could not be allowed to happen this time, and Kennedy knew Rapp was the one man in Washington who would tell the president in the roughest and most graphic terms that heads needed to roll.

FIVE

David took a sip of orange juice and looked out upon the vista of Monte Carlo. It was a place of serene beauty. With the warm sun beating down on him and the peaceful sounds of the harbor he could almost allow himself to fall asleep, but there was too much to be done. He checked his watch. In front of him only a few scraps of his exquisite breakfast remained. The prince had a team of chefs that accompanied him wherever he traveled. It had been thirty minutes since Devon had left to awaken the Large One, and although David did not expect the prince to bound out of bed and come meet him, he truly wasn't going to wait around all day.

The prince had summoned him in the midst of the final stages of preparation for their grand plan, and for that, David was not going to leave without exacting a heavy fee from his benefactor. Despite his irritation at the interruption, it was time that if they were going to discuss business, it was better to do it in person. Conducting such matters over the phone was always risky. One never really knew what the Americans could pick up with all those damn satellites of theirs.

David had many talents, but there was one area in particular where he was exceptionally gifted. It was getting wealthy people to part with their money. The key, David had learned, was to show them a return on their initial investment. He'd perfected that skill while working for a small venture capital firm in Silicon Valley after he'd graduated from the University of California at Berkeley. David had specialized in bringing in wealthy Saudi oil money, and that was how he had met the man whose boat he was now on.

He felt the prince before he actually heard him. A slight tremor rumbled across the deck and tiny ripples spread across the surface of his water glass. David looked over his shoulder just in time to see the Large One step through the glass sliding door and onto the covered part of the sun deck. The prince's ring-studded hand protected his eyes from the offending light of day. In Arabic he yelled a command, and instantly a man appeared at his side with a gold tray and a pair of sunglasses placed perfectly in the middle. The prince snatched them and somehow managed to squeeze them onto his fat head.

Looking at David sitting in the sun, Prince Omar began shaking one of his beefy fingers at him and cursing him in his native Arab tongue.

David stifled a smile and apologized effusively for interrupting the prince's sleep. Switching over to English he said, "You know, Your Highness, that I would not have interrupted you if it were not important."

Rather than come out into the sun, Prince Omar plopped his ample body down on a large couch overflowing with pillows. Chung, the mountainous bodyguard, took up his post on the other side of the sundeck so he could both keep an eye on things and stay out of the way of the servants who constantly buzzed about the prince. After adjusting his white silk robe, Omar began stuffing and throwing pillows about until his fleshy body was supported just right.

David watched all of this with amusement. He had seen photographs of the prince in his younger years. Omar had once been a handsome and slender man. He had been an international playboy. One of the world's wealthiest men, he jetted from one continent to the next, always attending the best parties. Now in his early fifties, he was a gluttonous wreck. All of the hard years had finally caught up with him. After his fiftieth birthday he entered a downward spiral of depression sparked by the realization that the party would not go on forever. With his depression came great mood swings and a seemingly insatiable thirst for a plethora of vices.

Three servants in crisp white tunics and black pants stepped onto the sundeck and formed a conga line just to the side of the prince. They all held gold trays overflowing with various things the prince might desire. Just serving the prince was not enough. These men were to predict his needs so that when the prince decided he wanted something it appeared as if they had anticipated his every whim. The first servant presented a tray with cigarettes. Omar snatched one and the servant held a diamond-studded gold lighter to it. When the cigarette was lit the man bowed and peeled away only to be instantly replaced by the second man who held a tray of drinks for the prince to choose from. There was an orange one, a red one, a pink one and even a blue one, and all them were perfectly garnished with skewers of fruit or vegetables. Omar's bejeweled fingers danced above the glasses while his tongue tried to decide which one it wanted. He picked the pink one, took a sip and then put it back with a sour expression on his face. Quickly, he zeroed in on the red one, which David assumed was a Bloody Mary.

After taking a long sip through the straw, he waved the servant away and stared at David for a long moment. Prince Omar admired the Palestinian. He had guts, he had brains and he was dashingly handsome. If anyone other than one of his family members had just awakened him, he would have told Devon to have Chung throw them into the sea. In fact, now that he thought about it, there were several family members he'd like to have thrown into the sea anyway, and they hadn't even interrupted his sleep.

Omar finally said, "David, come, tell me why you are in such a hurry." The third servant appeared at the prince's side holding a tray overflowing with pastries. Omar gestured for the tray to be placed on the table before him.

David walked across the sundeck and stepped under the canvas awning. He sat in a chair across from the prince and watched him devour a pastry with some type of cream filling.

"Why do you wish to irritate me like this, my friend?" asked the prince.

A Cheshire-cat grin spread across David's lips. He knew the prince liked him for the very reason he was scolding him. When you spend your every waking moment surrounded by sycophants it can be refreshing to be treated with a little insolence.

"Your Highness, I am almost ready to implement your plan." David referred to it as the prince's plan even though it was his own. "There are many things to be done, and as we've discussed there is little room for error."

The prince set his drink down and shifted forward in anticipation. "How close are we?"

"Close."

"Close," repeated the prince with irritation in his voice. "Don't tell me 'close.' I want details."

"You have all the details you need, my prince," David replied in an even voice.

The prince struggled in his sea of pillows to straighten up and in frustration barked, "Do I need to remind you who you are speaking with?"

Casually, David took off his sunglasses and placed them in his breast pocket. "I will never forget what you have done for me and my people, my prince. You are one of the few who truly care, and among those few you are the greatest of our heroes. But we have been through this before, and for your own good there are certain things you are better off not knowing."

The seemingly heartfelt homage appeared to calm Omar for the moment. "Come sit by me and whisper these things in my ear. I release you of your worries. I will decide what I am better off not knowing."

David did not move. "My prince, once I tell you, there is no taking it back. If things go wrong you could be implicated."

"I thought you were taking care of that."

"I am, and that is why I cannot stay here today and enjoy your gracious hospitality. I need to get to Amman for a meeting. A meeting that will throw the dogs off your trail if things don't go the way we've planned."

Omar plucked another pastry from the mound and took a large bite. With a red filling oozing from the corners of his mouth he asked in a quiet voice, "When will it start?"

While David pondered how much he should tell him, a servant stepped forward and handed the prince a steaming white hand towel. The prince cleaned his lips and jet black goatee and then tossed the towel to the deck.

David watched the servant pick it up and then said, "The action will start very soon, my prince."

"How soon?" Omar asked eagerly.

"Soon."

"Within the month?"

David shook his head. "Sooner."

"In weeks?"

Smiling just slightly he answered, "Within the week, my prince."

The prince clapped his hands together and nodded enthusiastically. "This is good news. This is wonderful."

As the prince reveled in the news, a nubile young woman with flowing blond hair stepped onto the deck wearing only a sheer robe. She approached the prince and ran her fingers through his hair. In French she asked him why he had left her. Omar pushed her away, telling her to go lounge in the sun until he was done. The woman stuck out her lower lip and walked past David, giving him a flirtatious wink.

The prince watched her with great interest and said, "David, turn around and look at her. She is perfect."

David looked over his shoulder just as the statuesque woman undid her robe and let it fall to the floor. The view was not bad. A pair of white thong panties were all that she wore. David admired her curves as she raised her hands above her head and stretched. Turning back to the prince he smiled and said, "Very nice."

Omar had a lascivious grin on his face. "There is another one just like her. If you stay tonight, you can have them both."

Yeah, and I'll bet you'll tape the whole thing, David thought. In addition to a fetish for taping his visitors, there were other things that worried him even more about the prince, but he did not want to dredge all that up right now. "Your offer is very kind, but I have too much to do, and besides I need to keep my mind clear."

The prince nodded knowingly. "When you are done then. I will present them to you as a gift."

David smiled graciously, but didn't say what he was thinking. That he would prefer to find his own women. Women who didn't need to be paid—women who hadn't been defiled by the prince's diseased sex organ. Getting back to more important matters he said, "There is something you could do for me at present."

"And would that have anything to do with money?" asked Omar with a stern look.

Not the least bit embarrassed, David replied, "Of course. You know how things are among our Arab brothers. As long as they get paid they are happy."

"What about the cause?" snapped the prince. "Isn't that enough?"

"For a select few, yes. The martyrs and the true believers, but they are not the type we want involved in this. As I've told you, we need professionals, not people who will simply blow themselves up."

"But I thought you said the martyrs are part of your plan."

"They are," answered David in a slightly irritated voice. "They will act like livestock spooked by a fire. They will be driven into action by rage, not by any orders that I give them."

Omar thought about this for a moment and then asked, "How much more do you need?"

David help up all his fingers and for the first time in all his negotiations with the prince he knew he would get exactly that much and not a penny less.

"Ten million," scoffed the prince. He began shaking one of his chubby fingers in the Palestinian's direction. "You have become far too greedy."

The prince was a billionaire many times over, easily

one of the hundred richest men in the world. Ten million was a pittance, but it was still the most David had ever asked for in a single sitting. "My prince, you are a man who understands value. My services do not come cheaply, and what I am about to embark on for you and my people will change the course of history."

"Five million."

David stood and joined the prince on the couch. With a sideways glance he noticed Chung moving closer in case he was needed. In a hushed voice, David said, "Prince Omar, what is the one thing in this whole world you would take the most pleasure in?"

The prince's eyes lit up at the question and David could tell he was going through a lengthy list. "My prince, think of the subject at hand. What we are about to embark on."

Omar smiled with a hateful lust in his eyes. "To see Israel destroyed."

"Exactly, my prince. Ten million dollars is a pittance, and for it I will give you a front-row seat to the self-destruction of the Zionist state."

Omar grabbed David's hand and squeezed it. "Half now and half when you are done. Tell Devon where you want the money wired and it will be done. Now, be on your way, and give me the gift I have waited a lifetime for."

SIX

The silver-haired gentleman appeared to have his nose buried in the European edition of the London *Times*. A soft breeze blew across the water, seagulls played above and the lines slapped out their rhythmic notes on the tall mast of the sailboat. To all outward appearances, Alan Church looked to be enjoying retirement. First observations with such a man, though, were always a bit tricky. The seventy-one-year-old Brit had spent the majority of his years trying to give people the right first impression—or the wrong one, depending on how you looked at it.

Alan was a mechanical engineer by training, but even that was only half true. He spent his twenties and thirties working for a large British energy conglomerate, and again this was only part of the story. During that time he traveled to the world's smaller and poorer nations in an effort to bring them hydroelectric power. It seemed for those two decades that Alan could be found wherever things were the nastiest, usually in a country where the transition from one ruling group to another was taking place and not in a peaceful democratic way. Most of those halcyon days, as he now somewhat sarcastically called them, were spent on the continent of Africa.

In truth, his time on the Dark Continent was anything but tranquil. He was robbed, shot at, kidnapped, twice caught malaria and once caught yellow fever. It was after the second bout of malaria that the powers back in London decided that it was time for Alan to take a new job in international finance. He'd spilled blood and toiled for the Crown, or more precisely, Her Majesty's Secret Service, for almost two decades. He was placed, without having to interview for the position, at one of Britain's finest banks where he eventually ended up keeping an eye on the financial comings and goings of The House of Saud.

Officially, or unofficially, depending on how you looked at it, Alan Church never worked for MI6, Britain's foreign intelligence service. To this day, if someone asked him the question he would laugh heartily and begin telling over-the-top tales of all the female spies he'd boffed in the service of the Crown. People who really knew him well, which weren't many, knew that there was a half-truth in almost everything Alan Church said.

Even now, as he sat on the deck of his sailboat, anchored just off the coast of the French Riviera, one had to look closely to see what Alan was really doing. At first glance he looked every bit the relaxed and retired gentleman casually perusing the newspaper as another day in paradise got under way, but upon closer inspection there were a few telltale signs that Alan had not entirely left the employ of his government. The first hint was a bit difficult to catch. It involved the unusual size of the radar dome that sat near the top of his mast and the odd-shaped antennae that sat next to it. The next sign that was a bit more obvious was that Alan wasn't really reading the paper.

Out of sight, but within reach, was a small control

panel with an array of dials. Plugged into this control panel was an earpiece. Alan at first listened intently to the conversation that was taking place between the prince and his visitor, manipulating the various controls in an effort to boost the effectiveness of the directional microphone concealed at the top of his mast.

He had dropped anchor the morning before just off the port beam of the prince's massive yacht, placing one other boat between his and the prince's. Under orders from London, he'd been loosely shadowing the prince for over a week. He'd even gotten to know a few of the crew members in the process. The captain of the ship was a retired French naval officer, as was much of his crew. Like most mariners, they were friendly to other sailors. While picking up provisions back in San Remo, Alan found out the ship was headed for Monte Carlo and then on to Cannes, a very common trip for the big yachts. Alan let it be known that he was headed in the same direction, so they'd probably be bumping into each other along the way. Things had progressed now to the point where the crew knew him on sight and waved as they went back and forth to shore in their power launch.

Headquarters was famous for being skimpy with the information they gave to their people in the field. They'd told Alan only to follow, observe, record and report. They didn't tell him why they wanted him to baby-sit Prince Omar, but then again, they didn't really need to. Alan knew enough about the dysfunctional House of Saud to know what his government was interested in.

The conversation that was taking place on the big ship didn't appear to be what they were after, and the dashing young man who had arrived less than an hour ago didn't fit the profile of an Islamic fundamentalist. With this in mind Alan checked his dials one more time to make sure everything was being recorded and then he began to read his paper, only half listening to the conversation that was going on in his left ear.

With the sun quickly warming the cool morning air, Alan let out a yawn and crossed his left leg over his right. The voice of a woman drew his attention away from the paper and he looked across the water to see what was going on. From his vantage point all he could see were the tops of several heads, and then a blond beauty came into view near the back of one of the upper sundecks. Without warning she dropped her robe and stretched her pale arms above her head, revealing a very nice pair of breasts. Alan lunged for his binoculars, but by the time he got them up she was gone. He laughingly shook his head. He was slowing down in his old age.

He was still smiling as he went back to his paper, and then slowly, his face turned more serious. The conversation between the prince and his visitor had without warning gone from mundane to quite noteworthy. Alan checked again to make sure the equipment was recording and then he went back to feigning interest in the paper. Whoever this David was, he would have to get some photos of him when he climbed back on board the launch to return to shore. As the two men continued their discussion, Alan decided that London would be very interested indeed in his next report.

SEVEN

M itch Rapp drove across the Key Bridge on his way to a meeting at the White House. His mood was tense and his patience short. He was not happy about what he'd learned this morning. The honeymoon was over. He'd been back in town for less than twenty-four hours and he was already looking to wring someone's neck. Ignoring his boss's orders, he'd left his bodyguard back at Langley and driven himself. He'd had some death threats lately, quite a few of them in fact, but despite the danger he needed some time alone to think before he met with the president. He'd promised himself that he wouldn't allow his new position of influence to be wasted.

The whole reason he had this new position was that his cover as a covert counterterrorism operative had been blown during his boss's confirmation hearing by a congressman who had no admiration for the Agency, and now every piece of crap from Boston to Baghdad knew who he was and what he looked like. His face had been broadcast across the airwaves. He was called America's first line of defense against terrorism. Virtually every newspaper in the country had reported his story and there had been several magazine covers. The entire thing was un-nerving to him.

The media spectacle his career had become went against everything he knew. Most of his life since the age of twenty-two had been a secret. Not even his brother had known that he worked for the CIA. Now, because of all the publicity before he even hit forty, he had been un-ceremoniously retired from the field, brought in from the cold and given a new job and a new title to go with it. He was now special assistant to the director of Central Intelligence on counterterrorism.

Terrorism had finally reached out and touched America, and her citizens were finally waking up to the fact that there were people out there who hated them, zealots who wanted to see the Great Satan toppled. The president and Rapp's boss, Director Irene Kennedy, had given him a mandate. In addition to working in conjunction with the Agency's counterterrorism center, they asked him to thoroughly study the nation's counterterrorism capabilities and come up with a recommendation on how to streamline operations and improve defenses. Rapp's first response had been to tell the president to start focusing on offense. So far the president had shown no signs of following that advice.

Kennedy, knowing Rapp better than anyone, admonished him to keep his temper and tongue in check. She told him to look at the study as a fact-finding mission. The ass-kicking would come later when he gave his report to the president and the National Security Council. That was when he could vent and let the truth be told, and Irene Kennedy knew better than anyone that the truth did need to be told.

If Rapp had learned anything during his lengthy study of America's counterterrorism efforts, it was that there were too many meetings. Too many meetings that accomplished nothing, and more often than not, created more red tape and hassles for the people who were on the front lines doing the important work. The meetings were a colossal waste of energy and resources. They never started on time and they always ran over, and that was the least of their problems. Now that he was on the inside, after spending more than a decade abroad working covertly for the CIA, he could see why so many in Washington thought the Agency had dropped the ball.

The Agency had become the antithesis of what Colonel Wild Bill Donovan, its founder, had designed it to be. It was a risk-averse haven for bureaucrats to put in their time so they could retire and collect their pensions. Sensitivity training and diversity workshops had taken priority over recruiting case officers with foreign language skills who had the chutzpah it took to run covert ops.

Thanks to Aldrich Ames, the FBI had been invited to join the Agency's Counter Intelligence Center. The brothers in dark suits had eviscerated the ranks of Langley's few remaining good case officers, for the simple reason that too many of the men and women in the directorate of operations were mavericks. Never mind that mavericks, independent thinkers, were exactly who Wild Bill Donovan and President Roosevelt had in mind when they started the Office of Strategic Services at the onset of World War II. Donovan and Roosevelt understood that you didn't hire decent, respectable, risk-averse family men to spy on the enemy. You hired risk-takers who were willing to put their lives on the line to get a piece of information that might make the difference. It was not a business for the meek, buttoned-up type. It was a business for daredevils who liked to gamble.

Signal and photographic intelligence now replaced eyes and ears on the ground. The billion-dollar satellites and ground intercept and relay stations were clean. They couldn't embarrass you the way a turned case officer could. They didn't bleed, they couldn't be kidnapped, they didn't lie and Congress loved them. The bright glossy photographs of terrorist training camps and scratchy audio intercepts of our enemies plotting to strike gave them great satisfaction.

The politicians marveled at America's technological superiority. There was one big problem, though; the enemy knew they were being watched and listened to, and went to great lengths to hide what they were doing from the big prying eyes and ears in the sky.

Everyone in Washington knew this, but it didn't stop groups like the State Department from pushing for more signal intelligence. The alternative was putting real men and women in the field and that could be very messy. Uncontrollable CIA case officers were a constant source of irritation for the State Department. They snooped around host countries, tended to drink too much, tried to recruit agents and generally behaved in a way that no gentleman or lady from Foggy Bottom would endorse. Even worse, if they got caught, the host country would expel innocent State Department employees along with the offending CIA case officer and the whole affair would upset the delicate dance of diplomacy.

The CIA had become just another Washington bureaucracy. A money-sucking black hole of political correctness. In short, the CIA was a reflection of the times and its political leaders. Now Rapp truly understood why Director Stansfield had done what he did. The recently deceased director of the Agency had fought hard to insulate the CIA from the political whims of Capitol Hill, but it was a Herculean task that no one man could perform. Seeing the winds of change approaching, Stansfield had created a covert counterterrorism unit known as the Orion Team. The group's mission was to operate in the dark and take the battle to the terrorists. Mitch Rapp had been the tip of that spear for the better part of a decade. He'd killed more men for his country than he could count, and he had come close to losing his own life more times than he dared to remember.

For the last several years he'd seriously considered getting out. Instinctively, he knew that one of these times, no matter how good he was, the breaks wouldn't go his way and he'd end up dead. The decision to make the move was finalized when he'd met Anna Rielly. She was only the second woman he'd ever loved, and the first had been a long time ago. Soon after meeting her he knew she was the one. It was time to get out of the killing business and get on with a normal life.

That had all been before the towers and the Pentagon were hit. Now he wasn't so sure. An anger burned inside him. He knew the face of the enemy better than perhaps anyone in the country. It was the hideous face of Islamic fanaticism. It had taken all the restraint he could muster to not get on a plane and go over to Afghanistan. Kennedy had convinced him not to. He was too important. She needed him right at her side, using his language skills and contacts in the region to run down leads and try to figure out what had happened.

Kennedy had vision, just like her mentor. She could see the goals of the competing agencies and interests in Washington and maneuver her way through the minefield. She knew that in the wake of 9/11 the politicians on the Hill would try to pin the whole thing on the CIA. Never mind that begining with the Church Hearings in the mid-seventies, it was the politicians who had pulled the CIA out of the spying business.

Then, in the eighties, it was the politicians again who told the CIA to break off any association with nefarious individuals, ignoring the fact that to catch the bad guys you actually had to talk to them and their associates from time to time. But the politicians on the Hill didn't want to hear any of it. The CIA either had to bat a thousand or get out of the hood. So ultimately, the politicians got exactly what they wanted. They created an agency that was afraid to take risks.

EIGHT

Who could have known in 1922, when Great Britain created the new country of Transjordan, that one day its capital of Amman would grow into a city of international intrigue? Amman, a city of over a million souls, was a dusty old town that had been cleaned up and dragged into the twenty-first century by the forward thinking King Hussein I and his son Abdullah II. Bordered to the east and south by Iraq and Saudi Arabia, to the north by Syria and to the west by Israel, Jordan was a cursed piece of land that was poor in mineral and oil deposits and plentiful in refugees. Palestinians, to be precise, and lots of them. For the first thirty or so years after the formation of Israel, Jordan moved in lock step with her Arab neighbors in calling for the annihilation of the Jewish state. But after getting decisively trounced in every military engagement with their Zionist neighbors Jordan began to think of Israel as a dog that was better left undisturbed, at least as far as outright wars were concerned.

If being cursed with a worthless piece of land wasn't enough, Jordan had to contend with a cast of neighbors that included the Middle East's most notorious despot, the ultrawealthy and schizophrenic Saudi royal family and the

Syrians, who for various twisted religious reasons hated the Jordanians almost as much as they hated the Jews. With no real resources or industry to build an economy, Jordan from its inception was dependent on foreign aid. At first it was the Brits, then the Arab League and then with the promise of better relations with Israel, the United States began to infuse millions of dollars in humanitarian, economic and military aid into the Hashemite Kingdom of Jordan.

King Hussein became masterful at playing both sides of the fence, taking money from both his Arab brothers and America. With great care he put his country on a course of neutrality and did not deviate even during the Gulf War. Despite immense pressure from the United States and Saudi Arabia, King Hussein chose not to jump into the fray. Publicly he proclaimed that he would not take part in the butchering of the Iraqi people, privately he told his keepers that it would serve them better if a channel of communication was kept open with Baghdad. King Hussein convinced President Bush that the Jordanian General Intelligence Department would provide him with invaluable information about what was going on inside Iraq. The Bush administration agreed and in return for cooperation with the General Intelligence Department the foreign aid spigot of the United States was only reduced instead of completely shut off.

At the time the agreement was reached King Hussein had no idea just how fruitful it would eventually be for his kingdom. During the years of sanctions that followed the Gulf War, Jordan became the lifeline of Iraq. Goods flowed in from Jordan like a river to the sea, and in exchange Jordanian coffers were filled with profits made from selling discounted Iraqi oil. Black market import-export companies sprang up in Jordan like weeds on an unkempt lawn. The French were the first to arrive, and they were quickly followed by many of their European neighbors and then the Chinese and the rest of the Pacific Rim and Asia. Jordan got a cut of everything and the entire racket became a massive boon to the Jordanian economy. All the while, with a wink and a nod, Jordan maintained her position of neutrality.

Amman was the place where Saddam's henchmen came to replenish the ruler's military supplies and shop for his grocery list of weapons of mass destruction. It was also where the CIA and Britain's MI6 focused an increasing amount of their resources. Amman had become the Middle East's version of Cold War Berlin. Any country that was big enough to care had spies on the ground in Amman, and with so many intelligence agencies operating in the city it was almost impossible to do business without someone noticing.

That was why David had chosen to meet his Iraqi contact in the Jordanian capital. He wanted to settle a score, send a message and muddy the waters in one fell swoop. David's connection to Prince Omar and the Saudi royal family needed to be protected at all costs. Yes, the Iraqis could provide money to the cause, but nothing compared to the Saudis. If the grand plan did not go as he hoped, David wanted to be able to point the Israelis and the Americans and anyone else who cared in the direction of Saddam Hussein. He did not want them to go looking in the kingdom of Saudi Arabia for him.

The green Range Rover snaked its way up Al Ameer Mohammed Street toward one of Amman's famous seven hills. Night had fallen on the city and they were headed for the Intercontinental Hotel. It was Amman's finest hotel, and the arrogant man David was going to meet would stay nowhere else. David sat in the backseat and went over the plan one more time. He had carefully applied a black beard flecked with gray to his face and had added a touch of gray to his eyebrows. Over his hair he was wearing the black-and-white keffiyeh of a Palestinian. As they neared the hotel he put on a pair of dark-rimmed glasses and checked his disguise with a small mirror. He looked a good fifteen years older. He had met with the Iraqi on six previous occasions and he had worn the same disguise each time.

David trusted very few people, and none of them were Iraqis. He had caught them in many lies during his business dealings with them, but in truth he had expected nothing less. They were the bullies of the neighborhood, and in the Middle East there was no shortage of bullies. The Iraqis made up the rules and then changed them again when they didn't like the way things were going. David despised them for the way they feigned concern over the Palestinian plight. The truth was that there wasn't a single Iraqi who truly cared for the Palestinians. To Saddam and his henchmen the Palestinians were nothing more than a lightning rod to attract anti-Semitism and hatred for America.

As the Range Rover pulled up to the front of the hotel, David was focused on the task at hand. Tonight the bloodbath would begin. If things went right it would be the first step in a long odyssey that would change the face of Middle East politics. It takes war to make peace and tonight would be the first shot in David's war.

He stepped from the vehicle and buttoned the jacket of his double-breasted blue suit. His posture slouched and his stride shortened, he moved toward the door of the hotel playing the role of an older man. The doors were opened by two bellmen who greeted David warmly. They knew him only as Mohammed Rashid, a Palestinian busi-

nessman who had strong ties to the PLO. David continued through the lobby, his Prada loafers clicking on the
marble floor. He entered the bar and peered through the
smoke-filled haze. The man he was looking for was seated
in the far corner, his back to the wall like he was some
cowboy in an American film. Two of his bodyguards were
seated at the adjacent table and were eyeing the rest of the
patrons, their menacing stares reminding everyone to
mind their own business. All three men had bushy black
mustaches, a prerequisite for anyone in Saddam's inner
circle.

David approached the table with feigned enthusiasm.
"General Hamza, it is so good to see you again."

Hamza did not offer his hand. He simply looked at the
chair opposite him and nodded for his guest to sit. The
Iraqi general took a drag from his unfiltered cigarette and
said, "You are late."

"I am sorry," David lied, "but I had a hard time getting
through the checkpoints."

Looking down at the two attaché cases on the floor
next to him, Hamza replied, "You'd better have a better
plan for getting back with these. If you lose them, I will
have your head."

David nodded effusively. "General, I will not allow
your money to fall into the hands of the Zionist pigs."

The general reached for his drink with the same hand
that held the cigarette. Never taking his eyes off the Palestinian he said, "For your own good, you'd better make
sure you do not allow that to happen."

David again nodded and eagerly assured the general
that no such thing could ever possibly occur. The two attaché cases contained a million dollars apiece in U.S. hundred-dollar bills. It was money for Hamas and Hezbollah
to continue their terrorist insurgency into Israel. General

Hamza was not a man to be taken lightly, but David was far from intimidated. The head of Saddam's Amn al Khas, or Special Security Service, was a brute, and brutes were easy to trick.

Hamza's thuggish behavior was legendary. In Iraq his name was spoken in whispers. He was responsible for entire families disappearing in the middle of the night, never to be seen or heard from again. On his orders, men and women were tortured and beaten for months simply because they knew someone who had been deemed a traitor to Saddam. Often, Hamza allowed those physically and mentally scarred subjects to live so that they could return to their communities and serve as living, walking, horrific, disfigured proof of what happened to people who went against Saddam. In any civilized society Hamza's behavior and tactics would be deemed inhumane at the least, but what made his actions all the more reprehensible was that the overwhelming majority of the people he had tortured and killed had done nothing wrong. In the twisted world Saddam had created for himself, he was convinced there were spies everywhere, traitors lurking in every city and every part of his government. There was a purge at least once a year and if the SSS didn't come up with bodies Saddam would turn his paranoid rage on the SSS instead. To avoid having his own head put on the chopping block, Hamza made sure his people found traitors. Guilty or not, they found them, they tortured them until they would say anything to stop the pain, and then they executed them.

It wasn't as if the Arab world was blameless when it came to such thuggery, it was just the brazen way Iraq went about it and the sheer volume of intimidation and torture that occurred. David could deal with brutality. He didn't like it but he could handle it. There was something else about the general, something that really turned his stomach, and it was for that reason alone that he would enjoy killing him.

A waiter approached and placed a napkin and a fresh drink on the table for Hamza. The man then asked David if he'd like something to drink. The general nodded his consent and David ordered a scotch and soda.

Hamza polished off the last few sips of his drink and then wiped several droplets of whiskey from his mustache. "I've decided to cut your fee. We're spending a lot of money on you and not getting enough back. You need to step up the bombing against Israel."

The fee the general was referring to had already been cut once. It had started at ten percent and dropped to five. It was David's cut for acting as an intermediary. David feigned concern. He had no personal use for counterfeit U.S. money, but he had to at least play the part. "But I have already cut my fee once."

"And you will cut it again." Hamza leaned back confidently and sucked on his cigarette until the end glowed a bright orange. After he'd exhaled the smoke in David's direction he smiled and said, "You are doing your people a service. The honorable thing to do would be to take no fee at all."

Honor had nothing to do with it. When David's fee was reduced the money was not passed along to Hamas and Hezbollah. It was pocketed by the general. David was tempted to point out that they were in this together. Arab brothers arm in arm doing battle against the Israelis, but he decided to leave the general's hypocrisy unchallenged. He needed the money for the next part of his plan and the fact that it was counterfeit was all the better.

His drink arrived and in a defensive tone he said, "But General, the cost of doing business in my land is very expensive. Many people need to be paid to assure the safe transfer of your very much appreciated funds."

"You should be paying no one," snarled Hamza. "You should slit the throat of the first person who gets in your way. Hamas and Hezbollah are on a mission from Allah and anyone who trifles with them should be dealt with harshly." The general shook his head in disgust. "You will never defeat the Israelis until you learn to control your own people."

Biting down on his tongue to restrain himself from smiling, David nodded thoughtfully. He and the general had arrived at the same conclusion, but for different reasons. David would unite the Palestinian people and he would start by killing the arrogant Iraqi brute who was sitting across from him.

NINE

Rapp was shown into the Oval Office by one of the president's aides. He found his boss, Irene Kennedy, and General Flood, the chairman of the Joint Chiefs, sitting alone on one of the couches with a series of folders spread out on the coffee table. Rapp could tell instantly that Kennedy had broken the news to the four-star general. The stony expression on the soldier's face said it all. It was hard enough to lose men in battle but it was beyond infuriating to know that it could have been prevented.

Rapp decided that given the subject at hand it was better for him not to speak. Before he had a chance to sit, President Hayes entered his office with a cortege of aides trailing him. At over six feet tall with a full head of salt-and-pepper hair, Hayes stood out in a crowd, and like most men who had reached his station in life, he exuded a real magnetism. The men and women who worked for him wanted desperately to please him. Hayes unbuttoned his suit coat as he strode toward his desk. By the time he reached it the coat was off. He turned to face the three aides who were arguing about the administration's education bill. Hayes held up his hands, palms out, and the three fell silent like well-disciplined kids obeying their father.

As Rapp watched the exchange take place he noticed, not for the first time, that the president had gained a little weight. It was a subject the two men had discussed on several occasions. Rapp, a former triathlete, still worked out six days a week and watched his intake closely. The president had confided in him that he was very wary of what his job was doing to his health. After all his official duties, which there was scarcely enough time for, there was still the Democratic Party and its incessant need to raise money.

Barely a day passed when there wasn't a fund-raiser of some sort, and where there was a fund-raiser one could always count on lots of food and booze. Rapp had designed a bare-bones workout plan that the president could do in forty-five minutes. The goal was to do it five days a week, first thing in the morning. As Rapp looked at the president's expanding waistline, he had a feeling the man had been skipping his workouts.

"I don't want to talk about this anymore," said the president firmly. "By the end of the day I want you all on the same page. If the three of you can't come up with a consensus, this thing will be dead before it reaches the Hill." One of the aides tried to get in a last word, but the president cut her off with a terse motion toward the door. The three left the room dejectedly and closed the door behind them.

Hayes dropped into his chair and picked up a pair of reading glasses from the desk. After quickly glancing over his schedule, he pressed his intercom button and said, "Cheryl, I don't want to be interrupted for the next fifteen minutes."

"Yes, Mr. President," came the always even reply of his gatekeeper.

Hayes looked up and waved for his three visitors to join him. "Pull up a chair. If you don't mind, I have to look over a few things while we talk."

Kennedy had called the meeting and she didn't object. She knew once the president heard what she had to say, she'd have his rapt attention. As they settled in, the president picked up a document from his desk, scanned it and then moved it to another pile. Looking over the top of his reading glasses he said, "Mitchell, you look tan and rested. I trust you had a nice honeymoon?" The president smiled.

"Very nice, thank you, sir."

"Good." Getting down to business, Hayes turned to Kennedy and said, "I get the impression that whatever it is you have to tell me, it's not good."

"That's correct, sir."

Before Kennedy had a chance to elaborate, the door to their left flew open and the president's chief of staff entered the room with a big cup of Starbucks coffee in one hand and a cell phone and stack of files precariously balanced in the other. "Sorry I'm late."

Rapp leaned forward and shot his boss a questioning look. He mouthed the words, *What the hell is she doing here?*

Kennedy made a calming motion with her hand and ignored Rapp.

Kennedy's cool attitude did nothing to still Rapp's apprehension over Valerie Jones. She was a pushy and obnoxious political operative. If she were a man she would be referred to as a tough bastard or prick, but since she wore a skirt to work she was simply called a bitch. Rapp couldn't remember a time when he hadn't been at odds with the woman. Her first reaction at the onset of any potential crisis was to ask how it would affect the president's poll numbers. It drove Rapp nuts that every issue had to be parsed, muddied and then spun.

Putting Rapp in a room with Jones was like one of those crazy chemistry experiments where you started pouring different things into a beaker knowing full well there would be an explosion, and ultimately a mess to clean up. With Jones now in attendance it was highly likely that Rapp's mood would go from sour to downright shitty.

Before the meeting was over things would get ugly between the two, and Kennedy was counting on just that. For things to work out the way she hoped, everyone needed to play their role, and in the end, she was confident where the president would come down. Irene Kennedy had learned many things from her old boss, Thomas Stansfield. He had been fond of reminding her frequently that they were in the secret business; both collecting and keeping.

Common sense dictated that the less one talked the more likely it was one would learn secrets rather than give them away. He also liked to say the outcome of a meeting is often decided before a single word is spoken. It is decided by who is asked to attend. That was exactly what Kennedy had had in mind when she invited Jones.

The woman could adopt a passive attitude if she absolutely had to. If a foreign head of state was visiting the White House she might tone her act down, but that was about it. Valerie Jones was an obsessive-compulsive workaholic who lived and breathed politics. It was her life. She wanted to be involved in every decision, for in the arena of politics, anything the president attached his name to would ultimately affect his chances for reelection.

Nudging a small bust of President Eisenhower out of her way, the president's chief of staff plopped her files down on the corner of his desk. Neither Rapp nor General Flood made an effort to get her a chair. In the P.C. world of D.C. politics both knew such a gesture could be misperceived, and they might get their balls chewed off. And besides, neither of them liked Jones enough to make the effort.

When the chief of staff was settled, the president looked at Kennedy and said, "Let's hear it."

The ever placid Kennedy cocked her head slightly and brushed a strand of her shoulder-length brown hair behind her ear. As had been the case all too often lately, she was the bearer of bad news. "Mr. President, General Flood informs me that you've been fully briefed on the failed hostage rescue in the Philippines."

"Yes," answered the president in a sour tone, "and needless to say I'm not happy about it."

"I'd like to remind everyone," interrupted the president's chief of staff, "that I thought that entire operation was a bad idea from the start."

Ignoring Jones, Kennedy held up one of the two red folders and said, "I think I can shed some light on what went wrong, sir."

Hayes, his curiosity piqued, placed his forearms squarely on the desk and said, "I'm all ears."

"In this file"—Kennedy held up her left hand—"I have a list of e-mail and telephone transcripts. You will remember that before launching the rescue operation we decided that for reasons of operational security our embassy in the Philippines would not be notified until the teams and the hostages were safely extracted."

Jones had just finished taking a sip of coffee and began to shake her head vigorously. "Again, I'm on the record as saying that was a bad idea. We're going to be smarting over that one for some time. This thing is a real mess. The press is getting more curious by the hour. The press office has already received three calls this morning, the Philippine government is demanding answers and our own State Department is furious."

The president also chose to ignore Jones for the moment and stayed focused on Kennedy, saying, "I remember the issue was hotly contested."

Without looking up, General Flood grumbled, "And you made it very clear, sir, that our embassy was not to be notified."

The president was caught a little off guard by the general's tone. The soldier was in an unusually foul mood, which was very out of character.

"Sir," said Kennedy as she opened the file and handed the president the first page. "This is the transcript of an e-mail that was sent by Assistant Secretary of State Amanda Petry to Ambassador Cox. In it she clearly states the time and date the operation was to commence." Kennedy gave the president a second to look over the text and then handed him another piece of paper. "This is Ambassador Cox's reply asking for more specifics, and this is Amanda Petry's reply that outlines the rescue operation in detail." Kennedy handed him the third sheet.

The president looked over the documents in silence, and a frown slowly darkened his expression as each word hinted at what may have happened, and the twisted dark road where this might take him.

Patience not being one of her virtues, Jones got up from her chair and stood over the president's shoulder. She began scanning the documents and trying to make sense of what Kennedy was up to.

Pulling his reading glasses down to the tip of his nose Hayes looked at the director of the CIA and said, "This is serious stuff."

Before she could answer Jones said, "The State Department is going to be livid about this. Beatrice Berg is a living legend . . . are you out of your mind?" Jones was referring to the recently confirmed secretary of state, who was quite possibly the most respected person in Washington. She was currently in Greece leading a delegation that was trying to jump-start the Middle East peace talks.

Kennedy nodded and said, "Valerie, none of us are happy about this."

"No," said Jones in an icy tone. "I'm not talking about the operation. I'm talking about you spying on State. You can't just go around intercepting State Department cables. I mean, are you insane?" Jones's face twisted into a scowl as she tried to calculate the damage that would be done if this were leaked to the press.

"Ms. Jones," General Flood gruffly replied. "It is routine business for the NSA to intercept embassy traffic. And beyond that I don't think the State Department is in much of a position to complain about anything."

"General, I don't like this any more than you do," the president's chief of staff said a little defensively, "but the State Department will not take kindly to being spied on by the CIA, the NSA or whoever."

"Tough shit," answered Rapp before Flood or Kennedy could say a word.

All eyes turned to Rapp, who was sitting on the opposite side of the desk. Jones, not one to be intimidated easily, said, "I beg your pardon?"

Rapp's dark penetrating eyes were locked on to the president's chief of staff. "Two sailors are dead and at least two more have had their careers ended due to the injuries they've suffered. Lives have been destroyed, Valerie. Children will never see their fathers again, two women have been widowed, and we still have an entire family of Americans held hostage in the Philippines, all because a couple of diplomats couldn't keep their mouths shut."

Jones snatched one of the pieces of paper from the president's desk and defiantly shook it. "This is not conclusive."

Rather than waste his time screaming at Jones, Rapp looked to Kennedy, anticipating the evidence that would silence the president's right-hand woman.

Calmly, Kennedy said, "Sir, there's more. After receiving the heads-up from Assistant Secretary Petry, Ambassador Cox phoned Philippine president Quirino." Kennedy handed the president a copy of the conversation. "An hour after that conversation took place Ambassador Cox arrived at the presidential palace where he stayed for approximately thirty minutes. We don't know what was said between the ambassador and President Quirino, but shortly after the ambassador left, President Quirino placed a phone call to General Moro of the Philippine army.

"As I'm sure you're aware, General Moro has been in charge of trying to track down Abu Sayyaf for the last year. He has repeatedly promised that he will free the Anderson family and deal harshly with the terrorists. On two separate occasions the general has had Abu Sayyaf cornered only to have them miraculously escape. Our military advisors in the region began to smell a rat and the DOD asked us to put the general under surveillance. This was over five months ago."

Kennedy opened the second folder and handed the president a fresh set of documents. "It turns out General Moro is not such a good ally after all. We didn't know it at the time, but he was a very active advocate of kicking the U.S. Navy out of Subic Bay. He wields great influence in a country where bribes are a way of life. We found several bank accounts, one in Hong Kong and the other in Jakarta. It looks like the general has been in the pocket of the Chinese for the better part of the last decade, and more recently we think he began extorting protection money from Abu Sayyaf."

Jones scoffed at the idea. "You mean to tell me that a bunch of peasants running around in the jungles over there can scrape up enough money to bribe a general in the Philippine army?"

"That's exactly what I'm saying," replied an even-keeled Kennedy.

"That's one of the most ludicrous things I've ever heard."

Kennedy resisted the urge to tell Jones that if she'd paid attention to her intelligence briefings she'd know that the idea was far from ludicrous. People in Washington had long memories and another thing Thomas Stansfield had taught her was to avoid making it personal. "Abu Sayyaf is not just some poor group of peasants. They receive millions in funding from various Muslim groups throughout the Middle East. Much of it comes from Saudi Arabia."

The president did not want to get into that mess right now so he focused his gray eyes on General Flood and asked, "Was General Moro informed by us of any aspect of the rescue mission prior to it being launched?"

"No," answered Flood. "For reasons that are all too apparent, the plan was to keep the Philippine army in the dark until we were on our way out with the Andersons." Flood shrugged. "We didn't trust them enough to bring them in on it and if we didn't ask for permission, they couldn't say no."

The chief of staff rolled her eyes and said, "I'd hate to think what the U.S. Army would do if a foreign country conducted a military operation on American soil without our permission."

Rapp leaned forward, almost coming out of his chair

entirely and looked angrily at Jones. "They wouldn't have to, because we'd never allow a group of terrorists to kidnap foreign citizens in the United States. We'd go kick the door down and solve the problem before you even had enough time to collect polling data."

Jones stood and crossed her arms defiantly. "Mr. Rapp, we're all aware that you are predisposed to using violence to solve a problem, but I would like to ask you where that has gotten us?" Not giving him a chance to reply she continued, "Our list of allies is shrinking. These little operations that you are so fond of have alienated some of our strongest supporters. The Filipinos are going to make some serious hay out of this, our own State Department is going to be livid with us for spying on them, and not letting them do their jobs, and before this is over"—she angrily pointed at Rapp—"you mark my words, there will be a congressional investigation into whose bonehead idea this whole thing was."

The blood rushed to Rapp's face, though he was too tan for it to be apparent to the others in the room. He stood to face Jones eye to eye. It took all his self-control to speak somewhat evenly. "Valerie, you have great political instincts, but you are an absolute moron when it comes to issues of national security. Your ideas are dangerous, your logic is flawed and nothing I've heard you say here today is based on sound moral judgment."

"Moral judgment?" she asked snidely. "You're going to lecture me on morality?"

The implication was clear. Rapp was a killer and thus should forfeit his right to judge. He ignored her condescension and said, "Here are the facts, Valerie. A family of American citizens was on vacation and were kidnapped by a well-known terrorist group that is a self-admitted sworn enemy of the United States. We now know that the

Philippine general in charge of freeing those hostages is taking bribes from the terrorists who hold them. We know that a decision was made to use U.S. Special Forces to free the hostages. That decision was completely legal and made by none other than the commander in chief." Rapp pointed at the president. "Part of those operational orders were that neither our embassy in the Philippines nor the Philippine government were to be informed of the rescue operation. Two senior State Department officials willingly disregarded those orders and as a direct result a platoon of SEALs was ambushed on a beach two nights ago."

With her arms folded defiantly across her chest, Jones asked, "Are you done?"

Rapp strained to keep from reaching out and slapping her. With a clenched jaw he replied, "No. This morning while you were yapping on your cell phone and picking up your triple mocha frappuccino, or whatever the hell it is that you drink, a cargo plane landed out in San Diego. Do you know what it was carrying?"

Jones glared at Rapp with unvarnished hatred. No one, not even the president, had ever spoken to her this way. "No."

"Two flag-draped caskets, Valerie." Rapp help up his fingers. "There were little kids, wives, and some grandparents there to meet those caskets. Their lives are turned upside down. The men they loved, the men they adored, the men they idolized are gone forever. They are feeling pain right now that you can't even begin to understand, and all because a couple of self-important bureaucrats over at the State Department couldn't keep their damn mouths shut!" Rapp's eyes were filled with rage. "If I had it my way, Valerie, I'd march Ambassador Cox and Assistant Secretary Petry out in front of a firing squad and have them shot."

Jones flapped her arms and roared, "I can't believe I'm hearing this." She looked around for someone to second her opinion, but no one backed her up. Dumbfounded, she looked back at Rapp and said, "I think you've lost it."

"I lost it a long time ago, Valerie, and I could give a rat's ass what you think of me. I've been on that beach thousands of miles away. I've crawled out of the surf wondering if I'm going to catch a bullet right between the eyes." Rapp marked the spot with his index finger. "I've seen a helicopter filled with young men blown from the sky because an arrogant senator couldn't keep his mouth shut."

Jones's arms were again folded across her chest and in a disinterested tone she said, "I'm well aware of what you've done for a living."

Rapp stood with his feet firmly planted, seething with anger. "I can take a lot of crap from people, Valerie, but one thing I can't stand is a lack of gratitude. I'm one of those guys on the beach getting shot at, trying to do the right thing, risking it all for love of country, duty and honor. Words that mean nothing to you. I've been there and you haven't." He pointed at her. "No Starbucks coffee, no dinners at Morton's, no warm baths. Just a lot of bugs, salty MREs and the comforting thought that there are a lot of self-centered Americans who will never be able to appreciate the sacrifice you've made.

"So, yeah, I guess I've lost it a bit," Rapp said in a calmer voice, "and that's why I'm not going to let you protect those arrogant assholes over at the State Department. The CIA had Ames, the FBI had Hanssen and now the State Department is going to have Cox and Petry. Things are going to get real uncomfortable for the ambassador and the undersecretary, and that piece of shit General Moro is going to get his, I can promise you that."

Jones still stood defiantly and asked for a second time, "Are you done?"

Rapp's face actually broke into a smile. He looked at the president for a moment. Hayes was notorious for letting his aides battle it out. His motto was that he'd rather get it all out in the open than let it fester under the surface.

Looking at Jones, Rapp thought, *I can't believe I actually saved this woman's life.* Shaking his head, he said, "I've got one last thing to say. If it wasn't for me, Valerie, you'd be dead." Rapp turned and started for the door. Over his shoulder he said, "So I'd appreciate a little more gratitude." When Rapp reached the door he opened it and looked back at Jones. "Oh, and by the way, you'd better figure out how you're going to spin this when it breaks, because I'm not going to stay quiet."

TEN

The room was located on the seventh floor of the hotel. David slid his passkey into the slot and when the light turned green he placed his forearm on the handle and opened the door. His meeting with General Hamza hadn't lasted long, and knowing what the future had in store for the Iraqi thug helped to make their encounter more bearable than usual. Fortunately, Hamza hadn't indulged in his usual hour of browbeating and self-aggrandizement. The general was very fond of reminding his contact of the Palestinian people's position in the Arab pecking order. In Hamza's exalted point of view, the Palestinians ranked just above camel dung.

When the general finished his drink and stood to leave, David knew what was causing him to cut short tonight's lecture. There was something in Hamza's room that the general wanted to get back to. It was for that reason that David was in a hurry. His spies had followed the general's men earlier in the day and had witnessed them once again kidnap a young girl.

He'd never left the hotel. After watching the general and his bodyguards leave, David waited a few minutes and then headed for the lobby. One of his people met him and took the cases. David then headed up to the room that he'd checked into three days earlier.

Grabbing a pair of latex gloves from his pocket, he went to work. In front of the bathroom mirror he peeled off the beard and wiped clean the gray dye from his hair and eyebrows. Both the beard and the damp washcloth were placed in a Ziploc bag. Next he took off the suit and shoes and grabbed a backpack from the closet. He put on a pair of black pants, black tennis shoes, dark shirt and coat and then rolled the other clothes up tightly and stuffed everything into the backpack. After going over the room one last time to make sure he wasn't leaving anything behind, David walked to the sliding glass door and yanked it open.

Before stepping onto the balcony he peered to his left and right to see if anyone was about. With the balconies on either side clear, David casually walked outside and continued his surveillance. From one of the rooms below he could hear loud music playing on a stereo. David's eyes burned with hatred at the thought of what might already be happening.

General Hamza was a vile, disgusting man in so many ways, but none more so than in his penchant for young girls. Prepubescent girls to be precise. David had discovered this perverse side of the general while he'd been watching him for the last several months. There had been at least two other occasions that David knew of where the general's bodyguards had snatched young Palestinian girls from the street and brought them back to the hotel so the general could have his fun with them. Using his contacts with the local Jordanian authorities, David dug around and found that the police had actually attempted to question the general about some of the girls who had been abducted. Several days later word had come down from the highest of places telling the police not to harass General Hamza. The Jordanians were not about to let the welfare of a handful of young Palestinian girls interfere with their relations with Iraq.

As David tied a climbing rope to the side of his balcony, he focused on the task at hand. This would not be the first time he'd killed and it certainly wouldn't be the last. He always operated with a calm precision that steered clear of either anger or pleasure. Tonight, however, he was finding it a bit difficult to suppress some of his feelings about the job at hand. The arrogance of General Hamza had gotten to him. The Iraqis had co-opted the Palestinian issue under the guise of Arab brotherhood for the simple goal of driving a wedge between the Arab states and America. If it was only that, David could live with it. He had a grudging respect for America and in the end felt they would do what was right. And if it was only the way the Iraqis lied with such vehemence, he could deal with it. Lying to other tribes was an accepted part of the culture of his people. What really boiled his blood, however, was the way the Iraqis treated Palestinians when the cameras weren't around. It was their arrogance and condescension, and on top of that the way they bullied their brothers in arms. When you fought your way through all the blustery dictums and rhetoric, the Iraqis were out for no one other than themselves.

There was one more thing about the Iraqi general that tested David's composure. It was his utter contempt of and downright hatred for women. Growing up in Jerusalem David was the only boy in his family. He had three older sisters. His father was Palestinian and his mother Jordanian. Both had been educated in Britain. His father was an attorney and his mother was a doctor. In a part of the world where equality between the sexes was still a long way off, David had grown up in a house where there was never a doubt that his mother and father were on the same footing. In fact, if pressed, David would probably admit that his mother was the more dominant of the two. All three of his sisters had gone to America and had become doctors. The two eldest remained in the States where they practiced medicine, and the youngest had come back to help her mother with her practice in Jerusalem. David held his sisters in the highest regard, and unlike many of his Arab brothers he did not adhere to the belief that women should be treated like property.

As David tied off the black climbing rope he muttered a curse and stopped fighting his anger. Nothing boiled his blood more than someone taking advantage of the weak. He pulled on a pair of leather gloves and splaying his fingers apart, worked the leather down firmly into one crook after another. After checking his weapons one last time he pulled a black balaclava over his head and adjusted it so only his dark eyes were visible. With everything in order, he swung one leg over the edge and then the other.

Loosening his grip ever so slightly, David slithered slowly down the rope until his foot touched the railing of the balcony beneath. Deftly he leapt from his perch and landed softly on the concrete surface of the balcony. What little noise he made was masked by the music coming from within the room. Cautiously, he leaned around the edge of the wall to see what was going on inside. The sheer curtain was drawn, but the heavy curtain was not. The room was lit with candles and David could make out a form hovering near what he knew to be the bed. David saw the form jerk in a forward motion and he thought he heard a muffled scream follow. Moving back quickly he took off his backpack and then placed his hand on the door. Slowly, he applied pressure and was not surprised to find that the door was locked.

Crouching, he reached into the backpack and extracted a thin piece of sheet metal with a notch in the end. David took the piece of metal and gently wedged it between the frame and heavy sliding glass door. Twisting it counterclockwise he waited until he had the right amount of tension and then lifted up. Not pausing to see if the general had heard the click, David slid the piece of sheet metal into his coat pocket with one hand and grabbed for his silenced 9mm gun with the other. With his eyes trained on the shadow on the other side of the large suite, he began opening the door. Moving the sheer curtain out of the way, he stepped into the room and was sickened by what he saw.

Standing naked over the girl, a sweaty General Hamza brought a riding crop high above his head and let loose with a wicked blow. The young girl was tied to the bed facedown, spread-eagle, with a gag in her mouth. Her entire body shuddered as the leather crop met her flesh. She tried to scream, but it only came out as another muffled cry. Her delicate skin had been breached in at least a dozen places.

David stared in horror at the long, bloody welts. Hamza, with his back to him, raised the crop above his head again, poised to unleash another blow. David suddenly wanted very badly to hurt him, not just kill him. Moving quickly, he reached Hamza just as the crop was about to strike the girl. His right hand came crashing down in a motion that mimicked Hamza's, but before the leather crop could strike the girl again, the black steel of David's pistol made contact with the base of the general's neck.

Hamza dropped the riding crop instantly, lurching forward and falling unsteadily to one knee. David hovered over him for a split second and then unleashed a second blow. This time the pistol grip landed on the top of Hamza's head. The general wavered for a moment like a tree that couldn't decide which way it would fall, and then before gravity could take hold David reached out and grabbed a handful of hair. Not wanting to alert the bodyguards in the next room, he carefully lowered the naked body of Hamza to the floor.

David grabbed a sheet and covered the young girl. As he looked down at Hamza with disgust and hatred a battle was raging within him. All of his instincts told him to finish off the general and then take care of the bodyguards. That would be the professional way to proceed. The vengeful voice in his head, though, wanted the general to suffer, and it was winning.

David moved for the door that connected the general's room to that of his bodyguards. Without a moment of hesitation he grabbed the handle and yanked it open. He knew the layout of the room, and his silenced pistol was up and already sweeping the area where he'd most likely find the two thugs, while he stayed in the doorway, hugging the frame to reduce his silhouette on the off chance one of the men might get off a shot.

Neither of them did. They were watching TV and looked up expecting to see their boss, but instead found a man wearing a black mask and pointing a gun at them. The weapon was fired twice in less than half a second. At a distance of just eighteen feet David never doubted his accuracy. Both 9mm, subsonic hollow-tipped rounds found their mark, hitting the bodyguards dead center between the eyes. The two Iraqis died instantly.

David closed and locked the door and then after another brief internal battle he decided on a course of action. From an assassin's point of view it wasn't the smart thing to do, but it was definitely the right thing to do. He would have to deviate from his well-planned script, but he wasn't about to leave this poor young girl behind in the hotel room to face further pain and humiliation when the police arrived. No, she would be coming with him. He was getting ahead of himself, though. First he had to think of an appropriate way to kill the naked Iraqi pig who was lying on the floor before him. David began cutting the young girl's bonds and with each slice of the knife the proper death sentence became more clear to him.

ELEVEN

Rapp's performance wasn't exactly what Kennedy had had in mind, but she could tell that it had an impact on the president. An added bonus was that Kennedy couldn't remember a time when she'd seen Valerie Jones so flustered. The president's animated chief of staff was silenced for once, waiting desperately for someone else to come to her defense now that Rapp had left. She looked from the president, to Flood, to Kennedy, and then back around again. Having found no comfort she settled on looking out the window and tapping her foot. Kennedy wondered if Jones honestly thought she would receive any solace from her or General Flood.

After several more moments of tense silence, Jones couldn't take it anymore. She looked at the president and blurted, "I warned you that having him around was a bad idea."

President Hayes looked at his chief of staff evenly. "I don't always agree with Mitch's opinions, but I do always value them."

"Robert, he doesn't see the big picture. He doesn't understand the negative impact this type of scandal will have on your presidency."

Hayes cocked his head a bit to the side and said, "I have a feeling that Mitch would say it's you who don't see the big picture."

Jones exhaled in frustration. "I'm not going to sit here and debate the big picture with some assassin from the CIA." Jones turned to Kennedy and said, "No offense, Irene, but I'm paid to put all the pieces of the puzzle together and minimize the president's exposure. You don't have to have a doctorate in political science to figure out what's going to happen when this story breaks. We are going to get eaten alive by the press, and then the committees on the Hill will begin to call for hearings"—she turned her attention to Hayes—"and they will make damn sure they drag you through the mud right up to your reelection."

To everyone's surprise Kennedy said, "I agree with Valerie."

Looking smug with her newfound support, Jones said, "Even his own boss agrees with me."

Kennedy held up a finger and added, "I do, but with one exception. You'll never be able to keep a lid on this. The press already knows something's up. By the end of today, they'll have a pretty good handle on this story, and we'll probably see our first installment in the morning papers."

"But we can handle that," Jones jumped in. "I already have our people working on the press release. The servicemen were lost in a joint training exercise with the Philippine army." Jones looked to General Flood. "This type of thing happens all the time, right?"

Before the general could answer, the president said, "The Philippine ambassador has already called twice this morning, and I assure you it wasn't to talk about the weather."

Jones batted away the concern with her hand. "They

need our aid to prop up their economy. All we need to do is throw them some more money, and they'll play ball."

Kennedy slowly shook her head. "Too many people know about this, sir. There's no way you're going to be able to keep a lid on it."

The president was leaning back now, tapping his fore-finger against his upper lip.

Before he could say anything, Jones jumped back into the debate. "Give me one week. That's all I'm asking for. One week and I'll have the press looking into something else, I promise."

Hayes looked to the chairman of the Joint Chiefs and said, "General, you're unusually quiet this morning. Is there anything you'd care to add?"

General Flood was an imposing man and even more so in his uniform. A few inches over six feet tall and pushing three hundred pounds he looked more like a retired foot-ball player than a man who still liked to jump out of planes a couple of times a year. It was evident from his face that he was trying to choose his words carefully. Keeping his eyes on the president he finally said, "Sir, I couldn't disagree with Miss Jones more emphatically."

The president was looking at Flood, but from the cor-ner of his eye he could see his chief of staff begin to squirm. Ignoring her he said, "Please elaborate."

"We have announced that we are at war with terror-ism. We have proof that at a bare minimum a Philippine general is taking bribes from a known terrorist organiza-tion that has taken a family of Americans hostage. We have proof that a State Department official, who was told in no uncertain terms that this rescue operation was to be kept secret, decided on her own volition to break federal law and discuss this information with an overseas State De-partment official. We have a U.S. ambassador, who took it upon himself to brief the head of a foreign country that U.S. Special Forces were about to conduct a covert operation on that country's soil. Any reasonable person would conclude that these actions clearly led to the deaths of two U.S. Navy SEALS. You have said it yourself, Mr. President, we are at war. This is serious business, and in my mind the ambassador and the undersecretary are traitors and their actions cannot go unpunished."

"I agree that they should be punished," Jones said quickly before anyone else could speak. "I say we ship them off to the worst posting we can think of. I say we not only make them take a cut in pay, but we make them pay restitution to the families of the two dead soldiers. I say—"

"Dead sailors," the general corrected her. Looking back to the president he added, "I happen to agree with Mitch. If it were up to me, I would have these two marched in front of a firing squad and shot, but I realize in today's world that will never happen. I do, however, think they need to spend some hard time in jail and they need to be publicly humiliated. They need be made an example of."

Jones, desperate to turn the tide of this conversation, weighed in once more. "General, I'm not saying I disagree with you, but again I don't think you're looking at how this scandal will affect this administration."

"With all due respect, Miss Jones, I'm more concerned with the welfare of this republic than any single administration. The two should go hand in hand, but as you've so passionately pointed out this morning, that's not always the case."

Jones glared at the general and said, "That was a cheap shot."

"No, it was a direct shot, but if I wasn't blunt enough

for you, let me spell this entire clusterfuck out for you in clear English." The general leaned toward the chief of staff and said, "This was a big operation. A lot of military and intelligence personnel knew about it beforehand, and since it went south a lot more people know about it today." Flood stuck out one of his beefy fingers with conviction and said, "I can guarantee you, if you try to whitewash this thing, someone in uniform, or over at Langley, is going to be so offended they will talk to a reporter off the record and they will set off a chain reaction that will do exactly what you're hoping to avoid. And that's if *Mitch* doesn't break the story first."

"You worry about your people, general," Jones shot back, "and I'll handle Rapp."

The sheer lunacy of the comment caused Flood to roar with laughter. "You're going to tell Mitch Rapp what to do? Let me know when and where, and I'll pay top dollar to witness that fight."

Before Jones could speak again, the president came forward in his chair and rested his forearms on his desk. "I've made a decision." He was talking to everyone, but was looking at Jones. "We're going to confront this thing head-on, and it's not up for debate. If we try to bury it . . . it'll only come back and bite us in the ass. I want the Justice Department to prepare warrants for the arrest of Assistant Secretary Petry and Ambassador Cox."

Jones began shaking her head. "Robert—"

Before she could continue the president cut her off and said, "Valerie, cancel my dinner plans for this evening and inform the congressional leadership that I'd like to meet with them."

Jones had a pained expression on her face. The president's demeanor suggested that any further protests would be unwise. She'd lost this one for now, but there was always later. When she had him alone she would try to get him to rethink his decision before he jumped off the cliff.

With strained pleasantness Jones asked, "What would you like me to tell them?"

"Tell them I need to brief them on an issue of national security."

"I'll get to work on it right away." Before leaving she turned to Kennedy. "You'll keep me informed of any decisions you reach with the DOJ and the FBI?"

Kennedy noticed it was more a demand than a question, but nonetheless nodded politely. Jones had been thoroughly defeated and there was no sense rubbing it in.

When the chief of staff was gone the president addressed Kennedy and Flood. "I'm sorry about that. Politics comes first for Valerie. She can't help it."

Flood shook his oversize head and grumbled something. Kennedy watched the general with pursed lips and then added, "No need to apologize, sir. You need people who will watch out for the political ramifications."

"That's true," agreed the president, "but that doesn't mean we have to check our morals at the door." Hayes's face twisted into a disapproving frown. "Valerie's tendency is to try to control everything. She doesn't understand that the American people will cut you a lot of slack as long as you're up front with them and they know you had the right intentions. In this situation it's pretty cut and dried."

Hayes laid his hands flat on his desk and moved several pieces of paper around while he pondered precisely how to proceed. "I want to do the right thing here. I want to be up front on this, and I want to move very quickly. I don't want some hotshot reporter breaking this before we get out in front of it, otherwise I'm afraid Valerie will be proven right and I'll be crucified on the Hill."

"If I may, sir?" asked Kennedy. The president nodded

and she said, "You might not want to wait for tonight. The general and I could begin briefing select members of the various committees this afternoon. Then when you meet with them tonight, you can give them the entire story. I would caution you, though, that we need to keep General Moro and his involvement out of this."

The president's expression went from keen to confused. "Why?"

Kennedy hesitated and then said, "Mitch has come up with a solution for dealing with the general. If you have time, I think we should get him back in here so he can explain it to you."

The president eyed the director of the CIA with great curiosity. Since diplomacy was far from Mitch Rapp's area of expertise, the president was very curious about what his top counterterrorism operative had in the works. Two navy SEALs were dead, a family of Americans were still held hostage and his presidency was on the brink of scandal. Right now, the idea of retribution seemed very appealing.

TWELVE

The little girl sat huddled in the corner, wrapped in a white robe, clutching herself tightly. David was sweating profusely under the black hood that covered his face. He grabbed one of Hamza's legs and arms and pulled him to the center of the bed. Hearing a muffled sob, he looked up to check on the girl. Her face was covered by the oversize white folds of the hotel robe. He felt a genuine ache in his heart at the agony she was suffering. He knew it wasn't just physical pain. Even worse, anguish and nightmares would probably follow her for the rest of her life.

David guessed that she couldn't be more than ten years of age. Right about now guilt and self-recrimination would be working their way into her innocent mind. She would begin to wonder what she had done wrong to warrant such treatment. The Muslim world dealt very harshly with sexual stigmas where women were concerned. In David's patriarchal society the distinction between a woman who willingly commits adultery and one who is forcibly raped is often lost. The honor of the family, which really means the honor of the father, is above all else.

David looked down at the poor frightened kid in the

corner and struggled over what to do with her. He knew he should have never untied her. He should have simply shot Hamza in the back of the head, dispatched the two bodyguards and left. If he'd stuck with his original plan he'd be long gone by now; miles of safe distance between himself and the crime. The maid would show up in the morning and find the young girl, and she would be taken to a hospital. Everything would have turned out just fine for her.

As much as he wanted to believe it, though, he knew that was far from what would really happen. The maid would have called the police, who would very quickly discover they had a dead Iraqi general on their hands. The media would find out shortly after that, and this little innocent girl would get swept up in the maelstrom that would follow. The police and reporters would talk to her parents and the entire neighborhood would find out that the young girl had been sexually assaulted. Through no fault of her own she would be shunned and treated as a pariah for the rest of her years.

David wasn't about to let that happen. When he'd started down this dangerous path years before, he'd made a promise to himself. David hadn't grown up in the camps, but his mother had been sure to bring him along whenever she visited the various clinics. She wanted him to see firsthand the squalor that Palestinian people were forced to live in. His mother, unique in more ways than he could ever count, used the long car rides to and from the camps to enlighten her only son on the politics of the most contested region in the history of mankind.

The camps were a breeding ground for discontent, corruption and anti-Semitism. The Jews were blamed for everything, both real and imagined, consequential and inconsequential. They were the evil greedy Zionists who had stolen the land away from the Palestinian people. The propaganda was insidious but his mother had been very careful to teach David about the complicated history of the conflict between the Palestinians and the Jews. In her mind there was more than enough blame to go around.

For a brief period in 1948 the Palestinians actually had a state, but instead of taking what the United Nations had legally mandated, they decided to attack the fledgling country of Israel with the help of five Arab armies. The decision proved disastrous. Israel trounced the Arab armies, seized the land that had been set aside for the Palestinian state, and deported most of the Palestinians who hadn't already left.

David's mother liked to point out that it was a little disingenuous of their people to cry that Israel had stolen their land. She was fond of asking him, "If we had won the war back in forty-eight, do you think we would have allowed the Jews to keep their land?" She never waited for him to answer. The reply was always a resounding, "No. The Arab armies would have killed every last Jew."

"The Jews are racists," she used to tell him, "but the Jordanians, the Egyptians, the Syrians, the Iraqis and the Saudis are all worse. The Jews hate us because we've given them no reason to like us, but what excuse do our Arab brothers have? They have none. We are beneath them, that is the way they feel. They have kept our people in these camps and stoked the flames of hatred toward the Jews to serve their own corrupt governments. We are servants to them. A useful tool in their campaign to keep their subjects' anger focused not on them, but on the evil Jews."

His mother's teachings had made David wary of all propaganda. He refused to allow hatred to drive his ambition. He would never allow himself to turn a blind eye to the truth. He would never allow himself to become just another cold-blooded killer. That was why he didn't just shoot Hamza and leave the poor girl to be discovered in the morning. David truly was a unique man. He was a pragmatist with a heart. The girl would be brought with him now, and an explanation and some cash would be given to her father later.

He finished tying the general's wrists and ankles to the bed and then hovered over him for a moment. General Hamza had spent the better part of thirty years inflicting pain on people, destroying lives and ruining dreams. A bullet in the head was too good for him. Hamza needed to experience the fear he had so perversely meted out to so many souls. David wanted to see real fear in the man's eyes.

He pulled his knife from its leather scabbard with his right hand and slapped Hamza's cheek with his left. The Iraqi thug's jaw hung loose. Reaching in with his thumb and forefinger David grabbed the tip of Hamza's tongue and pulled it taut. The general started to stir. David tightened his grip and angled the tip of the four-inch blade into Hamza's mouth. A quick upward slicing motion and a good seventy percent of Hamza's tongue was severed from his mouth. With perfect timing, the general's eyes shot open just in time to watch David tear the rest of his tongue out.

The Iraqi general, his eyes ablaze with fear and agony, let out a low guttural moan that because he no longer had his tongue never quite elevated itself to a scream. Immediately, he began to slash about like a landed fish in the bottom of a boat. He struggled against his bonds, trying to break free, struggling to comprehend what was happening. His last memories were deliciously good ones, and now he was tied to this bed with some masked man sitting on his chest dangling a piece of meat in front of his face. Making matters worse, his mouth was on fire with a pain that his brain could not identify. A warm liquid trickled down his throat and caused him to gag when it dribbled into his windpipe. Suddenly, the pieces fell into place. In a panic, Hamza lifted his head off the pillow and tried to speak. All that came out were a jumble of primitive noises. The masked man sitting on top of him wasn't holding a piece of meat, he was holding Hamza's tongue.

David dropped the fleshy organ onto Hamza's bare chest and reached into his own pocket. He grabbed a pack of crisp counterfeit hundred-dollar bills and waved them in front of the general's face. He didn't need to speak. Neither did the general, although he tried. There was instant recognition in his eyes. David crumpled a dozen of the new bills into a ball and with the tip of his blood-soaked knife he pried open the general's lips. He crammed the wad in and then added two more fistfuls of money until Hamza's mouth was overflowing with bills.

Moving quickly, he shoved another pillow under Hamza's head and then got off him. Taking a moment to relish the sadistic bastard's fear, David looked down at him and shook his head in disgust. He wondered if this butcher of Saddam's had ever granted someone a reprieve, if he had ever felt an ounce of guilt over his actions or pity for the people he had so brutally tortured. As David looked into Hamza's fearful eyes he knew the answer was no. Monsters like Hamza were wired differently. Their brains worked in ways normal people could never understand.

David felt no shame in what he was about to do. He felt no pity for Hamza. This would be justice in its purest form. Hamza would die in a manner commensurate with his crimes of brutality. David tossed the rest of the hundred-dollar bills onto the bed. They lay strewn about from one side to the other. Hamza looked down at the bills and tried to signal something with his eyes. David ignored him and walked to the foot of the bed, holding the knife up in the air. He stopped in between the general's spread legs and looked down. Placing one knee on the bed, he reached out with his gloved hand and grabbed Hamza by his genitals. The general's entire body convulsed in fear. Straining against his bonds he thrashed his head from side to side, a hideous noise rising up from his chest only to be stifled by the bloody bundle of worthless bills in his mouth. David did not hesitate or waver. He pulled hard with his left hand and reached out with the knife.

It took four slices, and there David stood with General Hamza's genitals in his hand. He held them before the Iraqi's horrified eyes and then simply dropped the bloody mess on his chest along with his tongue. Standing over him, David contemplated finishing him off, but decided against it. It was unlikely anyone would visit the room before morning and by then Hamza would surely have bled to death. It was more fitting to let him slowly die while staring at his lifeless sex organs, unable to scream for help, unable to move a limb to stem the bleeding. He would know the same helpless horror of his victims. And if someone came earlier and managed to save him, that wouldn't be all that bad either; Hamza would spend his remaining days a castrated, prickless mute.

THIRTEEN

The high billowing clouds had moved on and the midmorning sun was poking its way through the trees of the Rose Garden. The president sat behind his desk, elbows planted on the armrests of his Kevlar lined leather chair. His hands were clasped in front of his chin, the crisp white sleeves of his dress shirt forming a pyramid before him. He was engrossed in what he was being told by his guest.

Mitch Rapp, his dark suit coat open and his hands on his hips, strode back and forth across the blue rug of the Oval Office. The man moved with an athletic grace that hinted at his many talents. As he walked he laid out the operation for the president. Director Kennedy and General Flood sat in silence while Rapp paced behind them.

Rapp had been talking without interruption for nearly five minutes. He was about to go over the final part of the plan, but decided at the last minute to pause. Looking down at the chairman of the Joint Chiefs, Rapp said, "General, if you would like to excuse yourself from the room at this point, I would completely understand."

The general scratched his chin and in a surprisingly lighthearted tone replied, "I think I've got an idea where you're going with this, and I'm guessing you're not worried about offending me."

Rapp grinned. "General, I'm not sure it would be possible for me to offend you with words alone."

With a laugh, the general said, "As long as you leave my wife and children out of it, I'd say you're right. I assume you're offering me a chance to excuse myself from the really nasty part of this, in case it goes south."

"That would be correct."

There was a fairly long pause before the general answered and then he said, "My wife likes to accuse me of having selective memory." Looking up at Rapp he added, "You know what I mean?"

"I think I do." Rap smiled and then turned back to the president. "As long as I'm over in the Philippines, I think it would be a good idea to stop by and visit General Moro."

The president shifted uncomfortably in his chair. A voice in the back of his head was telling him to just nod, tell Rapp to have good trip and then get on with his day, but another part of him wanted to know more. "And what will you be discussing with General Moro?"

Rapp stopped with his shoulders squared to the president and looked down at his shoes for a moment. "Sir, does the first lady ever accuse you of having selective memory?"

"Ever since the day I met her, and truth be told she's right. But that's not the point." The president spun his chair a quarter turn and looked out the window. "Mitch, I'm not comfortable having you stick your neck out this far."

"Don't worry about me, sir. That's what I'm paid for."

The president nodded. "Yeah, I know you are, but that doesn't give the rest of us the excuse to say we were kept in the dark every time something goes wrong."

"Sir," said Kennedy with great sincerity, "that's the way it has to be."

"Well, that doesn't mean I have to like it, and to be honest, I'm not so sure eliminating General Moro will do anything other than satiate our short-term need for blood."

Rapp frowned at the president's words. In his tactical mind blood lust had no bearing on whether Moro deserved to die or live.

"Mr. President," Rapp said in a voice that was neither pleading nor condescending, "General Moro is a traitorous bastard who is directly responsible for the death of two United States Navy SEALs. And if you're worried about offending President Quirino, I can assure you that after she finds out Moro was a paid informant for both the Chinese and Abu Sayyaf, she'll be thanking us for getting rid of him."

The president tapped his finger on his lips a few more times and then leaning forward and grabbing a file announced, "Let me think about all this, and I'll get back to you."

Rapp didn't have to be a seasoned Washington bureaucrat to recognize a brush-off. Not one to give in so easily, he stood his ground and asked, "When will you have an answer for me, sir?"

Hayes eyed Rapp cautiously for a second and said, "In a couple of days."

Rapp shook his head. "That won't work, sir. Once the story breaks on the ambassador and Petry, our ability to move on Moro will be compromised."

Hayes again leaned back in his chair and exhaled. "Listen," he said in a no-nonsense tone, "from what you've told me this morning, this General Moro deserves to rot in a cell for the rest of his life, but as far as assassinating him goes . . . I'm not so sure. The fallout could be very ugly and to be honest with you, we really need the Philippine government with us in this fight. So as I said, I'm going to need a few days to consider our options." Having spoken his piece, Hayes spun his chair away from Rapp and opened the file he'd grabbed off his desk.

Rapp watched him with curiosity, and then looked down at Kennedy for guidance. She stood and motioned toward the door with a jerk of her thumb. She looked at General Flood and did the same thing. Reluctantly, Rapp followed her orders and began to leave the famed office wondering how many other people over the years had felt his same sense of frustration. As he placed his hand on the doorknob, he heard Kennedy say to the president, "Sir, I need to have a word alone with you."

Rapp grinned ever so slightly as he looked back at his boss. Kennedy, despite her subdued demeanor, could be surprisingly persuasive. He felt confident that by the time she left the office they would have the approval they were looking for.

FOURTEEN

David's demeanor was calm though perhaps slightly distracted as he walked down Via Dolorosa, passing from the Muslim Quarter of the Old City to the Christian Quarter. It was a walk he'd taken countless times. In his youth he did so without a care in the world, but as he grew older he began to see things, to notice the dangers that lurked in the entryways of the storefronts, in the eyes of the old men selling fruit and nuts on the street and the women running errands. There were spies and informants everywhere. It was in the thirteenth year of his life that innocence had been beaten from his body. He still carried scars from that day, both physical and mental, but he never spoke of them.

The eyes of the street spies no longer intimidated David as they had in the years after the beating. He was above reproach by such people. If he chose he could have any one of them killed with a single order, but that was not who Jabril Khatabi was. His parents had raised someone infinitely more judicious. He used his power with great care, discretion and patience. Now more than ever he needed those three traits.

More than twenty years past, he had been walking

down this same street in Jerusalem when he had been
snatched in broad daylight and thrown into the trunk of
a car. His own people thought he had been collaborating
with the Jews. Back then they had been wrong. David had
been nothing more than an innocent boy, walking
through the Old City on his way to meet his mother at
the hospital. Today all was different. If the PLO, or Hamas,
or Hezbollah or any one of a dozen groups had any idea
what he was up to they would torture him until he
begged to die.

Casually, he took a right onto Bab El Jadid and eyed
the checkpoint up ahead. The Old City was surrounded
by a fortresslike wall constructed by Suleiman the Magnificent in A.D. 1540. Through this wall there were just
seven gates. It was through these gates, over the centuries,
that the conquerors had controlled who and what came
and went from the city.

In the last century alone the city had been guarded by
four countries: the Turks, the Brits, the Jordanians and
now the Israelis manned the ramparts. Soldiers from the
Israeli Defense Forces, dressed in green uniforms and bul-
bous helmets, checked the IDs of everyone trying to enter
and leave the city. David remained calm as he continued
toward the gate and his meeting just beyond.

There were many informants lurking about on this
stretch of his journey. The Arab eyes were always watch-
ful, reporting everything they saw or suspected to the
Palestine Liberation Organization. The distrustful eyes of
his brethren haunted him, reminding him of the need for
his mission to succeed. The Palestinian people needed to
bury their hatred if they ever truly wanted peace for their
children, but in history's most oxymoronic way they
would first have to wage war.

At this appointed hour, however, David suspected that

there were also at least an equal number of Jewish eyes about. They wouldn't know who he was or the importance of the errand that he was on, though, for he was far too valuable to be trusted with any but Mossad's best and bravest.

Mossad, Israel's vaunted intelligence service, did not suffer the counterintelligence woes of other countries due to the simple fact that their agents were fiercely loyal to both country and cause. They were, however, not entirely out of harm's way. Agents had been kidnapped by Israel's various enemies and made to reveal valuable secrets. That was more than reason enough for David's contact to hold very close to his vest the identity of his most prized asset.

As David approached the New Gate, which had been cut into the wall of the Old City in 1887, he readied his papers. He presented them to a young Israeli soldier and was allowed to pass. He quickly crossed the street and after once again presenting his papers he was admitted onto foreign soil.

Notre Dame de France was owned by the Catholic Church and housed among many things the papal delegation to Christendom's holiest city. David's excuse for visiting such a place was less awkward than it might seem. He had explained many times to his Palestinian brethren that the delegation also held a branch office of the Vatican Bank. And no one, not even the Swiss, were as discreet when it came to banking matters as the Vatican. The leadership of the PLO did not question David in this regard. As long as he kept raising capital and funding their operations, they had little interest in the intricacies of international finance.

David was met by a youthful priest from Italy and escorted to the second-floor office of Monsignor Terrence Lavin. The short and portly monsignor tore his spectacles from his face and stood to greet his handsome guest.

"Jabril, how are you, my son?"

David clasped the monsignor's pale fleshy hand. "I am well, Terrence, and you?"

Looking up with his sparkling blue eyes, the older man said, "I would be better if we were having some fine French cuisine downstairs, but I have been told I am not allowed to ply you with food and wine today." The priest looked quickly at the closed door behind him and made a face.

Raising a conspiratorial eyebrow, David shrugged and said, "I would very much like that, but I'm afraid our mutual friend is calling the shots." David enjoyed Monsignor Lavin very much. A true Renaissance man, as they liked to say in the Church, he held advanced degrees in law, finance, theology and philosophy and was a connoisseur of fine wine, good food and classical music. David had met him many years ago through his parents and had often looked to the worldly priest to help expand his mind.

"Well," commented Lavin, "we will have to reschedule when you have some time." The priest grabbed a file from his desk and said, "The business that we supposedly discussed today." He handed it to David. "I've prepared a report of your holdings with us and how they've performed over the last month. The standard stuff. Take a look at it before you leave, in case your friends decide today is the day they feel like being educated." With that Lavin led his visitor to a dark-stained, heavy wood door behind his desk and opened it.

David thanked him and stepped into the shadowy windowless room. The Vatican took their security as seriously as any great nation. They had secrets that needed to be kept, relationships that needed to be cloaked and enemies that were none too fond of them. David had come to this room many times. Located on the interior of the second floor, its four walls were covered with massive old tapestries that he guessed hid counter-bugging devices. Like much of Jerusalem it smelled old. On this day, as on many others, the stale odor made him think of death.

An old wisp of a man sat silently at the far end of the table. A yellowed lamp in the corner cast a faint glow. The man's name was Abe Spielman. David had known him now for twenty-two years. Father Lavin had introduced them to each other, and David had never bothered to ask if that introduction was of the priest's own volition or if Spielman had pushed for it. Lavin had always acted as if it were his idea, but now that he was older and a bit wiser, David would have to guess that it was Spielman who had wanted to meet him. It would be very much in character with the old man. He was infinitely patient and had a knack for judging both people and situations far in advance of others.

Abe Spielman was a spy. At eighty-one he'd slowed down quite a bit, and if people took that to mean he was less than sharp that was fine with him. He had spent an entire career trying to get his adversaries to underestimate him, and to a great extent he'd succeeded.

You wouldn't know it by looking at this gentle grand-fatherly figure, but there had been a time when Abe Spielman had been a warrior of the finest order, both for Britain in World War II and then again during his country's fight for independence in 1948. His bravery throughout those heady days was legendary.

It was after the War of Independence that Spielman retreated into the shadows and went to work for his new country's intelligence service. He went on to become one of Mossad's most highly decorated operatives, but only a few people actually knew of his exploits and most of them were dead or near death.

Abe Spielman was a scholar. A writer of books and a professor of theology and history, who just so happened to moonlight as a spy. Or vice versa. He gazed down the length of the heavy wood table. The sight of the young man before him, so full of vigor and youth, reminded him of just how old he was.

"Excuse me for not getting up to greet you, Jabril." The voice was raspy and slightly unsteady.

"Don't be silly, Abe," laughed David. "You don't need to get up for me." He crossed around the room and extended a warm hand.

Spielman took it weakly in his own and said, "Please sit. Tell me how you've been, my friend."

"I've been fine." David dropped gracefully into the chair on Spielman's left. "And you?"

"Fine." He clasped his hands and added, "My graduate assistants do most of my work now so I can focus on my writing."

"Is that good or bad?"

Spielman frowned. "A bit of both, I suppose. I miss the kids mostly. Their youthful exuberance."

"But you don't miss the politics of the university?" David knew that his old friend felt very strongly about the takeover of Hebrew University by the ultraorthodox rabbis of his religion.

"They will be the end of us all. You know it as well as I. The zealots of Judaism and the zealots of Islam will drive us all right into the abyss."

David nodded knowingly. They had discussed it for years. After a long reflective moment he said, "If there were more people like us, peace wouldn't be such a problem."

"Problem." Spielman wryly noted the use of the word

in relation to peace. There was a time not so long ago when he thought he would see peace between the two peoples of Palestine, but now he felt that elusive prize slipping over the horizon. He'd dreamt of an armistice between Arabs and Jews for many years. He knew that for his tiny nation to survive long-term they would need to forge a real and lasting friendship with their neighbors. In recent years, though, that had all slipped away. "I do not think I will see peace in my lifetime."

David noted that there was genuine sadness in the old man's eyes when he spoke. In an encouraging voice he said, "It might not be as far off as you think, Abe."

Spielman shook his head. "No. There is no hope. Things are worse today than they have ever been short of the War of Independence. When teenage girls begin strapping bombs to themselves and blowing themselves up in public, we have reached a level of despair and hatred that the world has rarely seen."

"Not even with the Nazis?" asked David a bit skeptically.

"The Nazis were bullies; inhumane coldhearted butchers. They detested us, but in their minds we were beneath them." The professor paused for a moment and then added, "These martyrs that we are facing today hate us with every ounce of their being. But they also think that we are the villains, the cause of all their problems." He added sadly, "I warned my people years ago that these camps would someday be our undoing. Everyone ignored me, though. Apparently there were better things to spend our money on." Spielman frowned at the shortsightedness of politicians. "When you take away all hope, when you treat people as if they are no better than animals, undeserving of respect and compassion, do not be surprised one day when the whole lot of them rise up and shake off their bonds. It is the story of my own people being led from Egypt by Moses."

"Except the Palestinians," added David, "are already home."

"Exactly. They are not going anywhere. They want us to leave. For the first time they have seen hope in these so-called martyrs. They dance in the street when innocent Jewish women and children are killed."

"Are not innocent Palestinian women and children killed by your tanks and your missiles?" David parried.

Spielman eyed the younger man like a stern father. "You do not see Jews dancing in the street when a Palestinian baby is borne from the rubble."

David nodded. It was an ugly reality that his people not only rationalized the murder of civilians, but celebrated each death as if it were a glorious event.

"The day of a Palestinian state is not far off. The economy of Israel cannot hang on much longer. Tourism has all but withered away. If it were not for the Americans propping us up we wouldn't last more than a week. Yes, Jabril, you will get your state, and then there will be great bloodshed. Jewish settlers will refuse to leave the occupied territories and the bigots that your people look to for guidance will never be satisfied until all of Palestine is cleansed of Jewish blood. We will continue in this downward death spiral for years." He shook his head sadly. "And I'm afraid my people no longer have the stomach it will take for such a fight."

David nodded thoughtfully. Everything the elderly Jew said he agreed with; especially the last part. It was, in fact, the reason why he was here. "I agree with much of what you say but I am not quite so fatalistic."

"That is because you are young. You have many years ahead of you where I have only but a few. My faith in humanity has dwindled over this past decade. I feel as if we are settling into a dark period."

David reached out for the old man's hand. "Do not give up hope just yet." With a smile he added, "A meeting is set to take place tomorrow evening." David pulled a small sheet of paper from his shirt pocket and slid it in front of Spielman. On the list were eight names that were sure to grab the professor's attention.

Spielman donned a pair of reading glasses and glanced over the list. His mouth went completely dry. The list was a virtual who's who of terrorists in the occupied territories. It was more than he'd bargained for. When he began cultivating a relationship with Jabril many years ago he knew the young Palestinian had the potential to do great things. Jabril's parents were rationalists who placed a high value on education and shunned the violence and fiery rhetoric of the PLO. Spielman thought that Jabril might someday be a real leader of his people. But as much as he thought their friendship might someday bear the fruit of good intelligence, he never thought it would lead to such a staggering moment.

Mossad had kept an eye on him, discovering only recently the young Palestinian's successes at raising money for the various terrorist groups. All the while, Spielman had kept the backdoor relationship open through Monsignor Lavin. Along the way it had been very beneficial. He had gained a true friend in Jabril; a pragmatist who believed in peace.

Holding the piece of paper up in the air the sage Spielman said, "This is an interesting group."

"Very."

Spielman held the younger man in his gaze. "I suppose you wouldn't like to tell me where this meeting will be taking place?"

David bit down on his lip, and after some serious consideration he slid a second piece of paper across the table. It contained a sketch and the dimensions of an attaché case. "I need two of them. Have your people build them to my specifications, and I will meet you here again tomorrow to discuss the details."

Spielman cautiously surveyed the young Palestinian for a sign that his gesture was anything other than genuine, for if it was, Abe Spielman had just been given the golden nugget that every intelligence officer searches a lifetime for.

FIFTEEN

Rapp sat awkwardly over a laptop, his muscular arms contorted so he could peck at the keys. He stopped reading the profile on the screen and looked out the porthole of the Agency's Gulfstream V long-range jet. As far as the eye could see was an endless stretch of blue water. The plane was outfitted with a VIP package: plush leather seats, a couch, galley, head, bedroom and a secure communications system that allowed the team to stay in touch with Washington without fear of being intercepted.

Rapp didn't know how she'd pulled it off, but she had. Kennedy had convinced the president to give his approval to the operation, or turn a blind eye. Either way it didn't much matter to Rapp. He caught himself. That wasn't entirely true. He did care. It was infinitely better if the president turned a blind eye to the goings-on of the Orion Team and their dark operations.

As far as the American people were concerned, Rapp honestly felt that the vast majority didn't want to know what he was up to. America had been attacked. The country was at war, and war was ugly. They didn't want to see the gruesome details of how it was fought. They didn't start the war but they sure as hell didn't want to lose it. They wanted someone like Mitch Rapp to take care of the dirty work. The chief problem lay, as always, with the politicians.

They would use any issue to gain the upper hand on an opponent. Scandal is what they were in constant search of, so consequently the fewer people who knew at the White House, the better his chances of staying under the Washington radar.

If President Hayes wanted to insulate himself politically, so be it. From an operational standpoint it was a far more desirable situation. If the president didn't want to be associated with the op it would ensure that he wouldn't be discussing it with any of his advisors, and the probability of another leak would be reduced.

From the standpoint of morale it was a less palatable situation, however. Not that morale mattered much to Rapp. He didn't need his hand held, he didn't need to be pumped up, no pregame speeches were required.

Early in his career as a counterterrorism operative he'd once heard a Special Forces officer give his men a talk before launching a hostage rescue. The officer assembled his team and simply said, "If you need a pep talk right now, you're in the wrong line of work. We all know why we're here, so let's load up and get this done." No one said a word; no one needed to.

That scene had stayed with Rapp all these years. He was only twenty-three at the time. Twelve of the calmest, coolest badasses he'd ever met climbed onto two Black Hawk helicopters and went out and performed their jobs to absolute perfection. It was one of the most beautiful things he'd ever seen.

Despite his natural preference for operational security, Rapp couldn't help but feel disappointed in the president. He'd thought better of the man. Rapp was starting to wonder if Robert Hayes was losing his determination in the battle against terrorism. Up until now, Hayes's commitment had been unwavering. Why he'd now decided to get gun-shy was a mystery.

When Rapp had gone into the Oval Office this morning he'd honestly thought the president wouldn't need more than two seconds to sign on. When Rapp got back to Washington he'd make it a point to talk to Kennedy about the president. If anyone knew what was going on it would be her.

Kennedy was an amazing woman. Even after the president had given him the cold shoulder, he knew Kennedy would succeed. Her powers of persuasion were so total that Rapp liked to joke if she got tired of running the CIA she could go to work for the D.C. police talking jumpers off the ledge. Her ability to navigate her way through Washington's political maze was amazing.

With all this fresh on his mind Rapp had put the wheels in motion the moment he left the White House. His first call had been to the SEAL Demolition and Salvage Corporation, out of Baltimore, where he spoke to an individual who he'd worked with many times before. Since they were talking on an unsecured line the conversation had been brief and cryptic, but enough information was passed along that the man on the other end could begin to assemble his team and prepare to leave on very short notice.

The rest of the drive back to Langley was spent talking to his new bride. In her mind, the day they got married was the day her husband was to retire from field operations. And Rapp, at least, when they got engaged, thought so too.

The problem was, between the engagement and the wedding, he'd been forced to sit through an endless succession of meetings where little was accomplished. He was quick to come to the realization that retiring from the field might not be as easy as he thought. Simply holding down an office job was never going to cut it. He knew it and she knew it, but they were both in agreement that the really dangerous operations were out of the picture.

Rapp saw himself taking a very active role in planning operations. He might not be the man pulling the trigger anymore, but he sure as hell wasn't going to sit in his cushy office in Virginia doling out orders from thousands of miles away. There was a reason why military commanders favored the opinions of on-site commanders, and that was why Rapp would be running this op in person. There was nothing arrogant about it, but the truth was there was no one he trusted more to get it done right.

Anna, always the inquisitive reporter, asked a solid minute's worth of questions. Each one came from a different angle and each one was met with the standard, "You know I can't answer that." There was one question, however, that he could answer. Anna wanted to know if it would be dangerous. Mitch laughed and told her, "No," and to his way of thinking, at least, it was the truth.

There was little doubt, however, that if Anna knew what he had planned, she would disagree with him vehemently. Setting her opinion aside, in Rapp's brutally lethal world, this op didn't score too high on the danger list, and depending on how the final pieces were put into play, the op might actually present no direct threat to him whatsoever.

Something told him he wasn't being totally honest with himself, but at present he wasn't willing to explore it much further. Right now he had the calm sense of clarity he always felt before a mission. Like any predator, he was comfortable with only brief periods of inaction. He never felt more alive than when he was moving forward with a plan. His intellect came to life, he saw things with a heightened sense of awareness. Possibilities opened up before his mind, with paths to take, and options to choose from while the entire time he subconsciously calculated the odds for success and set the information aside.

There was something else, though. Something he'd never discussed with anyone, not even Kennedy. When he stripped everything away and forced himself to be brutally honest, he was left with the undeniable fact that he enjoyed killing men like General Moro.

At first he had been embarrassed by these feelings, uncomfortable with the knowledge that he took pleasure in something so brutal. But with time and maturity he had grown comfortable with the knowledge that he was killing men who had made a conscious choice to do harm. Moro was a traitor of his own volition, and when you plowed through all the political horseshit, the Anderson family had been minding their own business, breaking no laws, when they were snatched from their seaside resort. They were noncombatants in a war that had nothing to do with them.

Moro had decided to climb into bed with the enemy and because of him the Andersons were still held hostage and two U.S. commandos were now dead. Rapp knew that just planning this operation wouldn't be enough. He wanted to be there. He wanted to see the look on the general's face when he knew it was over. He wanted to reach out and tear the man's throat out with his bare hands.

Rapp's thoughts of blood lust were interrupted by a presence hovering over his shoulder. Reaching up he closed his laptop and turned to see who it was.

Special Agent Skip McMahon of the FBI placed one of his Popeye-like forearms on the top of the seat next to

Rapp and frowned. A bit of a fashion throwback, McMahon had on a short-sleeve, white dress shirt with a striped tie. In a deep gravelly voice he asked, "What are you up to, Secret Agent Man?"

Rapp smiled. McMahon was one of the few people he knew who had absolutely no problem giving him shit. "Just a little homework."

McMahon took a seat across from him, letting his tired, beat-up body slump into the leather chair. "Homework, huh?" he said in a skeptical voice. McMahon studied Rapp with his probing eyes. In his more than thirty years with the Bureau, McMahon had hunted bank robbers, kidnappers, killers, serial killers, terrorists, cyberpunks, spies, several federal judges and a few politicians to boot. He was a tenacious no-nonsense lawman who the Bureau often called on when they needed results. He was loved by the few people who truly understood him, and hated by the army of bureaucrats in dark suits who were more concerned with protocol than results.

But even the pension gang at the FBI had a grudging respect for McMahon. In a place where 99.9 percent of the employees had never discharged their weapon in the line of duty, McMahon had done so on more occasions than he cared to count. He wasn't a lawyer or an accountant, he was an old-fashioned law enforcement officer.

"So who's General Moro?" asked McMahon, his eyes staying locked on Rapp.

Rapp didn't answer at first. He cursed himself silently for allowing McMahon to read his computer screen and then he tried to figure out how much he should say. McMahon had been brought along to conduct surveillance on Ambassador Cox, and when Rapp gave him the word, he was to arrest the ambassador and escort him back to the United States.

The president had personally asked for McMahon at the urging of CIA director Kennedy. Kennedy and McMahon had a relationship that went beyond work. How far beyond, Rapp had never been comfortable in asking, but McMahon was ideal for the job. He had a reputation as someone who could turn a blind eye to certain things if need be.

Rapp figured McMahon could find out who the general was with one phone call, so he told him the truth. "He's with the Philippine army."

"No shit," McMahon said, feigning surprise. "I don't know if I ever could have figured that one out." McMahon scratched one of his hairy forearms and asked, "So what's your interest in the man? Is he friend or foe?"

Rapp smiled. "Tread lightly, Skip."

"Or what . . . I might step in dog shit?" McMahon's face contorted into an annoyed grimace. "Come on, Mitch, I step in dog shit for a living, and don't give me any of that need-to-know crap. I know plenty about you and"—McMahon leaned forward, pointing over his shoulder with his thumb—"I also know a fair amount about Blondie sitting up there. I don't know who the other guys are, but I can take an awfully damn good educated guess that they're pretty handy with a gun and they probably know all that kung fu shit they teach you guys. So"—McMahon leaned in even closer—"why don't we just cut to the chase and save each other a lot of time and effort."

Rapp shook his head with amusement. The "Blondie" Skip was referring to was Scott Coleman, the former commander of SEAL Team 6.

Coleman, retired from the navy, now ran an outfit called SEAL Demolition and Salvage Corporation. They did a fair amount of legitimate work training local police departments from Baltimore down to Norfolk on scuba techniques and underwater salvage, but unofficially they also worked from time to time as freelance operatives for the CIA. McMahon and Coleman had crossed paths several years back during a very high-profile murder investigation. The case had never been brought to trial, but both Rapp and McMahon knew the truth about the events that surrounded the sensational murders. Scott Coleman had been a major player in that drama.

McMahon had been chosen to come along for the very reason that he could be trusted. He wasn't some hotshot Fed who would try to burn the CIA so he could advance his career. McMahon understood that they were all on the same team. Nonetheless, Rapp wasn't all that comfortable with sharing highly classified information. "Skip, believe me when I tell you, you don't want to dig too deep on this one."

McMahon's frown turned into a scowl. "Mitch?" His tone left no doubt that he wasn't buying the tired old line. "I don't need bodyguards, and you sure as hell don't need bodyguards. I should be able to handle arresting the ambassador all on my own, so there's only one reason I can think of why you'd bring these four boy scouts halfway around the world."

Rapp slid his laptop off to the side and reluctantly made a decision. "You familiar with the Anderson kidnapping?"

"Yep." McMahon paused for a moment and then his eyes got real tight. He'd been briefed by Kennedy herself about why the ambassador was being arrested. He knew about the leak, the two dead navy SEALs and the failed hostage rescue. It didn't take him long to realize that General Moro was involved in this, and probably not in a good way.

"Is Moro a man we can trust?"

Rapp shook his head.

McMahon nodded slowly. "I see."

"Any more questions?"

The big FBI agent had a cheerful glint in his eye. Slipping out of his chair he patted Rapp on the shoulder and said, "No. I think I can fill in the blanks, but for Christ's sake, be careful."

Smiling, Rapp said, "Always."

SIXTEEN

The plane touched down at the old Clark Air Base at three in the morning. There was no fanfare, no military band, no diplomatic reception. The old base had been turned over to the Philippine government when they chose not to renew the U.S. Air Force's lease. This was an unscheduled, unannounced arrival. The Gulfstream was met by a tired-looking ground crew that was more concerned with rubbing the sleep from their eyes than who was on the plane. A fuel truck pulled up alongside the jet almost immediately and two men went to work filling the plane's tanks.

McMahon left the plane first. He was met by the embassy's FBI man, who, according to plan, should have been roused from a dead sleep just an hour ago and told to get his ass to the base to pick up someone important. McMahon was that man and once he was alone with the agent he would put the fear of God into him. No one at the embassy was to know he was in the country until he said so. McMahon was going to keep a real close eye on Ambassador Cox, and when the word was given he would slap the cuffs on him.

After McMahon was gone, Rapp walked down the

short stairs holding a file under his arm. Despite the sticky humidity, he was wearing an olive-drab vest, like the ones photographers wore. The lightweight vest was designed with plenty of pockets inside and out and was great for holding things like lenses and extra film. Or in Rapp's case, extra clips of ammunition, a silencer for his 9mm Beretta and a secure satellite phone.

A black Lincoln Continental sat in the shadows next to one of the large gray hangars. When Rapp reached the tarmac the sedan's lights flashed three times. Rapp took a look around and then nodded to Coleman, who was standing on the top step. The former SEAL ducked back inside and hit a button. The stairs retracted into the closed position and the sleek white jet began to move once again.

Rapp walked over to the car. The back door swung open, and he stopped to take one last look at the Gulf-stream, which was taxiing for takeoff. He stepped in, closed the door and turned to meet his contact. Lieu-tenant General Sergio Rizal looked back at Rapp with a pair of discerning dark eyes. Rizal was the head of the Philippine army. He was a graduate of West Point, and a staunch American ally. He and General Flood had a good working relationship that went all the way back to Viet-nam. Pudgy-faced and short-limbed, the fifty-eight-year-old had a little pot belly that strained against the buttons of his camouflage battle dress uniform.

Rizal was deeply concerned about his country. He had been sickened when in the early nineties the radicals in his government refused to renew the leases for the Amer-ican military bases. After twenty-one years of dictatorial abuse by Ferdinand Marcos and his wife Imelda the Fil-ipino people rebelled against the military and its Ameri-can backers. The radicals got their way, the Americans left, the aid dried up, and an already slumping economy worsened.

It wasn't long before the Muslim and communist guerrilla groups who had been kept at bay by the Marcos regime renewed their efforts to destroy the democracy. They concentrated on the outer islands and began wreaking havoc across the far-flung archipelago. Morale in the Philippine army worsened with each year, and with each subsequent decrease in funds. The communists were working their way into the government through the socialist party and were doing everything they could to frustrate the military in their campaign to keep the country unified.

After a decade of disastrous policy from the leadership in Manila, it had finally been decided that maybe it wasn't such a bad thing having the Americans around. The door was reopened a bit. Quietly, the United States military began leasing portions of the bases and the vaunted Green Berets began instructing the Philippine army on how to take the battle to the rebels. Much needed economic and military aid was increased, but in these tumultuous times, Rizal wondered if it was enough to turn the tide. The enemy forces were already formidable, and now this American was here to tell him he had a traitor in his own inner circle. For the first time in his military career, General Rizal felt that his country might be beyond saving.

Rapp made no effort to introduce himself. He'd read Rizal's profile twice. In addition, General Flood, who knew Rizal well, had told Rapp the man didn't trust people who talked too much. Instead, Rapp casually extracted a file from the flash bag on his lap and handed it over to him. He watched the general don a pair of reading glasses and then watched some more in silence as the man sitting next to him grew more and more irritated with each passing page.

General Rizal closed the file and removed his reading glasses. His expression was unreadable. In a very precise manner, the older man placed his reading glasses in a case and stowed them in his breast pocket. He looked down at the file resting on his knee and sadly shook his head.

"So General Moro is a traitor."

"Unless you have another explanation, that would appear to be the case."

The general frowned. "I have none." Rizal still had yet to make eye contact with Rapp. "In fact, when I look back on certain events, this makes sense." Rizal's stubby fingers tapped the file. "Abu Sayyaf, moving so freely, twice being cornered, but miraculously escaping both times. We were all convinced that if Moro and his vaunted commandos couldn't hunt down the rebels then no one could." The general shook his head. "How could I have been so blind?"

"Were you friends?" asked Rapp.

"No," said Rizal without emotion. "I never liked the man, but he has his supporters. He is very smooth politically, and his men love him. He has created his own cult of personality, something that has concerned me and a few others for some time."

Rapp liked the sound of that. Through the profiles that the CIA and Defense Intelligence Agency had provided, Rapp already knew Moro's commandos were fiercely loyal to him. This, combined with the new information that Moro had enemies within the general staff, made Rapp confident that he could sell his plan without having to twist any arms.

"What would his men do if he was relieved of his command?"

"I'm not sure." The American's implication was obvious. "I can recall him to Manila on any one of a dozen pretenses, all of them seemingly legitimate, but going public with arresting him, that will be the tricky part. He has many allies, some of them wildly popular and very anti-American. They will say that you framed him." Rizal sadly shook his head and added, "And there are many people in my country who will want to believe that." Looking out the window he added in a defeated voice, "Our military is very weak right now. I don't know how we will survive a scandal of this magnitude."

Rapp saw his chance. "There's another way out of this, sir."

For the first time Rizal made eye contact.

"Moro has broken his oath as an officer," Rapp started. "He's a traitor plain and simple." Rapp pointed to the file. "This is just the tip of the iceberg, by the way. If you brought him up on a court-martial he'd be buried under the evidence and ultimately sentenced to death. You can choose to go that route or we can try something else."

"I'm listening."

Rapp hesitated only briefly. "I want his head." His dark eyes never left the general's. "Two U.S. Navy SEALs are dead because of him, and a family of innocent noncombatants are still being held hostage because Moro has aided and abetted the enemy. If we arrest him he will be court-martialed, and despite the politics of the situation, he will be convicted and more than likely sentenced to death. But as you've pointed out, such a trial will severely damage our two countries' relationship and the image of the Philippine army." Easing back, Rapp added, "I think both of us would prefer to see this problem dealt with in a more subtle way."

Rizal thought about this for a minute. He knew exactly what the American was getting at. "What would you need from me?"

Rapp carefully examined the general and then began to lay out his plan. By midmorning the problem would be neutralized and the Philippine people would have a martyr to rally behind in their battle against the Muslim rebels.

SEVENTEEN

Cruising at 600 mph the Gulfstream jet made the relatively short hop from Manila to Samar Island in just under an hour, and touched down at an unlit private landing strip near the southern tip of the island. It came to a brief stop at the end of the runway, just long enough for Coleman and his men to deplane, and then raced back down the asphalt and into the star-filled sky.

The four men stood in silence as the roar of jet engines was replaced by the jungle's nocturnal murmuring. They were still well outside the combat zone, but they all instinctively spread out, each man putting his eyes on a different sector. They were in jungle fatigues, their faces smeared with greasepaint and their weapons dangling at their sides.

The airstrip and the acreage surrounding it belonged to a Japanese businessman. He'd bought the 1,200-acre plantation and built himself a magnificent home overlooking the ocean and an eighteen hole golf course for his private amusement. Rapp had his people at the CTC (CIA's Counterrorism Center) do a few discreet inquiries and discovered that the home was rarely used during the week and was currently unoccupied. There was a caretaker on the premises, but they would be long gone by the time he rubbed the sleep from his eyes and came to investigate.

Two of the former SEALs, Kevin Hackett and Dan Stroble, donned their night vision goggles and moved off in opposite directions, their MP-10 suppressed submachine guns hanging at their sides. Coleman chose not to put on his NVGs, looking off in the distance at the big house on the hill, now washed by moonlight. He took a small pair of field binoculars from his chest pocket to get a closer look at the house. A couple of exterior lights were on, but otherwise the place was black. A single light shone from the gatehouse across the drive from the main house. Coleman studied the structure for a time and was looking at the front door when the caretaker stepped outside. A slight frown creased his brow as he silently hoped their ride would arrive before he had to deal with this problem.

The fourth man arrived silently at Coleman's side. "The chopper's on its way in."

Coleman tilted an ear toward the sky, but heard nothing. He looked down at Charlie Wicker and nodded. He trusted Wicker's senses more than his own. In fact, he trusted Wicker's eyes and ears more than probably any other soldier he'd ever worked with. Barely five foot six, Wicker was almost elfish in appearance. He was the best sniper Coleman had ever seen in action and had been handpicked by Rapp for the operation. Wicker was the only active-duty man on the team. Rapp had sheep-dipped him from SEAL Team 6. When they got into position Wicker would be the star of the show.

A full ten seconds after Wicker had alerted him, Coleman heard the thumping noise of helicopter rotors against the heavy tropical air. The MH-60G Pave Hawk helicopter came in fast, skimming the tops of the trees and then passing over the heads of Coleman and his men. It flared out immediately like a horse being pulled back in by its reins, its tail landing gear looking like it would hit the tarmac hard. At the last minute the wheel stabilized a mere foot above the ground until the front landing gear came into line. The menacing bird set down gently without the aid of its heavy-duty shock absorbers.

Coleman and his men watched all of this with great interest. They expected the best, and it looked like they'd got it. The bird belonged to the Air Force Special Operations Command. It was part of the 353rd Special Operations Group out of Kadena Air Base in Japan. The specifics of the op had been taken care of on the flight over. Rapp had given Coleman the mission objective and told him to organize the details. Anything he needed was to be routed through General Campbell at the Joint Special Operations Command back at Fort Bragg. Coleman had one request and it was pretty simple, but very important. He asked for the best flight crew available. As evidenced by the failed mission to rescue the Andersons, the most dangerous part of any op was usually the insertion and the extraction.

Coleman stopped just outside the open door of the helicopter and slapped each of his men on the back as they bounded in. When they were all onboard he climbed in and stuck his head into the cockpit. The pilot turned to look at him, his night vision goggles perched atop his black flight helmet in the up position. Coleman handed the man a piece of white paper with a GPS coordinate on it.

"Bring us in low, just above the canopy and we'll fast-rope down."

The pilot nodded. Neither warrior attempted an introduction. All parties involved understood there would be no official record of what they were doing. The pilot punched the coordinates into the bird's advanced Pave Hawk avionics computer and Coleman buckled himself in for what he was sure would be a wild ride.

EIGHTEEN

When David entered Monsignor Lavin's office, the first thing he noticed was caution in the eyes of the normally jovial priest. It was not the sign the Palestinian was looking for. With everything he had worked for hinging on this evening's meeting, he was growing increasingly nervous as the appointed hour approached. One mistake now, one misread, would very likely lead to a brutal death at the hands of his own people.

Studying the priest with a discerning eye, David asked, "What is wrong?"

Lavin shook his head and said, "Nothing." He pointed at the door behind him and then looked at some papers on his desk.

Something was amiss, but what it was, David hadn't a clue. He hesitated briefly and then willed his feet to march him to the door. He had a feeling that on the other side of it something awaited him that he wouldn't like. When he opened the door his instincts proved correct.

There, sitting in the dim light, in his usual spot, at the far end of the conference table, was Abe Spielman. This time, however, a shadowy figure sat next to him. David could not make out any features, but he didn't need to.

The large bald head and bull-like shoulders could only belong to one man. It was Ben Freidman. The name alone inspired hatred and fear in many. In David's case, at least, it also inspired a begrudging respect.

In the entire West Bank there was perhaps no other man more loathed than Ben Freidman. As the director general of Mossad, it was Freidman's job to wage a covert war with Israel's enemies. The Israeli Defense Forces were in charge of dealing with the menagerie of terrorist groups within the occupied territories in a more overt manner, but it was Mossad's job to take on the particularly nasty operations.

Freidman had been the chief architect of many such actions over the last two decades. As David's eyes adjusted to the dim lights, he got a better look at the man. Though they had never met, the two enemies stared at each other with the familiarity of lifelong rivals. Neither spoke and the tension continued to build.

Spielman, nervous that his friend might turn around and leave, offered an apology for bringing a guest. "Jabril, I'm sorry for surprising you like this, but I can explain."

David's eyes left Freidman's and looked at his old friend. He decided, for now, not to reply. Even though he was caught off guard that their little two-person club had a new member, he knew he shouldn't have been. The information that he had given Spielman during their last meeting was bound to wake up some people at the Institute, as Mossad was commonly referred to by insiders.

Slowly, David walked closer to the two men and grabbed a chair, not the one right next to Spielman, as he normally did, but one a few away. The message was clear; he would listen, but it would not be business as usual. The other thing he hoped to convey was his mistrust of a monster like Freidman. Always the pragmatist, though,

David knew the director general of Mossad was a neme-sis that the bloodthirsty Palestinian leadership had created. It was a case of action and reaction.

Absent his normal charm, David looked to Spielman and said, "I didn't know we were allowed to bring visitors. I'm sure I could have found someone to join us."

Spielman didn't laugh. "Believe me, it wasn't my idea." In-side, the elderly professor was still seething over Freidman's dictum that he would accompany him to the meeting.

It made no difference that when Freidman was a case officer, he recoiled at any attempt by his superiors to meet one of his assets. In Spielman's harsh opinion, Freidman was a control freak and a bully, and a man who fanned the flames of Palestinian–Israeli hatred. He was exactly the type of person that could upset the hard-fought and del-icate friendship he had cultivated with Jabril.

Knowing Spielman well enough, David could tell that he was sincere. He gave him a slight nod, signaling that he was willing to take him at his word, at least for now.

Leaning forward, out of the shadows, Freidman placed his brawny forearms on the table and in a raspy voice asked, "Do you know who I am?"

"Of course." David maintained an almost disinterested attitude. He'd read the PLO's meager file on the man and had heard many stories.

Born in Jerusalem in 1949, Freidman went on to distin-guish himself in the Six Day War of 1967. After the war he was transferred to AMAN, Israel's military intelligence or-ganization, and then later Mossad. At Mossad he became a very effective kidon, or in the common parlance of the business, an assassin. He specialized in hunting down mem-bers of Yasser Arafat's Force 17. His tenacious ability to track people across multiple continents made him a greatly feared warrior in the struggle for his people's security.

"I have kept an eye on you," stated Freidman, "for many years, and have been looking forward to this day for some time."

David wondered if he meant simply meeting him, or meant wrapping his large hands around his throat and choking him to death. It was quite possibly a bit of both, for he had no doubt that Ben Freidman was cut from the same cloth as the militant terrorists who governed his own people. The enemy was the enemy, and there was no need to analyze it much further than that. There was no distinction or recognition of the individual. The condemnation was made of the entire Palestinian society, and conversely of all Israelis. It was this line of thinking that allowed these men to launch blunt attacks with no concern over who was killed. It was the rationale that allowed them to sleep at night and claim that their cause was the truly just one.

There were many directions David could take this. There were many questions in fact that he would very much like to ask the dark angel who was sitting across from him, but there were schedules to be kept, goals to be met and a country to be made. Besides, it was somewhat comforting to know that, during the course of the next two weeks, the man sitting across from him would feel pressure like he'd never felt before.

Eschewing anything controversial, and swallowing his pride, David said, "And I have looked forward to meeting you."

Freidman smirked as if to say he doubted the sincerity of the comment, and then said, "Tell me, Jabril, and excuse me if I sound distrustful, but it is my nature. This meeting tonight, why would all of these people risk gathering in one place?"

David wondered how good Freidman's intelligence was. It was highly likely that he had assets who could give him pieces to the complex puzzle. Those pieces on their own would prove nothing, but they might raise or lower his level of cynicism. Truthfully, he answered, "It is not that unusual for them to gather under one roof."

The bald man looked skeptical. "The leaders of Hamas, the head of the Palestinian General Intelligence and the leaders of Force 17 . . . this is a common occurrence that they all get together to plot the destruction of my people?"

David stayed the course. "Yes."

"I find it hard to believe they could stand the sight of each other."

"Let's just say they are united in their hatred of you . . . and their desire for money."

Things began to make sense for the head of Mossad. At first he thought Jabril was invited to the terrorism summit as a mere financial representative, but now he saw there might be more to it. It was possible that with his fund-raising prowess, he was able to call such meetings himself, in order to distribute cash. A recent piece of intelligence clicked in the back of his mind and he reminded himself to look more deeply into something one of his people had told him just this morning. Freidman eyed David and asked, "And what of you? What do you hate, or should I say who?"

"I try not to hate. It leads to poor decisions."

Freidman scoffed at the thought. "It can also be a great motivator."

"Yes, it can," replied David, "but look where it has gotten us." David watched as Freidman retreated back into the shadows, an expression of scornful disagreement on his face. Watching him react the way he did, David wished it was within his means to kill the man right this very moment. He could probably do it and forfeit his own life, or spend the rest of his days in an Israeli jail, being tortured and otherwise treated like a subhuman, but suicide was not in his plans. Maybe an opportunity would someday present itself, but for now he would have to make his deal with the devil. It saddened him, however, to know that Freidman would go on using his indiscriminant weapons of war to kill the people of Palestine. Ben Freidman held much in common with the men David was meeting with this evening. It was too bad he couldn't talk him into coming along.

A black attaché case appeared from under the table and then another. Freidman placed them both in front of David and said, "As you requested." He laid one of the cases flat, opened it and spun it around. "Each is lined with five pounds of C-4 plastique. You requested it, so I assume you know what you're doing."

There had been a debate between the top counterterrorism people and Spielman late into the evening yesterday. The question was, how would Spielman's asset pull this off? Was he going to use the cases as a suicide bomb, or was he going to somehow leave the meeting place and remote detonate the devices? The debate was evenly divided with Spielman saying it was impossible that Jabril Khatabi would commit suicide, and the analysts saying that their money was on the Palestinian turning himself into a martyr. This split among his own people led Freidman to take several precautions.

David nodded and examined the cases. They were basic black Samsonite attaché cases. He would weigh them when he got back to his apartment, and had little doubt that he would discover the Israelis had put more than five pounds of explosives in each. David extended his hand. "The detonator?"

"As you requested." Freidman handed over a black digital Casio watch. "Press the split reset button to arm the cases and then the start–stop button twice within three seconds to detonate."

"Thank you." David took the watch and studied it briefly before placing it inside the first case. "Just so you know, Mr. Freidman, I plan on making more than one stop."

Freidman frowned, not quite understanding what was meant by the remark.

David grinned. "I am not so naive as to think this watch is the only detonator. I also know that my life means nothing to you. So don't get any ideas about detonating the cases on your own. I will be led on a long journey tonight, changing cars often, and stopping at many houses until I reach my destination. Only I will know when the time is right, and although I know it is impossible for you to trust a Palestinian, believe me when I tell you that I want these men dead every bit as much as you do."

Freidman accepted the statement with a nod and said, "It's your operation. However you want to handle it is up to you."

"Is there anything else I need to know?"

Freidman hesitated. He had many questions, but now was not the time. If this Palestinian proved himself tonight and managed to survive the blast they could sit down later. He shook his oversized head and said, "No."

As David gathered the cases he heard the tired voice of his friend who was still sitting, observing the two strange allies. "Why, Jabril?"

David turned to look at Spielman. There seemed a genuine sadness in his eyes. "You do not know?"

"Maybe, but I would like to hear it from you."

David nodded thoughtfully. His mind rested upon the truth and he said, "These men who I am going to see do not want peace, and as long as they are the leaders of my people, we will only know hatred and death." With that, David grabbed the cases and left the room.

NINETEEN

The U.S. Air Force Special Operations helicopter streaked across the calm moonlit waters of Leyte Gulf. Up ahead loomed Dinagat Island and the site where two of their fellow warriors had been gunned down just days earlier. Only one of the men in the helicopter was on active duty but that didn't matter. Once a SEAL always a SEAL.

Coleman and his team were coming to settle the score, but somewhere else in the interior of the island, under the thick jungle cover, was an American family that was undoubtedly scared witless. The former commander of SEAL Team 6 wished he could do something to help them, but right now that was out of his hands.

Coleman and his men had moved to the side doors of the bird, two men to each side, their feet dangling over the edge, each man clipped to a safety harness in the event the helicopter had to make a drastic, evasive maneuver. They were all wearing night vision goggles, giving their eyes ample time to adjust.

In addition, Coleman was plugged into an in-flight headset so he could communicate with the pilots. As he peered out the port door he listened to the chatter. The pilots were reporting four contacts on the FLIR moving toward the island from the east. They were right on time.

To help mask their insertion Coleman had asked that choppers from the *Belleau Wood* make an overflight of the island while they were being inserted. The big CH-53 Sea Stallions would fly just south of the target area while the Pave Hawk came in from the north under a ridge line. Coleman wasn't at all worried about being picked up on radar. They would be flying too low for that. The problem was that when the sun came up they needed to be in position a little less than a mile from the general's camp.

In order to do that, the Pave Hawk would have to drop them off closer to the target than he would have liked. The sentries at the field command post would probably never hear the Pave Hawk's rotors in the heavy, humid tropical air, and if they did, they might think nothing of it, but if the general decided to send out scouts it could be a problem. Coleman wasn't in the business of taking unnecessary risks when a solution as simple as arranging a flyover was available.

The calm water vanished from beneath them and was replaced by a light sandy beach and then the thick jungle canopy. Coleman looked straight down, peering over the toes of his jungle boots. They were so low he felt as if he could reach down and grab a leaf. The helicopter began to climb as they worked their way up a ravine using their terrain-avoidance, terrain-following radar to hug the tree-tops. The pilot calmly called out one minute to insertion as the chopper weaved to the left and then back to the right as if it were meandering its way upstream.

Coleman tugged on his leather gloves to make sure they were tight and placed a hand on the heavy coil of rope that lay between himself and Kevin Hackett. The pilot called out thirty seconds to insertion, his voice just a touch tighter this time, and then asked his door gunners to report in. The men, one on each side of the bird, looked out past their ominous 7.62mm miniguns and scanned the area, reporting all clear after just a moment. One by one Coleman and his men undid their safety tethers and grabbed on to hand straps on the sides of each door.

Coleman's heart quickened and his chest tightened a bit as the helicopter started to slow. He'd gone through this drill hundreds of times and it never changed. He'd seen men die fast-roping in near perfect conditions. It was not something to be done half-assed. It was a task that needed to be performed with great care and focus.

The second Coleman heard the Go word from the pilot he chucked the thick rope out the door and tore off his in-flight headset. Without hesitation he reached for the rope with one hand and then the other. Coleman launched himself out the door, pulled the rope close to his chest, and then loosened his grip. He dropped like a stone for the first thirty feet and then with ten feet to go he put on the clamps and slowed his descent.

His boots broke the surface of the stream and he stopped knee deep in water. Coleman moved away from the rope, bringing his suppressed MP-10 up and sweeping the banks of the stream, his NVGs piercing the dark recesses of the area. Over his earpiece, he heard each of his men call out as they hit the ground, announcing they were clear. In the wake of the rotor wash the men moved quickly through the water to a predetermined rallying point on the east bank of the stream.

The Pave Hawk rotated 180 degrees as the ropes were pulled back up, and then started its descent back toward the ocean. Normally the ropes would have been dropped and left behind, but Coleman and his men didn't have the time to gather and bury them. They needed to get to their mountaintop before the sun came up.

The entire insertion took less than ten seconds. Coleman and his men moved out immediately, never looking up at the chopper as it left the area. Wicker took the point, followed by Coleman and then Hackett and Stroble. They moved in the stream carefully, picking their way through the rocks, their eyes and ears receptive to the slightest sign that they were not alone; their first order of business, to put as much distance between themselves and the infiltration point as possible.

THE PHILIPPINE ARMY HELICOPTER approached the island from the southwest, the edge of the rising sun casting an orange glow across the thin horizon. Rapp sat in the back of the Bell UH-1 Huey with a Special Force's colonel from General Rizal's staff. Rizal did not like the idea of sending Rapp into General Moro's camp unaccompanied, so he had sent along his most trusted aide to make sure nothing happened to the mysterious American.

Rapp wasn't crazy about having someone looking over his shoulder, but he had to admit, if anything went wrong it would be nice to have a high-ranking Philippine Special Force's officer around to settle things down. Rizal had assured him that Colonel Barboza was not a fan of General Moro. Barboza had served under Moro and was highly suspicious of his actions. The proof that Rapp had brought with him had confirmed some of what he suspected and much more.

Fortunately, Colonel Barboza wasn't a big talker. Rapp had been with him now for over two hours and the officer had scarcely spoken a word. They'd boarded General Rizal's jet back in Manila just before 4:00 A.M. and flown to Surigao in the Central Philippines. They then jumped onboard the Huey for the relatively short flight over to Dinagat Island.

Rapp had made only two calls on his secure satellite phone during that time. Both had been to Irene Kennedy. One confirmed that McMahon was in position to keep an eye on Ambassador Cox and the second confirmed that Coleman's team had been successfully inserted. Whether or not they were in place was still unknown. Rapp had the ability to contact them directly, but resisted the urge. Having spent most of his career in the field, he understood that they'd let him know their situation as soon as they were able. The plan was for Coleman to call him when he was in position.

TWENTY

David had been given very simple instructions. At 6:00 P.M., when the narrow streets of Jerusalem were choked with traffic, he was to be dropped off at the All Nations Church on Jericho Road and then walk north. His Range Rover pulled up in front of the church fifteen seconds early. David took a moment to gather himself and then after thanking his driver he stepped from the vehicle and onto the curb. He was resplendent in an expensive, dark-blue four-button Italian suit, white dress shirt, sans tie, and black shoes. His eyes were covered with chic black sunglasses and his thick black hair was slicked back behind his ears.

David's classic good looks ensured that he always stood out in a crowd, but waiting in front of the church, within view of the Al Aqsa Mosque, holding two identical attaché cases, he drew even more looks than usual. He set the two cases down, and fished out a pack of cigarettes. After lighting one, he stood there trying to look relaxed, one hand in his pocket, the other holding the cigarette. He took a few earnest drags and surveyed the area. The church that he was parked in front of was a favorite tourist spot for Christians. The All Nations Church, or

The Church of the Agony, as it was known by the old-timers, was not the ideal place to start such a journey.

Having grown up in the city, David couldn't help but be aware of the three religions. Each of them, he had noticed from an early age, loved to commemorate pain and suffering, but none of them more so than the Christians. David looked up at the ornate pediment that sat atop the church's colonnade. The gilded mosaic depicted the Agony of Christ as he prayed to his father the night before he was to be crucified. David glanced to the north at the small Garden of Gethsemane and its well-tended olive trees. They marked the spot where Jesus was betrayed by Judas and arrested. As the believers of the fourth major religion would have said, he was surrounded by bad karma.

He had little doubt that his Palestinian cohorts knew little of Christianity and Judaism, and what they did know were mostly lies propagated by racist caliphs, imams and sheiks. The Jews were of course the most savaged. The Muslim leaders repeatedly told their flock that during Passover Jews sacrificed young Palestinian children and drank their blood.

The ludicrous and unchallenged lies perpetuated themselves from one generation to the next. David looked to the place where Jesus had been betrayed. He knew of no Palestinian clever enough to intentionally start this journey from a place of such biblical importance. Besides, if they had the slightest clue that he had met with the head of Mossad, they would simply grab him and torture him until he revealed everything. They would never play some elaborate game. It was not the way of his people. They were too driven by emotion.

The early evening sun was still fairly high in the sky as he looked up and down the street. They were out there watching him; Palestinians and Israelis alike. David hoped that Ben Freidman wasn't so dumb as to try to trail him for the entire journey. Security for such a meeting was very tight. If the people who were to transport him got even the slightest whiff that they were being followed, they might easily abort.

Tonight's meeting, though, would be a bit different from the usual. They were all waiting on him this time, like greedy little children. They wanted their cash and that meant they would take risks to make sure he got there. Still, David wondered what Freidman and his spies from Mossad were up to. David had specified that no transponders be placed in the attaché cases. The reason for this was obvious. The security people in charge of the meeting would be carrying countermeasures that would detect just such a device. Freidman would know that, but David knew that Freidman would also never trust him enough to just let him wander off with fourteen pounds of plastic explosives.

He'd verified that weight as soon as he'd gotten back to his apartment that afternoon. Freidman's people had put seven pounds of the lethal explosives in each case rather than the five he asked for. The yield of each case had been increased by forty percent. This would make his mission all the more difficult to pull off, but he had a plan that would hopefully enable him to walk away unscathed.

After throwing his half-smoked cigarette into the street, David grabbed the two cases and started north. At the first intersection he crossed the street and continued on his way, passing the Tomb of the Virgin Mary on his right. He'd walked almost another block when without warning a blue Toyota van came to a sudden stop next to him and the side door slid open. David, having done this many times before, casually veered to his left and stepped into the waiting van. They were moving again before he was seated. Someone from behind threw the door closed and then the man in the seat next to him began frisking every inch of his body, starting with his left ankle.

TWENTY-ONE

Each step was taken with great care. Smaller rocks lying at odd angles were avoided while the men searched for firmer footing. They kept their separation at all times, Wicker setting the pace and each man in succession responsible for not falling too far behind or bunching up. This very act, this art form, of moving silently through total darkness, on an unblazed trail with a thirty-pound pack in hostile territory was perhaps the most difficult thing for a Special Forces soldier to master.

All four of the men picking their way through the jungle tonight excelled at this silent skill. They'd made steady progress since the insertion, but the terrain did not lend itself to a rapid pace. Coleman was beginning to doubt that they'd be in position by sunup. At the rare moments when the jungle canopy parted he could tell the sky was quickly going from black to dark gray. He checked his watch. The sun would be starting its crawl over the eastern horizon.

Clutching his MP-10 in his gloved hands, Coleman looked down through his NVGs, in search of firm footing so he could boost himself over a fallen tree. As he placed his right foot on the moss-slick tree he looked up to check on Wicker and froze. Charlie Wicker was standing completely still, his right hand held up in a fist. Coleman's own fist snapped up without hesitation, signaling the men behind him to freeze. The former commander of SEAL Team 6 searched in vain to see what had spooked his point man.

After several tense moments, Wicker gestured for Coleman to join him. He could have used his headset to call for him, but used hand signals instead. Coleman silently slithered over the log and carefully made his way to Wicker's position.

Wicker turned, cupping a hand over Coleman's ear and whispered, "There's movement up ahead."

Coleman's eyes strained to see what he was talking about, then whispered back, "I don't see a thing."

Wicker pointed to his ear, meaning he'd heard something.

"Animal?" asked Coleman.

Wicker shook his head. "Definitely human. I'm going to go sneak a peek."

Coleman nodded and shooed him on his way. Keeping his eyes on Wicker he raised his hand above his head and gestured for Hackett and Stroble to join him. If Wicker ran into trouble they needed to be in position to help him out. When the other two were at his side he briefed them on what Wicker was doing and then the three of them moved forward one by one.

They continued up the left side of the small creek to a point where it flattened. The rocks were replaced by a grassy bank. They moved forward in a crouch, treading lightly and staying close to the drooping branches of the trees. After rounding the next slight jog in the creek Coleman sighted Wicker about forty feet ahead of them kneeling next to a tree. He also, for the first time, heard the voices that had spooked his point man. It sounded like two men talking in hushed tones.

Coleman didn't like this development one bit. As far as islands went, Dinagat wasn't very small. Over thirty miles in length and twelve across, there was only one main road that ran north–south and they weren't anywhere near it. The odds of them accidentally running into a couple of locals at this remote juncture, and this early hour, were minuscule.

Coleman's thoughts drifted to the dark memory of the two SEALs who were lost on the beach not far from where he stood. He'd seen the proof of how that mission had been compromised, but for the life of him he couldn't imagine how this little covert endeavor could have been blown. Rapp had assured him that the circle of people who were in the know was tiny. And the number of people who knew the exact specifics, such as insertion points and times, was limited to just their war party and the pilots who'd ferried them in.

But still, they weren't alone out here in this jungle and it would be light soon. Coleman watched as Wicker turned toward him with the single lens of his NVGs protruding from his face. Wicker pointed toward his eyes with two fingers and then held three fingers up in the air, telling Coleman that he had three enemies in sight. Wicker then waved him up. Coleman turned to Hackett and Stroble, pointed at them and then held a clenched fist in the air. They both nodded their confirmation and then Coleman moved out.

It took him the better part of a minute to reach Wicker and on the way he noticed the smell of tobacco in the air. This made him feel slightly better. It was improbable that anyone waiting to ambush him and his men would be dumb enough to smoke cigarettes, but then again, Coleman had seen people do a lot of truly stupid things in the field.

When he reached Wicker's position he saw the men standing approximately fifty feet from them. They were on the opposite side of the creek next to what appeared to be a bridge made of fallen trees and stones. Water trickled from under the bridge as the creek dropped several feet into a circular pool of water that meandered its way toward them. A thin mist hung in the air.

Coleman noted the small waterfall and the noise it produced. The trickling sound would help conceal their own approach. The two tangos were carrying AK-47s with their distinctive banana clips, and the third man was carrying a rifle that he couldn't quite make out. The weapons were slung over their shoulders, muzzles pointed down. Coleman frowned at the stupidity of such a move.

Whoever these three Filipinos were, they weren't very smart, and if they'd ever received any formal military training, they'd already forgotten all the important parts. After watching them for another moment Coleman decided there was no way they were here to spring an ambush. They were more than likely Abu Sayyaf, and the way they were acting suggested they weren't too worried about security. If this was the best the Islamic terrorist group had to offer, the former SEAL Team 6 commander felt pretty good about the odds of the rescue operation succeeding.

There was also the possibility that the men were part of a local militia or workers for one of the island's farms. The intelligence dump he'd received on the island told him that with Abu Sayyaf roaming about, everyone had armed themselves.

SEALs were normally very good at patiently waiting and watching an enemy, but right now Coleman needed to get his team to the top of the mountain that was still a quarter of a mile straight uphill. There were three options. The first, most straightforward, and least desirable option was to kill the three men and get on with their mission. If he knew with any certainty that they were Abu Sayyaf, he'd gladly pull the trigger himself. The downside of that, however, was that they had to come back down the mountain when they were done, and three missing terrorists might bring some unwanted attention to the area.

The easiest course of action was to do nothing. Wait until the men moved on, and then proceed. But time was not a luxury at this point. They needed to get moving, and they needed to do it fast. That unfortunately meant back-tracking a bit and then moving through the jungle to get around the men. Any way he sliced it they were running out of time. Coleman didn't want to admit it yet, but it was looking more and more like they wouldn't be making it to the top of the mountain on time.

Coleman felt Wicker's hand on his bicep. He turned to see the point man walk two fingers in front of his face signaling that more people were approaching. The man's hearing was supernormal. Coleman, who was no novice in the woods, hadn't heard a thing.

Suddenly, the three Filipinos by the bridge threw their cigarettes to the ground and stamped them out with their sandaled feet. One by one they unshouldered their weapons and tried to look alert. Coleman heard someone speaking Filipino to the men from farther up the trail. Suddenly, there was another flurry of activity. Two of the men rushed to the other side of the small bridge and took up positions as the fourth man appeared from the jungle. Coleman saw that the man was carrying an M16 and . . .

Both he and Wicker ducked behind the tree at the same time. There was no mistaking the profile of the new man.

He had on a pair of night vision goggles. They lay completely still behind the tree listening for the slightest indication that they'd been spotted. After what seemed like an eternity, Coleman peered out from the opposite side of the tree. From his new vantage he could only see one side of the bridge. The man with the goggles was nowhere to be seen. Carefully, he slithered on the ground, backing up at first and then working his way toward the creek.

Once again, with a full view of the bridge, he found the man he was looking for. The man had flipped his NVGs into the up position and was talking in Filipino to the two men on the far side of the bridge. He pointed in the opposite direction from which he'd come and the two men immediately took off down the trail. The man with the M16 then pulled his goggles back down and began scanning the area. Coleman smoothly drew back behind the tree. The wisest thing for them to do right now was to sit tight. It was better to lie still than risk attracting attention.

Running down the list of possibilities, Coleman wondered if their insertion had been noticed and the guerrillas were attempting to set up a picket. If more men arrived and they began working their way down the stream it would be a foregone conclusion. Thinking ahead, the commander began to plot an ambush. If they had to, they could do it on the fly.

Coleman would leave Wicker where he was and the commander and Hackett would collapse to the middle. They'd let the enemy work their way down the stream far enough until they were fully flanked by his position and then they'd unload with Stroble and Wicker working their way from the outside in and he and Hackett the inside out. It would not be difficult for them to take down at least twelve men before a warning shot was fired.

Coleman was about to fall back when he felt Wicker tightly squeeze his arm and not let go. Looking over, Coleman saw that his point man was looking at the bridge from the other side of the tree. Slowly Coleman peeked out from behind the right side. He blinked twice in disbelief. It took him a moment to process what was happening on the small bridge and another moment to realize that his finger had moved off the guard and onto the thin trigger of his MP-10.

TWENTY-TWO

Coleman watched in disbelief as five Caucasians, two adults and three children, passed before him like a dream in the mist, their blond and red hair a stark contrast to the black hair of the armed men who walked with them. They were tied to each other, a sagging link of rope in between each frail, malnourished individual. The mom in front, two kids in the middle and the dad slowly bringing up the rear carrying the youngest of the brood. They looked ragged and underfed, but alive. The column moved across the bridge and down the trail. A rear guard loitered for a few seconds, then wandered off lazily after the group. And just like that, they were gone.

Coleman, who had just moments before cursed their bad luck, was now rejoicing in their fortune. In the midst of a jungle, in the middle of the Philippines, they had just stumbled across a family of Americans for whom thousands of men and women had been searching. Getting into position to support Rapp's mission was his priority, but this was an opportunity that he might not be able to resist.

Wicker leaned over and whispered in his ear. "I counted twenty-one plus the family."

Coleman nodded and then pointed for Wicker to move forward and check things out. With his hand cupped over his lip mike he said, "Kevin and Dan, get up here."

A minute later they were gathered near the bridge. The sky was getting lighter by the minute. While Coleman briefed Hackett and Stroble on what they'd seen, Wicker checked out the path to make sure no one was lagging behind or doubling back. When the point man returned Coleman quickly laid out their options. All four men looked to the top of the mountain where they were sup-posed to be by the time the sun was up, and then looked down the narrow muddy path where the family of kid-napped Americans and their captors had gone.

More than probably any other military outfit, SEALs were taught to think independently in the field, but none of them were prepared for this. They had a mission to ful-fill and Coleman wasn't about to leave Rapp to carry on alone, but he sure as hell didn't like the idea of losing the Andersons. His loyalty and respect for Rapp and the SEALs who had been abandoned on the beach was un-questionable, but so was the innocence of the American family held against their will for months on end. Strict protocol dictated that he get his team to the top of the hill as quickly as possible and radio in the sighting of the An-dersons. Common sense told him that this accidental sighting of the missing family was too good an opportu-nity to pass up.

Satellites and reconnaissance flights were incapable of penetrating the dense cover of the jungle, making any hope of searching for the Andersons by air hopeless. If Coleman radioed in their position it would take a day or more to insert a team. By that time the trail was sure to go cold.

Looking again to the top of the hill and then down the trail, Coleman continued to struggle with what to do. The answer suddenly came to him in the form of a question. What would Rapp do? The answer was obvious. The solution was less than perfect, but under the current situation, the best choice. The former SEAL Team commander gestured for his men to take a knee and then very specifically he laid out a course of action.

TWENTY-THREE

They had traveled north to Ramallah and then to Nablus, changing vehicles in each city. This was standard procedure. Both cities lay on the West Bank, and despite Israeli control, there were certain enclaves in each that the Jews would not venture into unless they were in an armored column spearheaded by tanks.

David hadn't a clue as to when or where the meeting would take place, only that it would definitely be after dark. Heading north could merely be a diversion before they reversed course, or they might simply meander through one city or the other until they were convinced they weren't being followed and then stop at the appointed place.

As darkness began to fall they pulled into a parking ramp. David was swiftly ushered from the yellow Palestinian taxi he'd been riding in to a white Israeli taxi parked next to it. David was asked to lie down on the backseat and a blanket was placed over him. The transfer complete, they sped from the ramp and began winding their way through the streets of Nablus.

Approximately twenty minutes later they stopped. The blanket was pulled from David and once again he was told to get out of the car. For a second time he found himself standing in a dimly lit concrete parking garage. He hadn't the slightest idea where he was other than somewhere on the West Bank.

Across the aisle, three men were standing by the trunk of a car smoking cigarettes. Two of them had machine guns slung over their shoulders and the third one David recognized instantly. His name was Hassan Rashid. He worked for Palestinian General Intelligence, which was the official intelligence organization of the Palestinian Authority. The agency was supposed to help combat terrorism and work toward a lasting stable relationship with Israel, but as with everything connected to the PLO it was rotten to the core.

Hassan Rashid was a street thug who had been a disciple of Yasser Arafat's since childhood. He'd grown up in Nablus and became very active during the first Intifada of 1987, but not in the way one would expect. As the conflict grew more violent Arafat saw an opportunity to consolidate his power, and he broke with the Palestinian extremist groups by calling for a Palestinian state to coexist alongside Israel.

This was Arafat's first real gambit to gain respect from the international community. It presented a real risk, however, since it was outright blasphemy for an Arab to want anything other than the complete destruction of the Jewish state. Because of Arafat's bold move the various groups under the loosely allied Palestinian United National Command splintered. Islamic Jihad and Hamas turned on Arafat and the blood began to flow. Rashid, who had one real talent in life, helped protect the PLO's standing in Nablus by brutalizing any and all Islamic extremists who stood against Arafat.

It took great effort on David's part to conceal his hatred for the man. As he stood with his two attaché cases, he watched Rashid flick his cigarette through the air. It hit the ground and cartwheeled toward him, the burning tip breaking apart and showering his feet with red sparks. David looked up slowly from his shoes. Rashid was looking back with a smug look on his scarred face. His longish hooked nose was pulled farther to the side by the lopsided smirk on his lips.

"Well, pretty one, what have you brought for us this evening?"

David decided not to reply. He had risen to untouchable heights, and if Rashid persisted in his schoolyard bullying, he would have to remind him of his place.

Rashid started toward him. "Come now, you're still not mad at me after all these years?"

"No," David feigned sincerity, "I love you like a brother."

"Oh, come now, pretty one. We all know you liked it."

"Oh, I loved it. In fact, maybe we could get together sometime and I'll shove a cattle prod up your anus. Knowing your affinity for little boys, I'm amazed you haven't already tried it." As David said this he saw the smile vanish from Rashid's face.

The man raised his right fist, and from two steps away began to let loose an emotional roundhouse punch. Taking David for an easy, defenseless target, he put little thought into his technique or balance. Most of the punches that Rashid had thrown in recent years had been at men tied to a chair or strung up. His street-fighting skills were not what they once were, so when his target made a swift side step, his wild punch missed its mark with such force that it spun him around.

David was done taking crap from the man who had plucked him from the street as a young teenager and tortured him for having too many Jewish friends. It had been twenty years since somebody had told the PLO that Jabril Khatabi was a sympathizer and they had dispatched Rashid, the street thug, to teach him a lesson. Now David was ready to repay the man who had destroyed his youth.

With a quick side step, he had avoided the punch, watching it sail past his face. Setting himself into a quick 360-degree spin, he kept the case in his left hand low and brought up the case in his right hand. He completed the spin just as an angry Rashid squared himself for another charge. The bottom corner of the hard black attaché case hit with a bone-splitting crack that smashed the man's nose and sent Rashid careening off his feet and into the trunk of a parked car.

THE WALL WAS AGLOW with screens relaying images shot from all around the West Bank and even a few taken from outer space. Ben Freidman was filled with anticipation. He had forced himself to use great restraint in deploying his assets. A deft hand would be needed to strike the blow he intended. Tonight he would avenge the deaths of hundreds of innocent Israelis. The Palestinians that Khatabi was going to meet were the masterminds behind the wave of suicide bombings that had rocked his country and crippled the Israeli economy.

Under Freidman's orders Mossad technicians had placed a highly sophisticated device in each case. In essence they were homing beacons connected to a GPS device and a timed burst transmitter. Every five minutes the devices turned themselves on for six seconds. The GPS recorded the position of the cases to within two meters and then the burst transmitter sent an encrypted message to a satellite in geosynchronous orbit. The devices then powered off so they wouldn't be picked up by an electronic countermeasure.

Freidman understood better than anyone the draconian measures his enemy employed to keep their activities secret. He, in fact, was the reason for much of their paranoia. He had hunted and killed them in such a wild variety of ways that it had now been several years since he had gotten anyone close enough to take real action against them.

The director general of Mossad had significant experience in the arena of assassination. In 1972, when eleven Israeli athletes were taken hostage during the Munich Olympics by the Palestinian group Black September, Ben Freidman had been there. He had stood at the side of his mentor, legendary Mossad Director General Zvi Zamir, while the German police bungled a rescue operation that resulted in the deaths of all the Israeli hostages.

To add insult to injury, the two surviving terrorists were later released by the German authorities for fear of reprisals. Israel had nowhere to turn for justice, so they looked to Mossad. It was Zamir who had convinced then Prime Minister Golda Meir that they must seek vengeance. Meir agreed and directed Zamir to hunt down the masterminds behind Black September and eliminate them. Over the next nine months the blood flowed and Ben Freidman proved himself to be one of Mossad's most efficient assassins.

His first hit was barely a month after the massacre of the Olympic athletes. Mossad wanted to send a signal to everyone, and their first target was Wael Zwaiter, a PLO representative in Rome. On October 16 Freidman approached Zwaiter from behind while the man was on a walk and put two bullets into the back of his head.

Two months later Freidman was part of a team that

killed Mahmoud Hamshari by placing a bomb in the phone of his Paris apartment. The device was detonated by remote control and the PLO representative was decapitated. Blood continued to flow and Freidman's crowning achievement came on April 13, 1973.

He was part of a select force of Mossad agents and army commandos that launched a raid into the heart of Beirut. The targets that night were three of the PLO's most senior officials. Muhammad Najjar, Kamal Adwan and Kamal Nasser were all gunned down in their homes. The success of the operation had implications far beyond the deaths of the three leaders. Information seized during the raids led to the assassination of three more terrorists with ties to Black September. The victory, however, was short-lived.

Just two months later Mossad was to suffer its most embarrassing public moment. The disaster occurred in the sleepy Norwegian ski village of Lillehammer. A team of Mossad agents were sent to investigate a possible sighting of the terrorist Ali Hassan Salameh. The inexperienced group incorrectly identified the target and then proceeded to kill Ahmed Bouchiki, a Moroccan waiter. If that wasn't bad enough, six of the team members were subsequently captured while trying to escape. The men and women were put on trial and five of the six were jailed. The international outcry was deafening, and Mossad was officially ordered to get out of the assassination business.

Fortunately for Ben Freidman, he had not been involved in the Lillehammer incident, for if he had, it would have marked the end of his career. Instead, the disaster in Norway served to remind him, and many others, that they needed to hone their skills further and redouble their efforts in their covert war against the Arab aggressors.

Despite the official ban on assassination, Freidman and

his group of kidons continued to hunt the terrorists that plagued his country. His crowning achievement came when one of his kidons infiltrated Hamas. One of the group's leaders, and bomb engineers, had been a particularly nasty thorn in the side of Israel for some time. His name was Yehya Ayyash. The Israeli assassin took a phone call for Ayyash on a phone that had been modified by the technicians back at Mossad. He then handed the phone to the Hamas leader and walked away. Seconds later a tiny charge of C-4 exploded, blowing a hole in the side of the terrorist's head and killing him.

Tonight the stakes were much higher. Ayyash had been but one terrorist, whereas this evening there would be many. Others would be sure to sprout up and take their place if he were successful, but it would take the enemy years to recover from such a blow. Hopefully by then, all Palestinians would be expelled from the occupied territories and a long tall wall would be built once and for all separating the two tribes. And then they could turn on each other. This Jabril Khatabi was a good example of what they were capable of. Freidman had no doubt that if they ever got to the point when they no longer had Israel to blame they would simply self-destruct.

Freidman's thoughts were interrupted by the voice of one of his people. "It looks like he's changed cars again."

The director general looked up at the wall of screens. On the left were twelve TVs, six high by two wide. In the middle were four large screens that measured four by six feet each and on the right there were again twelve TVs. On one of the big screens a red laser dot marked the roof of a white sedan that was moving through traffic. One by one screens flickered as they were changed from one camera vantage to another.

The advanced surveillance room wasn't all that different than a news control room. Right now the surveillance team's director and his two assistants were busy changing camera angles. At their disposal was an amazing array of surveillance equipment. Two satellites, over a thousand traffic and security cameras from all over the country, a specially equipped surveillance airplane circling the area at fifteen thousand feet, and several helicopters were about to join the fray just as soon as the sun slid over the long expanse of the Mediterranean.

Freidman watched and listened as his people worked computer consoles and joysticks, carefully directing teams in the field to attempt a visual confirmation that their man was still in the car. Freidman leaned forward into the glow of the screens and cautioned his people not to push too hard. The attaché cases were the key. He had to take Jabril at his word; that he wanted these men dead every bit as much as Freidman did. If he was right, Jabril would do everything in his power to prevent the money from being transferred to a bag or some other case.

TWENTY-FOUR

Rapp jerked open the helicopter door and stepped to the ground. He scanned the perimeter of the landing area looking for the general, even though he doubted the officer would be so polite as to meet his visitors as they landed. Colonel Barboza joined him and they walked underneath the spinning rotors of the Huey.

At the edge of the landing area the two men were greeted by an eager lieutenant dressed in BDUs, jungle boots and a black Special Forces beret. He saluted Colonel Barboza crisply and introduced himself as General Moro's aide-de-camp. With that brief introduction out of the way, the man did an about-face and led them down a path. The place was a standard military field camp. Located in a grassy clearing about the size of two football fields, it consisted of two rows of big green tents set atop wooden pallets.

From the satellite photos he'd studied, Rapp knew what each of the sixteen tents were for, which ones served as bivouacs for the troops to sleep in, which tent was the mess hall, medical tent, command center and most important, which was the general's tent.

What Rapp hadn't been able to glean from the satellite photos was what perimeter security was in place along the tree line. On the plane ride over, Coleman had mentioned it was very curious that there was no barbwire laid out around the camp's perimeter, and no foxholes or machine-gun nests dug into the obvious defensive positions. In Coleman's mind Moro was either derelict in his command or had very good reason not to fear an attack by the guerrillas.

At the expected tent the aide stopped and rapped his knuckles on a wooden sign that, amazingly enough, had the general's name on it. As a matter of course, U.S. Special Forces personnel in the field went to great lengths to hide the rank of officers. There was no saluting, rarely was rank displayed unless in a subtle way that could only be noticed up close, and men were taught not to all stand facing a commander as he talked. This last part was the most difficult to teach since the military had drilled the chain of command into their heads from their first day of boot camp.

Moro was either very proud of the fact that he was a general or he had no fear of letting the enemy know where to find him. Rapp suspected the sign on the door indicated a bit of both.

From inside the tent came the word, "Enter."

The voice was not menacing, casual or aloof. If anything, it sounded merely a bit curious. As he stepped into the dark tent he was forced to take his sunglasses off. There, sitting behind a small portable desk, was the general in a pair of camouflage pants and a green T-shirt. Rapp immediately noticed that the general was in tip-top shape. His arms were long and lean, with powerful biceps straining against the tight fabric of his shirt.

The general made no effort to get up and greet them and Rapp casually observed the interaction between Barboza and Moro. He watched the junior officer salute his superior in a way that was within the proper guidelines, but was noticeably lacking in both enthusiasm and respect. It was the bare minimum required by the military protocol and nothing more.

Barboza turned, waving an arm toward Rapp, and said, "This is Mr. Rapp. He works for the CIA."

The smallest of smirks formed on the general's lips. It may have been a smirk of recognition, or just a show of disrespect for the CIA. Rapp watched Moro with the detached analytical eye of a professional. The general made no effort to get up and shake his hand, and Rapp made no effort to extend his. The two men silently studied each other until the mood grew uncomfortable. Rapp had a strategy to employ and a crucial part of it was to keep Moro off balance until the time was right.

Moro sat motionless, his hands gripping the armrest of his wood and canvas chair. Rapp had played this game before, and he was sure the general had also done so countless times with his subordinates and probably even a few American military advisors and State Department officials.

What was different this time was that Rapp wasn't some American diplomat who was worried about offending the general's sensibilities. Rapp was intent on doing much more than that, and he sincerely hoped that in the process he would thoroughly upset the diplomatic applecart.

It was the general who blinked first. His smirk turned into a full-blown smile and he asked, "To what do I owe the honor of receiving the infamous Mr. Rapp of the CIA?"

Rapp took the insult as a compliment. He had two choices. He could either maintain the cold attitude of a

man who obviously distrusted Moro, or he could join the
general in his parlor game and try to gain his trust, or at
a bare minimum, ease his mistrust. He decided on the latter. With a smile of his own Rapp replied, "There is no
honor in receiving me, General. I am just a humble bureaucrat in the employ of my government."

This caused Moro to laugh loudly. "A humble bureaucrat. That is good." The general slapped his thighs enthusiastically and looked at a confused Colonel Barboza.
"Colonel, I see you have no idea of the fame of the man
you have brought to see me." It was obvious that Moro
enjoyed this advantage over the younger officer. "You
should read more. Mr. Rapp is an American icon. Mr.
Rapp is America's counterterrorist."

Rapp did not join in the general's laughter. He found
very little humor in what he did for a living. When Moro
had settled down, Rapp said, "General, if it's all right with
you, I'd like to have a word in private."

Moro looked from Rapp to Barboza. He studied the
colonel for a moment with a look on his face that hinted
of a deep-seated contempt. "Colonel, you are dismissed. I
will send for you when we are done."

Barboza remained impassive. He saluted the general
and then turned to Rapp. "I will be waiting for you outside."

When he had departed Moro offered his visitor a chair.
Rapp took a seat and settled in.

"I assume," Moro started, "that since you are America's
counterterrorist, that you are here to discuss the progress
I have made against Abu Sayyaf."

Raising an eyebrow in surprise, Rapp replied, "I wasn't
aware that you've made any progress."

The general chose to ignore the comment, instead
smiled and said, "Your Agency is famous for getting its

facts wrong, Mr. Rapp. I don't know what you have been told, but the terrorists have suffered over a hundred losses in the last month alone."

"So you say," replied Rapp with a straight face.

Moro could not let this pass. Indignantly, he asked, "Are you questioning my honor?"

Rapp wanted to say that it was worthless to debate an attribute that the general did not possess, but that might push him too far in the wrong direction. Ignoring the question Rapp said, "General, I am a practical man, and I have been told you too are a practical man, one with amazing capabilities." Rapp threw in the last part as a blatant attempt to flatter the general. "We both know what it is like to be in the field with politicians beating on us for results. I am not here to attack your integrity, but I do know for a fact that your men have not killed even half the enemy that you have just claimed."

Moro sat motionless for a moment, struggling between admitting the truth or sticking with his propaganda. He decided to do neither. "Mr. Rapp, what is your point?"

"My point is, General, that I know things about you that your own government does not." Rapp let the innuendo hang in the air. He could feel the comforting lump of his Beretta under his right arm. He would not hesitate to kill the snake sitting across the desk from him. Coleman and his team appeared to have run into some trouble, so it looked like it was up to him to handle the situation. He'd already pieced together a plan that he felt would work.

If Moro made the slightest move for his side arm, which was in its holster hanging from a peg on the tent pole behind the general, Rapp would have to ad-lib a bit, but he was still confident that he could accomplish his mission and avoid being torn limb from limb by the general's troops. Once he showed Moro the goodies there was a very real chance that things would spiral out of control.

With a furrowed brow, no doubt caused by Rapp's unsettling words, Moro tried to figure out why this assassin had come to visit him. The first and most obvious answer was quickly dismissed. Moro's men were fiercely loyal to him. The American would never make it out of here alive if he were to try to kill him. With a disarming smile, Moro said, "Mr. Rapp, you have me at a disadvantage. I have no idea what you are talking about."

SALTY SWEAT POURED DOWN Coleman's camouflage-painted face as he tried to keep up with Wicker. It was a hopeless task. Wicker, a decade younger and thirty pounds lighter, seemed to have an inexhaustible source of energy as he scampered up the mountainside. This was not to say that Coleman was past his day, it was rather that Wicker was a very unusual man. He could move through the jungle, in near silent fashion, at a pace that was impossible to match. Coleman was wise enough to factor all of this into his decision before they started their scramble up the hill and had told Wicker not to wait for him.

Back near the footbridge, Coleman had made the difficult choice of splitting his team in two. Stroble and Hackett were to carefully track the terrorists while Wicker and Coleman went on to support their primary mission. This was one of those battlefield decisions that would either be looked back on as ingenious and gutsy, or glaringly stupid. Like a football coach deciding to go for it on fourth down rather than kicking a field goal, the wisdom of such a decision is always dependent on the success of the gamble.

The physical screening process for SEAL candidates is

well known, but what is often overlooked is that the men who run the Naval Special Warfare Training Center in Coronado place an equal amount of importance on intellect and character. In short, a physically strong warrior who follows orders makes an ideal infantry soldier. In the modern battlefield their every move is monitored by a battalion, brigade and sometimes even a force commander. They are chess pieces on a very intricate board that need to be moved in a precise way.

The world of Special Forces, however, is very different. A physically strong warrior is a good start, but a strong, intelligent warrior is absolutely dangerous. SEALs are taught from Day One that operations rarely go as planned. It is drilled into them that quick, intelligent decision making will invariably enhance the chances for a successful mission, and contribute to the very survival of their unit.

They need to be able to operate behind enemy lines often without the aid of artillery and close air support. They are rarely involved in major battles unless their mission is to take out a select high value target prior to the launching of the main battle. In short, they are taught to operate independently from their command, within mission parameters, for sustained periods of time behind enemy lines.

It was not in Coleman's character to abandon Rapp, but the kidnapped American family had appeared like a gift out of the predawn mist. It was a gift he could not pass up. Coleman paused briefly to catch his breath and take a drink of water from his camel pack. He placed the small hose between his lips and sucked in a mouthful of water. Wicker was far ahead of him now. At least seventy-five yards. He caught a glimpse of him as he scrambled over a rock shelf and disappeared from sight. A shadow moving in the shadows.

Coleman started again in earnest, on all fours, pawing and pushing his way up the steep mountain. He was both thankful and leery of the cover provided by the trees that enveloped the landscape. They traveled in the same gully that ran from the top of the mountain all the way to the sea. At times it was like a gorge and at others a babbling brook. Up on this high steep part there were more exposed rocks and less grass and moss. The torrential rains of the region washed away anything that wasn't anchored down by the roots of the trees and the surrounding undergrowth.

It would be nearly impossible for anyone below to see them. They traveled just off to the side of the gully where the leafy limbs of the trees provided good cover. Coleman worried about what might be waiting for them at the top. Mountaintops are a prized possession among opposing forces. They offer a bird's-eye view of the lay of the land and provide crucial intelligence. They also offer a nice perch to set up a counter-sniping team.

Sniping in the Special Forces is a life-and-death game played at the highest intellectual level. A sniper does not fear machine-gun fire, artillery shells or bombs from the air. A sniper fears the bullet of another sniper. Snipers will lay in wait for days, slowly, cautiously scanning every inch of the landscape, section by methodical section, to make sure they don't become the target of someone staring back at them through a high-powered scope. Fear of snipers, more than any reason, was why they wanted to be in position by sunup. Unfortunately, that precaution was out of their reach. They would now have to hope that they were the only men around with long barrels.

Coleman pressed on, his thighs burning with each foot that was gained in his quest for the relatively short summit. The pain was ignored and the pace was quickened.

His lungs took in and exhaled a steady efficient supply of oxygen. He reached a sheer eleven-foot wall of rock. He was about to scale it when he noticed the trampled undergrowth to his left indicating Wicker's passage. Without hesitation he plunged through the foliage. When he got back to the gully he looked up and saw Wicker within striking distance of the summit. Coleman put his head down and redoubled his efforts. He figured it would take him no more than two minutes to reach the top.

TWENTY-FIVE

It looked like the roulette wheel would stop on Hebron, a Palestinian city of over one hundred thousand, twenty miles south of Jerusalem. In the fifty-plus years of Israeli statehood, Hebron had been a city caught in the middle. Located in a mountainous region, it was home to the Tomb of Abraham; a prophet revered by Muslims, Jews and Christians alike. A small community of Orthodox Jews lived near the center of the town, but they numbered less than a thousand and had to be protected by a garrison of Israeli Defense Forces.

The Palestinians resented the fact that a single Jew lived in their city and had tried countless times over the last century to rectify the problem by means that were less than humanitarian. The terrain lent itself naturally to urban guerrilla warfare; narrow streets that wound up and down hillsides flanked by multistory stone buildings with flat roofs. Blind corners abounded and streets stopped and started without warning. Israeli soldiers steered clear of much of the city knowing if they went in, there was a good chance they might not make it out. In short, Hebron was Palestinian-controlled territory.

It surprised David not in the least that this was where

the meeting would take place. His altercation with Rashid in the parking garage had been extremely satisfying. If Rashid and his men understood anything it was force. They had seen their boss bested, and bested easily, by a younger man who by virtue of the meeting he was about to attend was somebody important.

Still, David didn't give them much time to react as they gawked at the bloody Rashid lying unconscious on the floor. He yelled at the men to get moving and climbed into the white Israeli taxi. The men hesitated, not sure what they should do. "Leave him!" he ordered. "When I tell Mohammed Atwa what he has done, he will be grateful that you left him here."

This was a name that stirred genuine terror in the Palestinians. The three men did not hesitate to obey. Mohammed Atwa was the head of Palestinian General Intelligence; an organization that many Palestinians feared more than Mossad. The security service was known for torturing and killing suspected collaborators with impunity. Atwa had even resurrected the old practice of killing Palestinians who dared sell their land to a Jew. He also happened to be the same man who ordered the torture and interrogation of David when he was a young teenager.

David looked out the window of the sedan as they meandered through the canyonlike streets of Hebron. Darkness had fallen and they were no longer in the white Israeli taxi. Driving such a vehicle into Hebron would be akin to walking through Harlem in full Ku Klux Klan regalia. Instead, they'd switched to a yellow Palestinian taxi.

As they rounded a tight corner they came to a sudden stop. A group of masked young men immediately surrounded the car. They carried a variety of weapons from Russian-made AK-47s to American-made M16s. All four doors of the sedan were yanked open and everyone was told to get out. David was searched once again for a transmitter. When one of the men stepped up and tried to grab the attaché cases, David stopped him with a stern rebuke. He placed both cases on the trunk of the car and opened one and then the other. The packets of neatly bound one hundred dollar bills left the men momentarily awestruck. The nicely dressed young man they were dealing with was apparently someone very important.

David slammed the cases closed before the guards had time to gather their wits. Acting impatient, he grabbed each case and told the men he was not to be delayed further. With the vision of millions of American dollars still fresh in their heads, none of them argued. David was walked through the barricade and placed in the back of a minivan. The van raced up the street, turning several times. On each corner men stood watch with assault rifles at their sides.

Six blocks later they stopped in front of a three-story house. Both sides of the street were clogged with parked cars. David grew nervous for a second and then saw the vehicle he was looking for. The Mercedes sedan was parked just on the other side of a van. David breathed a sigh of relief, knowing that the armored car belonged to Mohammed Atwa.

Clutching the attaché cases, he stepped from the van and walked toward the house. His arms suddenly felt very heavy, and everything began to slow down. He looked down at the cracked sidewalk and then slowly up at the two masked men standing guard in front of the blue wood door with chipped and peeling paint. The men were gesturing for David to hurry but he didn't hear what they were saying. He just casually placed one foot in front of the other, and then the next thing he knew, he was in the house.

There were people everywhere. It was as if a party were

going on. Smoke and loud conversation filled the air. To the room on his left there was a virtual banquet; mounds of grilled lamb, shashlik, mussakhan and chicken liver. A middle-aged man who ran the Popular Liberation Committee in Gaza was popping baklava into his mouth and nodding enthusiastically to the head of Force 17. Over in the corner he saw two men sipping Arab coffee and discussing something in earnest. One of the men he knew to be the head of security for Islamic Jihad but the other man he didn't recognize. David felt his throat tighten a bit; this was the culmination of meticulous planning and great patience. It was almost exactly as he'd dreamt it would be.

He looked to the right and saw a big screen TV. It was tuned to Al Jazeera, but it seemed no one was paying attention. Three large couches were arranged around the TV. They were filled with men, some of whom David recognized. This was the closest thing David had ever seen to a terrorism summit.

There were representatives from the Gaza Strip, the West Bank, and at least one from Beirut. There were several new faces from the martyr brigades and many old faces from the PLO and its only true rival, Hamas.

Through the crowd David saw Mohammed Atwa approach. David forced a smile to his face and lifted the two attaché cases in the air. Atwa, the head of Palestinian General Intelligence, the torturer of thousands, grabbed David by the cheeks and standing on his toes, kissed the younger man's forehead.

With a flourish Atwa turned and waved a theatrical arm in the air. "He is here! Our son has returned from visiting our rich Saudi friends!"

Everyone fell silent for a brief moment and then the room broke into applause, toothy grins and nods of enthusiasm. This was the apogee of two years of hard work.

David had started small, working his way up the ladder of the Palestinian Authority. His first donation had been $10,000. From there it got bigger, and as his stature grew, he worked his way closer to Atwa; the power behind the power, the man whom he someday would kill.

David knew if he were to ever see a Palestinian state, Hamas would have to be dealt a vicious blow. The Islamic fanatics would never be happy until every last Jew was dead, and when that happened they would only be satisfied if a Palestinian state were run by clerics who enforced strict Islamic law. Even the radical PLO looked tame next to the crazed members of Hamas.

David had cautiously counseled Atwa to bring Hamas into the fold by providing them with capital. The agreement was that David would use his skills to raise money and Atwa would hand part of that money over to Hamas to finance their terrorist and martyr operations. As David's fund-raising prowess grew, so did Hamas's reliance on PLO support. David was so successful that Atwa was also able to entice some other groups to the trough. They included Islamic Jihad, the Popular Resistance Committee and Hezbollah.

Tonight had been billed as a watershed evening for the groups. The last month's fund-raising had been so fruitful that they would all gather under the benevolence of Atwa and the PLO to divide the spoils.

Atwa relieved David of one of the attaché cases and grabbed him by the arm. Excitedly, he led David between two of the couches to a spot in front of the big screen TV. Atwa turned his case around and opened it for the group to see. He nodded for David to do the same.

"Two million dollars, my friends!"

The room broke into shouts and praise for Allah. Men jumped to their feet and began hugging each other. The irony of seeing these cold-blooded killers act in a such a lighthearted way made David smile to himself. What idiots! Not only was the money counterfeit, courtesy of the Iraqis, but there was an even better surprise in store.

Atwa set the attaché case down on the table and David did the same. Turning to one of his lieutenants, Atwa handed him a sheet of paper that explained how the money was to be distributed. Then, overcome with the emotion of the moment, he grabbed David and hugged him. Patting him on the cheek like a son, he told David how proud he was of him.

David kept up his act and shrugged off the compliment. "It was no big deal."

"Yes it was, and don't say it wasn't." Atwa stuck a finger in his face to warn him against any more modesty. Then, looking around the room, he began to frown and asked, "Where is Hassan?"

David hesitated just briefly and then seized his chance. "I need to talk to you about that."

Atwa's lined face became concerned. "What has happened?"

David looked over one shoulder and then the other. "Not here. Not in front of the others." After looking around the room one more time, David gestured for Atwa to follow him.

The two men walked through the crowd, David stopping every few feet to accept another hug or handshake. He feigned reciprocity as the men showered affection on him, which was made all the more difficult by the fact that he was about to send them to their deaths. As they stepped outside, Atwa stopped; his look of concern now much deeper.

David pointed to the butcher's Mercedes sedan. "In private." David walked around the other side and climbed into the backseat. Atwa joined him and when both doors were closed David breathed a barely discernible sigh of relief.

TWENTY-SIX

Rapp was willing to play the general's game for a while. Moro would undoubtedly remain defiant right up to the moment he was confronted with the evidence. "Tell me, General, do you dislike America?"

Moro pondered the question with a puzzled look on his oily face. "I'm not sure what you are asking me."

"It isn't a difficult question. Do you like America? Yes or no?"

"That depends. There are things about America that I like, and there are things that I don't like."

"Fair enough. What about China?"

The Filipino's eyes screwed a bit tighter at hearing this. "I have no opinion on China."

"Really?" asked Rapp in a surprised tone. "That surprises me."

Any sense of Moro's air of amusement had evaporated at the mention of the world's most populous country. "What are you hinting at, Mr. Rapp?"

Changing gears, Rapp leaned back and said, "I would like to do business with you, General. As I said, I am a practical man, and I've been told you are too. I want Abu Sayyaf crushed, and I don't care what it takes. If I have to pay a certain person large amounts of cash to make sure the job gets done, then that's what I am willing to do."

"I am not sure," said Moro, squinting up at the tent's ceiling, "but I think I am offended by what you have just proposed."

Rapp looked him right in the eye and shook his head disbelievingly. "No, you aren't. As I've already said, I know certain things about you, and I know it is impossible that you are offended by what I just proposed."

Moro took in a deep breath and then exhaled slowly. It appeared that the American was privy to his business arrangement. Choosing his words carefully, he said, "What exactly did you come here for, Mr. Rapp?"

"I came to make you a better offer than the one you already have."

"I'm listening." The general leaned back and folded his arms across his chest.

"We know about your accounts in Hong Kong and Jakarta. We know you've been spying for the Chinese since the early eighties, and we know Abu Sayyaf pays you off so that you don't get too aggressive in pursuing them."

Moro studied Rapp with cautious eyes. Finally he said, "I'm still listening."

"As I've already stated, I'm a practical man. Although I'm not entirely comfortable with your connection to Beijing, I can live with it for the time being. Abu Sayyaf is an entirely different matter. That I cannot live with."

"Mr. Rapp, I still have no idea what you are talking about."

Rapp reached into his vest pocket while keeping his eyes locked on Moro. He pulled out an envelope and tossed it onto the general's desk. Rapp watched as Moro emptied the envelope's contents and began leafing through the various pages. They consisted of bank and phone records.

After Moro was done looking over the documents he placed them back in the envelope and set the package carefully in the middle of his desk. So the American did know his secret, or at least part of it, but Moro was not willing to admit guilt so easily. "I don't know what any of this is about."

In a deadpan voice, Rapp said, "There's more. We have radio and telephone intercepts. Your voiceprint has been matched beyond any reasonable doubt."

Moro stared unwaveringly at his adversary as he desperately scrambled for a way out of this ambush. After nearly a minute of silence, he decided there was only one option. "How many people know about this?" Moro nodded at the envelope.

"Enough."

"How many in my country?"

"A select few."

The sour expression on Moro's face betrayed his feelings about this piece of information. "Does Colonel Barboza know?"

Barboza knew something, to be sure, but Rapp wasn't sure exactly what. Not wanting to complicate things he answered, "No."

Moro nodded. The fact that the colonel was out of the loop seemed to offer him some comfort. "It appears you have me at a disadvantage, Mr. Rapp. Why don't we get back to what you were talking about earlier."

"The part about large amounts of cash."

"Yes," said Moro, smiling.

Rapp returned the smile despite the fact that he hated the man. "As I already told you, I am a practical man. Your relationship with the Chinese will be handled at a later date. For now my main concern is dealing with Abu Sayyaf."

Moro nodded.

"I want the American family back unharmed, and I want you to pursue Abu Sayyaf with such vengeance that they dare not take another American ever again. In fact I would prefer it if you wiped them out entirely."

"This will not be easy."

"Rotting in a Philippine prison for the rest of your life would be much more difficult."

The general's entire body tensed at the thought. "I did not say it couldn't be done."

Rapp nodded his approval. "General, fear can be a wonderful motivator, but it does nothing to build long-term relationships. That is why I am going to make you an offer that I think you will like very much." Leaning forward, Rapp lowered his voice and said, "If you return the entire Anderson family to us unharmed, I will see to it that one hundred thousand dollars will find its way into an account of your choosing. If by year's end you have managed to pursue Abu Sayyaf to my satisfaction you will receive an additional one hundred thousand dollars. If you succeed on both of these fronts we will sit down and explore the possibility of further compensation in regard to your relationship with Beijing."

With a wry smile Moro said, "You would like to turn me into a double agent."

"Like I said," said Rapp, shrugging, "let's see how our first two deals turn out and then we'll go from there."

Moro sat there for a long moment pondering the offer that had just been made to him. Rapp had played all of this out beforehand in his mind and had a pretty good inkling of what would happen next. In fact, he would be disappointed if Moro didn't do as he'd predicted.

Finally, Moro tilted his head back slightly and said, "Mr. Rapp, America is a very wealthy country. What you ask of me will take more resources than you have offered. If you wish to get the family of Americans back safely, I'm going to need more."

Rapp remained impassive, meeting the general's gaze with his own. Coleman and his men were obviously not in the position yet to carry out the mission or they would have called, so it was up to him. The entire time he'd been talking to Moro, he'd been refining a new plan. It would have to look like Moro had shot himself rather than face a court-martial for committing treason. The general carried the standard Special Forces 9mm Beretta pistol. Rapp would use his own suppressed 9mm Beretta to shoot him in the side of the head and then eject a round from the general's gun and place the weapon in his hand. Rapp would then ask Colonel Barboza to come into the tent. They would wait for a minute and then leave. Barboza would then instruct the general's aide-de-camp that the general was considering something very important and did not want to be disturbed under any circumstances.

They would then get on the helicopter and leave. Everyone would assume that the sound of the gun shot had been lost in the noise of the helicopter's departure. Then General Rizal would just have to make sure that only a cursory investigation of the body and the weapon took place. The general's body would be found sometime later along with the evidence of the bank accounts and phone records. It would be plain to even the most simpleminded officer that Moro had committed suicide rather than be publicly tried for crimes of high treason. The generals back in Manila would make sure the military investigators didn't delve too deeply into the forensics surrounding Moro's death. Most people would understand that the proud and arrogant general would rather commit suicide than face a humiliating court-martial.

Rapp finally answered the general. "I am prepared to go to two hundred thousand dollars to gain the safe return of the Andersons, but not a penny more."

Moro frowned. "That is still a little light. I'm afraid this is a game you are not well versed in, Mr. Rapp."

"Is that right?" Rapp asked in a doubtful tone. "General, I don't know if you've noticed, but I'm the one holding all the cards. My offer is final. Two hundred grand to get the Andersons back and another hundred grand when you have effectively decimated Abu Sayyaf."

"I'm not so sure," said Moro with a shake of his head.

"Well, I am," added Rapp quickly. "Push me any further, General, and you will be arrested right now and returned to Manila to face a court-martial. Colonel Barboza will replace you, and with the help of the U.S. Special Forces, he will free the Andersons and rid this island of any and every terrorist connected to Abu Sayyaf."

The general scoffed at his adversary's remark. "Colonel Barboza is an incompetent fool. If you want the Andersons back alive I am the man to do it. Give me three hundred thousand dollars and I will make it happen within forty-eight hours."

Rapp was straining to keep his temper in check. The sheer arrogance of Moro was getting under his skin. He flexed his hands and then clenched them into tight fists, reminding himself that none of this mattered. It was all a ruse to get Moro to relax. A look of calm washed over his face and he said, "All right, General, I'll agree to your terms."

"Good," said a jubilant Moro. "Now here is what we will do."

Rapp smiled and nodded as Moro enthusiastically

talked about how he would deal with Abu Sayyaf. He was saying something about arranging for the release of the American family. Rapp continued to look interested while his left hand slowly moved toward his gun. His fingers were just parting the folds of his vest when it happened. His hand froze with indecision, and Moro, noticing the change in his demeanor, stopped talking.

TWENTY-SEVEN

Coleman reached the summit of the small mountain huffing and puffing from the breakneck pace he'd kept for nearly twenty minutes. With sweat covering every inch of his body he took a knee and did a quick one-eighty of the relatively minute area before him. The summit was not big. A large, dark gray, almost black, rock occupied almost one entire side of the crest. It was covered with a few stubborn trees and bushes, their roots running down into the rock's deep fissures. Directly in front of Coleman lay a gently sloping shelf covered in grass and shielded from the sun by several twisted trees. On first glance he missed Wicker.

Positioned between the base of a tree and a clump of bushes, the soles of Wicker's jungle boots were all that was visible. Coleman dropped to his belly and crawled through the knee-high grass. When he reached Wicker he noticed that the more agile man had already unpacked and assembled his .50-caliber Barrett M82A1 rifle and was surveying the lay of the land through a pair of M19/22 binoculars.

Out of breath but not the least bit embarrassed by it, Coleman asked, "What's the sit rep?"

Wicker remained motionless as he peered through the powerful binoculars. "I did a quick check of the perimeter, and it looks like we're alone."

"Any sign of Mitch?"

"No, but we've got a Huey down there with a pair of hot engines, and a very nervous colonel standing outside of General Moro's tent."

Coleman frowned. "How in the hell do you know it's Moro's tent?"

"Because someone was dumb enough to hang a sign with his name and rank on it."

"You're shittin' me."

"Nope. Have a look for yourself." Wicker handed Coleman the binoculars and nestled in behind his high-powered rifle scope.

The former SEAL commander did a quick check of the camp and announced, "Well, if that isn't one of the stupidest things I've ever seen."

Wicker silently concurred while he used his scope to check out several likely spots where an enemy sniper might be lying in wait. He was a cautious man by nature, but he was also extremely confident in his skills.

This Philippine Special Forces group didn't appear to be a crack outfit. From the sign hanging on the general's tent, to the lack of perimeter security, it looked like a truly sloppy operation. The odds that they'd deployed a counter-sniper team seemed unlikely. Even more in his favor, though, was the distance of the shot that he was to take. There were only a handful of men in the world who could execute a head shot at this distance. If there was a counter-sniper team about they would be focusing on a perimeter of 500 meters, give or take 100 meters. Wicker was well outside that range. Even so, he was breaking many of his own rules.

They'd arrived while the sun was up, and he'd slithered into position without donning his ghillie sniper suit. Covered with netting and burlap strips in various shades of green the sniper suit allowed him to disappear into the terrain. If given proper time, he would have added the natural vegetation of his surroundings to the suit, ultimately making him invisible to even the most well-trained pair of eyes.

"What do you think?" asked Coleman.

"I think these guys aren't real worried about being attacked."

Next came the important question. "Can you make the shot?"

Wicker brought the crosshairs of his scope back to the general's tent and centered them on the colonel's head. Moving his eye away from the glass aperture, he looked to the east at the rising sun. The horizon was ablaze with a brilliant bank of storm clouds. For now the weather was acceptable. There was no wind yet, but that would undoubtedly change as the front approached.

Wicker eased his left eye back behind the scope and said, "Tell him I can handle it."

Coleman, who was still breathing heavily, marveled at the sniper's calm demeanor. After retrieving the satellite phone from one of his thigh pockets, he punched in a number and waited.

TWENTY-EIGHT

The director general of Mossad leaned forward and stared intently at one of the large screens. It showed a section of one of the nastiest neighborhoods in all of Israel. The analyst to Freidman's right spoke in hushed tones.

"Look at the roadblocks." With a laser pointer, the man marked the three avenues of access to the hillside neighborhood. "And look at the four men on this rooftop right here." He circled the roof of the building in red light.

"Lookouts?" questioned Freidman.

"That and probably more." The man said something into his headset and the rooftop was magnified. "I'm ninety percent sure two of those men are carrying RPGs."

Freidman looked at the grainy black, green and white image. It was being shot from the underbelly of a customized DHC-7 four-engine turboprop. Part of an aid package from the United States, the plane was outfitted with the Highly Integrated Surveillance and Reconnaissance System, or HISAR. The plane was designed to provide both image and signal intelligence in real time.

The men on the rooftop with rocket-propelled

grenades were not unexpected. Since the Black Hawk Down incident in Somalia back in 1993 every terrorist in the Middle East had realized how easy it was to shoot down a hovering helicopter. For this, and several other reasons, Freidman had ruled out sending in a team of commandos. There were other, less risky ways to handle the job.

Freidman shifted his glance to one of the other large screens. It gave a broader picture of Hebron. In the center of it a laser dot marked the roof of a sedan that was speeding through the streets. With each passing moment the tiny car worked its way closer to the hillside neighborhood that they'd already identified. It looked like things were going to work.

Suddenly, the sedan stopped at a roadblock that had gone unnoticed. The man on Freidman's right spoke into his headset and almost immediately the airborne low-light camera zoomed in on the roadblock. The room watched tensely as several people got out of the car. One of them walked to the rear of the sedan and placed two objects on the trunk. Others gathered around.

"Give me full magnification on the trunk of that car," barked Freidman.

Several tense seconds passed and then they were treated to a welcome sight. It looked like the two attaché cases were still in play. Freidman watched as they were closed. He muttered something unintelligible to himself and blinked several times.

The entire room watched in silence as the man with the cases was led through the roadblock and into a waiting van. The camera zoomed out, following the van as it wound its way up the narrow streets. A digital clock on the wall above the TVs crept downward from five minutes. In two minutes and twenty-eight seconds the burst transmitter would send confirmation of the location of the attaché cases and then the waiting would be over.

All at once the four large screens fell into sync, and at the center of each was the house they had expected to see. Freidman watched as the van carrying his instrument of retribution stopped directly in front of the target. Needing no further confirmation, he turned to the general on his left and nodded.

HOVERING AT 500 FEET, on the outskirts of Hebron, lurked two of the most efficient killing machines ever built by man, or more precisely, the Boeing Corporation of America. The AH-64D Apache Longbow helicopter was an unrivaled lethal machine. Its fire control radar target acquisition system allowed it to classify and prioritize up to 125 targets in just seconds. Even more impressive was the system's ability to designate the sixteen most dangerous targets and engage them with the Longbow's fire-and-forget Hellfire laser-guided missiles or AIM-9 Sidewinder air-to-air missiles. The Apache Longbow is the most advanced attack helicopter in the world, and in some people's minds the most advanced flying machine in the world.

The two birds had been on station for thirty-six minutes, patiently awaiting their orders. They'd lifted off from their airfield in the Negev and proceeded north, avoiding all towns and roadways. The Longbows that had been on station since late afternoon had returned to base to refuel.

Floating on the other side of a small ridgeline, eight kilometers from Hebron, the two choppers were running dark, their navigation lights extinguished. Each helicopter was configured for a multirole mission. They carried eight Hellfire missiles, thirty-eight Hydra 70mm folding-fin aerial rockets and 1,200 rounds of 30mm ammunition for their belly-mounted chain guns.

The amount of firepower that the Apache could carry was not what set it apart from other helicopters. The chopper, in fact, had rivals that could carry almost twice the amount of firepower. What set the Apache Longbow apart was its accuracy, stability and maneuverability. It was an all-weather attack helicopter designed to engage multiple targets with a focus on armor.

The Apache had been designed as a tank killer, but its designers had been so successful that its mission had grown. At the start of the Gulf War in 1991 it was the Apache that fired the first shots. Led by a Pave Low helicopter, a flight of Apaches snuck into Iraq under the radar and using their Sidearm anti-radar missiles, they punched a big hole in Iraq's air defense network. Through that hole poured hundreds of coalition fighters and bombers. Within hours, virtually the entire Iraqi air defense network was shut down.

And that was more than a decade ago. Since then the Apache had been given a complete overhaul that included the Longbow fire control radar, an improved navigation system, air-to-air capability, fire-and-forget missiles and increased battlefield survivability due to improved engines, electrical systems and avionics.

Taking on buildings and lightly armed men was not what the platform had been designed for, but the men flying the machines were not about to argue with the bosses in Tel Aviv. If they wanted to use a hammer to kill a fly that was their decision. The pilots and copilot gunners waited for their orders and monitored their various instruments.

The pilots looked out at the surrounding area with their Night Vision Sensors and monitored their ships' vitals, while the copilot gunners looked through their Target Acquisition Designation Sights. The surveillance plane circling above the city at 15,000 feet was sending a constant stream of information to the onboard fire control computers of the Longbows. Multiple targets were painted with lasers. All that was left to do was arm the missiles and engage.

The order to move came over the encrypted digital communications link. Simultaneously the twin General Electric gas turbine engines on each bird increased power and the helicopters began to climb. They moved over the ridgeline, closing on the city of Hebron at a cautious fifty knots. With each passing second the fire control computers effortlessly calculated a new solution to each target. In less than a minute the town of Hebron would be ablaze.

TWENTY-NINE

His fingers had just touched the cool black steel of his Beretta when he felt his satellite phone vibrate. Rapp froze for only a second but Moro noticed.

In an attempt to conceal his tension, Rapp smiled, and said, "I'll never get used to these damn vibrating phones." He withdrew his hand from the Beretta and grabbed the phone from his belt. "Excuse me, General, I've been waiting for this call."

Moro flashed a forced smile and nodded. He was now watching Rapp's movements with greater interest.

"Hello," Rapp answered. He listened for a moment and then replied, "Yes. It's a deal. He's offered to join forces with us." Rapp listened for another few seconds. "It's going to cost us slightly more than we talked about, but the general convinced me he could make it happen." Rapp smiled and nodded to the general. "Yep . . . O.K. . . . the ball's in your court. I can fill you in on the rest of the details when I get back." Rapp listened again briefly and then said, "Yep, it's a go . . . all right, good-bye." He pressed the end button and put the phone away saying, "They are very pleased, General. They're not crazy about you upping the price, but if you follow through on your promises no one's gonna complain."

"Good." Moro seemed to relax a bit.

"Now," Rapp said, getting up, "if you'll excuse me, I have to get back to Manila and take care of some more business. If you need any assistance in carrying out your missions, don't hesitate to ask."

Moro got up and extended his hand across the small desk. "Do not worry, Mr. Rapp, my men are some of the best in the world." He flashed Rapp a confident smile and pumped his hand.

Rapp forced himself to return the smile and ignore the fact that Moro was squeezing his hand a bit too firmly. He went to retract his hand, but Moro did not let go.

"Tell me, Mr. Rapp," hissed Moro in a conspiratorial tone, "is General Rizal on your payroll?"

Rapp tried once again to retrieve his hand, but Moro tightened his grip. Having absolutely no tolerance for such childish games, Rapp clamped down on Moro's hand with viselike pressure. Pulling the general toward him, he warned, "General, don't fuck with me."

With a gleam in his eye and a slick smile, Moro replied, "I am the one who you should not fuck with. I am sickened by your country and your arrogance, and let's be very clear about something, you will never own me. I will meet the agreement we made here today and that is as far as it goes. Tell that to your bosses back in Washington, and tell them if they don't like it the Andersons will never see their home again. Now get out of my camp before I decide to have you shot." Moro released Rapp's hand with a shove.

It took every ounce of restraint Rapp had not to level Moro with a left cross to the jaw. This man had psychological issues that ran much deeper than anything he had been briefed on. The only thing that prevented him from pounding his psychotic ass into the ground was the fact that the best damn sniper in the world was sitting on a mountaintop a mile away ready to bring this little drama to a much more final and beneficial conclusion.

With that thought in mind Rapp simply turned and left the tent. Just outside he found Colonel Barboza and the general's aide-de-camp conversing. Rapp jerked his head toward the chopper and kept walking. After several strides he pulled out his satellite phone and hit the speed dial number for Coleman. After a few seconds the connection was made.

"Did you see the tent I just came out of?"

After a brief delay, Coleman's reply came back. "Affirmative."

Looking ahead to the helicopter, Rapp twirled his finger in the air, signaling the pilots to start the engines. "That's where he is." Rapp was almost halfway to the chopper when he heard some shouting behind him. He turned to see Moro standing in front of his tent wearing his holster. For a moment he thought the general was yelling at him and then he realized his angry comments were directed at Colonel Barboza.

The colonel, who had already started for the chopper, was now stopped about midway between Rapp and the general. Rapp couldn't hear the specifics of what was being said, but it appeared that the higher ranking of the two officers wanted the junior officer to ask permission to leave the camp.

Rapp, fed up with Moro's behavior, studied the situation pensively, and then made a quick decision. Clutching the satellite phone, he asked Coleman one simple question.

COLEMAN RELAYED RAPP'S QUESTION to Wicker and waited. Wicker lay in the prone position, completely motionless. His left eye peered through the coated glass of his Unertl scope. He'd already lasered the range to the target and made the adjustments for windage and elevation. He was in a near trancelike state and his heart had already slowed to a meager thirty-two beats a minute. Wicker pulled the trigger back one notch and said, "Say the word."

Coleman took a quick look through his binoculars to make sure someone wasn't about to enter the line of fire. Satisfied that no one other than the target was at risk he said, "Take the shot."

Wicker inhaled a slow steady breath and then stopped all movement. Gently, evenly, his left index finger increased its pressure on the metal trigger. There was the gentlest of clicks and then a thunderous report as the massive fifty-seven-inch rifle let loose its Raufoss grade A round. The crack of the .50-caliber round shattered the calm of dawn and sent every bird in the valley screeching into the air.

ONE SECOND THE GENERAL was standing there, yelling at his subordinate, and then in the blink of an eye, he was yanked, as if by some unseen force, off his feet. There was a full second or two of confused inaction as brains tried to process the strange thing their eyes had just witnessed. Only Rapp knew what had happened. He was already moving, not toward the chopper, but in the opposite direction. The force with which the general's body was propelled to the ground suggested that Wicker's shot had done the job, but Rapp wanted to make sure, and he also wanted to have a word with Colonel Barboza before things got really ugly. The original plan was to be in the air when the shot was taken, but Rapp had seen an opportunity and taken it.

He reached Barboza just as the general's aide-de-camp began to realize what had happened. The lieutenant, after all, had the best view of the general's body. Rapp had his eyes on him as he reached Barboza's side. He could tell by the look of absolute shock on the young Filipino's face that it was likely his commanding officer had suffered a mortal wound.

Rapp grabbed Barboza by the arm, pulling him toward the fallen general. In a low voice he urged, "You have to take charge. There are enemy snipers in the hills. Get these men moving and then start chewing some ass." Rapp propelled him forward and the two men broke into a run.

Barboza's mind was moving fast, already wondering if this mysterious American knew more than he was letting on. Those questions would have to wait until later, for indeed it did appear that there was a sniper about. And nothing made a professional soldier's skin crawl more than the specter of an enemy sniper lurking nearby. Barboza had seen enough live combat to know a moving target was harder to hit than a stationary one, so he set a course for the shocked soldier in his path. Gathering speed he literally tackled the general's aide-de-camp and sent him sprawling across the dew-laden grass. "Take cover, you fool. There is a sniper shooting at us."

Rapp ran past the fallen body of Moro, taking a quick look to make sure the job was done. The evidence was stark; the entire back half of the general's head was missing. As Rapp continued along the side of the general's tent he felt nothing but satisfaction. Moro was a traitor to his country, his uniform and to the best ally his country had ever known. He had spilled American blood to suit his own selfish desires, and now he was lying in an expanding pool of his own. He alone had chosen his treacherous path.

THIRTY

David turned sideways on the plush leather seat. He had put a lot of thought into this moment while he'd been driven all over the West Bank. From this position he could better access the knife concealed in the heel of his right shoe.

"Where is Hassan?" asked an agitated Atwa.

David frowned and said, "I want you to know that I am not happy about this. It was he who provoked me. I simply responded in kind, and he being the pea-brained thug that he is decided to charge me."

"I said, where is he?" snapped Atwa.

David's fingers felt for the watch on his left wrist. "The last I saw of him, he was lying on the ground unconscious, but not seriously hurt."

"How?"

"I did it." David began pressing buttons on the watch. When he pressed the last button he closed his eyes and bowed his head as if he were ashamed of what he'd done.

The explosion rocked the car, catching Atwa completely off guard. As debris pelted the bulletproof Plexiglas, David dug a thumbnail into the heel of his shoe and pried open the secret compartment. Deftly, he snatched a small, sturdy switchblade. Before Atwa knew what was happening, David was on top of him. His left forearm pinned Atwa's head against the side of the car and the razor-sharp, three-inch blade slashed the older man's jugular vein deep and clean. Warm blood spurted from the wound and sprayed David in the face. As Atwa brought his hands up to cover the wound on the right side of his neck, David reached around the other side and slashed Atwa's left jugular vein. A fresh spray of blood erupted, splattering the window.

THE DIRECTOR GENERAL of Mossad sprang to his feet. Leaning over the desk in front of him he stared at one of the big screens with a maniacal intensity. He squinted his eyes in an attempt to decipher who the two men were who had just left the house. He swore one of them was Jabril Khatabi and there was something familiar about the other man. Before he could make up his mind they were gone, disappearing into the backseat of a parked car. Still on his feet and frowning, Freidman turned to the general on his left and barked, "Target that car!"

Freidman returned his attention to the screen and the parked car, wondering if it were going to pull away from the house. Suddenly, without warning, there was a bright flash and the entire street side of the house appeared to blow outward.

The confused frown vanished as Freidman realized what had just happened. The room quickly erupted in frenzied conversation as tapes were rewound and new commands were barked.

Freidman turned to the general and in earnest said, "Give the Apaches the green light."

"What about the car?"

Freidman looked back at the screens. All he could see was a cloud of dust and flames. He was fairly certain Jabril Khatabi was one of the men who had gotten into the car, and he had a good inkling who the second man might be. If it was who he thought, he doubted he would get another chance like this. With no reluctance, he said, "Destroy the car."

The analyst on Freidman's other side stood up and said, "What about our asset, sir? I'm almost positive he's in that car."

Freidman ignored the analyst and looking to the general said, "My order stands." Ben Freidman would lose little sleep over the death of Jabril Khatabi.

DAVID STEPPED FROM THE BACK of the Mercedes into a cloud of dust. His eyes fluttered, but closed immediately, stinging from the cement dust and cordite. When he tried to take a breath the result was much the same. Gasping through tight lips and clenched teeth, he brought his T-shirt up over his nose and mouth and tried again. After taking several breaths he reached back in, grabbed Mohammed Atwa's body and pulled him into the street. David could see almost nothing and stumbled over several chunks of stone as he dragged the body with him. To his left, through squinted eyes and the haze he could see several pockets of fire where a house once stood. He stepped on something that gave a little and on closer inspection he discovered it was one of the men who had been standing guard at the door.

David dropped Atwa next to the guard and then moved away to the other side of the street and down several doors. According to his agreement with Freidman he would wait around until the Israeli Defense Forces showed up and allow himself to be arrested. He was wondering how long it would take for them to fight their way through the roadblocks, when he heard a horrible shrieking noise. Instinctively, he dove to the ground, knowing what was about to follow.

THIRTY-ONE

The Philippine army helicopter approached the Amphibious Readiness Group from the west. In the middle of the formation sat the intimidating USS *Belleau Wood*. Rapp couldn't wait for his transport to land. The morning had gone from bad, to better, to good, to too good to be true, and then just when things looked like they would all fall into place he was thrown a curve ball. A little more than an hour after General Moro had been nearly decapitated, Coleman called to report an interesting piece of information. Initially, he regarded the news of the Anderson family as a gift, but then Rapp began to see a problem.

The Filipino Special Forces had been whipped into an uncontrollable frenzy by the death of their commanding officer, just as Rapp had hoped they'd be. The 200-plus-man force began loading up for war. Two counter-sniper teams had been sent out to see what they could find, while Colonel Barboza took charge and prepared to send out additional patrols to find the enemy. The men wanted blood, and as soon as they got a whiff of their opponent they were going to engage them with everything they had.

Rapp had watched all this unfold with a feigned grave concern. Inside he was very pleased. Everything seemed to be going according to plan. The Special Forces group would go after Abu Sayyaf with a rabid vengeance, and back in Manila, General Rizal would strongly advise that the U.S. military be allowed to join in the hunt. With this new cooperation they would locate the Andersons, rescue them and once and for all deal with Abu Sayyaf.

Coleman changed all that when he called to inform Rapp of the vision he'd witnessed in the wet predawn jungle of Dinagat Island. In addition, Coleman reported that the Abu Sayyaf camp was only four miles from the Filipino Special Forces camp. The original plan had been for Coleman and his team to take the shot and then move to the beach and swim out for an extraction. That was now off. Coleman did not want to lose contact with the Andersons and Rapp agreed.

So now they were left with an enraged group of Filipino Special Forces soldiers who wanted revenge. Sitting between them and their retaliation just happened to be four U.S. covert operatives. In addition, the Filipino soldiers were so agitated that Rapp doubted they would perform a well-thought-out, deft hostage rescue once they found the Abu Sayyaf camp.

If the two forces met, it could quickly disintegrate into a massacre with the odds of the Andersons making it out alive not good. Fate had moved all the players into a very tight area and moved up the timetable, as well, and if Rapp couldn't rein in the Filipino soldiers, his trip to the opposite side of the globe could quickly become a disaster.

Having just a few avenues open to him, and not able to talk freely at the Special Forces camp, Rapp made a single call. It was to his boss. Washington was fourteen hours behind, so while Rapp was already starting his day in the Philippines, Irene Kennedy was ending hers at Langley. Rapp made two requests. The first was that she get General Flood to lean on General Rizal in Manila to keep his troops in camp until they could come up with a strategy. The second request now loomed large beneath him.

The USS *Belleau Wood* churned through the Philippine Sea at twelve knots, its massive twin screws leaving a white frothy wake as far as the eye could see. Her escort and support ships were arrayed around her in a diamond formation that stretched for miles. To the east storm clouds loomed. Rapp cursed the weather at first, but then wondered if it could be used to their advantage.

The Philippine army helicopter landed on the massive nonskid deck of the USS *Belleau Wood* well forward of the looming superstructure. Mitch Rapp was out the door like a shot, heading straight for the only piece of ship that wasn't belowdecks. He'd been on U.S. naval warships before and knew for the most part where to go. When he neared the towering superstructure a navy lieutenant approached him and extended his hand.

"Mr. Rapp," yelled the officer, "I'm Lieutenant Jackson. Damn pleased to meet you."

Rapp allowed the officer to pump his hand with enthusiasm. Without having to look for the shiny trident on the officer's khaki uniform, Rapp immediately knew by the man's longish hair, physical build and goatee that he was a SEAL. "You're just the man I wanted to see, Lieutenant."

Jackson grinned. He, like most of his colleagues, knew all about Mitch Rapp. His appearance on the *Belleau Wood* was a good sign. "My orders are to bring you straight to the captain's quarters."

Jackson disappeared through the hatch and Rapp followed him. They walked down the metal stairs for several decks and then down a narrow passageway. They stopped in front of a gray door with the name CAPTAIN FORESTER stenciled in black.

Jackson rapped on the door twice with his knuckles and waited for permission to enter. It came almost instantly. Jackson crossed the threshold first and came to attention. He held a salute and said, "Captain, as you requested: Mr. Rapp."

Captain Sherwin Forester set down a book he was reading and stood. At six foot four, Forester looked cramped aboard the space-conscious ship. The ceiling of his quarters was only a few inches from the top of his head.

"Thank you, Lieutenant. As you were." Forester strode across the blue carpet, raising a bushy eyebrow as he sized up his visitor. With a grin he said, "Well, Mr. Rapp, today marks a first for me. In my twenty-one years of service I have never received a direct call from the chairman of the Joint Chiefs, and most definitely not while I've been at sea."

Rapp smiled. There was something instantly likable about Forester. "Is that a good thing or a bad thing, sir?"

Forester chewed on the question for a second. "I don't like waiting around sitting on my hands. Especially after what happened the other night. So I'm going to guess someone with a reputation like yours showing up on my ship like this just might be a good thing."

Rapp nodded. It appeared Forester was a warrior and not some bureaucrat masquerading as an officer. "I think you're going to like what I have to tell you."

"Good. Let's sit down." The captain led the way over to a couch and four chairs. The suite wasn't big by normal standards, but as far as ships went it was huge. Forester and Jackson took the couch while Rapp sat across from them in an armchair.

"So, Mr. Rapp"—Forester crossed his long legs— "what are you doing so far away from home?"

Rapp had already thought about much of what lay ahead. It was going to be a busy day and he needed these two men fully committed to what he would eventually propose. Having worked in an environment that was obsessed with secrets had not always gone over well with Rapp. He could appreciate the need for it, but there were times when the entire cause would be better served if the people in the field knew what was going on.

In Rapp's mind this was one of those cases, plus these two naval officers were not a security risk. They all wanted the same thing; in fact, Forester and Jackson probably wanted it even more. They'd been out here on patrol for more than a month with the Anderson family fresh on their minds, and it had been their brethren who'd been gunned down on the beach not too many nights ago. They could be trusted.

"What I'm about to tell you can't leave this room. In fact, if you breathe a word of it to anyone, it could end your career." Rapp clasped his hands in front of him and looked at both men to make sure they got his message. "Have I made myself clear enough?"

They nodded. "Good." Looking at Forester, Rapp said, "The SEALs you put ashore the other night that were ambushed . . . their mission was compromised by a leak that we traced all the way back to Washington."

After a long pause Forester asked, "Where?"

"The State Department. Some of this you're going to hear in the press. Assistant Secretary of State Amanda Petry sat in on the National Security Council briefings on the operation. She was told point-blank that she was not to share any information regarding the hostage rescue of the Anderson family with our embassy in Manila. Once the Andersons and all of our assets were safely out, we'd let the Filipino government know. If they got upset"— Rapp shrugged his shoulders—"our attitude was tough shit. The family's been held hostage for six damn months, and they haven't done shit to free them. In fact, we've discovered that they've actually hindered our efforts."

Hindered was a kind choice of words. "After our boys were ambushed Director Kennedy launched an investigation. It appears that for some time she's had people at Langley monitoring the situation out here. What she discovered you're not going to like. Prior to the rescue operation Amanda Petry e-mailed Ambassador Cox in Manila the general plans of the mission. Ambassador Cox in turn relayed this information to someone in the Philippine government."

"Who?" asked Jackson.

After hesitating Rapp replied, "That I can't say."

"Can't or won't?" asked the ship's captain.

"Won't," conceded Rapp, "but that doesn't matter. It's the next part that you're going to be most interested in. Have either of you met General Moro?"

Forester shook his head while Jackson said, "Several times."

"What'd you think of him?"

Jackson seemed to consider the question carefully and then said, "I think he had a real hard-on for me and my boys. A big chip on his shoulder."

"Yeah," Rapp agreed. "Like maybe he didn't like Americans running around on his little island?"

"That and the fact that he was always trying to prove that his boys were better than us."

Rapp sensed some potentially important information here. "Were they?"

Jackson laughed. "No way."

Rapp hoped the answer was based on more than bravado and unit pride. "Be more specific. How'd they shoot? How were they in the jungle? What was their discipline like?"

"They were extremely disciplined. Moro was a real sadist in that regard. They were in great shape. They could handle the long marches, with the big packs and not a one of them would piss and moan. I was a little disappointed in their shooting, but they don't fire anywhere near the amount of rounds as we do on the Teams."

This was important information. "How were they in the jungle? Were they good trackers?"

"It's funny you ask that," said Jackson, frowning. "They were great trackers. They'd pick up shit in the jungle before every single guy in my platoon with the exception of maybe one."

"Why's that funny?"

"Well, if they were such good trackers, why was it that they could never pick up the Andersons' trail? A couple times we strolled into camps that had been hastily vacated, and I'd urge Moro's men to press on, but there was always some excuse why we had to stay put. They'd sit on the radio for an hour waiting for orders while scouts fanned out looking for a trail."

"Did you ever try to pursue on your own?"

Jackson shot a sideways look at Forester. "Hell, yeah. Moro threw a real shit fit. He actually climbed into a chopper and came out to where we were. He reamed me in front of my men and his. Then he got ahold of my CO back in Guam and reamed him out too. I ended up with a letter of instruction in my file, and now they won't let me off the ship."

Rapp smiled. "Well, Lieutenant, I think I might be able to get that letter removed from your file."

"Huh?" asked a confused Jackson.

"Just remind me when this is all over, and I'll make sure the letter of instruction is purged. . . . In fact, I'll make sure it's replaced with a commendation." Rapp could tell Jackson wasn't following. "Your instincts were right, Lieutenant. General Moro was a traitor."

"Traitor?"

"That's right."

"I noticed," started Captain Forester, "that you used the past tense in regard to the general's status. Is that by accident or intentional?"

This is where things got tricky. The problem was not in acknowledging Moro's death. It would be public soon enough. The difficulty lay in who killed him and how they knew he was a traitor. Rapp decided to tell only part of the truth. "General Moro has been accepting bribes from Abu Sayyaf." Rapp left out the information about China. "As you pointed out, Lieutenant, he has no love for Americans."

"So Abu Sayyaf was paying him not to pursue them?"

"That's correct."

"Why that little—"

Forester interrupted the junior officer's cuss. "Did General Moro have anything to do with the ambush that was sprung on our men the other night?"

"I'm afraid so."

Forester remained calm despite the anger that boiled beneath the surface. "So back to my other question. Is General Moro still with us?"

"No," answered Rapp without the slightest hint of remorse.

Jackson, knowing Rapp's reputation and that he'd been at the Special Forces camp this very morning, asked in a hopeful tone, "Did you kill him?"

Forester cleared his throat loudly and eyeing Rapp said, "Lieutenant, I don't think we want to ask that question."

Rapp appreciated the captain's discretion. "That's all right. No, I didn't kill him. General Moro was shot by a sniper."

"A sniper," repeated Jackson.

"That's right. The camp's perimeter security was nonexistent. Abu Sayyaf got someone in close enough and they shot the general early this morning." Rapp paused to see how this was going over and added, "That's the official story. Now would you like to hear what really happened?"

Both men nodded, Jackson more enthusiastically than Forester.

"The information I'm about to share with you is highly classified. I can't stress this enough." Satisfied that they knew the stakes he said, "In the predawn hours this morning a U.S. Special Forces sniper team was inserted onto the island. They moved into position and sometime after sunup they took the shot."

Both officers took the news in silence.

"That's not all, however. While moving into position the team sighted the Anderson family and their captors. The four-man team split into two elements: one to follow the Andersons and the other to take out the general."

"We know where the Andersons are?" asked a cautious Jackson.

"Yep."

Forester uncrossed his legs and leaned forward. "We know precisely where they are?"

"Precisely," replied Rapp, "and we're going to go get them."

THIRTY-TWO

Light flurries floated down from the chill March evening sky as black stretch limousines cued up along Pennsylvania Avenue waiting to disgorge their important passengers under the north portico of the White House. The event was black tie; a state dinner for the Canadian prime minister. Irene Kennedy asked her driver to bring her around to the southwest gate. She didn't have time to wait in line. A private word with the president was needed before the festivities started.

Trust was not something that came easily to the young director of the Central Intelligence Agency. She worked in a profession where things were not always as they first appeared, where people and countries were constantly attempting to deceive her, and even when she did trust someone there were motives to consider. Mitch Rapp was one exception to her rule. He was one of the few people who Kennedy could rely on.

God knows they had a different way of going about things, but Rapp was effective and his motives clear. He had nothing but disdain for the people who ran Washington. As the failed rescue mission in the Philippines had proved, the nation's capital had a habit of getting too many people, and too many agencies, involved in matters that could often be handled by a very small group. It didn't take a master of espionage to realize that the more players involved in an operation, the greater the chance for a leak.

This in essence was why the director of the CIA needed to speak with the president and General Flood this evening. Rapp had called to give her the good news about the Andersons, but then had made a somewhat un-orthodox request. At first Kennedy didn't like it, but now, having had some time to think it through, she felt it held some real merit. It was classic Rapp and one couldn't really argue with his track record.

After a brief check by the Secret Service, the director's limousine was allowed admittance through the southwest gate. It pulled up West Executive Drive and stopped. Kennedy stepped from the back of the car clutching her black velvet wrap tightly around her shoulders with one hand and holding up the hem of her full-length evening gown with the other. A uniformed Secret Service officer opened the door for her and she hurried into the wel-come warmth of the West Wing.

Kennedy walked through the ground floor past the White House Mess and the Situation Room and then up a flight of stairs and past the Cabinet Room. Outside once again, she walked quickly down the Colonnade. This was the way the president walked to and from work every day. She entered the White House and waiting for her in the tropical Palm Room was Special Agent Jack Warch, the man in charge of President Hayes's Secret Service detail.

"You look very nice this evening, Irene," the always gallant agent said.

"Thank you, Jack, and so do you."

Warch, like all the agents working the detail this

evening, was dressed in formal attire. He offered his arm. "The president and General Flood are upstairs waiting for you."

Kennedy liked Warch. He was a hardworking professional who adored his family. "How are Sheila and the kids?" asked Kennedy.

"They're doing well. And Tommy?" Warch was referring to Kennedy's seven-year-old son.

"Growing like a weed . . . starting to get a little lippy." She shrugged. "You know . . . all the stuff that goes along with being seven." Kennedy thought of adding that it might be nice to have a father around, but she didn't. It was not her style to act like a victim.

They entered the elevator that would take them up to the second floor of the residence. Warch placed his back to the wall and clasped his hands in front. "How's my favorite counterterrorism agent?"

Kennedy looked at him sideways wondering if the comment was merely conversational or if Warch knew what Rapp was up to. He knew Rapp fairly well and in truth Warch could be trusted, but he was not in a *need to know* position. "He's fine."

Warch looked uncomfortable for a moment and then said, "His wife cornered me just a few minutes ago. She wanted to know where Mitch is."

"And?" asked Kennedy.

The elevator stopped and the door opened. "I told her I have no idea."

Kennedy stepped into the hall first. *"Do* you have any idea?"

Warch frowned. "No."

"Good," said Kennedy with a curt nod.

They both walked across the wide hallway that was more like a living room and stopped outside the door to the president's study. "Irene," the agent said in a concerned voice, "I think someone needs to have a talk with Anna."

"How so?"

"I just think you should talk to her."

"And tell her about what covert operations the CIA is running?" asked Kennedy in a sarcastic tone.

"No." Warch's face twisted in disagreement. "Of course not. But someone needs to tell her to stop asking all these questions."

"She's a reporter. That's what she does for a living."

"I know, but it's her husband, for Christ's sake, so it's only going to get worse. I think a little reassurance from you would go a long way."

Kennedy thought about what she might say. "She's here tonight?"

"Yep."

On second thought, with Mitch out of town this might be the perfect opportunity for her to set a few things straight with his wife. There had been a noticeable chill between the two of them and since both would be involved in Rapp's life for some time, maybe now was a good time for them to talk. "All right, I'll try to have a talk with her later."

Warch knocked on the door to the study, waited for a second, and then turned the old brass knob and opened the door. The chairman of the Joint Chiefs and the commander in chief were sitting by the fireplace playing a game of cards. General Flood had a glass half-filled with a brown liquid that Kennedy guessed to be Knob Creek bourbon. As for what the president had in his glass she had no idea. He was a social drinker with no particular favorite. She'd seen him drink wine, both red and white, beer, vodka, scotch and bourbon, but she'd never seen him exhibit a single sign of inebriation other than a tendency to get a little more vociferous than normal.

Both gentlemen stood and complimented the director of the CIA on how nice she looked. Kennedy reciprocated and took a seat on the couch while the president poured her a vodka on the rocks. Kennedy had learned that it was better to accept the drink and nurse it rather than decline and have to reaffirm that she didn't want a drink five more times.

The president settled back into his chair and picked up his hand. Looking over the top of the cards he asked, "Whose turn is it?"

"It's yours," replied the general.

Hayes started to pluck a card and then decided to put it back. "So, Irene, what's on your mind?"

"We have a situation, sir, that I think you need to be aware of." Kennedy looked briefly at General Flood to see if he'd told the president of their earlier conversation. He gave her no sign that he had.

Kennedy looked back to the president, who had finally decided on a card to get rid of. "Several hours before dawn in the Philippines we inserted a team into the jungle of Dinagat Island to take care of the situation with General Moro. While en route to their primary objective, the team stumbled across hostile forces that they identified as a column of Abu Sayyaf guerrillas."

Hayes set his cards down. He did not like the way this sounded. The last thing he needed right now were more U.S. forces killed in the Philippines. "Please tell me there wasn't another ambush?"

"No, sir, there wasn't. The team was not sighted by the opposing force. They allowed the column to pass, and then went on to complete their primary objective."

Hayes looked a little confused. "Then what's the problem?"

"Well"—Kennedy thought about it for a second—"I'd say it's more of an opportunity, sir, than a problem."

The president looked intrigued. "Let's hear it."

"The enemy column was transporting the Anderson family, all five of them."

"You're serious?" asked a suddenly eager president.

Kennedy found the question a little strange since she was not known for her sense of humor. "Yes, sir, the team split into two groups of two. One group went on to complete the primary mission while the other trailed the enemy column."

Now on the edge of his seat, Hayes asked, "Do we know where they are?"

Smiling slightly, she answered, "We have eyes-on intelligence, sir. We know exactly where they are. GPS coordinates and all."

Hayes stood abruptly. A day hadn't passed in the last six months where he hadn't thought of that poor family. "I want the National Security Council convened in the Situation Room in one hour." Hayes checked his watch. "I'll find an excuse to get over—" The president noticed Kennedy wincing slightly. "What's wrong?"

"I don't think we should go into crisis mode just yet."

Now the president was really confused. "Why not?"

"Mitch has requested that we keep this very low-key. He's onboard the *Belleau Wood* right now doing a tactical assessment while our team is on the ground giving him a constant stream of intel on the target."

"What exactly do you mean by low-key?" asked Hayes.

Kennedy hesitated and then asked, "Do you trust Mitch, sir?"

"Of course I do."

"Well, he thinks that the *Belleau Wood* battle group has

all the assets we need to pull off a successful hostage rescue, and in light of what happened the other night, he
thinks it best not to get the entire national security apparatus involved."

Hayes folded his arms across his chest and stared into
space for a moment. It was obvious he was torn between
his trust for Rapp and his natural instinct to manage the
situation. "What type of timetable are we looking at?"

"The Philippines are fourteen hours ahead of us, sir. It's
tomorrow morning there." Kennedy adjusted her glasses.
"The earliest we'd launch a rescue operation is after sun-
down, which gives us at least eleven hours to prepare.
Mitch is proposing that we give him the authority to put
a plan together on-site, and then report to us tomorrow
morning, our time, before we launch the rescue."

Hayes thought about this for a moment and then
turned to General Flood. "What do you think?"

The chairman of the Joint Chiefs looked at Kennedy.
"What are we up against?"

"Enemy strength is estimated at sixty armed men . . .
light machine guns mostly and a few RPGs."

As a soldier who'd been in battle, Flood was not a fan
of micromanaging situations from thousands of miles
away. He thought about the assets available and said, "The
Belleau Wood has more than enough muscle to handle the
job, sir. She has a task unit onboard, along with a platoon
of Force Reconnaissance marines, and there's also an entire battalion of marines onboard for backup if things get
hairy."

Hayes shifted his weight from one leg to the other.
"What's your recommendation?"

Flood checked his watch. "I'd say let Mitch put a plan
together. We can convene in the Situation Room in the
morning and get a briefing before we give it a green light.

Until then the best thing we can do is stay out of their way."

The president stood in front of the fireplace considering the advice he'd just been given. He shifted his gaze to Kennedy. "Irene, I assume you agree?"

Kennedy's predecessor had taught her many valuable lessons. One of the better ones was that men of power were best persuaded by their own words. "You've said it yourself before, sir. Mitch has a way of getting things done. I'd say the best person to handle this situation is right where we need him."

Hayes agreed with a curt nod. "All right. Let's plan on convening tomorrow morning. In the meantime I expect the two of you will monitor the situation closely."

Both Kennedy and Flood said they would.

"Good." Hayes nodded and then said, "All right, then, if you'll excuse me, I need to pick up my date."

THIRTY-THREE

Flood and Kennedy took the elevator down to the first floor. For reasons of decorum and tone, more than for national security, a little subtlety was now called for. It was only one flight, but the stairs opened out onto the wide Cross Hall, where visitors were gathered waiting for the band to play "Hail to the Chief" and watch the president, the first lady and the Canadian prime minister and his wife descend the long staircase. The crowd that was assembled in the Cross Hall consisted of foreign ambassadors, press, dignitaries, senators, congressmen, two Supreme Court justices and a bevy of celebrities and wealthy contributors.

The sight of the director of the CIA and the chairman of the Joint Chiefs descending the stairs together would lead to endless speculation that a crisis was brewing.

Kennedy and General Flood stepped from the elevator and were guided through the velvet ropes that cordoned off one end of the hallway. They'd gone no more than fifteen feet through the well-dressed crowd when the general was snatched from Kennedy's side by the majority leader of the Senate. Kennedy didn't slow for a second, lest the senator pull her into the group and begin pumping her for information. In her mind a state dinner was not the place to discuss national security. She continued into the East Room in search of a drink. Now that she was at the party itself, she felt an urge to take the edge off.

She'd almost made it to the bar when a hand gripped her arm. Kennedy turned to see a familiar and often unfriendly face.

"Hello, Director Kennedy."

Kennedy looked at the dazzling green eyes of the young reporter and smiled. "Anna, for the last time, please call me Irene."

"I'm just trying to be respectful," replied a less than sincere Anna Rapp. She instinctively disliked her husband's boss. When pressed on the point by Mitch she had to admit that much of it had to do with the fact that Kennedy knew him better than she did.

"Hmm." Kennedy frowned, not buying a word of it.

Cutting straight to the chase, Anna asked, "Would you please tell me where my husband is?"

Looking at the pretty young reporter and thinking of her conversation with Jack Warch, Kennedy decided that now might be just the right time for the two of them to have a good talk. "Anna, you look like you could use a drink." Grabbing her by the arm, Kennedy led her to the bar. "Two cosmopolitans, please." The bartender nodded and went to work.

"Irene, officially, I'm on duty. I don't think I should be drinking a cosmopolitan."

Kennedy glanced sideways at her. "Anna, I'm always on duty, and no offense, but my job's a little more important than yours. Besides"—she looked at Anna's strapless evening gown—"I don't think you're going to be standing outside in that little outfit giving any live updates."

Anna was slightly caught off guard by both the tone

and the message. This was the most she'd ever heard from the always polite, but tight-lipped Kennedy. "No, its not that, it's just that whenever I'm at the White House, officially I'm working."

Kennedy ignored her, grabbed the two martini glasses from the bartender and handed one to Anna. "Follow me."

Through the thickening crowd they went in search of a quiet place to talk. They garnered more than a few glances; both attractive women in their own right, Anna Rapp stunning and recognized by almost all, Irene Kennedy classy and reserved and also recognized by all, though for vastly different reasons.

As they continued through the East Room several people tried to stop Kennedy. Each time she smiled, apologized and kept moving. At the southern end of the opulent room they found a quiet spot and turned to face each other.

Kennedy held up her glass and in a conciliatory tone she said, "To your husband. One of the finest men I've ever known."

Anna wasn't sure how much she was supposed to read into the comment, but before she had time to really think about it Kennedy touched her glass and it was time to drink. The cold, fruit-tinged vodka went down smoothly. In a less confrontational voice the reporter asked, "So, tell me, where have you sent my husband off to this time?"

Kennedy took another sip while she thought of how best to handle this. Deciding on a bit of an unusual course, she asked, "Didn't he tell you?"

This threw Anna for a bit of a loop and then she caught the sarcasm. "No, he didn't tell me, and you know he didn't. So why don't you?"

Kennedy literally never lost her temper, but this pushy

reporter was begging to be put in her place. Where this lack of emotional control originated from she wasn't exactly sure, but she could hazard a guess. It lay somewhere in the belief that Mitch deserved better. In a chilly tone she asked, "Do you have any respect whatsoever for your husband?"

"Of course I respect him," snapped Anna.

"Then why do you put him at risk by walking around like a put-off high school homecoming queen?"

Anna bristled at the comment. "Don't condescend to me, Irene. This is my husband we're talking about."

"Exactly"—Kennedy moved in closer—"and if you really cared about him you'd stop asking people where he is. You'd remember that he's very good at what he does, and you'd honor him by keeping your mouth shut." Kennedy leaned in so her face was just inches from Anna's and in a low angry voice said, "His job is infinitely more important than both yours and mine. Do you have any idea how many lives he's saved over the years?"

Kennedy saw the defiance in Anna's eyes and said, "Sure, all your friends in the media like to call him an assassin, but have they ever stopped to count the lives he's saved?" Kennedy didn't pause long enough to give her a chance to answer. "Of course they haven't. He didn't just save your life that day upstairs, he saved dozens. Have you ever stopped to ask yourself that maybe right now he's doing exactly that? That he's saving lives?"

Kennedy eased back a bit and looked over her shoulder to see if anyone was trying to eavesdrop. Turning back to Anna, she added, "Right now there's a family of Americans whose lives depend on your husband. A mother and father and three little children. Think about that for a minute." Kennedy looked at Anna with commanding eyes. "Would you deny them the same gift of life that Mitch gave you?"

Anna was completely caught off guard. She knew that Kennedy was scheduled to attend the dinner. She had rehearsed this confrontation several times and it never played out this way. At no time was she ever supposed to be on the defensive. Kennedy was supposed to be back-pedaling. Kennedy was supposed to be listening. Anna was supposed to be in control.

Slowly, Anna began shaking her head. Her mind was flooded with memories of that night, not so long ago, when Mitch had saved her life. Her thoughts turned to the Anderson family that had gone missing in the Philippines. They had to be who Kennedy was talking about. She'd seen photos of them and their cute little redheaded children. Anna could not deny them their best hope. Standing up a bit straighter she struggled to find the right words. "Just knowing where he is and what he's doing, helps."

Kennedy nodded, satisfied that she had got the young reporter to think of more than herself.

"But I worry about him." Anna thought of her honeymoon and her husband's scarred body. Her eyes moistened. "I worry that one of these times he's not going to come home."

Kennedy honestly felt for the young bride. Clasping Anna's shoulder, she smiled and said, "I used to worry about him too, until I realized that it's the other guys who are in trouble."

Anna dabbed a tear from the corner of her eye and said sarcastically, "Great. That makes me feel much better."

Kennedy smiled. "Don't worry about him. I can tell you that he's nowhere near the action. He's helping plan the rescue, but will not be participating in it."

Distrustful but hopeful, Anna asked, "Really?"

"Yes," nodded Kennedy.

Anna let out a heavy sigh of relief. "Good. I just don't know if I could bear losing him."

Kennedy tried to see things through Anna's eyes. It had been so long since she'd been in love, and it was a very real possibility that she had never felt as deeply for her husband as Anna did for Mitch. Theirs was a passionate marriage born in the heat of battle. He had saved her life, and then she had given him the one thing he secretly yearned for: a real life.

There had been plenty of times when Kennedy had worried about Rapp when he was on operations. She loved him like a brother and stayed up late at night hoping he would return safely. Kennedy gave Anna an unusually warm smile and said, "I know how much he means to you, and if at any time I can help ease some of your worries, if I can answer some of your questions, then I will."

Anna was shocked by the generous and uncharacteristic offer. All she could do was smile and say thank you.

"All off the record, and never to be discussed with anyone else, of course," Kennedy said with a very serious expression.

"Of course." Anna took a drink of her cosmopolitan and studied her husband's boss. Maybe she'd misjudged Irene Kennedy.

THIRTY-FOUR

Coleman and Wicker had descended the mountain without incident and then very slowly and deliberately worked their way through the thick jungle with the goal of linking back up with Hackett and Stroble. Using the various paths that snaked their way through the plush vegetation was unwise, so even though they were going mostly downhill, it took a full two hours before they reached their comrades.

The last hundred or so feet was navigated on their bellies. Thanks to their secure Motorola radios and GPS devices, they were able to locate the well-concealed Hackett and Stroble without needing them to reveal their position. The two former SEALs had picked a spot atop a small ridgeline among the roots of a large mangrove tree. Their vantage of the Abu Sayyaf camp was ideal.

When Coleman reached the hide, he was surprised to find how lax the enemy's security was. A cooking fire puffed smoke into the air and the men lounged about with no apparent concern that they might be attacked. At first glance there appeared to be no perimeter patrol. Coleman took this as further evidence that General Moro had been under their payroll.

Looking through binoculars he counted four dilapidated lean-tos and two green tents that appeared to be of the U.S. army surplus type. Two men were busy tying down a blue tarp over one of the lean-tos as they prepared for the storm that was coming. The color of the tarp was further evidence that contrary to the intelligence reports they'd seen, these guerrillas were not a crack outfit. Coleman guessed the site was an abandoned village of some sort. Methodically, he scanned every foot looking for the Andersons. He checked each dwelling and saw no sign of the family. This meant they'd already been moved to a different camp, or they were inside one of the army tents. Coleman prayed it was the latter.

Knowing they had a long day ahead of them, Coleman ordered Hackett and Stroble to get some shut-eye while he sent Wicker to reconnoiter their left flank, and see if he could confirm the location of the Andersons.

As Wicker squirmed away, the former commander of SEAL Team 6 got Rapp on the secure net and began the process of meticulously relaying the location of each structure, the precise terrain of the camp and the exact strength of the enemy. Neither man communicated the obvious. Come nightfall they would be launching one of the most delicate and challenging of all military operations: a hostage rescue. Unlike almost every other military engagement, this one needed to be exercised with great restraint. It needed to be carried out with extreme skill and precision, or the hostages would get mowed down in the cross fire.

THE EXPANSIVE NONSKID DECK of the USS *Belleau Wood* pitched and rolled as the seas intensified with the oncoming storm. Standing on the aft section of the flat-top, Rapp picked up a suppressed MP-5 submachine gun that was lying on a tarp with several others. He held the weapon in his hands for a second getting a feel for the balance, and then pulled back the slide. After checking the chamber he released the cocking lever and listened for the click of a 9mm round being chambered.

In front of him were eight cardboard silhouette body targets. Rapp thumbed the selector switch from safety to single shot. He paid no attention to the men who were standing behind him. Moving with the confidence of someone who had done this many times before, he brought the weapon up into the firing position. His right foot moved slightly in front of his left, his entire body crouched a bit and he leaned forward. With the butt of the weapon nestled firmly to his left shoulder he looked down the black steel and through the hoop sight.

The ship rolled under his feet and with his knees flexed, Rapp found the rhythm. He squeezed the trigger once and a bullet spat from the end of the thick black silencer. Thirty feet away the projectile tore a hole in the center of the head of the paper target. Rapp squeezed off two more rounds that enlarged the hole created by the first bullet. Then flipping the selector switch from single shot to fully automatic he began moving down the line, spraying the targets with lead. Each paper silhouette varied in distance from thirty to fifty feet but it didn't seem to affect Rapp's marksmanship. By the time he reached the end all eight heads were shredded.

Pausing for only a second, Rapp did a speed load on a fresh thirty-round magazine and started back down the line, this time shooting with one hand and moving at a much quicker pace. When he reached the end he stopped and analyzed the fresh set of holes he'd added to the chest of each target. Satisfied with the weapon he turned to the chief and said, "This one will do just fine."

Lieutenant Jackson, who'd been watching with great interest, smiled and said, "Not bad."

Rapp grinned. "It was easy. They weren't moving."

As Rapp walked toward the superstructure Lieutenant Jackson fell in. "Do you want to tell me what you're up to?"

"What do you mean?"

"Somehow I get the feeling you're not going to sit this one out on the sidelines."

Rapp kept walking toward the superstructure. He'd been on autopilot all morning, diligently putting the op together. It was now after noon and things were gelling nicely. Coleman had confirmed that the Andersons were in one of the army tents, both SEAL platoons were ready, the insertion had been planned, the backup was in place and the extraction was ready. Now all they had to do was wait for nightfall.

The only thing that was left for Rapp was to be honest with himself. He was drawn toward the action like a surgeon to the operating room. He didn't have to go; Coleman and his men were some of the best in the world, as were Jackson and his SEALs. But as good as they were Rapp knew he was better, and Coleman would be the first to admit it.

Rapp knew if he didn't do everything in his power to save that family he'd never forgive himself. Anna would never understand that, but she didn't have to know. That, combined with being on the other side of the planet, made it easier to make the decision.

"Yeah," said Rapp, "I'm going." One concern had consistently come up in the operational planning meeting. The Abu Sayyaf group that was holding the Andersons was not the only guerrilla element on the island. The way they were armed made it highly unlikely that they were the force that had ambushed the SEAL team several nights earlier. With that in mind Jackson was concerned about landing his platoon on the beach. Like any leader he had no desire to lead his team into an ambush.

The most readily available solution to the problem was to be inserted by helicopter farther inland as Coleman and his men had been the night before. Rapp, however, ruled this out immediately. Neither Jackson nor Captain Forester knew the real reason why Coleman and his team were on the island. They both thought it was to track down the Andersons.

If they knew the whole story, as Rapp did, they would probably come to the same conclusion. And that was that Coleman's helicopter insertion had more than likely spooked the Andersons' captors into moving them. If the guerrillas decided to move again, the rescue would have to be postponed until another plan could be drawn up.

Coleman offered to send one of his men on the three-mile hike back to the beach to check things out in advance of the landing, but Rapp also ruled this out without hesitation. He wanted Coleman and his men focused on the target. If the guerrillas decided to move again he would need all four of them on the hunt. There was also the remote possibility that they might be discovered by the guerrillas and if that happened Coleman minus even one man could mean the difference between survival and annihilation.

There was a readily available solution to the danger of the landing. Rapp had been tossing it around in his head for several hours and decided now was the time to make it known. Looking at Jackson he asked, "How tall are you?"

Jackson looked a little confused. "Five-eleven. Why?"

Rapp gave him the once-over from head to toe. "One hundred and seventy-five pounds?"

"One seventy-eight."

"Good." Rapp slapped Jackson on the back and said, "You wouldn't mind lending me some of your gear, would ya?"

THIRTY-FIVE

Rain fell in heavy sheets as the United States Marine Corps CH-53E Super Sea Stallion helicopter cruised toward its destination. The wipers worked furiously to clear the cockpit windscreen but it was useless. The pilots were flying by instrument. At a standstill, visibility was a scant two hundred feet, but flying at 110 mph it was reduced to zero. Fortunately, the wind was manageable. The slow-moving front had stalled over the Philippines, dumping rain from Manila in the north to Davao in the south. Nothing was moving that didn't have to.

While most people sought cover, and either cursed Mother Nature's power or watched it in wonder, there were those who embraced it. Twenty-five such individuals sat in the back of the cold, sterile cargo hold that was designed to carry up to fifty-five marines. All were dressed in black neoprene scuba suits. Twenty-four of them were U.S. Navy SEALs and one was an employee of the CIA.

The rain was a real blessing, enabling Rapp to move up his timetable and launch early. Nightfall was still several hours away, but you couldn't tell. Emboldened by the weather and the updates from Coleman that it looked like

the guerrillas had settled in to wait the storm out, Rapp
jumped at the opportunity to get things moving. He considered alerting Kennedy that they were starting the op
but decided against it. It was three in the morning in
Washington and that would involve waking her up and
then bringing her up to speed. He had neither the incli-
nation nor the time to open the door to suggestions from
the strategists and politicians back in Washington. At this
point they would more than likely complicate the mission. As far as getting final approval went, he wasn't worried. The precedent had been set when the president
authorized the rescue operation earlier in the week. The
United States wanted its citizens back and the aggressors
would pay.

The original plan had been to take two Sea Stallions,
load up the operators and four zodiacs, and drop everyone
off five miles from the beach one hour after sunset. When
the front finally moved in Rapp consulted with the pilots
and Jackson. The pilots felt the storm would mask their
approach to the point where they could get in close
enough to drop them a mile from the beach with no fear
of being spotted or heard.

Rapp and Jackson had no problem coming to the same
conclusion: lose the zodiacs and put everyone on one
bird. These types of operations were complicated enough.
Any chance to simplify was an opportunity that had to be
taken. The men were more than capable of off-loading the
zodiacs in the roughest of seas, but it was nonetheless
something else for them to do. And then once ashore they
would have to take time to stash the boats. All of this was
preferred to a five-mile swim when they were up against
the clock, but that was no longer an issue. A one-mile
swim for the men was nothing.

One of the crew members came through the cabin

holding up two fingers. There was no sense in trying to yell over the three turbine engines and six rotor blades. Those who hadn't already strapped on their fins began to do so. At the one minute mark the back ramp of the big chopper was lowered into the down position. On Jackson's command all the men stood and steadied themselves as best they could.

At the back ramp one of the crewmen was tethered to the chopper by a safety harness. He leaned out the open hatch and called out the bird's slow descent via the in-flight headset. The pilots could see almost nothing through the windscreen. Instead of holding a true hover the bird crept forward at five mph. This was intentional, so the men wouldn't land on top of each other as they entered the water. At ten feet above the drink the pilots decided they were close enough and ordered the crew chief to get the men out.

In twos, the warriors, wearing their big black fins, waddled like penguins to the sea. Jackson counted the sticks as they jumped off the ramp and when he and Rapp were the only two left, he grabbed the spook by the shoulder and in they went.

As the helicopter climbed into the storm, the men paired off and lined up for the swim to shore. A quick head count was taken, their position was verified by GPS and compasses were consulted. Jackson ordered them to move out and the twenty-five waterborne warriors began slicing through the water.

Three hundred feet from the beach the formation halted. The landmass was but a darker shadow through the curtain of rain. Jackson briefly tried once again to send in two of his combat swimmers to reconnoiter the beach, but Rapp overruled him and took off on his own. Using only his feet he kicked his way through the salty water until his hands touched the bottom. He took off his dive fins, secured them and then removed and stowed his mask. Reaching under the neck of his wet suit he grabbed and donned the headset of his secure Motorola radio. Lastly he retrieved his suppressed MP-5 submachine gun from the swim bag and took it off safety.

He'd outfitted the weapon with an AN-PVS17 night vision sight and after turning it on he did a quick check of the jungle. He'd opted for the gun-mounted scope over wearing the goggles. The reasons were twofold. First, it was harder to shoot wearing the goggles and second, there was a good chance the goggles would help to precipitate a headache. He'd rather trust his eyes and use the gun-mounted scope as he needed it.

Warm fresh water pelted his face as he looked up and down the beach. There was nothing but the rain; rain splashing into the water about him, rain pelting leaves of the jungle, rain hitting the beach. It was a serene, steady patter that would deaden almost any man's senses if exposed to it long enough. Rapp was counting on it to put the guerrillas to sleep.

So much rain had fallen that the beach was streaked with gullies of water pouring from the jungle. Rapp stood there in the water, his senses alert to all that lay before him. After less than a minute of observation he decided the chance that Abu Sayyaf was keeping an eye on this one spot of beach, in this torrential downpour, was minuscule. The SEALs had been killed the other night because of an intelligence leak, and this time he'd made sure no such leak could take place.

After picking his spot he radioed back to Jackson that he was going feet dry. Holding the MP-5 in the ready position he came out of the water and darted across the fifty-odd feet of white sand and through the first line of palm trees. Standing next to one of the long bent trees he paused and listened. After ten seconds of silence he moved a little farther inland and worked his way up the beach and back. Satisfied that the landing area was clear he radioed for the others to come ashore.

A few minutes later, Rapp watched as four heads appeared out of the mist. The four SEALs stayed partially in the surf and trained their weapons on the jungle while behind them other black-clad men began rising out of the water two at a time. Each pair of swim buddies ran up the beach, some faster than others, depending on their loads. In less than a minute the entire element was off the beach and concealed.

As per plan, a defensive perimeter was set up and the men began donning jungle fatigues and boots while dive fins were collected and buried. The wet suits were kept on under the camouflage BDUs to help preserve body heat. It would be a long night in the rain, and even though the temperature was in the eighties, being soaked for so long would slowly sap the men of their valuable energy.

After donning his fatigues, Rapp pulled a floppy camouflage hat down over his head. Drops of water poured from the brim. Suddenly, the wind picked up. With it came a roar through the trees and the rain intensified. The drops falling from his hat turned into streams and Rapp's thoughts turned to Coleman. He and his men would be soaked to the bone by the time they hooked up with them.

Adjusting the lip mike on his headset, Rapp toggled the transmit button on his digitally encrypted Motorola radio and spoke. "Strider, this is Iron Man. Do you copy, over?" Rapp waited for a reply, cupping a hand over his free ear.

"Iron Man, this is Strider. What's your situation?"

"We're on the beach and about to move out."

"ETA?"

Rapp looked down at the rain-soaked ground and then up at the rising terrain. What would normally be a forty-minute hike on dry ground might easily now turn into a three-hour jaunt. Rapp tried to remain optimistic. "If we don't run into anybody, I'm guessing two hours, maybe a little less."

"We'll be here."

"What's your sit rep?"

"Same as last time. No one's moving."

Rapp was tempted to ask him how he and his men were doing, but decided not to waste their time. Coleman would say they were fine regardless of how miserable they were.

Jackson appeared at Rapp's side. "My point man has already found a path and everyone else is ready to go."

Rapp nodded and covered his lip mike. "Let's move out." Taking his hand off the mike he said, "Strider, we're on our way. I'll give you an update in thirty minutes."

The first squad of eight SEALs started up the narrow footpath into the thickening jungle with the men spaced a little closer than security would normally dictate. Jackson and the second squad, along with Rapp, came next and then the third squad brought up the rear. All twenty-five heavily armed men quietly disappeared into the jungle and the pouring rain.

THIRTY-SIX

Something wasn't right. David's eyes fluttered open for a second and then snapped shut. The air was thick with dust and his ears were ringing. Having no idea where he was or what he'd been doing, David tried to sit up, but couldn't. Again he blinked his eyes open, this time only to a thin squint. All of his senses seemed to be off with the exception of his sight, and even that was a little blurry.

David rolled his head to his left and saw nothing, and then to his right, where through the clouds of dust and smoke he saw fire. The flames jogged his memory. He was in Hebron at the meeting. The attaché cases were filled with the Iraqi counterfeit money. He had stepped outside and climbed into the armored car with Mohammed Atwa and then detonated the cases. A smile crept onto his lips as he remembered the look on Atwa's face when he'd stabbed him in the neck. David remembered the blood spraying from the man's throat. What a joy it was to see genuine horror on the face of a man who had brutalized thousands.

His eyes fluttered. The haze lifted a bit. He tried to move his left arm but it didn't budge. He struggled with his right arm and after a moment it broke free. David lifted his head and realized that his lower body was covered in rubble. His thoughts again returned to the attaché cases and the explosives. The technicians at Mossad must have packed even more C-4 than he'd expected into the cases. The entire house where the meeting had taken place appeared to be leveled.

David held his head up and looked up and down the street. The destruction was massive. Half the block appeared to be destroyed. *The attaché cases could not have done all this,* he thought to himself. Then he remembered the noise. A noise he had only heard once before, but a noise that was impossible to forget.

With one of his arms free, David propped himself up and looked around. His head was awash with pain and either his ears were ringing very loudly or there were sirens blaring not so far away. From his new vantage point he took in the devastation and was shocked to see the utter destruction. At least three homes in addition to the one where the meeting had taken place were completely demolished; piles of rubble, with pockets of smoke and flames.

The reality of what had happened hit David like a building had fallen on him. He did not mean for all of these innocent people to be harmed. The attaché cases would have been more than enough to handle the job, but that bastard Ben Freidman wanted to make absolutely sure that he killed everyone.

He'd tracked him to the meeting. This was not a surprise to David. The fact that Freidman would try to follow him was a foregone conclusion, but David felt the man would not press too hard for fear of blowing what already amounted to the best gift he had ever been given. Somehow he'd managed to follow him, and then to make sure no one made it out alive, including David, he'd launched missiles into the neighborhood. That was the noise he'd heard right before everything went black. The horrible shrieking noise of a missile, a harbinger of death and destruction.

David cleared several smaller stones from his legs and then a few larger ones. Where his black dress pants were torn he could see blood mixing in with the dust from the stones that had covered him. Slowly and carefully he pulled himself out from under the remaining rubble and took an inventory of the various pains that were shooting through his body.

The ringing was still in his ears. David looked around in search of an emergency vehicle but saw none. He came to the conclusion that the explosion had probably damaged his hearing. Carefully, he tried to stand, but quickly found that all was not well with his right leg. David placed only a fraction of his weight on it and hobbled over to what was left of a parked car.

The destruction was horrendous. Half of the block was leveled and of the homes that were still standing, most were either burning or in danger of catching fire. The number of innocent people killed would be enormous. It was time to flee. He did not want to be around to answer the questions of whoever it was who showed up, whether it was the Palestinian Authority or the Israelis. As David limped gingerly down the sidewalk, skirting rubble and leaning on whatever he could find for assistance, he saw an opportunity. Ben Freidman undoubtedly thought he was dead. Maybe there was a way to use that to his advantage.

David picked up the pace, wincing in pain as he put more pressure on his bad leg. Through the smoke and the dust he spotted a woman wandering toward him with a blank expression. As he neared her he noticed she had something in her arms. The look on her face told him she was in shock. Resisting the urge to approach her, he pressed on. When they were within a few feet of each other he glanced at what was in her arms and instantly wished he didn't. He wanted to believe the tiny frail body was that of a doll, but he knew better. It was a baby and David knew the poor infant would be visiting him in his dreams for years to come.

Peace did not come without a price, he told himself. He continued saying this over and over as he hobbled away from the scene of devastation. Ben Freidman would someday answer for his callous brutality. It didn't have to happen this way. The children did not have to die. David knew the perfect way to hurt such a man. All he had to do was get to America. Once there he would put into motion a series of events that would bring about the birth of a Palestinian state and the end of Ben Freidman.

THIRTY-SEVEN

Coleman was one of those steady types: never too up and never too down. He had an air of quiet authority about him that commanded a respect among his men. He was never overbearing or brusque, just calculating and decisive. But right now, more than anything, he was wet. The poncho that was draped over him had long ago become useless against the torrent of rain that was coming down by the bucket. The ground was so soaked, it was as if he was sitting on a plump sponge.

With the onset of nightfall and the deluge of rain, visibility had been reduced to the point where they could no longer see the enemy camp. Coleman had moved Stroble and Hackett to a forward position an hour ago to keep an eye on things. They'd reported back exactly what the former SEAL team commander had expected; that nothing had changed. With their report in mind, Coleman dispatched Wicker on a mission to circumnavigate the camp so he could get a better feel for the entire area.

As a general rule, when the weather was inclement people stayed put. It didn't matter if it was the South Pacific or the South Bronx. It was human nature to seek shelter and try to stay either warm or dry or cool depending on the conditions.

SEALs were the exception to this rule. Knowing that they could and would be called on to perform an operation at a moment's notice, regardless of the weather, they took it upon themselves to train in the worst of conditions. It was also why they had to endure hell week during their selection process.

Candidates were deprived of sleep for days on end and marched continually into the cold surf of the Pacific at all hours, in soiled sandy uniforms. Most of them could handle the physical torment, the academic rigors were challenging, but not overtaxing, and the verbal assaults from the instructors were for the most part ignored. It was the cumulative effect of all of these, however, that got to the SEAL candidates.

By the time hell week arrived they were already in a weakened state. Their bodies were sore, their nerves were frayed and then the very bedrock of mental stability was jerked from underneath them. They were robbed of sleep and warmth, and when the human body is deprived of those two basic necessities individuals began to do strange and unpredictable things.

This was when most of the men broke and rang the bell, signaling that they were dropping out. To the average citizen, waking up a group of young men by slamming metal trash can lids together at 2:00 A.M. was cruel enough, but after you added in the fact that the men had just gone to bed thirty minutes earlier and had not been allowed more than an hour of sleep in three days, it seemed downright inhuman.

But the SEALs weren't looking for just anyone. There was nothing nice or normal about warfare. It was mentally and physically exhausting and it was all done without the comfort of a bed, a hot shower and warm food. Most important, it was unlike almost any other job for one plain reason; you couldn't just quit. If you were working for the airlines and you got sick of throwing heavy suitcases around, you could at a moment's notice walk away from it all. If you didn't like your boss at work, you could easily quit.

In Scott Coleman's world, however, there was no quitting, because quitting usually meant that you had to die or someone else did. That more than anything was what hell week was about. The men who ran the Naval Special Warfare Center in Coronado needed to find out who could take it, because in the real world of special operations quitting was not an option.

As miserable as Coleman was right now, he took a small amount of comfort in the fact that he'd been in much worse situations. He did have to admit one thing to himself, however; he wasn't a young stud anymore. Now that he was past forty, it seemed there was a new ache added to his list every month or so. He'd led a hard life for almost twenty years and it was catching up with him.

As he leaned against the base of a hardwood tree he could tell his lower back and knees had stiffened considerably. He looked out into the faint gray light and checked his watch. The sun wasn't even down yet, but it might as well have been. Coleman judged his visibility was a scant twenty feet. Fishing a small packet from his pocket he tore it open and popped two Nuprin into his mouth. The anti-inflammatory drug would help ease the aching in his back and knees. Rapp and the other warriors would be arriving shortly, and it would be time to move.

Suddenly a whispered voice carried through the air. "Coming up behind you, boss."

Coleman heard Wicker's voice and turned to see the sniper standing just ten feet away. The fact that he had gotten so close unnerved the commander. Either he was slipping or Wicker was the sneakiest little bastard he'd ever met.

Coleman got to his feet and looking at the diminutive Wicker said, "You know that's a good way to get shot."

Wicker smiled, his teeth a brilliant white against his camouflage-painted face. "You have to hear me in order to shoot me."

"How long you been standing there?" demanded Coleman.

"Long enough to watch you pop a couple of pills."

"Shit." Coleman shook his head.

"Boss, don't sweat it. With this rain falling I could sneak up on a buck and kill it with my knife."

I bet you could, Coleman thought. Wicker was a hunter of both the four- and two-legged variety. Having grown up in Wyoming he'd hunted everything from caribou to black bear to timber wolves.

"What'd you find out?"

"I don't want to come off as being too confident, but I think I could have walked right through their camp unnoticed."

"You're serious?" asked Coleman.

"Yeah. It's this rain. It dulls the senses. It dampens the travel of noise to start with, but then after several hours like this it becomes hypnotic."

Coleman nodded while he thought of something Rapp had said on the radio earlier. "What about that ridge on the other side of the camp?"

"A couple of footpaths and that's it."

"No sentries?"

"None," Wicker said with a disgusted shake of his

head. "And I took my time. I mean they don't have a single person out checking their perimeter. They're all sitting in those shacks or under the lean-tos. It's a joke these guys didn't get their asses kicked off this island a long time ago."

"Well, when the guy commanding the opposing force is in your back pocket it makes things a little easier."

Looking through the mist in the direction of the camp, Wicker added, "I think the four of us could go in there right now and get this done."

Coleman suppressed a smile. He'd already thought the same thing, but he'd prefer to wait for the additional twenty-five shooters that were on their way. With a little luck they might be able to pull it off, but if there was a single miscue they'd get shredded. "Any other observations?"

"Yeah." Wicker tilted his head back, looking up at the dark sky through a hole in the canopy. Raindrops pelted his face. "I don't think this thing is getting any weaker; in fact I think it's intensifying."

Coleman agreed, and looking skyward he said, "The gusts are definitely more frequent."

"And stronger." With caution in his voice he added, "If it gets worse we might want to think about a different way to get home."

Just then a strong gust swept the treetops, shaking loose a curtain of rain. Coleman looked toward the ground to avoid getting his face doused and instead got a stream of water down the back of his neck. It had already been a long wet day and now it looked like things were only going to get worse.

THIRTY-EIGHT

Rapp was relieved to see Coleman. He wasn't crazy about jungles. They were great for concealment, but that went both ways. Behind every tree and bush loomed the threat of death. Moving through a jungle, even in the best of conditions, was physically draining. The humidity, the bugs and the heat all took their toll, but that wasn't the nastiest part. It was the manifestation of paranoia that really wore you down. The psychological toll it took on your nerves was far greater than the way the heat and humidity sapped your strength. The constant threat of ambush or booby trap meant that every single footfall on the path was taken with trepidation. Every bush and tree potentially concealed an enemy waiting to cut you down.

Throughout the two-hour march from the beach Rapp took comfort in the fact that Coleman kept reporting that the enemy appeared to be sitting the storm out. Hopefully, any of the MILF guerrillas on the island were doing the same. An ambush was unlikely, but a booby trap was still a real possibility.

They'd stopped twice for brief breaks so Jackson could get a head count and check in with Coleman. The storm seemed to gain strength as they made their way inland.

Both Rapp and Jackson understood what this could mean, and they'd already discussed it with Captain Forester. Back on the bridge of the *Belleau Wood* Forester had a much better handle on the big picture.

Gale-force winds were now buffeting the flattop with speeds hitting forty miles per hour. And that wasn't the end of it. The ship's meteorologist was giving even odds that the front might turn into a full-blown tropical storm with winds hitting seventy-plus miles per hour. With the increased threat the amphibious group was now steaming toward Surigao Strait and the relative protection of the leeward side of the island. The weather had been an asset until now, but it could quickly become a hindrance to a very important part of the operation.

Jackson's men were spread out in a defensive perimeter around Coleman's position. Radio silence was to be strictly obeyed unless there was something important to report. This had nothing to do with a fear of their conversations being intercepted. Neither Abu Sayyaf, MILF or the Philippine army had the technology to decipher their transmissions. Radio silence was simply standard operational procedure so the commanders could concentrate on the task at hand and keep the airwaves open.

Brief introductions were made. Rapp had already brought Jackson up to speed on Coleman's distinguished Special Forces career, and Coleman was still connected enough to the teams that he personally knew all of Jackson's commanders.

"To start things off," said Rapp, looking mostly at Jackson, "I want to establish the chain of command." Glancing at Coleman, he continued, "Scott, you're running the show. No offense, Lieutenant, but he has more experience with this type of stuff than you."

"No offense taken," Jackson replied with sincerity. He

was not so dumb as to think he was going to give orders to the former CO of SEAL Team 6, retired or not.

Wicker was brought in on the discussion to try to give them the best picture of what they were up against, and then the four men headed off through the soaked jungle to get a firsthand look at the enemy encampment. Coleman alerted Hackett and Stroble to expect visitors. A short while later four rain-soaked figures slithered on their bellies into a position just abreast of the other two men. It was now so dark that the recesses of the camp could only be seen with the aid of night vision devices.

Rapp placed a wet eyebrow up against the rubber cup of his gun scope. He was treated with a picture of the camp illuminated in shades of green, gray and black. It was pretty much what he'd expected from listening to Coleman's reports: four ramshackle lean-tos and two large tents. Faint light shone from under the bottom of both tents and the lean-tos were lit with lanterns. From their position Rapp could see directly into two of the lean-tos. He counted eight terrorists in one structure and nine in the other.

Taking his eye off the scope, Rapp asked, "Which hut has the hostages in it?"

Coleman was wearing a pair of night vision goggles with a single protruding lens, the type that made the wearer look like an insect. "The one on the right."

"Anyone in there with them?"

"There was." Without looking away from the village, Coleman asked Hackett, who was lying next to him, "Kevin, how many tangos are in the tent with the family?"

Whispering, he replied, "Eight at last count."

Coleman relayed the number to Rapp, who estimated the size of the hut and then tried to imagine how the people would be laid out inside. "Is the total enemy count still at sixty?"

"Give or take a couple," replied Coleman.

Rapp looked at the two tents and four huts. If the numbers were right, he'd accounted for twenty-five of the sixty terrorists. That left roughly thirty-five others divvied up between the other tent and two lean-tos. Fortunately, it appeared those three structures could be assaulted without the hostages being caught in a cross fire.

"What are you thinking, Scott?"

Coleman took a while to answer. He'd been thinking about his strategy all day. "We send two four-man teams around each side of the camp. They take out the lean-tos while a four-man team takes out the one tent and a five-man team handles the rescue."

Rapp ran the numbers. "That leaves a cover force of only five."

"We could increase the cover force if you want to just lob grenades into the other structures, but my guess is you won't like that."

Rapp frowned. He instinctively disliked anything that made too much noise. "It might attract some unwanted attention."

"Shit," answered the young lieutenant on Rapp's other side. "Who's going to hear it on a night like this? Besides, we're going to have to blow some trees to clear a landing area for the choppers."

This was a part of the plan that Rapp had never much liked. There was a small clearing about a quarter mile from where they were that was to be used as their extraction point. In order to make it big enough for a CH-53 Sea Stallion to land they would have to enlarge the landing area by attaching explosives to at least a half-dozen trees and shearing them off. It was sure to attract some attention, storm or no storm.

"I'd prefer to avoid the grenades if possible."

Coleman flipped his goggles into the up position and looked at Rapp. "Then we stick with a five-man cover force." Rapp still seemed not entirely enamored with the plan. "Trust me on this. We'll use one of the SAWs to hit the big tent and take the other two and set them up for cover. In addition to that I'll be up here with Kevin and Slick Wicker. They've already got their line of fire figured and the camp divided into three sectors. If anything pops up they'll take care of it before you even know it's a problem."

The SAW Coleman was referring to was the M249 Squad Automatic Weapon. A light machine gun, the SAW was capable of firing up to 700 rounds per minute and in the hands of a trained operator the weapon could lay down a withering amount of suppressive fire.

Rapp nodded. "You know more about this stuff than I do."

Flashing his teeth behind his painted face, Coleman smiled and said, "Yeah, you're a real Girl Scout. Let me take one guess where you're going to be during all this."

Rapp allowed himself a small smile. Coleman knew him well. "Let's get back to picking your plan apart for a minute."

"Nope. Not until you tell me what you've got planned for yourself."

"You know where I'm gonna be. Someone has to go in there and check things out before we hit the tent."

"Aren't you married now?" asked Coleman in a smart-ass tone.

Rapp ignored him. Coleman knew the answer. "Let's get back to the CP and put the finishing touches on this thing before this storm gets any worse."

THIRTY-NINE

Rapp didn't like what he was hearing. Odds were a big thing to him. He was by no means risk averse, but he liked the probability stacked as much in his favor as possible. Invariably, what bothered him most were things that were out of his control, and the weather was typically one such thing. Captain Forester had just informed them that the storm was in fact growing in strength. Gusts were now topping 60 mph and until they got around to the other side of the island all flight operations were suspended.

Forester assured Rapp, however, that the extraction was still on. The captain maintained that his pilots could handle the winds. The ride just might be a little bumpy. This did absolutely nothing to assuage Rapp's concerns. Bravado and blustering were one thing but reality was something entirely different. Could the captain's pilots pull off the extraction? Yes, was the answer, but could they also crash? Most definitely. Nighttime helicopter operations were delicate even in calm weather, but throw in a little wind, rain and a mountainous terrain and you had a recipe for disaster.

As Forester spoke of the competency of his aviators, the CIA counterterrorism operative was acutely aware of one vital statistic: more U.S. Special Forces personnel had been killed in helicopter accidents in the last two decades than in all other mishaps combined.

Rapp, Coleman and Jackson were all kneeling under the relative protection of a large dense tree. Covering his lip mike, Rapp looked at Coleman and said, "I've got a bad feeling about our extraction." Rapp could tell immediately by the look on Coleman's face that the man shared his concern.

"I'm not crazy about it either, but what are our alternatives? Do you want to wait to see if this thing blows over and go in just before first light?"

That option also didn't sound good to Rapp. "No, we're not going to wait. Now's the right time to hit 'em."

"We brought along plenty of explosives," offered Jackson. "We could try expanding the perimeter of the landing area."

"That might help," conceded Rapp, "but I'm still not crazy about getting on a helicopter in this weather."

Coleman was struck with an idea. "What if we march back to the beach?"

"That's fine if we're not pursued or worse." Jackson pointed over his shoulder toward the Abu Sayyaf camp. "If they manage to get off a radio transmission that they've been hit, we could get cut off on our way to the beach, and even then we still have to get on a chopper."

"Not necessarily," said Coleman. Thumbing the transmit button on his radio he asked, "Captain, what are the seas like on the leeward side of the island?"

There was a brief delay while the captain radioed one of the ships in the group that was out ahead. "Right now we're looking at ten-foot swells."

He knew the answer to the next question but asked it anyway. "Any problem launching the Mark Fives in those seas?"

"No. I can turn the ship into the storm, and we'll have no problem."

"What do you think?" Coleman looked at Rapp. "If the takedown goes off clean we can have the captain launch the Mark Fives and meet them on the beach. It'll take us at least an hour to get there. That should give them more than enough time to launch the boats and pick us up. We can bring the boats right in on the beach, load up and head out to the *Belleau Wood.*"

"And if we run into any resistance," added Rapp, "or we think they've alerted their comrades in arms, we call for the helicopter extraction."

"Exactly," answered Coleman.

Rapp looked at Jackson. "What do you think?"

"I like it. It gives us some options to work with."

"Good." Coleman was also relieved. Lifting the handset of the secure radio he said, "Captain, here's what we're going to do."

While Coleman worked out the details with Forester, Rapp took the opportunity to discuss something very delicate with Jackson. He hadn't given the subject much thought until he'd got a good look at the enemy camp, but now, in light of the fact that they might need more time to get off the island, the sensitive issue needed to be dealt with.

Rapp looked the younger man square in the eye. "Lieutenant, have you ever seen combat before?"

Jackson hesitated briefly as if he'd been waiting for the question. "No," he finally admitted.

"That's all right," replied Rapp. "We all have to start somewhere. How many of your men have seen action?"

Again, Jackson hesitated while he tallied the number. "Five of the twenty-three."

This was not exactly what Rapp wanted to hear. In his

mind he started moving people around like pieces on a chess board. Hackett's experience was too valuable to attach him to the cover force. His steady gun would be needed down where the action was taking place, and for that matter it would be nice to have Coleman at his side too. The only problem there was that Coleman needed to be in a position where he could take in the whole picture.

Coleman got off the radio with the captain and Rapp apprised him of his concerns. Before considering them, Coleman asked Jackson to bring his men in for a final briefing.

When the young lieutenant was gone, Rapp said, "He's never seen action."

Coleman seemed unfazed by the revelation. "It doesn't surprise me."

With a detached look in his eyes Rapp added, "I'm going to need some hardened guys down there with me to mop up when we're done."

The two men looked at each other and communicated an unspoken thought. "Yeah, I know," said Coleman. "No prisoners. No survivors." He'd been through the drill before. "I'll make sure I communicate it to Jackson and the chiefs. Believe me, he's green, but he's heard it before."

"Yeah, hearing about it's one thing, but until you've had to put a bullet in a wounded man's head . . ." Rapp frowned and looked down at the ground. "It'd be nice if we could spare the kid from having to think about it for the rest of his life."

Coleman agreed. "Don't worry, I'll take care of it."

Jackson came back to the group and his men started appearing through the underbrush. When everyone was assembled, Coleman and Jackson began briefing the men on the specifics of the mission. Few questions were asked. The men had all gone through the drill before. Contingencies were addressed and for a final time they went over handling the hostages and getting them out of the line of fire and secured as soon as possible.

Coleman went on to state in very clear terms this was more than a hostage rescue. He explained to the men that if they wanted to make it back to the ship they needed to decimate the enemy. They were an inferior force in numbers and could offer no aid or quarter. The men had all heard this before from their various instructors, but for the majority of them it was the first time it held such relevance.

The last thing Coleman did was point to his own forehead and say, "Remember ... double taps to the foreheads and keep moving."

Then one by one he ordered each element to their jumping-off points. Coleman then directed the cover force into position and when everything was ready he gave the word to move out. Rapp led the group up the middle. Crawling on their bellies, they slid from their elevated position down toward the rushing creek. Before the rains had come the creek could have been crossed with one step; now it was a raging waist-deep river that would have to be forded with caution.

Even with the cover noise of raindrops hitting the thick jungle leaves, the men moved with great care. Footing was so slippery that everyone had been ordered to crawl, lest someone slip, go tumbling down toward the creek and possibly alert the terrorists. Behind Rapp followed Lieutenant Jackson and ten of his men. The remaining twelve SEALs who were not assigned to the cover force were now working their way into position to flank the camp. As per the scouting report that Wicker had given them, six men had gone to take up position on the west end of the camp and six more to the east side. These two groups were to watch the two main paths that led into the village and then strike the four lean-tos when the order was given.

All twenty-nine men in the operation had been briefed on the entire scope of the operation. This was crucial, not just so that they could carry out another man's assignment if he fell, but to understand where everyone else was. With so much firepower concentrated in such a small area, the men needed to be aware of what the various elements were up to, lest they shoot one of their own.

When they reached the overflowing banks of the creek, Rapp waited to hear from the two flanking elements that they were in position. He looked out from under the brim of his jungle hat across the rain-peppered rushing stream and toward the village. From his vantage he could see directly into one of the lean-tos without the aid of his gun-mounted night vision scope. The men inside appeared to be playing a game of some sort under a single hanging lantern. At the moment one of the men appeared to be yelling at one of his companions about something. The others stood about and laughed boisterously at the angered man. As Rapp watched he couldn't help but think that the discipline of this group was really lax. It was really an embarrassment that someone hadn't freed the Andersons sooner.

While waiting for the go-ahead Rapp's thoughts turned briefly to his wife. If she knew what he was doing right now, she'd cut his nuts off. Instinctively knowing that there was probably a pretty good case to be made that he was an irresponsible and somewhat dishonest husband, he decided to not explore the issue further. At least not for now. The awkward denials and recriminations could wait until he was back in Washington.

It was always questions with Anna. She had an insatiable desire to know things, and the more she was told something didn't matter, the more it mattered. This trait, of course, treated her well in her job as a reporter, but in their relationship it was something that had to be monitored closely. Anna was a very passionate woman. Nothing was done in a halfhearted manner. If it was worth doing it was worth doing to the fullest. In this regard, Rapp wasn't all that different; he just went about things in a more analytical, stoic way, whereas Anna was more passionate and determined.

Coleman's voice crackled over his earpiece, pulling him back to the present. "Teams three and four are in position, Mitch. Let me know when you're ready."

Cradling his suppressed MP-5 in his arms he edged forward, entering the rushing water headfirst. The force of the stream rushing down the mountain was stronger than he thought it would be. He hoped it wasn't any deeper than his waist or they might have a more difficult time getting across than they'd planned. As the water deepened, Rapp found his footing and carefully picked his way across, ready to drop down into the water at a moment's notice if someone appeared from one of the two tents.

Fortunately, the water never got above the middle of his thighs. As long as none of the other men lost their footing, they would have little difficulty in fording the stream. When he reached the other side he crawled up the grassy bank and took up a cover position a mere thirty feet from the hostages' tent. Using hand signals he gestured for Jackson to bring the other two teams over.

This had been Jackson's idea. The original plan was to send Rapp over on his own and see if he could get close enough to the one tent to somehow tell them where the hostages were positioned inside. They all agreed that most likely the Andersons were huddled together at the far end of the tent. Nonetheless, it would be nice to know exactly where they were.

SEALs regularly trained in shooting rooms set up for hostage rescues. They'd have to burst through a door, window or sometimes even a wall, and in a matter of a second or two differentiate between the hostages and the terrorists and then kill the latter.

Jackson's suggestion had been to get the remaining two teams across before Rapp tried to sneak a peek. This way if things went wrong they'd be in a much better position to execute the takedown. No one wanted to return without the Andersons, so Jackson urged that they hold nothing back.

Rapp looked over his shoulder and saw Jackson reach his side of the creek and then gesture for the next man to follow. As he waited for Jackson to join him he was startled by a flash to his left. Rapp's whole body tensed as light spilled out from the other tent. Looking through the grass he saw a man holding back the flap of the tent and relieving himself.

Rapp didn't bother to train his gun on the man. He knew Wicker would have already done so. Looking over his shoulder he could barely make out one of Jackson's men crouching down in the middle of the rushing water.

With no fear of being heard due to the falling rain, Rapp whispered into his lip mike, "Everyone relax. This guy can't see more than twenty feet."

When the guy finished his business and let the flap of the tent close there was a collective sigh of relief. The fording continued and before long all of the men were across and in position to move should Rapp be discovered.

Sitting atop the slight ridge just 200 feet from the village, Coleman had an unobstructed view. He'd watched intently as Rapp and then the others crossed the rushing stream. Both flanking elements were not visible as they worked their way through the jungle. Wicker had already scouted that terrain and reported that it was free of booby traps. When each element was ready Coleman spoke to Rapp.

"Mitch, when you're ready, go sneak a quick peek and then get out of there. Lieutenant, have your conga line ready." The conga line Coleman was referring to was an entry technique the SEALs used. The men lined up as if dancing the conga and then entered the structure, every other man peeling off and responsible for clearing a given area within the room. It was a tried-and-true technique used by all hostage rescue teams.

Whispering into his mike, Rapp let Coleman know he was going in. Crawling through the grass he inched his way forward toward the tent. Now out in the relative open, protected only by darkness and rain, he moved quickly. Across a muddy path and then up a slight slope of shorter grass, he was careful to keep the barrel of his weapon clear. Less than ten feet from the tent now, he began to hear voices. He continued toward the far side of the tent where the Andersons were most likely situated. He was now within the stakes.

Carefully, he crept up to the edge of the tent. A thin sliver of light spilled out from under the green canvas where it floated just above the wet ground. Rapp made no effort to look under the side at first. Instead, he repositioned himself so he was lying in the right direction and listened to the voices.

Over the din of the rain pelting his hat, the tent and the ground, he could barely make out the voices of men speaking Filipino. Rapp crawled toward the other end of the tent and the voices grew louder. He also saw shadows cast from the interior down along the gap at the bottom. Satisfied that they'd guessed right, he scooted backward through the grass and mud to the other end.

Before looking under the side of the tent, Rapp stared momentarily at his suppressed MP-5 with its night vision scope and long thirty-round magazine extending from the underside. If he had to shoot, the weapon might be difficult to bring up under the side of the tent. Rapp laid the weapon down on the ground in front of him and reached for his silenced 9mm Beretta. After quietly drawing it from his thigh holster, he held the weapon lightly in his left hand. Unlike the movies, there was no need to chamber a round, take the weapon off safety and cock it. Rapp operated with his weapons hot at all times.

He listened for another moment, but gleaned nothing further. If the hostages were inside they weren't making any noise. Cupping his hands over his lip mike he whispered, "I'm going to sneak a peek. Be ready to move."

Twisting onto his back he positioned himself so he could look under the side by pulling the bottom up slightly with his right hand, leaving his left hand free if he needed it. Laying his head almost on the ground he took a look. He was rewarded with nothing more than the sight of the rotten wood boards that served as a floor for the tent.

Cautiously he lifted the side of the tent. Only an inch at first, though he was confident that the wind and rain would conceal any noise that he made. Rewarded with an up-close look at a dirty foot, he paused, not knowing if it belonged to a Filipino or an American. Raising the side another inch, and pulling it out slightly, he saw part of a hairless calf encrusted in mud and bug bites and a separate foot that was so small it could have belonged only to a child.

Rapp's spirits instantly rose and he pulled back the bottom of the tent a little farther. As in the other tents, a single lantern hung from the ceiling. In the dim light he spied two of the children and the back of the mother, their red hair making them instantly recognizable. Rapp continued to scan for the father and the other child. Knowing exactly where everyone was would allow them to execute a clean takedown.

Rapp thought he could make out part of the father's leg on the far side of the tent. Pulling on the side a little more he lifted his head to try to get a better angle. Suddenly he was met with a pair of wide eyes, and that was when it happened.

FORTY

Coleman watched everything from his perch. Even in the relatively warm air, he was chilled. He ignored the physical signs that he needed to find a dry, warm place. His body had been through worse. Even at his age, he knew he could tolerate quite a bit more.

Silently, he urged Rapp to hurry. It was important that they verify the position of the Andersons, but it was not imperative. He'd never gotten used to the anxiety that went along with these types of operations. That was probably a good thing, but one would think that after all the operations he'd been part of, it would get a little easier.

Looking through the scope of his M4 carbine, he watched Rapp draw his pistol and then roll onto his side. Then he heard Rapp's voice warn everybody to be ready. Coleman kept the scope on Rapp. His finger was nowhere near the trigger. If things got hot, his eyes and commands were more important than his shooting skills. That was unless they were routed into a full retreat. In Coleman's mind that wasn't even a possibility. Not with surprise on their side and the skill of the shooters he'd deployed.

As someone who had often commanded men in battle,

Coleman had a real feel for when things weren't going well, and conversely, when they were. So far all seemed to be going very well.

That sentiment instantly died when a scream came clamoring over his earpiece. Coleman instinctively winced at the sound of something so ominous and unwanted. Before he had a chance to find out what was going on, Rapp began shouting orders over the net.

RAPP SAW THE LOOK OF FEAR begin to form on the face of the young redheaded girl cradled in her mother's arms. In an effort to forestall the inevitable, Rapp smiled at the girl and mouthed the words, *it's okay*. It was about this time that he remembered his face was smeared with green, black and brown paint. He could smile at this young child all he wanted, but it wouldn't change the fact that he looked like a monster coming to get her and her family.

As soon as the little mouth started to open, Rapp knew what would follow. He hesitated for only a fraction of a second and then brought his gun up just as the girl let loose a bloodcurdling shriek. A subsonic 9mm round spat from the end of the silencer striking the nearest kidnapper in the side of the head, instantly dropping him into the lap of the man who was sitting next to him. The terrorists were sitting around a rickety table, and for the briefest of moments they froze.

With a tone of urgency, but not panic, Rapp shouted the Go word over and over into his lip mike, as he moved from one target to the next. His gun moved as an extension of his arm, efficiently seeking out targets, sweeping from left to right. The pistol carried sixteen rounds, one in the chamber and fifteen in the grip. Each depleted round registered in his mind as its brass casing was ejected.

He got off three clean head shots before the tent became so filled with terrorists diving and lurching every which way that he had to resort to aiming for chests and backs. One of the men got hold of his weapon and Rapp shot him in the shoulder, sending him sprawling and the gun clattering to the floor.

Remembering Jackson and his men, Rapp yelled, "Spray down the right side of the tent! The hostages are all down by me!" The last thing he wanted was to hit one of them with a stray bullet as they came through the tent. Or worse, have one of them hit him coming the other way.

Rapp saw two muzzles coming around. One was tracking toward the hostages, but Rapp couldn't get a clear shot. A body was in the way. Screaming "Shoot at the damn tent!" he squeezed off three quick rounds directed at a target he couldn't fully see.

The terrorist teetered backward, the dead body of his comrade knocking him off his feet. His finger squeezed the trigger on the way down, sending a three-round burst tearing through the wall and roof of the tent. Rapp saw more movement to his right. His eyes moved faster than his gun. He saw the flash of the rifle muzzle and then the wood floor in front of him splintered with the impact from a bullet, followed by another flash and another. The man was shooting the assault rifle on full automatic, shredding the rotten floorboards before him.

Rapp rushed his first shot, hitting the man in the shoulder. He needed only a split second more to place the terrorist's head in his sights, but he never got the chance. The searing pain of a bullet slammed into his flesh, sending his shot wide of the target.

Before he could react to what had just happened, a fusillade of bullets ripped through the canvas wall of the tent, sending the terrorist who had just shot him into a spastic sideways dance. No fewer than six shots propelled the man over a plastic chair and to the ground. The bullets did not stop coming for another five seconds, over a hundred of them in total.

Rapp finally called out for Jackson and his men to secure the hostages. Keeping his weapon and eyes trained on the mass of bodies at the other end of the tent, he tensed as the first wave of pain radiated to the extremities of his every limb.

He watched as Jackson's men came into the tent. Several quick shots were fired from the end of the thick silencers, but most of the work had already been taken care of. They were just mopping up. Letting his head rest on the ground, he looked over at the huddled family in the corner. He was about to call out over the radio that he'd been hit, but stopped. The other elements would still be in the thick of it. Coleman didn't need the distraction just yet. No, Rapp decided he would just lie there and relax for a bit.

FORTY-ONE

A slight headache gnawed at the base of Kennedy's brain. She knew in truth it was due to the second cosmopolitan that she'd had with Anna Rapp. It had been worth it, though. Her private conversation with Anna had broken through some barriers.

The two women had reached an understanding of sorts. Mitch was their link. They both loved him, and if they truly cared about him they would make the effort to get along. Kennedy was magnanimous in her understanding of Anna's plight, but insistent that Mitch would not be happy leading the indolent lifestyle of an intelligence analyst. He was an incredibly talented individual who just so happened to be in the business of counterterrorism. His skills and his commitment had aided countless individuals and led to the prevention of death and destruction.

Now, as Kennedy was returning to the scene of last night's festivities, she wondered how she could look like anything other than a liar to the woman whose confidence she had just gained. She'd gone to great lengths to calm Anna's fears over her husband's safety. Speaking with true conviction in regard to Rapp's talents and penchant for survival, she'd told Anna that Mitch had been involved in much more dire operations, and that he, in fact, would be nowhere near the point of battle while on his current mission. Since he had already succeeded in eliminating General Moro, she felt this was close enough to the truth. Others would be taking care of the hostage rescue, and Mitch would be monitoring the operation from a safe distance.

That had at least been her understanding of how things would proceed. All that changed when her phone rang this morning at precisely 5:00 A.M. Jake Turbes, the director of the CIA's Counterterrorism Center, awoke his boss to inform her that the operation in the Philippines had been a success. This fruitful conclusion to an international situation was all a very big surprise to Kennedy, since the operation wasn't supposed to have begun yet. After thanking the director of the CTC, and giving him no sign that she'd been somehow left out of the loop, Kennedy pulled herself from her bed and went straight to Langley.

When she got there the puzzle of what had occurred some six thousand miles away began to fall into place. The mission had been a complete success. The Andersons and all of the operators were safely onboard the *Belleau Wood* sitting out a rather ferocious tropical storm, and there was only one injury to report. All things considered, Kennedy should've been very pleased with the outcome.

On the surface she appeared her calm, cool self; nodding at the right times and asking only the most pertinent of questions, but inside, she was seething. Someone had been shot, and as luck would have it, it was none other than Mitchell Rapp.

Kennedy was furious. How in the hell did Rapp get shot when he was supposed to be sitting on a warship ten miles off the coast, and more important, why in the hell was the timetable for the rescue operation moved up without her knowing about it? Kennedy resisted the urge to call General Flood and ask if he'd given the green light. She would need some time to gather her thoughts, and her intuition told her that Flood had also been left out of the loop. Asking half-cocked questions that she didn't know the answers to was a good way to invite inquiry into how she ran her agency.

Mitch Rapp was going to have to answer some very tough questions when he got back. Kennedy's only solace right now was that ultimately, Rapp would pay for his cowboy attitude far worse at home than he would at work. At Langley he was the golden boy, capable of doing no wrong. A mythology had been structured around him. He was a walking, talking legend, a man with rugged good looks who could point to a dossier of more successful clandestine operations than any operative in perhaps the history of the Agency.

That résumé would protect him. There wasn't a person at Langley who would dare lock horns with him, and only a handful of politicians on the Hill who would even consider taking such a risk. Not that this most recent incident would offer them any real opportunity. Rapp was a hero, and Americans loved their heroes.

As her predecessor Thomas Stansfield had taught her, Kennedy suppressed the desire to get Rapp on the phone and read him the riot act. It would be better to cool her emotions and let him sweat it out for a while. Maybe even the entire long flight home.

No, Kennedy would let the one woman who truly mattered to him take care of things. It didn't matter how good Mitch was, his little powder keg of a bride was going to kick his ass like it had never been kicked before. It would almost be worth it to bug his house just to hear the interrogation. No matter what Rapp said or did, he could not lie his way out of what he had done. He couldn't hide behind national security because Kennedy wasn't going to let him, and unless he kept his clothes on for the next month, there was no way he was going to be able to hide the fact that he'd been shot.

In an effort to keep up her newfound friendship with Mrs. Rapp, she called Anna shortly before 6:00 A.M. and told her that the mission was a success and that her husband would be on his way home shortly. Anna, grateful for the call, thanked the director of the CIA profusely. Kennedy, in return, thanked Anna for being so understanding and told her to call if she had any questions.

This sudden coziness between his boss and wife would give the intensely private and compartmentalized Rapp reason for pause once he found out about it. Kennedy took a certain amount of devious comfort in that and in the fact that Rapp would be dreading how to explain what had happened.

As Kennedy stepped off the elevator on the third floor of the Executive Mansion she was prepared to do what presidential advisors had done for centuries: spin. She didn't care for the tactic, but one of her most trusted and loyal employees had put her in the awkward situation of having to do so. The alternative would be to tell the president the stark truth, which could potentially have some ramifications that she didn't need to deal with right now.

The outcome of the operation was just what the president had wanted. The Andersons were safe, the United States had suffered no casualties and a message had been sent to the terrorists. Using Rapp's line of logic, or defense as Kennedy was more inclined to say, it didn't much matter how they got there, just so long as they got there.

Kennedy entered the fitness room and after sidestepping a weight bench approached the president, who was hunched over the console of a stair-stepper.

Hayes tore his eyes off one of three TVs mounted on the wall in front of him. He'd seen Kennedy enter the room in the reflection of the mirrored wall. With sweat pouring from his face he snapped, "What in the hell happened in Israel last night?"

Kennedy was only momentarily caught off guard. On her way over from Langley she'd scanned the Presidential Daily Brief, a top secret document compiled by the CIA that kept the president and his top national security advisors apprised of what was happening in the world.

"I've already put a call in to Ben Freidman, but he hasn't gotten back to me yet."

The president frowned at the mere mention of Freidman's name. He was well acquainted with the head of Mossad. He in fact detested the man, and if it wasn't for Kennedy, the president would have demanded that Prime Minister Goldberg fire the bastard.

The president wiped a film of sweat from his face with a towel and growled, "It still burns my ass that he has a job."

Kennedy instantly regretted mentioning Freidman's name. The previous year he had been caught giving intelligence to, and aiding, one of the president's chief political adversaries. It had taken a great deal of skill to convince the president that it would be better to keep Freidman in his post and use his guilt as leverage.

Hayes looked at the clock. "What time is it over there?"

"They're seven hours ahead of us, sir. It's two-twenty in the afternoon."

"How long ago did you call him?"

"About thirty minutes ago." Kennedy folded her arms in front of her. She'd actually put in the call about an hour ago, but saw no reason to get the president more agitated than he already was.

"Well, call him back again," snapped Hayes. "And tell him I want some answers!" Pointing at one of the TVs he said, "They leveled an entire city block, and they're saying the death toll could surpass one hundred people, for Christ's sake."

Kennedy looked awkwardly at the floor and then back at the president's reflection in the mirror. He had grown considerably more irritable lately.

"Sir," she cautioned, "you know the Palestinians always inflate those numbers."

Hayes gripped a black bar with one hand and with the other he lowered the speed of the machine. "Have you seen the footage?" he asked a little less confrontationally.

"Yes."

"And you don't think it looks bad?"

"Yes, it does, sir, but let me get some more information before we jump to any conclusions."

Hayes nodded and began to breathe a little easier. Realizing he'd been a little hard on one of his most trusted advisors he asked, "So, did you have a good time last night?"

"Yes, I did. It was a very nice party, sir."

"Good." He mopped his brow again and asked, "What's happening over in the Philippines?"

Kennedy forced a smile and adjusted her glasses. "I have good news. The Anderson family is safely onboard the *Belleau Wood* as are all military personnel who participated in the operation."

As if someone had delivered an unexpected gift, a mix of joy and confusion spread across the president's face. He glanced at the clock on the wall and said, "I thought the rescue wasn't set to take place for another hour or two."

"Well, there were some developments during the

evening, sir, that caused us to move up our timetable."
Fortunately, Kennedy knew the president was a man who
never punished success. Like most good chief executives
he delegated authority and wanted results.

"A tropical storm blew in," she continued to explain,
"threatening to ground our aircraft. At the same time, the
rain provided the cover needed to sneak our ground forces
into position earlier than we had anticipated. Not wanting
to lose the opportunity we gave the green light and it went
off without a hitch." Kennedy was tempted to mention
that Rapp had been shot, but for now she wanted to keep
that little nugget of information to herself.

The president's face lit up. "That's great! When will
they be arriving stateside?" The politician in him was already looking forward to greeting the family.

"They have to wait for the storm to break and then
they'll start back. They could be here as early as tomorrow
or Monday."

"And how are they doing?"

"Fairly well," answered Kennedy. "A little malnourished and covered with insect bites, but otherwise stable."

The president stopped the machine and climbed off.
He moved over to a treadmill and climbed on. "How are
they psychologically?" Hayes pressed several buttons and
the tread started moving.

Kennedy could only guess at the horrors they had suffered. From her intelligence reports on other kidnappings,
Abu Sayyaf and MILF were fairly humane in the sense
that they seemed to avoid rape and torture, especially of
Americans. But still, being held captive thousands of miles
from home in extremely primitive conditions would have
taken its toll.

"I'm not sure, sir. For now I bet they're just happy to
be free."

"Yeah, I suppose." The belt picked up speed and the president began walking faster. He pumped his arms and said, "Do me a favor and brief Valerie on this." The president glanced at the wall clock. "She's usually in by eight on Saturdays."

The president needed his chief of staff. Kennedy understood better than most how Washington worked. Political effectiveness rose and fell with the tide of positive or negative media attention. This was too good of a story not to manage properly. Kennedy would brief Valerie Jones and then Jones in turn would mobilize the formidable White House communications and press people. They would prod and squeeze this story into a five-point jump in the polls.

"Anything else, sir?"

The president hesitated and then sighed. "I suppose we should have the NSC meet for a full briefing."

Kennedy nodded. If the president hadn't suggested it she would have. The various cabinet level departments needed to be brought up to speed, especially the State Department. Somebody needed to tell President Quirino in the Philippines what the United States had just done, and in light of the sensitive subject it would be wiser if that person were the secretary of state rather than the president. "What time would you like me to schedule it for?"

"Let's say eleven o'clock downstairs . . . and oh . . . if you talk to Mitch before then, thank him for me."

Kennedy nodded.

"He's an amazing man."

Kennedy did not hesitate to reply. "Yes, he is." Any man brash enough to usurp the authority of the director of the CIA, the secretary of defense and the president all in one evening was an amazing man indeed.

FORTY-TWO

T rust was a word that David wasn't very fond of at the moment. Ben Freidman had broken their agreement. There could be little doubt based on the news reports that the head of Mossad had wanted his newest informant to die in the attack that had taken place on the previous eve. Extending that logic, and understanding the brutality that Freidman was known for, David felt the need to get out of Israel as quickly as possible.

After stumbling away from the site of the bombing, David didn't make it far; only two blocks to be precise. A ruptured eardrum caused him to walk as if he were drunk. His dust-covered suit, listless walk and bloodied face caught the attention of a paramedic, who after a quick examination thrust him into a waiting ambulance. Upon arrival at the hospital David gave a fake name.

Mossad had spies everywhere and if they weren't lucky enough to have one at the hospital, they could hack into the patient files with little effort. One of the first people to arrive after the attack, he was treated right away. The gash in his leg and neck were cleaned and stitched up with great speed. More seriously injured people were being pulled from the rubble and on their way.

Having grown up around hospitals David had no problem finding the doctors' lounge. He moved without fear of being discovered. The staff would be working at a crisis pace for the next day or more. His clothes were no longer useful, so he threw them into the garbage and cleaned up. The only thing he kept were his undergarments, shoes, and a money belt that contained cash and documents for an assumed identity. Next he searched the lockers until he found one that contained clothes roughly his size. David changed into them and took the car keys sitting on the top shelf.

Out in the parking garage he went to the first level where the physicians parking was located and hit the door lock button on the keyless entry twice. Up ahead on his right a pair of headlights flashed and a horn honked. David left Hebron as directly as possible. Various Palestinian groups had already begun setting up barricades to keep the Israeli Defense Forces from entering the city and he was lucky to find a way through them.

By sunup David had made it all the way to the south and crossed the border into Jordan at Arava. Feeling only slightly safer, he called the prince and requested that he send his plane to the seaside town of Aqaba to pick him up. The prince, comatose from a night of festivities, was unable to speak, so it was his always efficient assistant Devon who sent one of Omar's five private jets. By noon he was safely out of Freidman's reach and on his way to France. He landed in Nice in midafternoon and was taken by limo to the Carlton Hotel in Cannes, where Devon had booked him a suite.

The first order of business was clothing, so after an hour of shopping along de la Croissette and billing everything to his hotel room, and ultimately the prince, David returned to the solitude of his plush room and collapsed out of exhaustion. Sometime later, he was awakened by the fleshy soft hand of none other than Prince Omar.

David rolled over onto his back and tried to blink the weariness from his eyes. As the room came into focus he realized it was nighttime. Omar reached out and pawed the side of David's neck. The touch stung the tender skin around the stitches. Out of reflex David slapped the prince's hand away. Almost instantly he was aware of someone else in the room. Someone large by the size of the shadow they cast against the wall.

Chung, the obedient Chinese bodyguard, was making his presence known, lest David try anything stupid. Prince Omar, however, was not bothered by the slap. He was too amused by the mark on David's neck and the implications it held.

"I think someone has been up to something." Omar cupped David's cheeks in his hands and said, "I want to hear all about it."

David shooed Omar's hands away. His head was killing him and the last thing he wanted right now was the prince touching him. "Hear about what?"

"About last night!" proclaimed the Saudi prince with a twinkle in his eye.

"I don't know what you're talking about," David groaned.

Omar stood up laughing. He was dressed immaculately in a very expensive silk suit. "Oh . . . you know what I'm talking about. Now get your duff out of bed and get ready for dinner." Omar gestured with his hands toward the bathroom. "Come now . . . hurry. I am very hungry and I have been watching Al Jazeera. I want to know everything. We will eat and celebrate tonight. I will be waiting for you downstairs." Omar, as giddy as a schoolgirl, left the room with Chung in tow.

By the time he got into the shower his spirits had lifted a bit. He was famished. Maybe a nice feast with Omar wouldn't be so bad. Shaving proved to be a bit more of a challenge than he would have liked, but with Omar skipping it was not an option. The prince was a stickler for appearances. He wanted to be surrounded by beautiful people and that meant well-groomed and well-dressed people.

David put on his new clothes: a white shirt, four-button black suit, and blue tie. The tie was a bit tricky but as long as he didn't turn his head too much it was manageable. A large flesh-colored Band-Aid over his stitches helped keep blood off the collar.

David found Omar downstairs in the bar. He was sitting in a corner booth squeezed in between four women, two on each side. Two other men sat at each end of the U-shaped booth. They were both Arab and more than likely were several of Omar's three-thousand-plus cousins. As for the women, they were undoubtedly high-priced hookers that had been secured for however long the prince chose to stay in Cannes, or until he tired of them and replacements were obtained.

David almost didn't notice Chung, which was no easy feat considering his size. Somehow he'd managed to conceal himself on the other side of a large potted fern and column. David winked at him, just to let him know he wasn't fooled. Chung's sphinxlike face remained utterly impassive.

As David approached the table, Omar released his always groping hands from two of the girls. Reaching out, he held his palms up in a gesture of enthusiastic welcome. "David, I am so glad you could join us." Looking to his guests he said with a conspiratorial wink, "David is a man of many talents, and he is soon to be very famous." The two Arab men nodded as if they knew more than they should.

The girls looked at him with playful eyes and then began giggling and muttering to each other in French. David ignored the women and gave the prince a disapproving look.

Omar, not wanting his little party spoiled by the often too serious David, rushed to say, "Sit!" The prince gestured to one of his cousins to make room. "Come sit with us. We will celebrate." Looking to the waiter standing obediently near the booth, Omar yelled, "Champagne ... more champagne!"

David held up his arm, freezing the waiter before he could fill the order. With a smile, and a slight bow at the waist, David said, "My prince, if I may have a moment of your time in private?" David's forceful dark eyes conveyed that his words were not a request but a demand.

"Of course." Omar clapped his hands twice and gestured for the table to be removed. He was not about to slide his plump form out of the booth.

The waiter snapped his fingers and two busboys rushed over and removed the table. Omar left his guests without saying a word and grabbed David by the elbow. With a look of deep concern, he asked, "What is wrong?"

David strained to look at ease. He was willing to bet double or nothing on the ten million dollars that Omar had given him not even a week ago, that the prince had shared their secrets with other members of the Saudi royal family.

"Who are those two men?"

"Cousins, of course."

"Ah . . . just as I thought. And what have you told them?"

"Nothing."

David stared doubtfully at Omar.

Caught in an obvious lie, Omar said, "Nothing of consequence. I simply told them you are a great man who is changing the world. A true warrior for the Arab people."

David sighed uncomfortably. He had to have a serious conversation with Omar, but he would need his undivided attention for at least an hour. "I am very hungry, and I need to speak with you."

Omar looked back the table. "Good, then let's sit—"

"No. Not them. Just the two of us." The prince looked back and forth between David and the table several times, reluctant to leave the women.

Reading his mind, David said, "They can wait. You will have all night to enjoy them. All I need is one hour of your uninterrupted time."

Omar finally agreed. After waving one of his cousins over and explaining the situation, Omar and David were led to a private table in the far corner of the restaurant.

David was unsure of how to proceed. He had stressed many times how important it was to share their plans with no one. As a brother to the crown prince and high-ranking member of the Saudi royal family, Omar had always done whatever he wished. This was why David had to handle him with kid gloves.

Even so, there were times when it was simply impossible not to speak his mind. As the last twenty-four hours had shown, this was a very dangerous game they were playing, and although it was David who was currently on the front line taking the risks, circumstances could change very quickly. If the voyeuristic prince wasn't careful he just might end up closer to the action than he would ever wish.

After choosing his words carefully, David said, "It flatters me that you say such noble things about me, but I can't stress enough that you must cease all conversation regarding our plans."

"But, David, there are people who care deeply about the cause. People who we can trust."

"People like your cousins?" asked David with a raised eyebrow.

"Of course. I trust them with my life."

David studied his benefactor. "What did you tell them?"

"I bragged about you a bit," Omar answered in a sheepish tone.

"Did you happen to mention that I may have been involved in something that happened last night?"

Omar smiled. "Maybe."

David clutched the ornate armrests of his chair so ferociously that he thought they might snap. His mind off and running, he imagined these two ninnies pulling out their cell phones and calling their friends and family back in Saudi Arabia, bragging about their cousin and the clandestine operation he was launching to finally rid them of Israel.

David never wanted to get rid of Israel. He wanted Palestine to coexist with the Zionist state, but that would never be enough for Omar and the majority of his relatives. They wanted the complete destruction of the Israeli state and the annihilation of the Jewish people.

As they always did, David's thoughts returned to the phones. "My prince, I have warned you before and it is not just to protect me. It is for your own good." David shook his head sadly. "You cannot tell people what we are doing. I know you can trust your family, but you are missing the point. I do not think your cousins are going to run to the Americans and tell them what we are up to. No, I don't believe that for a moment. I think the Americans, however, will monitor their phone calls and they will catch them bragging to other relatives."

Omar frowned and shook his head. "Impossible. The Americans do not spy on my country."

David was taken completely aback by Omar's overconfidence. "You do not think the Americans spy on your country?"

"No," answered the prince in his same confident tone. "We have an agreement with them."

David stared in disbelief, that someone as worldly as Omar could be so naive. "I hate to break the news to you, Prince Omar, but America spies on Saudi Arabia."

"They do not, David. I have spoken with my brother about the agreement and our intelligence service monitors things very closely." With a smug nod, he added, "I can assure you."

"They may not have people on the ground, they may not be actively spying on you, but that does not mean they are not passively spying on you."

"What do you mean . . . passively?"

"Satellites," answered David. "They pick up everything. Their National Security Agency listens to everything."

Omar seemed to think about this for a moment and then asked with a frown, "How is it possible with so many people talking on phones?"

David tried not to show his shock over the prince's stupidity. Omar was not a very bright man, which in addition to his wealth was one of the reasons why David had picked him. He was a gambler with a very large bankroll. He had amassed his personal fortune, one separate from his family's, by getting out of real estate and into stocks at just the right time and then vice versa a decade later. His instincts in terms of knowing when to buy and when to sell were uncanny, but his knowledge of espionage was almost nil.

"Trust me on this. They can do it, and every time you brag to one of your relatives we have no idea how many other family members they call." David detected a gleam in the prince's eye and something clicked. Notoriety was the real reason for his loose lips. He had not been chosen as the crown prince, despite his financial successes, and so he now worked doubly hard to try to build his reputation within the dysfunctional House of Saud. One of the reasons he had been overlooked as a serious candidate for crown prince was his playboy lifestyle. In a country where over ninety percent of the residents were fervent Muslims, it was important that the king at least appear to follow the teachings of Muhammad.

"Prince Omar, trust me when I tell you we do not want the Americans to find out what we are up to, or for that matter the French, the Israelis or anyone else."

With a sour look on his face Omar said, "I am not afraid of the Americans. They wouldn't dare touch me. My family could flush their entire economy right down the toilet." Omar snapped his fingers contemptuously.

David was tempted to point out that the Saudi royal coffers weren't what they once were. In addition, the Saudis had so much money invested in America that they would be cutting their own throats if they turned off the oil spigot. Omar was nowhere near as safe as he thought, but David would never be able to convince him of that. His life of opulence had given him a false sense of importance.

"Please don't forget," pleaded David, "that the key to our success is to get the international community to think that Israel is out of control."

Omar shook his head. "The key to our plan is getting

my brother to threaten America with an oil embargo. That will wake them up."

"Yes, that is very important, but if you want our plan to succeed, then we need to make sure the Americans don't find out what we're up to."

Grabbing his menu, Omar nodded with a frown of irritation on his face. "Enough of this talk. I thought you were hungry." Omar gestured to the menu sitting untouched in front of David. "We will eat and you will tell me about last night."

David grabbed the menu and glanced at the first page. Based on a conversation he had had with Omar some months earlier, he decided to make one more attempt at getting him to shut his mouth. Looking over the top of his menu David said, "Omar, trust no one completely, not me and most definitely not your family. You have said it yourself that you have relatives who are far too cozy with the Americans. You know as well as I that there are people in your family, pro-westerners, who are very jealous of your success. They would gladly sell you out to the Americans."

Omar slammed his menu down. The water glasses on the table jumped and the candle flickered. "And what would the Americans do about it?" spat Omar. "Kill a member of the Saudi royal family? Never!"

David nodded, if for no other reason than to calm the prince. His slight outburst had attracted some unwanted attention. Omar was probably right. The Americans were unlikely to assassinate him, but they might find someone else to do it. On the other hand, the Americans wouldn't think twice about killing David.

David looked over his menu and decided it was best to change the subject. "How are things with the ambassador?"

"Fine," snapped Omar. "Devon has already wired him

half the money and he will get the other half on Monday. We own him."

David was pleased to hear this. The ambassador would be a vital part of their overall plan. Things were going exceedingly well but David knew he should temper his optimism. Hebron had worked out beyond David's wildest dreams. Freidman had overplayed his hand and now had a massacre to explain. Tomorrow he would fly to America to carry out the next phase of the operation.

IT WASN'T THE AMERICANS, the French or the Israelis who were currently on the job, but the British. Alan Church's sailboat was berthed in the harbor not far from the massive yacht he'd been following for weeks. His most recent report had stirred some guarded interest back at MI6 in London. His orders were to maintain surveillance, and see if he could identify the man who had met with Prince Omar. Apparently the photographs he had snapped in Monaco were either not good enough to get a positive identification, or the man was unknown.

Church had been sitting at the bar keeping an eye on the prince and his guests when in walked the very man in whom headquarters had shown an interest. The handsome Arab spoke to the prince in a manner that suggested he was more than just another one of Omar's abundant sycophants. After a brief exchange Prince Omar and the mysterious individual went unaccompanied to the dining room where they were seated at a remote table.

A longtime follower of the Saudi royal family, Church was more familiar than most with the turmoil and tumult that bubbled just beneath the calm veneer of the very private clan. The spoiled consortium of relatives numbering just over 5,000 sat atop a powder keg of some twenty-three million subjects who were growing increasingly impatient with the excesses of the ruling family.

For years, the House of Saud had tried to placate religious fanatics in their country by building them lavish mosques and madrasas. The ultrafundamentalist Wahhabi sect prospered more than any other group during this time, and now held great sway and power with an increasingly unruly populace.

Church was unsure if he would see it in his lifetime, but he was confident that the days of the Saudi monarchy were numbered. They had sowed the seeds of their own destruction by funding religious fanatics who would never tolerate their secular ways and gluttonous lifestyles. Omar was one such royal. Living in the lap of western luxury he tried to assuage his guilt by paying penance to the ultraconservatives of a faith that he was born into, but one that he had never seriously practiced or believed in.

Church informed the maître d' that he was ready to be seated for dinner. Cannes was a town where people partied well into the night, and the evening dinner crowd was still light. The man escorted Church through the restaurant to a table that was surprisingly closer to the prince than he would have liked. Church noticed the prince's guest give him a suspicious glance.

Knowing the limitations of his listening device, and not wanting to raise undue suspicion, Church stopped the maître d' and pointed to a table that was closer to the bar and farther away from the subjects. The two men reversed course and left Prince Omar and his guest to talk without fear of being heard.

Sitting with his back to the wall, the British agent now had a perfectly good view of both the bar and the prince and his acquaintance. Personally, he was more interested in the four women the prince had left in the bar, but duty was duty, so he turned his attention to the matter at hand.

He retrieved a case from the breast pocket of his suit coat and donned his reading glasses. After fumbling with the case for a second he placed it on the table with the open end pointed directly at the two men conversing in the far corner of the restaurant. With the tiny directional microphone and recorder now doing the tough work for him, Church opened the wine menu and began searching for a nice expensive bottle of Bordeaux, courtesy of the British government.

FORTY-THREE

Kennedy was back at Langley sitting in her large corner office on the seventh floor. It was nearing three in the afternoon, and on most Saturdays she would not be in the office this late, but it was pouring outside and her son Tommy was at a friend's house until five. Her seven-year-old was getting more and more independent, which to Kennedy was both good and bad. Good, because he was a little less demanding of her time, and bad, because he was a little less needy of her affection.

At seven, Tommy was coming out of his shell. His reserved manner had worried his teachers more than it had his mother. Others assumed it was the divorce that had caused young Thomas to be so shy, but Kennedy thought it had more to do with the fact that his mother didn't really speak for the first five years of her life, and to this day opened her mouth only when she really needed to.

Kennedy looked at her son's shy demeanor as a positive. Just like his mother he was very cautious around strangers, slow to anger and deeply introspective. The boy had a wonderful imagination, and was capable of playing by himself for hours on end. On the other hand, he was also capable of burying his mother under an avalanche of questions when it was least expected.

Now in the first grade he was making friends, playing sports and getting perfect marks, which was no surprise considering the IQ of his parents. While his father may not have been the most responsible and selfless man, he was nonetheless very smart. Fortunately, he didn't come around often. In Kennedy's mind he was a distraction from an otherwise tranquil and loving home.

There were other male role models around. Tommy adored Mitch and just so happened to have a crush on his new bride. Mitch constantly prodded her son to get involved in sports and loved to take him up to Camden Yards to watch the Orioles. Next summer Mitch had promised to teach Tommy how to water ski, and now that she and Anna had reached an understanding, it was likely that they would see more of each other.

There was also the quirky Frenchman a few doors down, Mr. Soucheray, who hung out in his garage all day listening to the radio, tinkering with an endless array of gadgets and pursuing his lifelong fascination with the internal combustion engine. Thanks to him, Tommy probably knew more about cars, motorcycles and anything that ran on gasoline, than probably any seven-year-old in the country.

Kennedy closed the file on her desk and put her pen down. With a yawn she took off her glasses and rubbed her tired eyes. If she left now she could probably sneak in a quick nap before Tommy returned from his friend's house. She grabbed several red folders off her desk and spun her chair around. After placing the files in her safe she locked it. She was about to get up when her large white secure phone rang.

She looked at the display and frowned. Ben Freidman was finally returning her call almost nine hours later. The man had gall. She possessed enough information to destroy him and still he played these games. She was sure he would have some excuse to explain why it took him so long to call her back.

Kennedy looked out at the falling rain and grabbed the handset. "Irene Kennedy."

"Irene, it's Ben. I'm sorry I couldn't get back to you sooner, but as I'm sure you've seen on TV, I've had my hands full over here."

"Yes, we've been watching."

"We took out a bomb factory last night and now we're bracing ourselves for reprisals."

There were times when Kennedy wished she were more like Mitch Rapp. If she were, she'd tell her Israeli counterpart that he was full of shit. The news outlets were reporting that the Israeli Defense Forces attacked a bomb-making factory in Hebron and that was why the damage was so extensive. The Palestinians were denying any such factory existed and claimed the Israelis had attacked a civilian neighborhood without provocation. The truth, as always, lay somewhere in the middle. Jake Turbes from the CTC had briefed her only an hour ago that they did not think a bomb factory was the target. They'd picked up cell phone chatter that the real target was a high-level meeting of Palestinian terrorist groups. She also had in her possession satellite imagery that showed Israeli helicopters showering the neighborhood with missiles.

Ben Freidman was lying to her, but in the hall of mirrors that was her life, she wasn't about to reveal what she really knew. Instead, she simply said, "The president is very alarmed by the amount of people killed in the raid last night."

In his standard defensive tone, Freidman said, "Irene, we had no idea that the secondary explosion would be so large. They had enough explosives there to level the whole block."

Obviously, she thought. The latest intelligence reports indicated that the Israeli Defense Forces were not in control of the site. Various terrorist and militia groups around Hebron had set up roadblocks to keep the Israeli army out and they had maintained their position just long enough for the media to show up and begin filming the carnage. The Israelis had fallen into this public relations nightmare before and immediately pulled back. Footage of tanks crushing teenagers and young men, no matter how just the cause, did not play well for the rest of the world.

Freidman was playing a dangerous game here. If the Palestinians were telling the truth about the number of dead, they would have quite a case to take to the UN. When she spoke to the president she would have to apprise him of the possibility. No sense going too far out on a limb to defend Israel if they weren't going to tell the truth to their best ally.

She decided to prod him just a bit. "You know that the Palestinians are saying you attacked a neighborhood without provocation."

Freidman scoffed. "I could have written their press release for them before the operation was even launched. It's the same lies every time."

"Yeah, I know," Kennedy answered with well-feigned sincerity. *The only problem is,* she thought, *that they in turn could have written your press release for you.* "You know the timing of this is very bad."

There was a long pause and then Freidman asked in an agitated tone, "How so?"

Freidman's frustration was not lost on Kennedy. Her Israeli counterpart was an unusually blunt man, but something in his voice told her that he was under a lot of pressure. He had his enemies in the cabinet, doves who wanted to disengage and start real peace talks. She was sure they were none too fond of this current operation.

"The president is meeting with the crown prince of Saudi Arabia next week," offered Kennedy, "and the main topic of discussion was going to be a renewed peace initiative in the Middle East . . . but now that we have dozens of Palestinian women and children being pulled from the rubble the whole thing might be a nonstarter."

"Irene, it was a damn bomb factory."

"And it has taken the president months just to get the crown prince to sit down."

"You know as well as I do," spat Freidman, "that the crown prince will never support real peace. The day he recognizes Israel is the day he ignites the revolution in his country and slits his own throat."

"You think we don't know that?" asked Kennedy, maintaining her neutral tone. "The president wants assurances on other fronts. We want to see a real crackdown on the terrorist groups operating out of Saudi Arabia. We want to see the funding of these groups stopped."

"Irene," Freidman interrupted her and let out a sigh of frustration. "We've been over all this before. I appreciate the efforts you make on our behalf, but this is our war. We are on the front line. We are the ones facing terrorist bombers every day. We will not sit on our hands. When we receive solid intelligence we are going to act, and if these cowards insist on hiding behind women and children, then so be it."

"Ben, I am well aware of your difficulties, but you can't go it alone. You need to do a better job of keeping us in the loop."

"I am keeping you in the loop," he replied earnestly. "What do you think I am doing right now?"

Kennedy was not about to let him know that she knew he was lying to her, so she simply said, "You're calling me nine hours after I put a call in to you stating that the president of the United States wished to know what was going on." Kennedy let the statement sink in and then added, "Now come on, Ben, you and I are veterans at this. There's only a couple of reasons why you wait that long to return a call, and none of them are good from where I'm sitting." Kennedy listened intently while she pictured Freidman squirming on the other end of the line.

Finally, he said, "There's something I've been working to confirm . . . something that's very important. I didn't want to call you until I knew for sure."

"And what is that?"

"This goes no further than you. I don't want you telling the president until I can verify it. We had intelligence that a high-level meeting was taking place last night."

"How high?"

"I'll send you the list, but suffice it to say that there were key players from Hamas, the Popular Liberation Committee, Force 17, Islamic Jihad, leaders of the martyr brigades and possibly Mohammed Atwa, the head of Palestinian General Intelligence."

"You're serious?" Kennedy acted surprised. "So the story about the bomb-making factory is—"

"True! We did not know it was there. Our rockets set off secondary explosions that were unavoidable."

Kennedy wondered why it had been such a struggle for Freidman to tell her about the real intent of the operation and why, according to her facts, he was still lying to her about the bomb factory. "When will you have confirmation on who was taken out in the strike?"

"By tomorrow I should have a good idea. I have an

asset posing as a cameraman who's photographing the dead. Those pictures, along with the intercepts we're picking up, should give us a fairly complete list. Listen now," said Freidman reasserting control, "I have to go now. If I find anything else out, I'll let you know."

"All right." Before she could say good-bye Freidman was off the line. Kennedy sat there for a moment staring at the handset, trying to separate the fact from the fiction in an effort to discern what the head of Mossad was up to. In the end it could be nothing more than his inability to play things straight. There were plenty of people like him in the business. Never tell the whole story, only parts of it. Or it could be much deeper than that. Kennedy would have to monitor the situation closely.

Turning to her computer she fired off a quick e-mail to Jake Turbes that she wanted him to personally look into the events in Hebron, and do so without the aid of Mossad. She wanted clean untainted facts by which to judge Freidman's honesty, or more likely lack thereof.

FORTY-FOUR

Ben Freidman sat on the porch of the house sipping a glass of water and looking out at the rolling terrain under the moonlit evening sky. He desperately wanted a drink, but one had not been offered to him. It had been a very long day trying to manage the situation in Hebron. There were people in his government who didn't appreciate the victory he had achieved. They were weaklings. Men and women who didn't have the stomach to fight for the preservation of Israel.

The man he was waiting to see had the determination, though. The ranch in the Jordan Valley belonged to Prime Minister David Goldberg. Goldberg, the head of the conservative Likud Party, had been elected by an overwhelming majority of the Israeli people despite the fact that his party held only a handful of seats in the 120-member Knesset. That had been two years ago, when the people had seen how duplicitous the Palestinians were. The Israelis extended the olive branch and Yasser Arafat took it from them and slapped them in the face. He used the new Palestinian Authority to secure his hold over the Palestinian people and bring in weapons and explosives to help wage an even bloodier war against the Jews, all the while he feigned a lack of control over the so-called martyr brigades.

Goldberg had been swept into office as a hard-liner who would crack down on the Palestinian terror groups and restore some security to the country. Unfortunately things had not gone as planned. They were up against a new form of terror. One that so far they had been unable to stop. The steady stream of homicide bombers had crippled Israel's fragile economy and frayed the nerves of even some of the stoutest patriots. The martyr brigades needed to be stopped, and Ben Freidman was willing to be every bit as ruthless as the enemy to get the job done.

He was worried about his old friend and current prime minister, though. There had been signs lately that Goldberg was beginning to crack under the pressure. His cabinet was filled with backstabbers and even his own party was asking if the old general had what it took to deal with the crisis. And then on top of that the damn Americans were giving him orders to back down.

Freidman had seen it all before. He understood the visceral hatred the Arabs felt toward him and his country. In Freidman's mind it was based on jealousy. The Arabs and their closed patriarchal society couldn't handle being bested by the Jews. The Palestinians had held on to this land for thousands of years and had done nothing to improve it. The Jews came back to their homeland and in one generation turned much of the arid landscape into plentiful farms and orchards. They had tried to negotiate a fair peace, but the Arabs would have none of it. There would always be a large and influential segment of the Palestinian people who would never be satisfied until Israel ceased to exist. It was Freidman's job to make sure that never happened.

This was the important mission of Freidman's life. It

was his vocation to make sure Israel survived, and he was willing to go to great lengths to ensure success. Doing it alone, though, was not possible. He needed help. He needed allies who would pacify the bleeding hearts in his country, those naive imbeciles who actually believed that peace was worth risking the entire security of a nation, of a people who had narrowly avoided extinction.

He needed lobbyists in America to lean on the right people. People who could get to other people who controlled the lifeblood of politics: money. People who could deliver the three states that every presidential hopeful wanted: New York, Florida and the crown jewel, California. He needed America's support more than ever and he would work diligently to make sure it was there when the time came.

Right now, though, the thing he needed most was a strong prime minister who would stay the course. He'd seen signs lately that his old friend was losing his stomach for the fight. This could not be allowed to happen. Prime Minister Goldberg needed to hold true to his commitment and stave off another attack from the liberals.

David Goldberg stepped onto the porch holding two bottles of Goldstar beer. He handed one to Freidman and apologized for making him wait. Even though Freidman would have preferred a stiff drink, he took the beer and watched his friend take a seat in the rocking chair next to him.

On the face of it, Goldberg was the most unlikely hawk you would ever meet. His plump fleshy appearance made him appear too soft for a war hero. He had a mane of white hair, which framed a tan face and heavy jowls. He was a large man, but not muscular and it was easy to see him as the grown-up version of the pudgy kid in school who was always picked on. This was a mistake. The man's temper and valor were legendary. Never one to shy away from a fight, Goldberg had the disposition of a bull. He had distinguished himself many times on the battlefield, and for that at least, he had the respect of his countrymen. Unfortunately, though, his valor did not indefinitely guarantee their support.

Goldberg took a swig of beer and said, "Ben, you have created quite a stir."

Freidman listened to a dog barking in the distance and said, "Don't I always?"

"Yes, you do, but these are delicate times."

Freidman already disliked the tone of their conversation. "When haven't they been?"

The prime minister disagreed by shaking his head. "We have never seen the international pressure we see now."

"Forgive me for being so blunt, David, but the international community can kiss my ass."

"Believe me, I share your feelings, but we cannot ignore them. What you did last night is causing me problems."

Freidman looked away from his old friend and took a drink from his beer. "David, you asked me to hit back, and did I ever find a way to hit back. It will take them years to recover from this."

The prime minister wasn't so sure anymore, not since these she-devils started blowing themselves up. More and more Goldberg was starting to think in terms of withdrawal from the West Bank and the occupied territories. There were only two things that prevented him from doing so. The first was the settlements. Thousands of Jews had moved into the areas and would die rather than leave. The second reason he wouldn't support the withdrawal and recognition of a Palestinian state was that he feared for his life. The man sitting next to him on the porch, along with many others, would have him killed if he were to gamble so recklessly with Israel's security.

Knowing he had to be careful with how he dealt with Freidman, he said, "The attack was the crowning achievement of your career, Ben." Goldberg held out his bottle for a toast.

"Thank you." Freidman clanged his bottle against the prime minister's and said, "But?"

Goldberg finished his drink and in a confused tone asked, "But what?"

"Don't protect me, David. Remember I hear everything. I know your cabinet is furious with the number of casualties."

"They are rarely in agreement on anything."

"Well, if you'd like me to address them I am more than willing."

Goldberg considered this for a moment. It wasn't a bad idea. Ben Freidman could intimidate even the staunchest opponent. "Maybe later, but for now I am more concerned about explaining to the international community how so many innocent civilians died."

He was tempted to remind him that the Palestinians living in the neighborhood were hardly innocent, but the director general of Mossad decided against it. Goldberg the warrior had transformed into Goldberg the politician. Instead he said, "They are an unfortunate casualty of war."

"But sixteen Hellfire missiles, Ben. What were you thinking?"

Freidman shrugged. "This was a once in a lifetime chance. I wasn't about to let a single one of them escape if I could help it."

"I've been told your infiltrator had enough explosives in those cases to take out everyone at the meeting."

Freidman was more than a little surprised that Goldberg knew about the specifics, but he covered it well. He had intentionally told him little prior to the mission with the tacit understanding that if things went wrong, the prime minister would have deniability. Now someone within his own agency was talking to the prime minister and Freidman would have to find out who.

"David, don't tell me you've lost your stomach for this?"

A scowl formed on Goldberg's face. "Don't confuse the issue, Ben. I'm hearing things from other sources. I'm hearing that you went overboard on this thing . . . that we could have avoided killing all the innocent civilians."

Freidman stopped rocking and looked harshly at his old friend. "Do me a favor and stop calling them innocent. They have been blowing up women and children for years, and you know as well as I that the only way to make them stop is to hit them harder than they hit us."

Goldberg wasn't so sure anymore. When he'd been a young tank commander, he'd thought so. When he'd taken the reins of the country just a few years ago he had thought so, but now, after all the homicide bombs, he was wavering in his conviction. "Ben, these are delicate times. The eyes of the world are upon us."

Freidman was disgusted by what he was hearing. He was tempted to tell Goldberg to step down if he didn't have the constitution to see it through. Instead he said, "The eyes of the world have always been on us. It shouldn't matter any more now than it has in the past. We are not the aggressors here, David, and you know that. They are the ones who have continued to attack us, and both of us have been around long enough to know the only thing they respond to is force."

"But it has to end at some point. We need to find a way."

"What?" snapped Freidman. "Do you want to pull out and build your stupid wall? Have you paid no attention to history? All you will be doing is giving them land that they will use to someday attack us from. You will be remembered as the Neville Chamberlain of Israel."

"I am talking about doing no such thing," replied a terse Goldberg. "And don't sit here and lecture me about being Neville Chamberlain, when just last night you killed a hundred innocent women and children. I've been briefed by the army, Ben. I know there was no bomb factory. Those people did not need to die."

Freidman did not intend for this meeting to head in this direction, but he was not about to back down. "I will admit that some of those deaths are regrettable, but again, only a few. The overwhelming majority of the people who were living on that block were either terrorists or supporters of terrorists. I will lose no sleep over my decision, and I will gladly stand before your cabinet and defend my actions."

"It is not the cabinet that I am worried about," snapped Goldberg. "It is the UN, and it is the Americans. If they decide to look into this, and they find out that there was in fact no bomb factory, you will have done us great harm."

"They will not look into it," promised an irritated Freidman. "I can handle the Americans. I always have and I always will, and as far as the UN is concerned they are a bunch of impotent dilettantes. A week from now this will all be forgotten." Freidman took a swig of beer and confidently added, "I can promise you . . . this will all blow over. Right now, though, we need to stay on the offensive. In the wake of an attack such as last night they will make mistakes. They will seek vengeance and we must be ready to pounce. This is what I propose we do."

Goldberg rocked in his chair and listened as the head of Mossad laid out his plan for how to keep the various Palestinian groups on the defensive. The prime minister was torn as he listened. The old soldier in him very much wanted to press the advantage, but there was another voice in his head that was preaching caution. It was the voice of a politician who had the support of less than half of his country.

So far the only reason he hadn't received a vote of no confidence was because there was no clear challenger willing to step into the ring. His opponents were circling, though, and it wouldn't be long before they pounced. For the time being he would have to keep a close watch on Freidman. If the UN found out what had really happened in Hebron, his cabinet would turn on him in a second, and Israel would once again be forced back to the peace table with weak leadership at the reins of power.

FORTY-FIVE

It was Sunday night, it was late and Mitch Rapp sat awkwardly behind the wheel of his sedan, his body contorted in such a way as to keep his right butt cheek from touching the seat. Medically speaking, the ass was not a bad spot to be shot; no vital organs, just a lot of muscle and fat. In terms of general comfort, though, it sucked. To the amusement of Coleman and his men, Rapp had flown all the way back from the Philippines either standing or lying on his stomach.

With the mission a complete success, and Rapp's long-term health not an issue, the men were able to make light of his situation. For the most part Rapp took the ribbing well. The humor was at least a welcome distraction from having to dwell on what awaited him when he got home.

Relationships, he was finding, were tricky things. He'd already learned that often his recollection of what had been said, or promised, varied greatly from his wife's. He'd been searching his memory for the last day trying to remember if he had ever specifically promised to stay out of situations where he might be shot. Most of these conversations were vague by nature of the secrecy that went along with his job, but he seemed to remember some reassurances he'd made that he wouldn't do anything stupid. Something told him that she would classify getting shot in the ass as downright moronic.

Ultimately, however, he realized that this legalistic approach, while an inventive defense, was worthless. Nothing specifically had ever been agreed upon or said, but there were clearly expectations in place. Anna was not a judge or jurist, so any case pleaded on the grounds of technicalities would be unwise. She was his wife and no amount of truth or logic would save him from her wrath.

This briefly led him to the conclusion that he would need to stall and fabricate a story. The Anderson family was currently recuperating at the naval hospital in Pearl Harbor. Rapp had told Kennedy that he wanted to stay with the family for a few days and handle their debriefing. He was hoping to stretch the debriefing into a full week of recuperation for his own tender wound. In addition to that, he felt it would be fairly easy to fake a surfing accident on a coral reef. All he'd need to do was shred a pair of swim trunks and scrape himself up with some coral. It would hurt like hell, but it would pale in comparison to what his wife would do to him if she found out he'd been shot.

Kennedy had dismissed his request immediately, saying that something had happened in Israel, and she needed him back in Washington immediately. A plane would be waiting for him in Pearl Harbor and he wasn't to waste a minute. Ever since that conversation he'd been struggling to find a way out of an impossible situation. Somewhere over the western United States he'd come to the awful conclusion that he would have to face the wrath of his wife head-on.

This was all new to him, this feeling of dread. Relationships for Rapp had always been fairly uncomplicated. Since the death of his college sweetheart, he had never allowed anyone to get that close to him. Part of it was his job. Intimacy involved honesty, and his job precluded allowing any woman to really know him.

There had been a torrid affair with Donatella Rahn, an Israeli spy, that had lasted on and off for several years. In certain ways Donatella knew him better than anyone. It was a volatile relationship prone to great highs and depressing lows, and in a certain sense they were too much alike to ever marry, although she sure would have liked to have tried.

There had been plenty of other relationships, but never one so serious as to make him want to change. Anna had altered all that. Before her, if someone asked too many questions, or demanded too much of him, he found the nearest exit and never looked back. Relationships had always been easy, because they were always on his terms, and as soon as those terms were challenged or questioned it was over.

Now, everything was different. There was no walking away, no my place and your place, it was now their place. He had married Anna because he wanted to spend the rest of his life with her. She made him want to be a better man, and deep down inside he knew it was for all the right reasons.

But right now, driving down this dark, rural Maryland road he dreaded seeing her reaction. In a way he hoped she would lash out at him and get it over with. The alternative was too painful to think of. Anna was a fiercely stubborn woman. The worst thing she could do to him was withdraw her love and affection.

Rapp turned into their driveway and swallowed hard. He'd called her earlier in the day when they'd landed in California to refuel, and told her he'd be in around midnight. It was now closer to one o'clock and he hoped she would be asleep. The front porch light was on but that was about it.

Rapp parked on the new pad next to the single-car garage so Anna could get her car out in the morning if she left first. Carefully, Rapp rolled out of the car seat and stood still for a moment. Every time he placed weight on his right foot it felt like someone was sticking a knife into the wound. The doctor onboard the *Belleau Wood* gave him a pair of crutches that he'd left at the airport. This whole shot in the ass thing was going to be handled on a need-to-know basis, and Anna was the only one who needed to know. As far as everyone else was concerned he'd pulled his hamstring.

After grabbing his bag from the trunk he limped over to the front door like an invalid. When he inserted his key, the dog began barking. Rapp opened the door and quietly greeted his mutt.

"Hi, Shirley." Rapp patted her head and then keyed in the code to turn off the alarm.

Somewhere in the house he thought he heard music playing. Anna had left the small light over the kitchen stove on, but other than that the first floor was dark. In the faint light cast from the porch Rapp saw a piece of paper sitting on the stairs. He picked up the linen card and opened it. It was addressed, *My Dear Husband, I've missed you terribly. Hurry upstairs!*

Looking at the note, Rapp let out a long sigh and then started gingerly up the stairs, his left foot taking each upward step carefully followed by his right. By the time he reached the top step he could tell the music was coming from the bedroom. He approached the open doorway with trepidation, torn between a deep yearning to hold her in his arms and the fear of how she would react when she discovered his wound.

The room was lit with candles and there she was, lying in the middle of the bed in a black silk nightgown propped up against an array of plush pillows with one leg languidly crossed over the other. She gave him a devilish smile and held out her hand.

Rapp's brain was racing in opposite directions. Part of him wanted to tear off his clothes and jump into bed with her, and another part of him was saying that he needed to explain a few things before he got naked. For the short term, the path of least resistance and most enjoyment won out. Rapp moved across the room smiling at his gorgeous wife.

Stopping at the side of the bed he reached out and held her hand, and for a moment all of his worries melted when he looked into her sparkling emerald eyes. She tugged, pulling him closer. Rapp bent at the waist only a few inches and was instantly shocked back to reality. The fresh wound stopped him in his tracks, sending signals screaming to his brain not to bend farther.

Rapp recovered by pulling Anna toward him. She got up on her knees and wrapped her arms around his waist. "I missed you, honey."

"I see that," replied Rapp as he cupped her face in his hands and kissed her on the lips.

"Did you miss me?"

"You know I did." Rapp smiled. "More than you can imagine."

"Oh, I think I can imagine." She wrapped her arms around his back and squeezed tight.

Rapp held her head against his chest and laughed like a little boy. "Did you have a good week?"

"No." Anna reached up and slid his jacket over his shoulders, letting it fall to the floor. "How could I have had a good week without you?" Next she grabbed the leather holster of his Beretta and slid it over his shoulders. The daughter of a Chicago police officer, she knew enough not to let the weapon drop to the floor. Carefully, she lowered it and set it on the jacket.

Rapp admired her slim figure under the thin black silk and let his hands begin to explore. Anna tugged at his shirt and began unbuttoning it while she tilted her head back and offered her lips to her husband. Rapp kissed her, knowing he should stop her from undressing him and explain what had happened, but he couldn't. He didn't want it to stop.

Anna tore off his shirt and broke away from the kiss. Pushing herself back she ran her hands over his bare chest and down around his sides. She took in his lean strong body and let out a lustful moan. Before Rapp could react, her hands slid from his sides down and around to his butt. Anna looked into his eyes with a playful hunger and squeezed with a force that matched her passion.

There was a split second in Rapp's mind where time stood still. Everything froze and his mouth and eyes opened in anticipation of what was about to happen. And then the pain emanating from Anna's grip shot through his body like a lightning bolt. His entire body went rigid and he reached for his wife's hands. Prying them loose, he stepped back and closed his mouth and eyes as a wave of nausea washed over him.

"What's wrong?" asked a startled and concerned Anna.

Rapp held on to her hands and waited for the pain to subside. In a weak attempt to lighten the situation, his painful expression lessened into a grimace but not quite a smile. "Um . . ." His brain searched for the right words but they weren't coming.

"What's wrong? What did I do?" Anna stepped off the bed, holding her hands out gently.

"You didn't do anything," Rapp managed to say. "It's just something that happened to me."

"You're hurt?" Anna looked confused. "Why didn't you say something to me . . . what's wrong?"

The questions kept coming, as she moved closer and he backed away, in a weak attempt to buy some time. "Honey, it's not a big deal . . . I just suffered a little injury while I was in the Philippines."

"What kind of injury . . . let me see it."

Rapp held on to her hands. "No . . . you don't need to see it. It's no big deal."

Anna detected the look of guilt on his face and seized upon it. "What do you mean I don't need to see it? I'm your wife."

"Honey," Rapp said in a lame attempt to calm her, "it's really no big deal."

Anna released him and took a step back, placing her hands on her hips. With a menacing look she stared him right in his face and said, "You are trying to hide something from me, Mitchell Rapp, and you'd better come clean right now, or we are going to have serious trouble."

Rapp let out a nervous sigh. He was boxed in with nowhere to go. Defeated and embarrassed he said, "I was shot during a hostage rescue and—"

"Shot!" screamed Anna. "Oh my God, where? Are you all right?"

"Yeah . . . yeah, I'm fine."

Concerned and puzzled, Anna asked, "So where were you shot?"

"Um . . ." Rapp hesitated and then in a slightly embarrassed tone said, "In the ass, but don't worry, I'll be fine . . . it just hurts a lot."

Confusion spread across her face. "How did you get shot?"

"I can't talk about that," Rapp replied with as much confidence as he could muster. "It's classified."

Anna placed her hands on her hips and looked angrily at her husband. "Classified my ass! You're my damn husband for a week, you come home one night and tell me you have to leave town on an urgent matter and that, oh by the way, you won't be doing any more of that James Bond stuff that you used to do." She stabbed a finger at his chest, backing him into the corner. "You lied to me, Mitchell."

"No"—Rapp kept his hands out in front of him— "that's not true, honey."

"Don't bullshit me, Mitchell! And then to add insult to injury I run into your boss at the White House on Friday night and she tells me you're over in the Philippines supervising the rescue of that family of Americans. Irene told me you were on some ship and out of harm's way." Folding her arms tightly across her chest she added, "I can't believe I was dumb enough to trust her."

Rapp was completely caught off guard that his boss had confided in his wife. Shocked, he asked, "Irene told you about the mission?"

"Yes." Anna got right in his face. "And don't try to change the subject, or hide behind all that national security crap. If you want this marriage to survive you'd better come clean with me right now. How in the hell did you get shot?"

There was no more room to maneuver. "I was shot during the hostage rescue."

"So you weren't on the ship, you were right there in the thick of it?"

After hesitating for a second he said, "Yes."

Anna began shaking her head. Through clenched teeth she snarled, "That bitch. She lied to me." Looking her husband in the eye, she said, "Your boss sat there and lied to me at the White House. She ordered you to lead this hostage rescue, and then had the audacity to tell me you were safe." She clenched her fists and let out an angry scream. "You're done working for her, and when I see her . . . *boy*, am I going to let her have it."

Rapp held up his hands in an effort to calm his wife. Caring too much for Irene to let her take the heat for something she didn't do wasn't his style, and in addition, something told him that when the two most important women in his life got together and compared notes they would discover that it was not Irene's fault.

"Anna, don't blame this on Irene."

"Why shouldn't I?" she snapped.

"Because . . . as far as she knew I was not directly involved in the operation."

Anna took a moment to try to decipher the importance of what her husband had just said. "What do you mean? She's your boss!"

"Well . . . she . . . just . . . um . . . she's busy. She doesn't have time to micromanage something that's happening thousands of miles away." Rapp watched nervously as his wife's face twisted into a skeptical frown. Trying to stop her from scrutinizing his words too closely he said, "Hey, the important thing is I'm home, and I'm safe." Smiling, he added, "I've got a little scrape that you won't even notice in a week or two."

"What are you talking about?" shouted an incredulous Anna. "You were shot in the ass!" She reached out to take a swat at his butt, but he blocked her.

"Honey, let's calm down."

"Don't honey me! And don't tell me to calm down! A couple of inches in the other direction and you could have been hit in an artery, or maybe even your dick . . . you stupid macho jerk."

"But I wasn't. I'm fine . . . don't worry about it . . . it won't happen again."

"Yeah, right," snarled Anna without an ounce of sincerity. "So tell me something, Mr. Big Shot . . . Mr. Tip of the Spear." Anna used her fingers to make mocking quotation marks in reference to several articles that had been written about his role in America's battle against terrorism. "You're pretty high up on the totem pole. In fact the last time I checked you only take orders from two people. "The president and Irene. Isn't that right?" Anna poked him in the chest with a finger.

Rapp chose not to answer the question.

"So if Irene didn't order you to be involved in the rescue, then who did? I doubt it was the president."

"Um . . ." Rapp hesitated, then decided to keep his mouth shut.

"You did, didn't you?"

Slowly he began to nod and then said, "Yeah."

"You asshole. You lied to me."

"No, I didn't," Rapp said, shaking his head.

"Don't even try it, Mitchell." Anna shook her fist at him. "You told me you were done with this type of stuff."

"No . . . I never said that."

Anna took a deep breath trying to gain some composure, and then let out a bansheelike scream. Rapp put his hands out to grab her shoulders and try to calm her, but she retreated too quickly.

She shook her fist at him, saying, "Oh, I swear to God, I could hit you right now." Anna's jaw was set and her fists were clenched in rage. She needed to get away from him, to sort things out, to try to make sense of how she had been so naive. She turned and took a step toward the door.

Rapp let his hands fall and started to follow her. "Anna, don't worry. Everything is going to be fine."

The *don't worry* part was what really got to her. It was only her life they were discussing. The man she loved more than anyone in the world had lied to her and then got shot and she was being told not to worry as if they'd had some slight misunderstanding. It was too much to handle. Her entire body tight with rage, she spun and delivered a clean punch to her unsuspecting husband.

Rapp would have been able to block the blow if his eyes had been open, but unfortunately, they were closed while he cursed himself out for being so monumentally stupid. The blow stopped him dead in his tracks, causing him to stumble back a step. Instinctively, his hands snapped up in defense as he prepared to grab hold of his wife's wrists, but she was done with him. She stormed from the room with tears welling in her eyes. Rapp was left alone in the bedroom to ponder the mess he had created.

FORTY-SIX

"Trust me, I'm not happy about it either," said an unusually agitated Irene Kennedy into the phone that she was clutching.

Mitch Rapp stood in the doorway of his boss's office following the conversation in complete shock and trying to make sense of what was happening. It appeared that his worst nightmare was taking place before his very eyes. Things were spiraling out of control and, for Mitch, who was very much accustomed to being in charge, it was unnerving.

Rapp's body was stiff from sleeping on the couch, and his rear end hurt almost as badly as it had right after he'd been shot. His left eye was slightly swollen, and a headache seemed to be just over the horizon. Rapp stood on the threshold of the sun-filled office, and wondered what forces had allowed this cruel alliance to form against him. The more he listened to his boss the worse things looked for him.

"No." Kennedy shook her head while holding the phone. "No . . . Oh, that's great," the director of the CIA said with rare sarcasm. She looked up at Rapp disapprovingly from behind her brown glasses. "No, he didn't bother to tell me that he'd been shot in the *ass."* She scowled at him, and pointed sternly at a chair in front of her desk.

In all of his years of knowing Kennedy, he had never seen her show this much emotion. Last night, with his wife, was bad enough, but Kennedy had always been someone he could depend on. This just might be intolerable. Rapp stepped into the office and closed the heavy soundproof door. The administrative assistants didn't need to hear this. He walked slowly across the large office as his boss continued discussing his bad behavior with his wife. The whole thing was very unsettling.

"No," Kennedy said, "you don't need to apologize to me. I can see why you thought it was my fault." She stopped talking and listened for a few seconds. Then in response to whatever it was that Anna had said, she replied, "Well, that is very nice of you to say. I feel the same way, and believe me you can count on me for the same thing. I think the two of us are more than up to the task."

Rapp closed his eyes and let out a low groan. He felt like he was back in grade school, standing in the school office listening to his principal and mother conspire against him on the phone.

"Yes, I'll be the judge of what is classified and what isn't." She spun her chair around, turning her back to Rapp. Then shaking her head she said, "Yes. Don't listen to him anymore. If you have any questions pick up the phone and call me." Again Kennedy paused to listen and then said, "Exactly! I couldn't agree more. I might even recommend that he spend some time with one of our in-house psychiatrists."

Rapp stared at the back of his boss's head and said, "Over my dead body."

Kennedy spun her leather chair back around and shot

him a glare. "All right, Anna. I'll see you in a couple hours, and I've got you down for drinks on Thursday at six. Thank you. . . . Okay. Oh, and I wouldn't worry about that other thing. He's tough, and as I already said, he more than had it coming." She nodded several times, and then said, "All right . . . bye-bye."

Kennedy slowly replaced the handset, keeping her inquisitive eyes locked on Rapp. "Well, that was an interesting conversation."

"I bet," replied Rapp with no effort to conceal his displeasure.

Kennedy looked at his face. "Nice shiner. Where'd you get it?"

Doubting her sincerity he said, "I slipped in the shower."

"Really. At least you didn't fall on your behind." Kennedy pointed to one of the chairs in front of her desk and said, "Sit."

Rapp shook his head. "No thanks . . . I think I'll stand."

"Sit," replied his boss in a voice more stern than anything he'd ever heard from her.

Rapp carefully lowered himself into one of the chairs and with a fake smile said, "There. Are you happy?"

"Hardly." Kennedy snatched her glasses from her face and placed both elbows on her desk. "You have got some major explaining to do." The reserved, analytical Kennedy was amazed at how good it felt to let her pent-up anger out.

Rapp, put in the unusual position of having to remain the calm one, said, "I think everyone needs to relax a bit."

"Nice try, but you were way out of bounds on this one. When in the hell were you planning on telling me that you were shot?"

"Oh, come on, Irene, you've got enough stuff to worry

about with running this place." Rapp dismissed her concerns with a wave of his hand as if one of her top advisors and best operatives getting shot was utterly trivial. "You don't need to worry about every little injury to one of your people in the field."

An offended, angry expression fell across her face. Her brown eyes focused intently on him and she said, "That hurt."

Rapp was completely mystified. His head hurt, his eye hurt and his ass was absolutely killing him. How could a few words "hurt"? "What are you talking about?"

"You," she started in an angry tone, "are not just simply one of my many employees. Next to my son and my mother you are probably the dearest friend to me in the entire world, so I would appreciate it if you wouldn't insult my feelings by portraying me as some detached boss who has no concern for her employees."

"That's not what I meant," said Rapp as he shook his head.

"That is what you said, and what you meant, and don't insult me further by trying to re-tailor your words."

"Oh, for Christ's sake." Rapp started to stand. "I can't take all of this estrogen."

Kennedy stood abruptly and yelled, "Then take a little testosterone! Sit your ass back down, Mister!"

"My ass hurts too much to sit, thank you very much!"

"Don't try to turn this around on me, Mitchell. This is not my fault. When you called me requesting that I get full authority for you to plan the hostage rescue you knew exactly what you were doing. You waited until the real chain of command was asleep, and then you went in and launched the rescue, without our final approval." She angrily pointed a finger at him and said, "And you put yourself right in the thick of it."

Looking down at her desk, she picked up a file. "This is the after action report filed by Lieutenant Jackson. Did you think I wasn't going to find out?" She threw the file down onto her desk. "You crawled into that damn camp by yourself and almost got killed."

"Almost got killed," Rapp mocked her. "Where the hell have you been for the last fifteen years? Every time I walk out the door I almost get killed. That's part of my job."

"Not any longer. You're not twenty-five anymore. We have other people who can lead the charge. You're not some buck private storming the beaches. You have one of the best counterterrorism minds in this entire town, and we can't afford to lose you over some macho need to be right in the thick of it."

"Are you done?" Rapp looked at her defiantly. He knew there was some truth to her words, but he was sick of being on the receiving end of another tongue-lashing. "Could you try to see past your bruised ego at being left out of the loop for a few hours and thank me for a job well done? General Moro is dead, an entire sixty-plus-man force of Abu Sayyaf guerrillas has been silently exterminated, we have a new commander of the Filipino Special Forces who will vigorously take the war to the Muslim terrorists, the Anderson family has been rescued, and not a single asset was lost in the process." Rapp held up his hand. "The only problem was that yours truly got shot."

Kennedy decided to remove some of the emotion from the discussion. As good as it felt at first, she knew it was counterproductive. Especially when dealing with a bull like Mitch. He needed to be finessed, not pounded on. Thoughtfully, she nodded and said, "Thank you for a job well done."

Rapp immediately relaxed. He did not enjoy fighting with Kennedy, especially on the heels of what had happened last night. She had always understood him—probably even better than he understood himself. "And I'm sorry if I hurt your feelings. You know I think of you and Tommy as family. . . . It's just that . . ." He shook his head in confusion. "I've always been on the front line. You know that. I've always been left alone to make decisions as I see fit in the field. We handled the General Moro thing without consulting you, and I saw no reason why I needed to call Washington and ask for the green light on the hostage rescue."

"You didn't want to consult with us," answered Kennedy, "because you didn't want to hear us tell you that you couldn't go on the mission."

Rapp thought about it for a moment and then admitted, "Maybe."

"Well, let's just chalk this one up as a learning experience. You're probably having a more difficult time transitioning into your new duties than either of us predicted."

Rapp shook his head and frowned. "I'm not having any problems."

"Yes you are. In not-so-subtle ways. We need to sit down and clearly outline the parameters of your job." She watched Rapp frown and said, "Don't worry, I just don't want any ambiguity in the future. You're too valuable to this country, and too valuable to me as a friend, to be risking your life needlessly."

Somewhat reluctantly, Rapp replied, "All right."

In a conciliatory tone Kennedy asked, "Is there anything else you'd like to discuss?"

"No . . . not really. I'd just like a little less screaming and a little more gratitude."

"I can work on that." Kennedy smiled. "And as far as the gratitude thing is concerned . . . well, I think you're going to get plenty of that."

FORTY-SEVEN

R app had never really taken the time to look around the Oval Office. He was usually ushered in, sat where he was told, and then left as soon as his audience with the president was over. This time, having declined to sit, he meandered around the room checking out the various pieces of art and waiting for the president to appear.

It was painful knowing that Anna was downstairs in her office. During the ride over from Langley he had relayed his version of last night's events to his boss. She informed him in the gentlest of ways that he had neglected to do the single most important thing, which was to simply say he was sorry.

Rapp told Kennedy he felt torn. Yes, he was sorry that he'd hurt his wife's feelings, but she didn't marry an advertising executive. His injury shouldn't have been entirely unexpected. Kennedy stressed that, expected or unexpected, it didn't change the fact that in her mind Anna could have lost the man she had just promised to spend the rest of her life with. Kennedy asked Rapp how he would feel if the shoe were on the other foot and it was Anna who had been shot.

The thought of losing Anna sent such a pain through

him that he began to see her point more clearly. When he was done with this meeting he would have to find her and apologize. Maybe he could even milk the shiner for a little sympathy. Despite his injury, he desperately wanted to be alone with her.

Rapp was studying a portrait of Thomas Jefferson when Valerie Jones entered the office. For some reason she was all smiles, which as far as Rapp could recollect was a first.

"Good morning, Irene," she said.

Kennedy replied with a simple, "Hello, Val."

Jones turned her attention to Rapp. "How are you, Mitch?"

Rapp remained facing the portrait of one of America's greatest presidents. Instead of turning around he looked over his shoulder at the chief of staff. He and Jones had never gotten along. In fact, he could think of no other woman who he currently detested more.

Regarding her suspiciously he answered, "I've been better," then returned his attention to the portrait of Jefferson.

"Oh . . . that's too bad. How'd you get the black eye?"

Fortunately for Rapp the president entered the room before he could answer. "Sorry I'm late." Hayes dropped a leather-bound folder on his desk and hurried over to greet Rapp.

"Mitch, once again you saved the day. Great job over there in the Philippines."

"Thank you, sir." Rapp took his hand.

The president's attention locked in on Rapp's shiner. "Did things get a little rough for you over there?"

"Not too bad." Rapp shrugged it off.

"It looks like it hurts."

Rapp shook his head. "No . . . not really. I've had worse."

The president nodded. "Yes, I suppose you have. Well, listen, have a seat." Hayes gestured to the couch opposite Kennedy and Jones. "There are a few things we want to discuss with you."

"If it's all right with you, sir, I'd prefer to stand."

Hayes stopped and gave Rapp a questioning glance.

"It's my back, sir. If I sit down, I might not be able to get up."

"Oh I see. By all means . . . stand if it feels better." Hayes took his usual chair in front of the fireplace. "Well," said the president, "at eleven o'clock the secretary of state and the attorney general are going to hold a joint press conference announcing the prosecution of Assistant Secretary of State Petry and Ambassador Cox."

Rapp was shocked. He'd figured the president would string him along for another few weeks, and then let the issue die down. "That's good news, sir."

Hayes looked up at Rapp, who was standing behind the couch on his right. "I'm told Mr. McMahon has Ambassador Cox in custody, and is on his way back?"

Rapp nodded. "That's right. The embassy staff was told the ambassador had to rush home for a family emergency."

"Good. The National Security Council is meeting next door as we speak. If you're still up for it I've arranged for you to be present when Assistant Secretary Petry is arrested."

"I wouldn't miss it for the world."

Hayes nodded and then turned to Kennedy. "Now on to an issue that isn't so good. . . . What in the hell is going on in Israel?"

"I'm working on that, sir." The director of the CIA retrieved a file from her briefcase and pulled out a single sheet of paper. She handed it to the president and said, "That is a list of the terrorists who were killed in the attack."

Hayes put on his reading glasses and scanned the names. "Holy cow! Is this for real?"

"As far as I can tell, yes, but the CTC is working to verify the names through other sources."

President Hayes stood to reread the list for a second time. "What's the death count?"

"Again, the CTC is trying to verify the number, but right now the Palestinians are saying over one hundred people were killed."

"Is that possible?" asked a skeptical Hayes.

Kennedy hesitated and then said, "Yes."

"But I thought they always exaggerated those numbers."

"They might not have to this time."

Hayes kept studying the list, even though he was thinking about something else. "Of those hundred people, how many were terrorists?"

"Right now we're guessing anywhere from twenty to forty, but I stress that is only a guess."

"And the whole bomb factory story that the Israeli's have been putting out?"

Kennedy shook her head. "It doesn't hold up. We have satellite imagery and radio intercepts of the attack. There was an initial explosion that we haven't been able to pinpoint. That blast destroyed the house where we think the meeting was taking place, and then there were a series of explosions that followed."

"Where did those come from?" asked the president.

Kennedy hesitated for a second, knowing the president would not like the answer. "They appear to have come from helicopter-launched missiles."

"Appear to have?" Hayes wanted a more precise answer.

"The imagery people are saying they were Hellfire missiles launched from Apaches."

"Back up a minute," ordered the president. "Freidman told you that his people found out about this meeting and fired two missiles into the target area that ignited a secondary explosion that leveled the entire block. Correct?"

"That's what he told me, sir."

"And now you're telling me," said Hayes with a frown creasing his brow, "there was an initial explosion that we have not been able to identify, that was followed by a series of explosions that were caused by Hellfire missiles."

"Yes."

"How many?"

"Sixteen of them, sir."

"Sixteen?" asked an incredulous president.

"I'm afraid so."

"Why so many?"

"I have absolutely no idea."

"Have you asked him?"

Kennedy considered the question. "No I haven't, sir. I wanted to discuss it with you first."

"Well, by all means"—Hayes gestured to the bulky secure phone on his desk—"get him on the phone."

"Sir," cautioned the director of the CIA. "I'd like to do a little more digging before we confront him."

Hayes was not in a patient mood. "The Palestinian ambassador to the UN is going to address the assembly this afternoon and demand that the UN make a full inquiry into this mess. The Saudi ambassador called me this morning to protest the slaughter of hundreds of innocent civilians." Hayes shook his fist in anger. "This thing is not simply going to go away. I can get our ambassador to delay a vote by the Security Council until the end of the week, but we will not be able to put it off indefinitely. I need real answers, and I need to know what in the hell the Israelis are up to. I also need to know what our allies know. If we know they're lying, there's a good chance a few other countries know it too."

"I'll get started on it right away, sir."

"And Freidman," snarled the president. "I want him to either start playing by the rules he agreed to, or we will terminate our arrangement and he can kiss his ass goodbye."

Kennedy nodded and told herself now was not the time to disagree with the president. The entire relationship with Freidman was fraught with potential disaster. The president could call up the Israeli prime minister and demand that Freidman be removed from his position as director general of Mossad, but even with the evidence they had, it might not work. Ben Freidman had files on everybody. She had a sneaking suspicion that if Freidman was ever really backed into a corner he would use those files to take down anyone and everyone. There wasn't a thing that he wouldn't rationalize if it was done to help preserve either himself or his country.

In a confident voice, Kennedy told her boss, "We'll find out what really happened over there, sir."

"Good." Only slightly satisfied, the president turned to Rapp. "And, Mitch, I want you to take a very personal interest in this thing. You know a side of Freidman that no one else at Langley does. I want to know why he's lying to us, and I want to know what you think we should do about it."

"Yes, sir." Rapp had a few ideas, but they would take some looking into. In the meantime he was betting on his initial suspicion. Ben Freidman had only one master, his country, and no matter how closely they held his feet to the fire, he would never betray Israel.

FORTY-EIGHT

The National Security Council was one of those
Washington terms that encompassed many things. In
its truest sense the Council was made up of the president
and a handful of very senior advisors. In a broader sense it
represented an entire staff that coordinated the flow of intelligence between various agencies and departments
under the executive branch and the White House. One
such group within that staff was the Counterterrorism
Support Group. As their name indicated they were
charged with handling all issues involving terrorism, such
as the kidnapping of the Anderson family by Abu Sayyaf.

Due to the leaks that occurred at the State Department
during the initial hostage rescue, the Counterterrorism
Support Group had been left out of the loop during the
second and successful hostage rescue. This intentional
breach of procedure was missed by no one. In a town
where being in the know was the ultimate sign of power,
there were a lot of bruised egos. The rumors had been fast
and furious as to why, and through a few well-designed
leaks, all were led to believe that their exclusion was due
to a power play by none other than Mitch Rapp.

These leaks, and his reputation in general, were the

cause of the icy reception that awaited Mitch Rapp
when he entered the National Security Council conference room on the fourth floor of the Old Executive Office Building across the street from the West Wing. The
attendees, over a dozen of them, all stopped what they
were doing and looked up at the unannounced visitor.
The Department of Defense, the FBI, the CIA, the State
Department and Homeland Security were all represented. These were people just two rungs from the top.
They carried great responsibility, they worked tirelessly
and they received very little public recognition. Of the
people in the room, only Jake Turbes from the CIA knew
Rapp.

They all knew of him, to be sure, but not a one of
them had ever said more than hello to him. Some of them
respected him, a few despised him, mostly due to the embarrassment they were now forced to endure, but to a
one, they all feared him. Here in their midst was a cold-
blooded killer, who had dealt with the national security
issues they wrestled with every day, in a much more real
and final way.

He was a man who came to meetings unannounced
and rarely spoke. He was a man who had the president's
ear, respect and gratitude. He was a man who each feared
could end any of their careers if he so chose. So when
he entered the long narrow room all of the attendees
squirmed a bit, and to make matters worse, instead of
taking a seat at the table, he remained standing.

Rapp positioned himself in such a way that he could
observe Assistant Secretary of State Amanda Petry. Of all
the attendees only two, besides Rapp, had any idea what
was in store. Jake Turbes of the CIA and Don Keane of the
FBI were both in the know. Rapp kept himself from making eye contact with them and instead looked to Patty

Hadley, the deputy national security advisor. He nodded for her to continue with the meeting.

She smiled a bit awkwardly and said, "Well, you're just the man we were looking for." Her comment was followed by some uncomfortable laughter.

Rapp allowed a wry smile to form on his lips. His problem was not with Hadley. "Fire away."

"We're all trying to figure out why we were kept in the dark on this one."

Rapp directed his response to Hadley. "A decision was made to keep this operation as close to the vest as possible."

She listened to the answer and then after a moment asked, "Why?"

"Let's just say that our previous rescue attempt didn't go over so well."

After a long moment of silence, Steve Gordon, the coordinator for counterterrorism at the State Department, was the first to speak. His pride had been damaged enough that he felt he had to speak for the group. "I hardly think the people in this room were responsible for the failure of the first rescue attempt."

"Really?" asked Rapp, his tone a bit menacing.

Gordon was slightly taken aback. He mustered up a bit more courage and reiterated his point. "Yes."

"I wouldn't be so sure," said Rapp as he leaned against the wall and folded his arms across his chest, a red file shoved under his left arm. "Any other questions?" This time he looked directly at Amanda Petry. He knew her type. Her righteous indignation would never allow his accusation to go unchallenged.

She looked back at him, barely able to conceal her contempt, and completely oblivious to the role she'd played in the disaster of a week ago. The false belief that the rest of the group supported her gave her the confidence to say, "Mr. Rapp, you may not think very highly of us, but you should at least respect the fact that we care about this country every bit as much as you do, and we work very hard at our jobs."

Rapp was simmering for the moment. He would blow later. This was a role he relished. It was an opportunity to remind everybody just how high the stakes were. What unfolded in this room in the next five minutes would be spread all over Washington by week's end. It would be whispered about around the coffeepots and water coolers, and it would grow and become more sensational with each retelling, and in the end people would be reminded that national security was something to be taken very seriously.

"To respond to your first point, I doubt very much that you care about this country as much as I do, and as far as your second point is concerned, I have no doubt that you all work very hard, but that by itself doesn't cut it. You people aren't on the board of some corporation. You are entrusted to help protect the national security of this country, and to be brutally honest with you, working hard isn't enough." Rapp's eyes never left Petry's.

Her nostrils flared just a bit and unable to contain herself, she said, "The State Department plays a very important role in this country's national security, Mr. Rapp, whether you like it or not. And for us to do our job, we need to be kept abreast of what is going on."

"Kept abreast," Rapp repeated her words and slowly bobbed his head as if he were taking them very seriously. "Tell me, Ms. Petry, can you think of a single reason why the rescue operation was launched without consulting this committee?"

"I'd say somebody such as yourself advised the president that we be kept in the dark," answered Petry with a look of disdain on her face.

"Exactly!" said Rapp, his tone rising a bit. "And can you tell me why I would have advised such a move to the president?"

There could be little doubt, by the expression on her face that she hated the man who was questioning her. "I have no idea."

Rapp opened the file under his arm and threw two five-by-eight photographs down on the table. They were head shots of the two dead navy SEALs. "Do you have any idea who these two men are?"

"No," replied an indignant Petry.

"Irv McGee and Anthony Mason. United States Navy. They were killed last week on a little sand beach in the Philippines. Both were married and combined they left behind five kids." Rapp made no effort to retrieve the two photos sitting in the middle of the table. This was as close as any of them would ever get to the two dead warriors, and he wanted to make sure everyone in the room looked at their faces.

"Ms. Petry, can you tell me how these two men ended up dead?" Rapp paused just long enough to see that she wasn't going to answer his question. "I'll tell you how they died," his voice boomed out in anger. "Someone in this room disregarded operational security because they felt the rules didn't apply to them." Petry didn't crack a bit and Rapp asked her, "You have no idea what you did, do you?"

Petry's face was now flushed but she had yet to register what was happening. Blinded by her own belief that she was being wronged, Petry said, "You'd better have a pretty good explanation for this, Mr. Rapp."

The red file flew open and out came the copies of

Petry's e-mails to Ambassador Cox. Rapp slammed them down on the table and yelled, "The *president* decided last week that our embassy in Manila was not to be told in advance about the hostage rescue! You ignored that order and sent Ambassador Cox an e-mail alerting him to the specifics of the rescue! Well, I guess since you work hard, and care about your country, you don't have to adhere to operational security!"

Petry looked at her own e-mail and still refused to admit any wrongdoing. "I hardly see how this ended up causing the deaths of these two men."

"Because, you idiot," screamed Rapp, "Ambassador Cox alerted President Quirino about the operation, who in turn notified General Moro, who just so happens to be a paid asset for Abu Sayyaf! If you would have done what you were told those two men would be alive right now. You and your fucking diplomatic arrogance got them killed, and that's why this committee was kept in the dark."

Rapp stood at the end of the long table, his fists clenched in rage. No one attempted to speak. Amanda Petry sat in shock looking at the two photos, still refusing to believe that a simple e-mail could have caused their deaths. Rapp knew that there were those in Washington who would think what he'd just done was unprofessional and insensitive, but he couldn't have cared less. In his mind this town, especially the national security apparatus, could use a whole lot less sensitivity.

Rapp turned and opened the door. Two FBI agents were waiting outside to arrest Petry. He passed them and started down the hall, his thoughts turning to the two dead SEALs. Their families deserved his sensitivity and sympathy, not Petry.

FORTY-NINE

David had practiced the routine precisely eight times.
He looked like just any other New Yorker as he
walked up Park Avenue, his shoulders set with determination and the collar of his black trench coat turned up both
to conceal his face and to ward off the bite of the cool
March evening air. The pedestrian traffic had died down
from its post-workday peak, but at a quarter past seven
David was far from alone.

Unlike in Jerusalem, however, David did not feel as
though he were being watched. There was an outside
chance that the FBI was trailing him, or an even slimmer
chance that Mossad had somehow followed him to
America, but David was confident in his ability to both
elude and detect surveillance. No, he was alone. He'd
seen the footage of the massacre in Hebron. Ben Freidman would think he had killed his Palestinian informant. The destruction in Hebron was so complete it
would be some time before all the bodies were accounted for.

And as far as the Americans were concerned, they had
their hands full chasing Arab students on expired visas.
David had already changed identities twice since leaving

Hebron and was now traveling with a French passport. His first-class ticket from Nice to Paris to New York had been purchased with an American Express card that matched the name on his passport. He was now Charles Utrillo, a mergers and acquisitions specialist in town to meet with J. P. Morgan. The cover was not deep. If he was arrested, and the FBI looked into his credentials, they would quickly discover it was a sham. The passport and credit card were merely there to ensure entrance into America without raising any suspicion.

This portion of his plan had been relatively easy to put together. The West Bank was rife with arms merchants, and for the right amount of cash almost anything was obtainable. David's purchases were never very large or exotic. Mostly small arms, silencers, ammunition and one very expensive rifle. He preferred dealing with the Russians. They were hungry for cash and despite their recent cooperation with the West, they were still capable of keeping their mouths shut and records closed.

Getting the weapons to the United States had been a little more difficult, but not much. The import-export business, worldwide, was known for not asking too many questions. David had shipped a crate of rugs to a warehouse in Philadelphia and picked it up back in January. Broken down and rolled up within the various rugs were two handguns and a Russian-made VAL Silent Sniper rifle. The weapon fired a 9mm subsonic heavy bullet and was capable of defeating standard body armor at distances up to 400 yards. According to David's information his target wouldn't be wearing anything so cumbersome. The man had reason to celebrate this evening and he wasn't about to put on a bullet-proof vest to dine at his favorite restaurant.

As David crossed 65th Street he glanced to his right.

Halfway down the block stood an old brownstone with bars and steel mesh over all the windows. In front of the house, on the sidewalk, the New York City Police Department had erected a blue and white guardhouse large enough for only one person. A police officer manned the post twenty-four hours a day, seven days a week, just to make sure no one tried anything. David knew this was more to deter protestors and pranksters. The real security was inside the house.

David had been invited there as a guest on many occasions. The brownstone was home to the Permanent Observer Mission of Palestine to the United Nations. The Palestinian ambassador was a friend of David's or, more precisely, a business acquaintance. Ambassador Hamed Ali was a childhood friend of Yasser Arafat's. The posting had been given to Ali as a reward for a lifetime of commitment and loyalty to Arafat. Ali was seventy-five and had a smoker's hack that made it abundantly clear to anyone who cared to listen that he was not long for this world. That helped to ease David's conscience a bit. That and the fact that in his younger days, Ali had sown plenty of death and destruction.

The Palestinian Authority, due to its inability to raise money through taxes or tariffs, depended greatly on foreign aid and charity. David had proved his worth by personally delivering to Ambassador Ali a quarter of a million dollars in the first three months of the year alone. Ali often complained to David that being an ambassador was a very expensive job. Diplomacy was almost always conducted under the pretense of a meal and never a cheap one.

David responded by opening an account for the ambassador at his favorite restaurant, La Goulue. The French restaurant, one of New York's finest, was only two blocks from the ambassador's residence. David just so happened to know that Ali would be dining there this evening. He had spoken with the ambassador earlier in the day, congratulating him on his address to the UN. David had intimated that a celebration was in order. Ali agreed and invited David to join him and several friends at La Goulue. David noted the time, but turned down the invitation. He told the ambassador he needed to catch a flight to the West Coast.

Ali had spoken to a rapt General Assembly, proclaiming that for a real and lasting peace in the Middle East the UN must intercede. He decried the unprovoked attack of innocent Palestinians by the Israeli aggressors over the weekend and demanded that the UN make a full investigation. In response to Israeli claims that the number of casualties had been grossly exaggerated, Ali read off a list of independent journalists and aid workers who were all reporting a death toll in excess of one hundred people.

As soon as Ali was finished, the Israeli ambassador took the floor and assured the assembly that, as a sovereign nation, Israel was more than capable of conducting their own investigation into the matter. In a parting shot the Israeli ambassador recommended to Ali that in the future they should locate their bomb-making factories in less populated areas so as to avoid so much bloodshed. The ambassador's quip was met with jeers and catcalls by the various Arab delegations.

Right on cue Ambassador Joussard of France took to the floor pleading for civility and decorum. In the end, he promised the truth would be known. With the eyes of the international community focused on Hebron, France would work with the other permanent members of the Security Council to get to the bottom of what had happened. When David was finished tonight the UN would be that much closer to intervening. And once an international force was on the ground, a Palestinian state would be that much closer to a reality.

David crossed 66th Street and looked up at the towering behemoth before him. The Seventh Regiment Armory was a colossal architectural throwback. Planted between Park and Lexington Avenues and 66th and 67th Streets, the nineteenth-century building was built to house New York's first regiment sent to fight in the Civil War.

The massive building was no longer home to just the National Guard. It housed a women's shelter, various local and state social services, a restaurant, several nonprofits and a catering business that could handle groups of up to several thousand people.

David turned up the front steps behind a man roughly his age. Taking the steps one at a time he was very conscious of what was under his trench coat. When he entered the building the first thing he noticed was the roar of a crowd coming from the drill hall straight ahead. He didn't bother stopping to investigate. Earlier in the day he'd read the marquee announcing a class reunion for Brooklyn Prep.

David kept moving, turning to his left and going to the end of the hall, past the torn and battled-scarred regimental flags, past the elevator and into the stairwell. In all of his previous visits he had yet to run into someone on the staircase, which was a bit of a surprise considering the condition of the elevator, and the fact that there was a good chance you'd have to share the small metal cage with someone who either suffered from a mental illness or an addiction to crack.

He reached the top floor and then continued up another half flight where he was confronted with the locked door that led out onto the roof. David paused, turning on the two-way radio in his pocket and donning a flesh-colored earpiece. The digitally encrypted device was already programmed to monitor the same channel that the ambassador's security detail was using. David listened for a moment. There was no chatter so he checked his watch. It was 7:21. Ali's reservation was for 7:30, but the man almost always ran five to ten minutes late.

David retrieved a lock pick from his jacket and went to work. He worked the tumblers to perfection. Having done it before, he knew where each one would fall. With the door opened he stepped out of the dim stairwell and into the dark night. After placing a strip of duct tape over the metal frame, he allowed the heavy fire door to close. Standing in the glow of the city lights David casually lit a cigarette.

Several apartment buildings looked down on the Armory. If any of the occupants cared to look out their windows, all they would see was just another desperate smoker trying to enjoy his vice. Slowly, David moved over toward the turret jutting out from the southwest corner. He puffed on the cigarette and looked around, scanning the adjacent buildings for anyone who might be watching him. So far so good.

He had it down to a science. It took Ali anywhere from eighty-three seconds to three minutes and forty-eight seconds to walk from his residence to the restaurant, depending on whether or not he made the lights at Lexington, Park and Madison. David had time. It took him just twenty seconds to assemble the rifle, fifteen if he was really pressed. He would wait until they were on the move before he did that. If by chance someone was watching him, he didn't need them to call the cops.

At 7:29, David heard the familiar voice of one of Ali's bodyguards come over the earpiece. The man was going out to check the street. David took a deep breath and reminded himself of his cause. To make peace, one often had to make war. He repeated the phrase over and over. Men like Ali and Arafat and Freidman would never agree to a real peace. It would take huge pressure from the international community, and America had to be a part of that. They were the only country that could force Israel to sit down and grant the Palestinian people a state, and after tonight the tide would continue to swell.

More chatter came over the radio. The second bodyguard announced that the ambassador was coming out. David had no idea who or how many people would be with him, or if he was meeting his guests at the restaurant. This was the part that he needed to be flexible about. It was out of his control. He started the stopwatch mode on his wristwatch, took one last drag from his cigarette and then stabbed it against the wall of the turret. Well versed in American investigative techniques, David placed the butt in a plastic bag and put it in his pocket, as he had done with each cigarette he had smoked while on the roof. He would leave as little behind for the FBI as possible. From one of his pockets he grabbed a sock filled with rice and placed it in the base of the notch in the wall. It would help to balance the weapon and prevent leaving metal residue from the barrel.

David opened his trench coat, grabbed a thick black barrel and undid the Velcro that held it in place. He slid the barrel into the receiver and twisted it ninety degrees until it clicked into place. Next came the 10-power Leupold scope and a twenty-round magazine. David extended the stock into the locked position, pulled back on the cocking handle and then released it, chambering one of the special 9mm bullets.

Casually, he checked his watch. He was at twenty-nine seconds and counting. David took one last look around and then placed the heavy rifle inside one of the notches in the stonework. Like a medieval archer perched atop a castle wall he prepared himself to take out the enemy. David looked through the scope to make sure everything was as he wished. The range had been checked for the southwest corner of Park and 65th. He'd zeroed the rifle in himself at a state park two hours north of the city. David was extremely accurate with the weapon up to 300 yards. A better marksman could probably take it up to five hundred yards, but David had no kind of need for that distance. Tonight his target would be roughly 145 yards from him.

It was an easy shot with one exception: Ali would be moving and there would be people around him. David checked his watch again. They were coming up on a minute and a half. They must have missed the light at Lexington. David eased his grip on the rifle and scanned the street without the aid of the scope. He would see the bodyguard first, walking several paces ahead, clearing the way.

As expected, the man appeared and stopped at the red light. David eased his eye in behind the scope and put the bodyguard in the center of the crosshairs. Then he moved the weapon to the east and soon found what he was looking for. The ambassador stopped just behind the man and David let out a curse. Ali was with a woman. She had her arm hooked in his and she was standing between David and his target.

The light turned green and group began walking across Park Avenue. One bodyguard in front, the other behind, and Ali and the woman in the middle. David kept breathing in a steady manner and kept his hand relaxed as he followed the group, looking for a shot that wasn't there. When they stepped onto the curb on the other side of Park he made his decision. He hadn't come this far to not take the shot, but neither was he going to kill a woman he did not know. He did not like it, but it was a contingency he'd planned for. He quickly maneuvered the rifle, bringing the crosshairs to bear on the head of the trailing bodyguard.

David squeezed the trigger and the rifle bucked just slightly as the heavy bullet spat from the end of the thick black barrel. He instantly chambered a fresh round and a split second later David had found his next target. The man ahead of Ali was still walking, oblivious to the fact that his friend had suffered a mortal wound and was at this moment falling to the ground. Again, David squeezed the trigger, sending another round on its way.

The rifle settled as another round clicked into the chamber and David steadied the scope on his next and last target. Ali took two more steps before he realized something was wrong. The woman took two and a half steps before she noticed the man falling in front of her. That extra half step that she took was all David needed.

David watched as Ali turned, looking behind him for help from his other guard. The expression on the ambassador's face turned from one of shock to horror as he discovered that he was without protection. Before Ali could react further, David pulled the trigger for a third time and sent a final silent bullet into the head of his intended target.

FIFTY

It was dark outside and the wind was howling off the big bay. Rapp stood in front of the full-length mirror in his bedroom and carefully pulled the bandages back from his wound. It looked like he'd been stepped on by an elephant. The bruising covered almost his entire right butt cheek and had already started to seep down into his leg. The doctors wanted him to stay off his feet for this very reason, but both he and the doctor knew the advice wouldn't be followed. He'd keep taking antibiotics and applying ice when he had the time and he'd make it through just fine. He threw on a pair of sweatpants and a thick cotton T-shirt and carefully made his way down to the kitchen.

Anna was on her way home from work and Rapp was praying that she had calmed down enough that they could talk about last night without getting into another fight. Rapp wasn't much in the mood for any more screaming. He'd thought on and off all day about how he should have handled things with Anna. He'd screwed up to be sure, but he wasn't completely off base. Anna knew who she was marrying. She'd seen him in action before and knew it could be rough. And on top of that her father and two of her brothers were cops. The Philippines had been a successful trip. The Andersons were safe and on their way home, the deaths of the SEALs had been avenged, General Moro had been dealt with, Abu Sayyaf had been routed on their own turf and General Rizal had requested the aid of the CIA in ferreting out any other traitors. It had been a good couple of days for the Agency.

On another front, however, things were not so good. Tensions between the Israelis and the Palestinians were approaching a dangerous level. There was a movement afoot in the United Nations to send in a team of independent inspectors to review what was already being called the Hebron Massacre. New footage was being released by the hour of tiny bodies being pulled from the rubble.

The outrage was building to the point where several Jewish groups had taken to the airwaves protesting the heavy hand of Prime Minister Goldberg. Having been on the receiving end of perhaps the most horrific act of mass genocide in the history of mankind, Jews were very sensitive to the murder of women and children. As a people they held the moral high ground when it came to suffering, and the last thing many of them ever wanted to see was their own people committing atrocities that drew comparisons to the Nazis.

After returning from the White House, Rapp had gone straight to the CIA's Counterterrorism Center on the ground floor of the new headquarters building where he was brought up to speed by Jake Turbes. He had been Kennedy's replacement when she'd vacated her post to become the new DCI. Kennedy had handpicked him with the consent of President Hayes. Turbes was a veteran of both Laos and Afghanistan. He was one of the few people left at Langley with any real field experience. This probably more than any other reason was why Rapp got along with him.

It was amazing that Turbes, a maverick from Louisiana, had survived the Agency's purges. The risk-averse CIA of the nineties did not treat case officers like Turbes well. He was a real throwback, and Rapp suspected that Turbes had only survived the various shakeups by keeping a low profile and a little black book.

Rapp had confirmed a rumor that one of Turbes's bosses had indeed tried to fire him. The boss, a slick climber, didn't like Turbes's rough style and gunslinger attitude and wanted him out. With thirty years under his belt Turbes was informed that he was being forced into early retirement. Turbes politely declined. The boss told him he didn't have a choice. Turbes then told the boss that he knew all about the girlfriend he kept in Cathedral Heights and that he would be more than happy to tell both his wife and the counterespionage guys that he was keeping a flame on the side. The boss decided to rethink Turbes's early retirement, but that wasn't enough for the fifty-three-year-old veteran. He told the supervisor he had twenty-four hours to resign from that Agency or he could kiss his reputation and family good-bye. The next morning the boss resigned.

Right now Turbes was very unsettled about what was going on in the Middle East. Prior to the terrorist attacks of September 11, the director of the CIA's CTC was afforded a fair amount of anonymity. That was no longer the case. Congressmen and senators now called frequently demanding to know what dangers were lurking on the horizon and what the CTC was doing to thwart them. Turbes had been forced to hire six extra people just to handle all the increased liaison duties between the Hill and the various federal departments. Turbes agreed with the belief that intelligence wasn't any good unless it was shared with the people who might be able to do something about it, but the politicians by and large did not fall into the category.

As far as Turbes was concerned there was one absolute about Washington, and that was that politicians loved to hear themselves talk. No matter how many times you told them that something was classified there was always someone else they felt they could confide in. A wife, a girlfriend, a staffer without the proper security clearance, the list was almost endless.

There were a few rare exceptions. A select number of senators and congressmen could really keep their mouths shut, and they were the people who for the most part had gravitated toward serving on the intelligence committees. The real plums for the egos on the Hill had always been Judicial, Appropriations, Finance and Armed Services. These were the committees that were most likely to garner them air time and enable them to funnel pork back to their districts. But with the new war on terror a few of the opportunists had forced themselves onto the intelligence committees so they could capitalize on the committees' sudden higher profile.

Turbes kept a close eye on these people and had shared many of his concerns with Kennedy and Rapp. Just today he had sat on two pieces of intelligence that were so inflammatory he didn't feel he could trust them with the committees until Kennedy gave the go-ahead. Kennedy had agreed wholeheartedly and had already scheduled an early meeting at the White House so they could brief the president. The first piece of intelligence involved the gruesome murder of an Iraqi general in the Middle East and counterfeit money and the second involved the most taboo subject in the entire Hayes administration—the Saudis. Rapp knew when the president heard what they had to say he was going to blow his lid. OPEC for the most part went the way of the Saudis, and a warm relationship with the Saudis could go a long way toward keeping oil prices stable.

Rapp grabbed a pot from under the stove, filled it with water and placed it on the burner. While waiting for it to come to a boil he decided to check to see if they had any messages. There were two for Anna and he saved them both. After adding the rigatoni noodles to the boiling water he uncorked a bottle of red wine and started making the sauce. Shirley the mutt sat on the floor watching him intently, waiting for any scraps that might fall her way. The extent of Rapp's culinary skills were limited to three or four pasta dishes and steaks on the grill. After he had the sauce going he put two place settings on the breakfast bar. He would have to eat standing for a few more days.

Anna arrived home just as the noodles were coming off the stove. She greeted Shirley and then set down her heavy black bag. After hanging her coat in the front hall closet she entered the kitchen with arms folded and stopped on the other side of the small center island. Looking down, she fingered a stack of mail, most of it junk.

Rapp dumped the noodles into the colander sitting in the base of the sink and looked through the rising steam at his wife, who so far had not acknowledged him. Deciding to take Kennedy's advice he said, "Honey, I just want to let you know I'm very sorry about last night. I shouldn't have blindsided you like that, and in the future I'll try to do a better job of letting you know what's going on."

Anna did not look at him. She kept her eyes down, and continued to finger the stack of mail. She had her hair pulled back in a tight ponytail and slowly she began to nod. It was less of an acceptance of the apology than an acknowledgment that she'd heard him.

Rapp watched her intently, not quite sure how this little game was supposed to proceed. With each passing second of her silence he grew a bit more irritated. He'd made the first step and she could at least thank him for trying. In a voice void of his earlier conciliatory tone he asked, "Is there anything you'd like to say?"

She shrugged her shoulders and continued looking through the mail. "I don't like this," she said without looking at him. "I don't like being so out of control. No one has ever made me this angry. This is not who I am."

Rapp wasn't sure if he should reply, but something told him he should just keep his mouth shut and listen.

"I've never known anyone like you. There's no relationship book out there on how to be married to a spy."

Rapp smiled. "I'm not a spy."

"You know what I mean." She kept her arms folded and looked him in the eye for the first time.

Rapp nodded in silence.

"I understand that I didn't marry a businessman. I know who you are, and I respect you and love you for everything you've done, but you have to remember, you didn't marry a nincompoop who waits dutifully for you to come home every night and never asks a single question other than 'How was your day?'" Anna pointed to herself. "That's not who I am . . . that's not who my mother was. I'm not going to live a separate life from you. I need to know what you're doing. I need to be kept in the loop." She paused at the sight of her husband frowning. "Mitch, contrary to what you think, I know how to keep my mouth shut, and I'm sure as hell not going to say anything to anyone that might jeopardize your safety."

"What about national security?" he asked.

"I'm not asking to know the names of the CIA's informants in Iraq. I want to know about you. The hardest part about all this is having no idea where you are, or what you're doing."

It was all so strange for Rapp. He'd spent his entire adult life never having to explain to anyone anything about his job. It was something that he'd always kept tightly segmented from his personal life. The entire idea of opening up and sharing any of it with anyone was foreign to the point of making him almost claustrophobic. Even though he felt this way he knew she made sense. If she were to suddenly leave the country with barely a moment's notice, and give him no explanation of where she was going, how long she would be gone, or what she'd be doing, it would drive him insane. There had to be some type of a middle ground where they could meet.

Finally he said the only thing he could. "I can't argue with a single thing you've said, but you have to understand it won't be easy for me. I'm not exactly a great communicator."

This made Anna laugh. "No you're not, but admitting it is half the battle."

Seeing her smile made him feel better almost instantly. "Well, I promise I'll work on it, but you have to promise me you won't push too hard. Spouse or not . . . there are certain things I can't tell you."

"And you need to promise me that you're not going to lead any more commando raids."

Rapp sighed and agreed. Anna and his boss were right. Though his job would never be a safe one, though he would certainly find himself in the eye of the storm again in the future, it had been plain stupid and unnecessary to involve himself so directly in the hostage rescue. It just wasn't his job anymore. "I promise." He held out his arms and Anna came to him. He grabbed hold of her and held her tight. "I'm sorry, Anna."

"I know you are." Anna embraced him and kissed his chin. "I'm glad you're home, and now you're never going to leave again."

Rapp ignored her and asked, "Are you hungry?"

"I'm starving."

"Good. Have a seat." Rapp pulled out a barstool for her and poured a glass of wine. Efficiently, he prepared two plates of steaming noodles and added a healthy dose of red sauce to each. He grated a little Parmesan cheese and sprinkled it on top of each plate.

Giving him one of her piercing looks, she said, "So what do we have to do to make sure you never get involved in something like this again?"

Rapp wasn't exactly crazy about his wife's choice of words. He was a man of action, and the phrase "never get involved" had far too much finality to it. To buy some time, he said, "Irene and I are going to talk about it . . . go over some guidelines for what I should and shouldn't be involved in."

Anna took a drink of wine. "I know this isn't easy for you, honey, but you've sacrificed enough. It's time to let some other people carry the load. My dad's been a cop for over thirty years. He didn't spend all of them kicking down doors and chasing bad guys."

Rapp knew she was probably right, but it didn't mean he had to like it. If the Philippines had proved anything to him, it was that he wasn't ready to call it quits. Somehow he would have to sort all this out before another assignment came up, or he would make the same mistakes.

Anna was about to say something else when the phone rang. Rapp walked over and looked at the caller ID. The call was from Langley. He grabbed the handset. "Rapp speaking." He listened for a moment and then said, "Jesus Christ. You can't be serious." After listening again for a few seconds he said, "All right. I'll be there as soon as I can," and then hung up the phone.

"What is it?" asked Anna with genuine concern.

"Someone just assassinated the Palestinian ambassador to the UN."

FIFTY-ONE

The last train for Washington D.C. left Penn Station at 10:05 P.M. and arrived at Union Station at 1:20 A.M. David had purchased the ticket earlier in the day with cash and then gone about preparing for the evening's focal point. With the Palestinian ambassador now dead, he was ready to move on to the next part of his plan. David regretted having to kill the two bodyguards, but there had been no other way. He tried to take comfort in the fact that their deaths would hopefully result in the birth of a nation.

After leaving the armory, David had calmly walked back to the Sheraton Hotel on Seventh Avenue, just a few blocks south of the Park. He had chosen the hotel for its proximity to the theater district, the main hub of tourist activity for New York. With so many visitors from all over America, and the rest of the world, it was effortless to come and go unnoticed.

Once up in his room David had sanitized the rifle one last time even though he had never touched the weapon without wearing gloves. Each piece was placed individually in large green garbage bags, wrapped tightly and then packed in the outside compartments of his wheeled suitcase. At 8:30 he left the hotel without bothering to check out. The room was under a credit card and would be billed automatically. He'd spied several construction Dumpsters on 52nd Street earlier in the day and he headed west in search of them.

As he approached the first Dumpster he checked to see who was about and then casually unzipped one of the outer compartments of the black wheeled case. When he passed under the scaffolding that protected pedestrians from falling debris he found himself alone. David hurriedly threw two of the plastic bags into the cavernous receptacle. A moment later he found himself standing next to the second Dumpster. Quickly he chucked the other two bags up and over the side, where they landed with a thud at the bottom.

David continued west and caught a cab on Ninth Avenue. He placed his suitcase in the trunk and then settled into the cramped backseat. The cabbie asked him where to and was visibly disappointed when David told him Penn Station rather than one of the airports. David settled in for the short ride and ignored the recorded voice of some celebrity he'd never heard of telling him to buckle his seat belt. The easy part was over. Now he had to go to Washington and execute the most difficult aspect of his plan.

FIFTY-TWO

M itch Rapp had seen the president in various states of anger, but this morning he appeared to be especially upset. Michael Haik, the president's national security advisor, had put out the word. President Hayes wanted everyone at the White House by 7:00 A.M. sharp. Kennedy had brought along Rapp and CTC Director Jake Turbes. She made it clear to both of them that she wanted them to keep a low profile during the initial meeting with the president's national security team. The information that the CTC had collected would be discussed later when the group was of a more manageable size.

The large conference table in the Cabinet Room was surrounded by brown leather chairs, each of them exactly alike with the exception of one. The president's chair had a higher back and was placed in the middle of the table so that he was the focus of attention. This morning, with his strained face and clenched jaw, he was very much the center of attention. Bloodshed in the Middle East was one thing, it wasn't good, it wasn't acceptable, but it wasn't a surprise either. The assassination of a foreign ambassador in New York City along with two of his bodyguards was absolutely shocking and unacceptable.

President Hayes listened to FBI Director Roach relay the facts surrounding the assassination of the ambassador. When Roach was done the president tapped his pen on a legal pad for a few seconds and then asked in a very disappointed tone, "That's all we know?"

Director Roach, the consummate professional, looked back at the president stoically and admitted, "For now, that's all we have, sir."

In an unusually testy tone Hayes replied, "I learned that much reading the *Post* this morning." Dismissing the FBI director with a shake of his head, Hayes looked one person over to Roach's boss, Attorney General Richard Lloyd. "Dick, I want this case solved, and I want it solved in a timely manner." The president stared at his old friend and added, "I don't care what it takes. Find out who did this and put them on trial and do it quickly."

The president then shifted his gaze back in the other direction and settled on Irene Kennedy. Rapp watched all of this from a few chairs down. The president was sitting with his back to the window; his national security advisor, Michael Haik, on his left and his chief of staff, Valerie Jones, on his right. Across the table and next to the attorney general were Secretary of State Beatrice Berg and Secretary of Defense Rick Culbertson.

Hayes kept his eyes fixed on Kennedy, his agitation clearly visible in the way he tensed his jaw. "What have the Israelis had to say about this?"

Kennedy was prepared for the question. If the president wanted to know what the Israeli response was to the killings, he would have asked Secretary of State Berg. Instead he'd asked the director of the CIA, which meant he wanted to know what Mossad had to say about the assassination. She'd already spoken to Ben Freidman three times, and on each occasion he had vociferously denied having had anything to do with it.

"Sir, Director General Freidman denies categorically that Mossad had a hand in what happened last night."

The president looked doubtful. "Why should I believe him?"

The question could be answered in many ways, none of them good. Freidman had wasted what little trust the president had in him, and Kennedy doubted there was anything she could say or do that could rebuild the damage. She would have preferred to stay quiet on the issue, but the president wanted an answer. "I don't think Mossad would risk doing something this brazen."

"And why's that?" asked Hayes.

"Simple cost-benefit, sir. Killing Ambassador Ali gains them very little and as we are sure to see as the day progresses . . . it will cost them greatly in the international community."

"That line of reasoning would work if they actually gave a rat's ass what the international community thought, but as we saw with the attack on Hebron over the weekend . . . I'm not so sure they much care what the rest of the world thinks."

Valerie Jones nodded. "I would agree."

Several other people seconded her opinion. Secretary of State Beatrice Berg, however, dissented. "I don't see it that way. They might think very little of the UN, but they certainly care what we think."

The president immediately turned his attention back to Kennedy. "Everyone here is familiar with what Israel says took place in Hebron over the weekend, correct?" All the attendees nodded. Hayes turned his gaze on Kennedy. "Now, Irene, would you please share with the rest of group what really happened."

Kennedy sighed ever so slightly. This was compartmentalized information and she had no desire to dissem-
inate it to the various agencies represented in the room.
She knew, though, that any attempt to try to convince the
president otherwise would be useless. Reluctantly, she
began. "Through assets on the ground and reconnaissance
photographs we have discovered that there was no bomb-
making factory in Hebron." Kennedy looked through her
glasses at the confused expressions of the other high-level
officials. "The damage that was done was not caused by a
secondary explosion."

"Then what in the hell was it caused by?" asked Secretary of Defense Culbertson.

After a brief hesitation, Kennedy said, "Sixteen Hellfire
missiles were fired into the neighborhood."

With a confused frown on his face Culbertson asked,
"Why?"

"That's the million-dollar question," replied the president in an unfriendly tone.

"Well . . . what does Freidman have to say about all of
this?"

The president leaned back in his chair and looked to
Kennedy for the answer.

"He's sticking with their story that there was a bomb-
making factory."

"How sure are we," asked Secretary of State Berg, "that
there was no bomb factory . . . that all of the damage was
caused by the missiles?"

"The evidence is pretty clear-cut."

"How clear-cut?"

Kennedy thought about the satellite images and the reports she'd received from their people on the ground. She
normally preferred to avoid going too far out on a limb
but on this one she felt confident. "I'd say the evidence we

have convincingly contradicts the story that is being put out by the Israeli government."

"So what you're telling us," interjected Culbertson, "is that we can't trust what our only ally in the region is telling us."

The president nodded. "That about sums it up. Beatrice, what does the Israeli ambassador have to say about last night?"

Berg had not called Prime Minister Goldberg nor had she called the Israeli ambassador. In the skilled game of diplomacy the higher-ups avoided asking questions of each other that might force lies to be told. So one of Berg's underlings had called the deputy chief of mission for an unofficial response to the assassination of the Palestinian ambassador. The ambassador's number-two man had dismissed any involvement by Israel as ludicrous. This was only the first round and the answer was expected. As the drama unfolded, tougher questions would be put to people with more weighty titles.

"The embassy," started Berg, "is saying exactly what we'd expect them to say."

"That they had no involvement," answered the president.

Berg nodded.

"Irene," asked the president, "what do we know about Ali? Is there any reason that we know of why the Israelis would want him killed, or more precisely why Ben Freidman would want him killed?"

"As with all things between the Israelis and the Palestinians, there is ample motive. Ali grew up in Gaza and was an active member in the terrorist group Force 17 and then later with the PLO. The Israelis claim that like Arafat, he was a terrorist and still is a terrorist. More recently there have been accusations of fund-raising for the martyr brigades and some questionable acquaintances with people who run in the wrong circles."

"What kind of circles?" asked Hayes.

"People who deal in arms trafficking."

Valerie Jones, who had been quiet up until now, asked, "Is that information we collected on our own, or intelligence that was provided by the Israelis?"

"That's information we gathered through our own sources."

"So," began the president, "do you see anything in Ali's recent history that would warrant Mossad wanting to kill him?"

The president was fixated on Freidman, and Kennedy couldn't really blame him. Despite Freidman's denials, Kennedy had been thinking quite a bit about the possibility that he had ordered the assassination of Ali. There were many logical reasons why Freidman should not have ordered such a bold move, but on the other hand, recently he had proven to be increasingly unpredictable and brazen. The president was looking to Kennedy for an answer and she settled on an honest if somewhat cautious course.

"A year ago, sir, I would have not thought Ben Freidman capable of such a drastic move, but today I'm not so sure." Kennedy hesitated for a moment as if she were about to say something else and then stopped.

The president picked up on this and said, "What is it?"

"I'm trying to step back and see the big picture from the Israelis' point of view. It's been a bloody couple of years for them. The homicide bombers have taken a massive toll in both life and morale. Israel already receives almost no support from the international community, so in that regard they risk almost nothing. They could be expanding the war . . . an extension of their attitude that if you hit them they will hit you back even harder."

President Hayes nodded. "Hit the Palestinians where they feel safest, and keep them off balance."

Kennedy shrugged. "It's a possibility. One that I think is a bit of a stretch, but a possibility."

Hayes seemed to like this line of thinking. It gave him something he could get his hands around to explain why Freidman would do something so reckless. In a final effort to draw out any disagreement, Hayes asked, "Can anyone right now come up with a suspect other than Mossad?"

Rapp had been listening keenly to the discussion, and despite his complete lack of faith in Ben Freidman, he thought there were quite a few other possibilities that should be explored. He also knew a few things that the others didn't, but under orders from Kennedy he was to keep his opinions to himself until they were alone with the president.

FIFTY-THREE

Prime Minister Goldberg had never in his life felt so beleaguered. This was worse than the Yom Kippur War, when he had been surrounded by Syrian forces and shelled until his ears bled, and ordered by his commanders to hold his position until a counterattack could be mounted. He had hung on for three days without sleep. He and his men were fighting a much larger Syrian force in a bloody battle for the Golan Heights. The counterattack eventually arrived and an angry Israeli army threw the Syrians back across the border and closed to within spitting distance of Damascus.

Then the United States and the Soviet Union had stepped in and tried to separate the belligerents like fighting children on a playground. Goldberg would never forget the lesson he learned in 1973, and that was to never trust his Arab neighbors. They had attacked on the holiest Jewish holiday of the year, when Israelis were either at home or in their synagogues praying. For the first three days they had hammered the Jewish people, and then when the Israeli army regrouped and pushed both the Egyptians and the Syrians back across their borders, the Arabs screamed for international intervention. They launched a sneak attack and then whined for peace and of course wanted their land back even though thousands of Israelis lay dead.

Under the pressure of an Arab oil embargo the United States had forced Israel to pull back and concede much of the land they had captured in a war they did not start. How many times did the world have to see proof that Arabs could not be trusted? It frustrated Goldberg to no end that the leaders of Europe refused to see things as they were. It saddened him deeply that despite everything his people had been through on that cursed continent that they did not come to the aid of Israel. All Goldberg wanted for his people was a safe place to live. And if things weren't already bad enough having to deal with suicidal Palestinians and bigoted heads of state, he now had to contend with dissenters within his own government.

He was tired. The years of leading the fight had taken their toll and Goldberg's energy was beginning to wane. At the rate things were going there was a good chance he wouldn't survive the week without being subjected to a vote of no confidence. To start with, the UN and a healthy number of his cabinet members were up in arms over the events in Hebron, and now someone had assassinated the Palestinian ambassador in New York City.

One of Goldberg's aides had briefed him on the assassination during breakfast, and his private reaction to the news had been one of desperate fear. The very first person who came to mind was his old friend, and the director general of Mossad, Ben Freidman. Goldberg had been asking himself all day if Freidman was capable of launching such a disastrous operation on his own. The answer was a startling *yes,* which made him all the more uncomfortable with the meeting that was about to take place. The prime minister would have preferred to let the prob-

lem fade away. There was enough bloodshed in the Palestinian–Israeli conflict that the ambassador's death would
fade to the background sooner than one would think, but
unfortunately, for the next month or two, things were sure
to get worse. It was still early in America, but Goldberg
had no doubt that as the day progressed President Hayes,
or more likely Secretary of State Berg, would be on the
phone demanding assurances that Israel had had no hand
in the brutal act.

Goldberg was tempted to bury his head in the sand,
but that would be foolish and contrary to his character.
He needed the truth from Freidman and then after that
he could decide what to say to the Americans. He ran a
frustrated hand through his thin white hair and looked at
his wall clock. It was approaching 2:30 in the afternoon.
Freidman was late, which was not a surprise. The head of
Mossad came and went as he wished.

IT WAS A FEW MINUTES LATER that Freidman finally arrived to find a nervous prime minister sitting behind his desk. Freidman knew what this was about. He
was the prime suspect in the assassination of Ambassador
Ali. In contrast to the prime minister's suit, Freidman was
dressed casually in slacks and a loose-fitting, short-sleeved
dress shirt. As always, the shirt was untucked to conceal
the .38-caliber revolver he carried in a belt holster at the
small of his back. Freidman never went anywhere without it.

Slowly, he lowered himself into one of the two arm-
chairs opposite Goldberg's desk. The beleaguered expression on his friend's face did not go unnoticed. "David, you
do not look good."

Goldberg had the type of face that had surrendered to
gravity almost completely. It was hard to believe that this

roly-poly man had served in combat. He shook his head, heavy jowls sagging. "I am in the fight of my life."

Freidman interpreted this comment as the exaggeration of a politician who had lost perspective. In a voice void of any compassion or sympathy, Freidman said, "This is nothing."

Looking up under hooded eyes, Goldberg studied the supremely confident head of Mossad and felt a bit of anger spark from within. "Maybe you haven't noticed lately, Ben, but my cabinet is about to fall apart. The UN is screaming for inspectors to be sent into Hebron and after what happened in New York last night, it's a foregone conclusion that they will pass a resolution."

"And you can tell them to stick their resolution—"

Goldberg slammed his fist down on his desk, cutting Freidman off. "I will be able to tell them no such thing," he yelled, "because I will no longer be prime minister! Thanks to you I will be long gone before the first inspector arrives."

"You're exaggerating," responded Freidman with a disgusted shake of his head.

"Exaggerating," snapped Goldberg. "I'm doing no such thing. You have gotten me into this mess due to your overzealous actions in Hebron!"

"Don't criticize me for being *overzealous*. The whole reason you were elected was because the Israeli people wanted someone who would be overzealous."

"You didn't need to level the whole damn neighborhood," Goldberg shot back.

"Yes I did!" screamed Freidman. "Remember Falid Al-Din? We sent a missile right into his car, and he walked away. I wasn't going to make that mistake again."

"So you destroyed an entire neighborhood!"

"You're damn right I did! This is a war!"

Goldberg let out a frustrated sigh and through gritted teeth said, "I know it's a war, but there are other issues to consider."

"Like what?"

"Like our allies."

"You mean our allies who firebombed Dresden and Tokyo and then dropped atomic bombs on Hiroshima and Nagasaki?" Freidman stared back at the prime minister with righteous conviction. They'd had this discussion many times before and their views were identical. "War is ugly, and sometimes you save more lives in the long run by being more brutal than your enemy. We should expel every Palestinian from the occupied territories and not allow them back until every major Arab state signs a peace treaty with us . . . and damn the international community."

The prime minister shook his head. "You know better than that. The political will to launch such an operation isn't there."

"Why don't we find out?"

Goldberg was angry at himself for getting so far off track. Freidman had once again shown that he was willing to go to great lengths to get what he wanted. *Maybe,* Goldberg thought, *he would even be so devious as to put me in a position where I had no choice but to lash out.* He looked hard at the director general of Mossad and wondered just how far he'd go to get what he wanted. The answer, he knew, was that he would go very far indeed.

"Look me in the eye and tell me what role you had in the death of the Palestinian ambassador."

It was easy to offend some people, but not Ben Freidman. Goldberg might as well have asked him what he'd had for lunch. "I had absolutely nothing to do with Ali's murder."

Goldberg searched for some hint that his old friend

was lying to him. After only a second or two he knew it was a worthless exercise. He'd seen the man on too many occasions lie with the same impunity as he told the truth. "Did Mossad have anything to do with the ambassador's death?"

Freidman shook his head. "I might be crazy, David, but I am not stupid. Why would I be so dumb as to kill the Palestinian ambassador to the UN while he is in America?" He frowned dismissively. "I do not mourn Ali's death. He was a two-bit thug dressed up as a diplomat. He's in Ramallah almost every month. If I wanted him dead there would be easier ways to do it, with far fewer repercussions."

These words had the opposite effect on Goldberg than he had intended. Through Freidman's defense the prime minister glimpsed the very reason why he might have thought he could get away with killing the ambassador. Sound-minded people would eventually decide that the director general of Mossad would never risk offending the Americans when he could simply kill the ambassador when he was visiting the West Bank. Now Goldberg was truly worried. What if one of his closest advisors was working behind the scenes to provoke an all-out war?

Freidman could tell that Goldberg was not buying his denial. In a more ingratiating tone, he said, "I promise you, David, I had nothing to do with this. I have already spoken to Director Kennedy and she believes Ali's assassination may have something to do with a business deal gone bad." Freidman was stretching the truth a bit, but felt it was needed.

Goldberg gave him a skeptical look. "What kind of business deal?"

"Ali has been known to deal in arms from time to time."

"Weapons?"

"Yes." Freidman was happy to see this seemed to give the prime minister some hope.

"And you say the Americans knew about these activities?"

"Yes, as do the French, British, Germans, Russians and I'm sure quite a few other intelligence agencies."

"I would like to see Ali's file as soon as possible and give the Americans everything we have on him."

"It's already in process."

Goldberg felt a little bit better, but he still had the Hebron disaster to contend with. "Assuming we are fortunate enough to be cleared of any wrongdoing in Ali's death, it will still be too late to help us with the Hebron thing. With the current political mood the UN is sure to vote for inspectors by today or tomorrow."

"Have the United States stall."

"They won't. Not right now."

"Then just deny the inspectors access."

Goldberg had already thought it through and discussed it with his closest political advisors. Dejectedly he replied, "I can't. It would be political suicide. My cabinet would fall apart, and I'd get a no-confidence vote within twenty-four hours."

Freidman knew he was right, but wasn't willing to give in so easily. The two men sat in silence, both of them trying to find a way out of this complicated mess. Freidman had come up with only one option when his thoughts were interrupted by a muffled rumble coming from outside the building. Both he and the prime minister got to their feet and went to the window, just as another explosion was heard in the distance. Unfortunately, this was a noise that they had become all too familiar with.

Within minutes, reports were streaming into the prime

minister's office. Three suicide bombs had gone off within minutes of each other. Two in West Jerusalem and one in Tel Aviv. The damage and death toll was unknown, but expected to be high. Emergency response teams were at each site and searching frantically to make sure no other bombs were set to explode. It was a new and particularly evil trick of the martyr brigades to set secondary devices to detonate later and kill the paramedics who rushed to the scene to help the victims.

Freidman grabbed Goldberg by the elbow and led him into a corner out of earshot from his aides. "This is your opportunity."

"How could this be an opportunity?"

"Send in the army and declare a curfew on Hebron. Secure the area and leave the rest up to me. By the time the UN inspectors arrive there will be ample evidence of a bomb-making factory. You will stifle the critics in your cabinet and the UN will be appeased."

Goldberg thought about it for a second, then slowly began to nod. It was his only option. It was war, and in war the truth was almost always the first casualty.

FIFTY-FOUR

The rest of the meeting at the White House was dominated by what would happen at the UN. They all agreed that Israel was about to be strung up and that for the first time the United States might not be able to stem the backlash. Valerie Jones gave everyone a stern warning about the press. No one was to give any interviews without checking with her first. The last thing they needed right now was individual cabinet members and administration officials contradicting each other. Storms like these could be weathered, but only if everyone hung together. They could not afford to have the Hayes administration look as if it were in disarray.

When the president ended the meeting by standing, Kennedy caught Jones's eye and held up five fingers. The president's chief of staff nodded and looked down at her appointment book. The president's day was already running behind, but Jones was more than up to the task of juggling meetings and canceling or shortening events. Kennedy didn't ask often and considering the events of last night her request was undoubtedly important.

Jones looked over at her boss, who was talking to Secretary of State Berg. They were standing under a portrait of Theodore Roosevelt. The chief of staff returned her attention to Kennedy and said, "Wait in the Oval and I'll bring him in as soon as I can tear him away."

Kennedy thanked her and then left the Cabinet Room with Rapp and Turbes. As the three of them entered the Oval Office, Rapp said, "He already has his mind made up on this thing."

"Yeah, I know."

"He's not going to like what we have to say," added Rapp.

"No, he won't."

Before the three of them had a chance to settle in, the president entered the office, with Jones and his personal secretary. The president went straight to his desk and deposited a leather folder. His personal secretary began reciting a list of things that needed his attention while Jones stood off to one side looking through a stack of pink message slips that one of her people had just handed her. She froze on one and then looked up to the president.

"The Saudi ambassador wants to see you as soon as possible."

Kennedy suddenly became very interested in what the president had to say to his chief of staff. She took several steps forward and listened.

Hayes had a very warm relationship with the Saudis. Almost without thought he replied, "Set it up."

"Sir, if I may." Kennedy stepped even closer. Looking to the president's secretary the DCI said, "Betty, would you please excuse us." The secretary honored Kennedy's request without hesitation. Once she was gone and the soundproof door was closed, Kennedy said, "Sir, there have been some developments that I think you need to know about before you schedule that meeting with the ambassador."

Hayes raised a suspicious eyebrow. "Such as?"

Kennedy gestured toward the two couches by the fireplace. "I think we should sit. This might take some time."

Hayes paused for a moment as he looked down at the workload on his desk but then agreed. Kennedy and Turbes sat on one couch while Jones and the president took the other one. Rapp chose to stand rather than sit.

Kennedy started by saying, "Early this morning we received some intel from the Brits. As you know per our informal agreement with the Saudis we do not spy on them in an active fashion. The Brits, however, have no such agreement and are kind enough to share with us whatever they dig up."

Kennedy never wasted the president's time so he assumed this was good. "And what did they dig up?"

Kennedy opened a red file marked EYES ONLY and was about to hand it to the president when she decided it would be easier if she showed it to him. Getting up she moved to the other couch and sat on the president's left. She pointed to a five-by-eight, black-and-white photograph and asked, "Do you know who this is?"

Hayes studied the photo of a plump man wearing a suit and walking into a hotel, surrounded by several people, including one very large Asian man. It was obvious from the quality of the shot that it was a surveillance photograph. There was something oddly familiar about the man in the suit, but the president couldn't place him. After a moment he shook his head, and said, "No."

In a way this surprised Kennedy, and then again it didn't. Prince Omar had a very strange relationship with his royal family. Kennedy had yet to figure out if his lack of official association was by choice or by the edict of his brother, the crown prince. "His name is Prince Omar. He's a bit of an outcast from the royal family."

"Why?"

"He's led a very flashy life over the years. He's a big gambler, a womanizer and recreational drug user."

"He sounds like quite a few of the other family members."

"Yes, but he's the direct brother to the crown prince and fifteen years ago was in real contention with his brother to become king. He's very outspoken and unlike many of his cousins, uncles and nephews, he's actually made a fortune all on his own."

"That is unusual," admitted the president. The 5,000-plus Saudi royal family was notorious for their lavish spending habits, not for their ability to support themselves. "How did he make his money?"

"Banking and real estate."

Hayes looked at another photo of the prince and said, "So why is he an outcast?"

"He's very critical of his brother in regard to cooperating with the West in the war on terrorism."

Hayes nodded knowingly. He was no stranger to the hypocrisy of many of the Saudi royals. They were educated in the West, they vacationed in the West, they spent as much time as possible in the West, enjoying the fruits of free democratic societies and then returned home to bash the West and pander to the neo-conservative mullahs and imams.

"So why are you bringing him to my attention this morning?"

"In light of what happened in New York last night, I thought you should see this right away." Kennedy reached over and flipped through a few more photographs until she found the one she was looking for. "Last week Prince Omar's yacht was anchored at Monte Carlo. MI6 had him under surveillance, and photographed this man being ferried to his yacht."

"Why did they have him under surveillance?" asked Jones.

"The Brits didn't offer, and I didn't ask, but if the opportunity presents itself, I'll find out."

"Who is this guy?" asked the president. He pointed to a photograph of a handsome man sitting on the back bench of a power launch.

"That, sir, is what we are trying to find out. The Brits were able to pick up some low quality audio of the prince talking with this unknown individual and it is very interesting. The prince was easier to understand because he was louder." Kennedy flipped the photo and revealed a typed transcript of the discussion between Omar and his visitor.

The president donned his reading glasses and followed along.

> SUBJECT ONE: Your, highness, I am . . . implement your plan. There are . . . things to be done . . . little room for error.
> PRINCE OMAR: How close . . . ?
> SUBJECT ONE: Close.
> PRINCE OMAR: When will it start?
> SUBJECT ONE: Within . . . week, . . .

Kennedy passed over several paragraphs as they were unimportant and found the next important passage.

> SUBJECT ONE: There is . . . you could . . . for me . . .
> PRINCE OMAR: . . . would that have . . . money?
> SUBJECT ONE: They are . . . they . . . driven into action by rage, . . . I give them.
> PRINCE OMAR: How much more do you need?

SUBJECT ONE: *Response Unintelligible.*

PRINCE OMAR: Ten million. You have become far too greedy.

SUBJECT ONE: *Response unintelligible.*

PRINCE OMAR: Five million.

SUBJECT ONE: Prince Omar, what . . . one thing . . . you . . . most pleasure in?

PRINCE OMAR: To see Israel destroyed.

SUBJECT ONE: Exactly . . . ten million . . . pittance, and for it . . . self-destruction . . . Zionist state.

President Hayes slowly took off his glasses and looked at Kennedy cautiously. "Do we have the actual audio of this conversation?"

"Yes. Our people are working on it right now, but I doubt they'll be able to do much more with it than the Brits already have."

The president grabbed one of the photos and asked again, "Who is this man?"

"We don't know yet."

Turbes leaned forward. "Sir, I've got the best people at the CTC looking into this. I'm hopeful we'll get an ID on him within a day or two."

"There's one more thing, Mr. President." Kennedy closed the file. "The Brits say the prince and this man met again in Cannes last Saturday. Apparently they had some problems with their audio surveillance so the tape of their conversation has yielded very little, but they were able to confirm one thing."

"And what is that?"

"The Brits say the man was headed for America."

"Why?" asked Hayes in confusion. "I thought he stated in the transcript that the target was Israel."

Kennedy shook her head. "I don't know, sir. We're trying to sort this all out."

"Irene," the president said with a bit of a disappointed tone. "I know I've told you countless times to keep me in the loop, but I think all you've done here this morning is confuse me."

"I would have much rather taken a day or even a week to flesh this out, but considering what happened in New York last night, I wanted to make you aware of it as soon as possible."

"But why?" Hayes shook his head. "This transcript tells me the target of these two is Israel, not the United States."

"Then why did John Doe leave France for the United States?" Rapp paced slowly behind the couch, not bothering to look at the president or his boss. "If his goal is Israel then he should be headed in the other direction, or maybe MI6 is reading too far into this or we're taking the wrong meaning from it." Rapp looked down at the president. "Arabs are famous for being shameless braggarts when it comes to Israel. They puff up their chests and throw around wild brutal ideas, but rarely do they ever follow through on them. What if all we heard on that tape was a business transaction that—" Rapp thought of something Kennedy had said in the meeting. "What if Prince Omar was involved in an arms deal with Ali and he got burned?"

Hayes looked at Rapp with a skeptical frown and asked, "Do you really think that's what this is about, Mitch?"

"I'm not sure, sir. It's too early to tell. . . . I'm just trying to throw out some other possibilities, before we get swept up in this blame Israel storm."

The president didn't feel like hearing any dissension

this morning. Ben Freidman had abused the trust of his country's greatest supporter and until someone gave him hard evidence to the contrary, Freidman would continue to be the focus of the president's ire. "Mitch, do you trust Ben Freidman?"

Rapp didn't waver for a second. "Of course not."

Hayes nodded. "And you think he's capable of something this reckless?"

This time Rapp took a moment to consider the full breadth of the question. "Absolutely. If it means protecting his country . . . I think he's capable of almost anything."

The president concurred with a firm nod.

"But," Rapp added quickly, "one thing doesn't quite make sense. I think the fact that the assassination took place in New York City leaves some doubt."

"Why, because you don't think he'd risk offending us?"

"Yeah."

Hayes scowled. "I don't think Ben Freidman worries about offending anyone."

"But Prime Minister Goldberg does," answered Valerie Jones. "His coalition cabinet is ready to fall right over the edge of the cliff. If he gets implicated in this the Knesset will vote him out like that." Jones snapped her fingers in the air.

"Sir," warned Kennedy, "all we're trying to say is let's be very careful about what positions we take until we know more."

After sitting back Hayes thought about Kennedy's cautionary words and sighed. Her advice went against his instincts. He'd lost all patience with Ben Freidman and his lying ways, but he knew Kennedy was right. He looked at her and nodded. "All right . . . for now we stay quiet about all this, but," looking to Rapp and Turbes he said, "find out who this man is and if he had anything to do with Ambassador Ali's assassination."

Rapp nodded, but Turbes was preoccupied with reading an e-mail off his Blackberry. The director of the CTC glanced up from the small screen, a grim expression on his face and announced. "Three suicide bombs just went off in Israel."

President Hayes placed a hand over his face and said, "Oh, God . . . this just keeps getting worse."

FIFTY-FIVE

The old house wasn't in the nicest neighborhood, and it wasn't in the best condition, but it served its purpose. It was right on the bubble where North D.C. bordered Northeast D.C. Compared to the southeast quadrant of the city, the neighborhood was tame, but trouble could still be found if you didn't pay attention to where you were going at two in the morning. That was the Washington take on things, but having spent most of his life living under occupation, David found the neighborhood to be extremely safe.

He'd passed himself off to the landlord as a French software designer who owned his own company and was trying to break into the U.S. market. He would only be in D.C. sporadically, as meetings with his lobbying firm and the Department of Commerce dictated, but when he was in town he would need ample space to continue his work. The rent was reasonable and the landlord didn't balk when David handed over the first two months plus deposit in cash. In the five months since then David had wired the rent to the landlord from a dummy account in Paris that matched his false identity of Jean Racine.

David's only request, which he offered to pay for, was

to upgrade the electrical service in one of the upstairs rooms and get the house wired for high-speed Internet access. The landlord, who lived a little more than a mile away, objected to neither and stayed true to his promise that he wouldn't bother David as long as David was a quiet and respectful tenant.

Now David sat in the converted office on the second floor of the Victorian home and concentrated on the array of visual equipment before him. Mounted on the wall were eight Sony twenty-one-inch flat-screen monitors costing over a thousand dollars each. Two workstations were set up on the long folding table that served as a desk. The station on the left was for checking e-mail, managing his funds, which were spread out at various financial institutions around the world, and keeping an eye on a certain online news service that provided almost instantaneous access to what was going on at 1600 Pennsylvania Avenue. The other workstation was dedicated to controlling the other seven monitors as they fed him live feeds from traffic cameras around the city.

That part of the plan had been achieved with less effort than he had anticipated. Simple bribery had bought him access to the Washington D.C. Department of Motor Vehicles' traffic camera network. At any given moment he was just a few key strokes away from accessing any one of the more than one hundred cameras located throughout the District. The password to enter the system had cost him only $2,000. The DMV was a true menagerie of immigrants, most of whom had come from Third World countries where government salaries were often augmented by bribes and payoffs. The young Palestinian who he approached leapt at the chance to make a little extra money and never once asked why the stranger from his homeland wanted access to such information.

The man could have thrown out a decent guess, but he would have assumed wrong. David had his eyes set on a very ripe target. One that would enrage the United States and unite the Arab world. The pressure for peace in the Middle East and a free and autonomous Palestinian state was about to reach an apogee. David just needed one simple meeting to take place and he would spring the trap.

FIFTY-SIX

Rapp followed Turbes down the sterile hallway of the New Headquarters Building of the George Bush Center for Intelligence. The CTC had been recently relocated from its relatively small space on the sixth floor of the Original Headquarters Building to the bottom two floors of the south wing of the new structure. This massive increase in space, staff and budget was a reflection of just how seriously Washington was now taking the threat of terrorism.

To Rapp's mind this was a mixed blessing. The new funding was great for buying high-tech equipment and training new people, but it also brought with it more oversight, more accounting, more red tape and in general more people getting in each other's way. Rapp was an advocate of small specialized teams that could react quickly and plan operations with as little interference as possible. Instinctively he recoiled against large organizations and for that reason more than probably any other he always felt a little uncomfortable entering the new CTC.

Turbes stopped at a door and slid his ID through the magnetic card reader, while Rapp loosened the knot of his tie and undid the top button of his dress shirt. They had barely entered the CTC and analysts were already lining up to have a word with Turbes. Somewhere near the back of the line Rapp spotted Marcus Dumond and Olivia Bourne. Dumond was the CTC's resident computer genius, and Bourne was the senior regional analyst for the Gulf States. Officially, she had nothing to do with Saudi Arabia. Unofficially, she kept as close a watch on the Saudi royal family as politics would allow.

When Rapp had been brought in from the field and named special assistant to the DCI on counterterrorism, Kennedy had sat him down and given him an overview on the CTC. At the top of the list of the center's most valuable people, Kennedy had placed Olivia Bourne. The thirty-nine-year-old West Virginian had an undergraduate degree from Brown and a graduate degree from Princeton. She had literally no field experience, but was a walking encyclopedia when it came to tracking the Islamic Radical Fundamentalists, or IRFs, who they hunted.

Kennedy hadn't bothered to brief Rapp on Marcus Dumond since it was Rapp who had recruited him. Rapp had met Dumond while he was a graduate student at MIT with Rapp's brother. At the time of his recruitment Dumond had been a twenty-seven-year-old computer genius and almost convicted felon. The young cyber genius had run into some trouble with the Feds while he was earning his master's degree in computer science at MIT. He was alleged to have hacked into one of New York's largest banks and then transferred funds into several overseas accounts. The part that interested the CIA was that Dumond wasn't caught because he left a trail, he was caught because he got drunk one night and bragged about the looting to the wrong person.

When the Feds came and broke down his apartment door, Dumond was living with Steven Rapp. Rapp heard about the incident from his brother and alerted Kennedy, who was then the director of the CTC, that the hacker was worth a look. Langley doesn't like to admit the fact that they employ some of the world's best computer pirates, but these young cyber geeks are encouraged to hack into any and every computer system they can. Most of these hacking raids are directed at foreign companies, banks, governments and military computer systems. But just getting into a system isn't enough. The challenge is to hack in, get the information and get out without leaving a trace that the system was ever compromised. Dumond was a natural at it, and his talents were put to good use in the CTC.

Both Bourne and Dumond were gesturing to get Rapp's attention. Bourne held up a piece of paper and pointed eagerly to the face on the printout. Rapp bypassed the line and went straight for Bourne. Grabbing her by the elbow, he pulled her away from the crowd.

Keeping his voice hushed, he asked, "What's up?"

Bourne smiled. "We've got a bead on Prince Charming."

Rapp's first reaction was to turn and see what Turbes was doing. It looked like two CTC employees were wildly explaining a problem to the head boss in hopes that he would referee their dispute. Rapp looked to Dumond and Bourne and said, "Follow me."

The three of them walked down the side aisle of the large open room that held a sea of cubicles. The maze of plastic and fabric dividers was affectionately known as the Bull Pen to those who worked counterterrorism. When they reached Rapp's office he unlocked the door with a key and then entered. Glancing at Dumond he said, "Close the door." Once it was shut Rapp turned to Bourne who spoke both Arabic and Farsi fluently and asked, "What did you find?"

Bourne handed over the printout. "Our boy flew from Nice to Paris to JFK on Sunday."

Rapp looked at the grainy black-and-white image. "Where'd we get this?"

"Custom's surveillance camera at JFK. We scanned the Brits' photos into the facial imaging recognition system and let the computers go to work. We started with our in-house database on known or suspected terrorists and came up blank, so before checking with our allies I decided to run a search with Customs on the hunch that if this guy had anything to do with the Palestinian ambassador he would have had to enter the country on Sunday or Monday at the latest."

Rapp nodded and looked at the grainy photo. "Are we sure this is him?"

"Ninety-eight point six three percent sure," replied the hyperanalytical Dumond.

Holding the photo up, Rapp asked, "Does he have a name?"

"Charles Utrillo," Bourne replied.

Rapp turned his attention to Dumond, knowing his little hacker would have already done a full background check. "I suppose that's not his real name."

"Nope." Dumond shook his head. "I checked several French government databases and came up with nothing."

Dumond handed over a printout. "Here's the information on the credit card he used to pay for the plane ticket. We're running a search on rental cars and hotels within a hundred-mile radius of New York City. If he used the card again we'll know sometime in the next thirty minutes."

"Are you tracing the card on the other end?" asked Rapp.

"Yeah. It was set up for automatic payments from a

bank in Paris. The account has a little less than eight grand in it."

Unfortunately, Rapp thought he knew the answer to his next question, but he asked it anyway. "And how did that money get into the account?"

"Four separate cash deposits."

Rapp cringed. This guy was covering his tracks like a real pro. Speaking from experience Rapp said, "The name's a dead end. Wherever he is now, he's using a different identity."

"Even so," asked Bourne, "do you want us to flag his passport and alert the FBI?"

"Flag his passport," answered Rapp, even though he doubted it would do any good, "but hold off on the FBI for a bit. Let me talk to Irene first and see what she wants to do." Rapp paused and put himself in the shoes of the assassin for a moment. He tried to guess what the man's next move would be. His options were to either stay in New York and wait until things settled down or leave immediately. If it was Rapp he would have left immediately. Canada would have been his first choice, and then head back to Europe, or if he had time, head west.

"Start checking security cameras at the three major airports from eight last night until this morning. Concentrate on outgoing international flights . . . especially anything bound for Canada."

"We're in the process of doing it right now," answered Bourne. "Do you want me to check with the DGSE or Mossad and see if we can get a match on the photo?"

Normally Rapp wouldn't think twice about checking with either the French or Mossad, but given the current situation he hesitated. "Not yet. I need to run this by Irene first." He checked his watch and then asked, "Anything else?"

"Yeah," said Bourne. "Ask her if we can bring the Feds and local law enforcement in on this."

Rapp nodded. Remembering something, he asked Dumond, "How are you coming with the prince's finances? Ten million bucks is a lot of money. There has to be a sign of it moving from one account to another."

Dumond shook his head in frustration. "Ten million bucks is nothing to a guy like this. It'll take me the rest of the day just to try and identify all of the various accounts he uses and even then I could miss a few that I'm sure he keeps hidden."

"I don't care what it takes, get it done. Pull all the people you need for the busy work, and I'll get Irene to authorize it. I want to know who this guy is and unless Olivia gets lucky, the best way to catch him is to follow the money trail."

FIFTY-SEVEN

The sun was down and rush hour was over as Rapp turned onto the Chain Bridge and hit the gas. His turbo Volvo S80 shot across the low-slung bridge like a rocket. When he reached the other side he hung a right and again floored it. He was already fifteen minutes late for his 8:00 dinner date with his wife. At Reservoir Road he hung a left and shot across a lane of traffic and into a residential neighborhood just north and west of Georgetown University.

Anna had picked the restaurant. It was in Glover Park on Wisconsin Avenue. Austin Grill was a little hole in the wall that served great margaritas and decent Mexican food. Unfortunately, Rapp wouldn't be drinking any margaritas tonight; as soon as dinner was over he'd have to head right back to Langley. They were no closer to finding out who Prince Omar's minion was than they were eight hours ago.

Kennedy had given them the green light to bring in the counterterrorism people at the FBI, but had decided against alerting France or Israel. Bourne had done a routine search through Interpol's database, shuffling John Doe's photograph in with a half dozen others they were interested in. The intent was to make Interpol think it was a standard query, and nothing to get excited about. Against everyone's hopes, the search came up empty.

The pressure from the White House wasn't helping. If they didn't know more by tomorrow morning, Rapp was prepared to get on a plane and fly to France. He had a few ideas about how he could crack this thing open and his best hope lay with Prince Omar's personal assistant, the effeminate Devon LeClair. The Brits had provided a brief bio of the man, and it appeared he was the most likely person to handle Omar's nefarious activities. Rapp was willing to bet he could get the guy to crack inside of five minutes. In the meantime he'd given Dumond orders to take a close look at the Frenchman.

Rapp took a left onto 37th Street, braking for several students who were lollygagging in the crosswalk and then accelerated up the hill. Less than a minute later he turned, heading south onto Wisconsin Avenue and grabbed the first available spot. Climbing out of the car he winced slightly as he put weight on his bad leg and then did a quick three hundred and sixty degree check of the area.

Rapp entered the bar with the collar of his jacket turned up and his head down, trying to look as inconspicuous as possible. He squeezed past the young crowd that was bellied up to the bar. Even on a Tuesday night the place did great business. With every step he scanned faces and checked things out. He headed for the balcony where they always sat and hobbled up the stairs.

Just like a good girl he found his wife sitting in the corner with her back to the wall. Rapp smiled without hesitation, his deeply tanned face showing a pair of creased dimples. He hurried over to her and said, "Sorry I'm late, honey."

Anna smiled and offered her lips. She was usually the one who was late so she couldn't complain.

Rapp kissed her and took off his jacket, careful not to let his suit coat open too far and alarm any of the other patrons by revealing the gun in his shoulder holster. He took a seat next to his wife so they both had their backs to the wall. Taking her hand he asked, "How was your day?"

Anna took a drink of water and said, "Pretty hectic. People are really freaking out about the Palestinian ambassador."

"Tell me about it," responded Rapp.

"I heard the president went ballistic when he found out."

Rapp thought about it for a second. "He wasn't happy, but I don't think I'd describe it as going ballistic."

Anna wasn't sure if her husband was spinning her or telling the truth. "You guys have any idea who did it?"

"We've got a few leads . . ."

"Nothing you can talk about," finished Anna.

Rapp smiled and kissed her again. "You're figuring this game out."

She laughed and said, "Oh, I'm not done with you yet." Staring at him with her emerald eyes she said, "The word on the street is that the president thinks the Israelis are responsible."

Inside Rapp felt his gut tighten. The president had no business letting a rumor like this get started. At this point, any suspicion aimed at Israel was based on the president's hatred and distrust of Ben Freidman and nothing more. What little evidence they had pointed in a very different direction, and one that he could not share with his wife.

"We have very little to go on right now, but I don't think the Israelis did it."

A waitress showed up at the table and dropped off a red, white and blue swirly margarita. She asked Rapp what he wanted and as tempted as he was to follow suit, he settled for a bottle of Lone Star beer instead.

When the waitress was gone, Anna asked, "Why don't you think Israel did it?"

Rapp frowned. "Let's change the subject. How's your mother?"

Anna took a sip of her drink and said, "You never ask about my mother."

"That's not true. How is she doing?"

"She's fine . . . now tell me why you don't think the Israelis did it."

Rapp was about to put up the stone wall and then remembered where it had gotten him lately. She was his wife and as long as he didn't get into details, there was probably no harm in explaining his opinion. "I know a lot of Israelis, and although they're a little crazy at times, they are far from stupid. Unless there's something about Ambassador Ali that we don't know, I see no benefit to Mossad taking him out."

"Unless," said Ana, "they feel so isolated their only choice was to lash out."

Rapp was already shaking his head. "Not here in the United States."

"What if they're thumbing their nose at the UN?" Anna took another sip.

"Why not kill him when he's in the West Bank and avoid offending their one true ally?"

"Maybe they couldn't get at him when he's in the West Bank?"

Rapp laughed. His wife obviously knew very little of Mossad's capabilities. "Trust me, Mossad could have taken him down any one of a dozen times in the last year."

"Well," Anna said a bit defensively, "I'm hearing the president is pretty convinced it was the Israelis."

Rapp was tempted to tell his wife that the president didn't know what in the hell he was talking about, but discretion won out and he simply said, "We'll know a lot more in a few days, and until then I think we should all keep our theories to ourselves."

Anna smelled dissension and pounced. "So the CIA and the president are in disagreement."

Smiling and shaking his head, he said, "You're awful. I never said any such thing. You asked your husband his personal opinion and that's what I gave you. In no way does it reflect the official opinion of either the president or the CIA."

Anna made a funny face while sucking on her straw. When she came up for air she said, "Nice try. I'm going to lead the news with it in the morning." She held her drink in front of her mouth like a microphone. Using her fake on-air voice she said, "Breaking news here at the White House. Major dissension between President Hayes and the CIA."

Rapp almost took the bait and then caught himself.

"By the way, aren't you wondering how my ass is doing?"

Anna shook her head. "Nope. Your current ailment is nobody's fault but your own. You'll get no sympathy from me."

Rapp pulled a woebegone face. "My doctor tells me I might never be able to have sex again."

Anna tried her best not to smile. "The divorce papers will be on your desk in the morning."

Rapp burst out laughing. It was the first time in several days and it felt great. As he looked into his wife's eyes he wished he didn't have to go back to the office, but he did.

He had to find out who this guy was and when he did he would demand that the president allow him to launch an operation that set an example, an operation that would send a warning to people who wanted to finance terrorism. He knew the president would be reluctant to grant him the authority to do what he wanted, so he would have to work that much harder to make sure he had overwhelming evidence and sound reason on his side.

FIFTY-EIGHT

It wasn't quite 7:00 on Wednesday morning when David entered the tiny garage behind the house he was renting. Inside was a stripped-down white Ford minivan with no seats or windows in the rear passenger area. David had done all of his dry runs without the van. Even though he was confident the bomb wouldn't go off unless it was armed, he erred on the side of caution and kept it locked up in the garage. As he slid the key into the ignition he couldn't help but catch himself worrying that starting the engine might bring about a premature end to his plans.

The concern was foolish. He'd read all the manuals ad nauseam. There were ample materials available on explosives if one was willing to look, and besides, his people had become experts on bombs over the last two decades. The more difficult aspect of the plan had been obtaining the amount of explosives he needed and then getting them into the United States. The now deceased General Hamza had been kind enough to supply him with three separate shipments of Iraqi-made Semtex, a very powerful plastic explosive, and then using a series of export companies he had shipped a large cargo container from Jordan to Indonesia and then finally to the busy port of Los Angeles.

From there the container had made its way east to Richmond, Virginia, where it sat in a storage facility for two months while David made sure it wasn't being watched. Twelve forty-pound blocks of the claylike Semtex sat in the back of the van under a canvas painters' tarp. Underneath the tarp was a maze of det cord and blasting caps that would ensure the near simultaneous detonation of the 480 pounds of explosives.

David backed up slowly until he reached the street and then headed south. Due to all the government jobs, D.C. was not a city of early risers and the traffic was still light. He cut down a cross street and then turned the van onto Georgia Avenue. A short while later he passed Howard University and then Georgia turned into 7th Street. He was now less than a mile from the White House. After stopping for a red light he took a right onto Rhode Island and continued in the right lane avoiding as many potholes as he could.

He was more nervous now than when he had killed Ali. There was something about D.C. All the cameras and various law enforcement agencies each presented the possibility of capture. To David it was truly unbelievable that a city with so many cops in it could have such a high murder rate, but that was America.

He tried not to be overly optimistic about his odds of succeeding. He'd covered his tracks diligently and monitored the FBI's Web site hourly waiting for a photograph of him to appear at any moment, but it hadn't. They had no idea who he was, and if the papers were to be believed, the entire world, even the Americans, believed that the Israelis were responsible for the assassination of Ambassador Ali. Everything was going according to plan. Now all he needed to do was make one last grand statement. An act of pure violence that would force Israel to concede.

He turned onto the desired street less than a quarter mile from the White House and slowed for a car that had abruptly pulled out in front of him. David continued north for two more blocks in search of the optimal parking place. Much of the credit for this last bold move had to be given to Omar. He had convinced David that the best way to force Israel to the table was to enrage the Americans. Spill blood on their soil and watch them lose their patience with Israel.

Now more than ever David was convinced it would work. The French ambassador to the UN was scheduled to bring a resolution for Palestinian statehood before the Security Council at 11:00 this morning. So far everyone was onboard, minus the United States, but unfortunately that wasn't enough. As a permanent member of the Council, the American ambassador had veto power. As things stood right now, the Americans were not ready to back the French resolution, but that was about to change. After David was done this morning the vote would probably have to be postponed, but its odds of passing would be greatly increased.

David carefully parallel-parked the van and then plugged the meter with enough quarters to last into the afternoon. Standing next to the parking meter he took one last look at the van and made sure he'd done everything. The tabs were up-to-date, the meter was full and the bomb could not be seen from the front window. As casually as his nerves would allow, he turned and began walking away from the vehicle. He would wait to arm the bomb when he got back to the house. After he was sure his target was on the way.

FIFTY-NINE

Rapp stepped out of the shower in the men's locker room of the New Headquarters Building and grabbed a towel. He'd managed to sneak in a few hours' sleep on the couch in his office, and right about now he was wondering if that had been such a good idea. Due to his wound he'd had to sleep on his side with his head up on the armrest. The contorted angle of his neck had given him a kink that a steaming hot fifteen-minute shower had done nothing to fix. As he dried off he told himself to ignore it. There were bigger problems to deal with, like finding this prick who worked for Fat Omar. That's what Rapp had taken to calling the Saudi prince, refusing to grant him his regal title.

With the aid of a full-length mirror, he taped a new bandage over his wound and got some clean clothes out of his locker. It was common for those who worked in the CTC to keep a change of clothes at work. When a crisis erupted there usually wasn't enough time to sleep, let alone go home and get changed.

Rapp was standing in his boxers when the locker room door flew open and a disheveled Marcus Dumond burst in yelling Rapp's name. "Mitch . . . Mitch!"

"Over here," yelled Rapp.

Dumond skidded to a stop at the end of the aisle. "You gotta get upstairs! Olivia found something!"

Rapp pulled his pants on. "What?"

"She's got a lead on this guy, and you're not gonna like it."

RAPP STOOD OVER BOURNE'S SHOULDER, his thick black hair wet and uncombed, staring at the flat screen monitor. For the third time in a row he watched the man walk across the expansive floor of Penn Station, and for the third time in a row he asked Bourne, "Are you sure it's him?"

She smiled confidently and said, "Yep. The software mapped his face and gave us a lock on the surveillance photos the Brits provided."

Rapp watched the man in the dark trench coat. The times worked out. Kill Ali, get away from the area, dispose of the weapon and then catch a train out of town. Or go to the station and make everybody think you got on a train, then duck back outside and disappear. Rapp had used the trick himself on more than one occasion. "Have you checked to make sure he didn't turn around and come back out?"

"No need to," replied a confident Bourne. She made a couple of key strokes and more black-and-white surveillance footage came up on the second monitor. Bourne handed Rapp a printout that showed the schedule of trains leaving Penn Station for the night in question.

Rapp looked down at the one she had circled and squinted to read the small type.

"Going off of that," offered Bourne, "I pulled the footage at Union Station. The train left New York at ten oh five and pulled into D.C. at one-twenty in the morn-

ing." Bourne hit her Enter key like a concert pianist striking the final note of a glorious performance and then sitting back she crossed her arms and watched the digital
video stream play across her screen. "That's our guy walking across the lobby right there."

Rapp didn't bother to ask if she was sure this time.
"The bastard's in D.C.," he mumbled more to himself
than Bourne. His mind instantly seized, not on who he
should call, or where the man might be, but rather on
who he was after. When you stripped away all the bullshit,
Rapp was an assassin. He was also much more than that,
of course, but in the most raw, blunt way he was an assassin. He understood the thought processes involved in running an operation virtually alone. It was his preferred
mode. That way he didn't have to worry about anyone
other than himself screwing up. This guy looked like he
was operating alone, and if Rapp was guessing right there
was only one reason why he would come to D.C. He
wasn't done killing.

"Do we have any more footage on him?"

"No, this is it."

"Dammit," swore Rapp. "Have you told Jake?"

"No. He's on his way up to the Hill to brief the Intel
Committee."

"Irene?"

"No. She's on her way to the White House."

Rapp stood up straight and looked across the sea of
cubicles at the far wall to see if Tom Lee, the CTC's
deputy director, was in his office. If Rapp had been a typ-
ical government employee, he would already be racing
across the Bull Pen on his way to tell Lee everything he
had just learned. Needless to say, Rapp was more than
some bureaucrat worried about covering his ass and making sure his government pension was protected at all costs.

This was a tricky situation. Lee was not an employee of the CIA, he merely had an office in the building. He was FBI and with the FBI came a lot of rules on how things were handled. Rules that Rapp felt got in the way.

Rapp had to make a quick decision. They needed to catch this guy, but they didn't want to spook him. Plus once they told the FBI about him there was no taking it back, no flexibility in how to handle the situation.

He decided on a cautious course for the moment. Looking down at Bourne and Dumond who were seated he said, "Call the cab companies and find out who was working the station at the time this guy stepped onto the curb, and"—Rapp lowered his voice—"keep it within our little group right here."

Both Bourne and Dumond nodded. They were CIA and knew exactly what Rapp was talking about.

"And, Marcus, keep working on Fat Omar's accounts. There should have been a large chunk of change moved sometime in the last week. If anything comes up call me on the digital." Rapp grabbed the printout of the surveillance photo and a train schedule and started for the exit.

"Where are you going?" asked Dumond.

Rapp folded the printouts and shoved them into his pocket. "The White House."

SIXTY

Pesident Hayes sat behind his desk with a phone to his ear while his national security team sat on the couches and waited for him to join them. Kennedy was sitting next to Valerie Jones pretending to read a file. In truth she was listening to what the president was saying, or more accurately what he wasn't saying. The senior senator from New York, a state the president had barely carried, had called to advise him not to come down too hard on the Israelis for their incursion into Hebron.

Hayes didn't even want to take the call, but Jones had practically demanded it. When he was up for reelection they would need New York. This was not the first call placed to the White House this morning on behalf of Israel. The powerful Jewish lobby was in crisis mode trying to avert a potentially disastrous vote that was to take place at the UN later today. Every member of the National Security Team had fielded at least two calls from influential power brokers pleading the Israelis' case. Secretary of State Berg had been solicited the hardest, followed by Chief of Staff Jones and then Secretary of Defense Culbertson. Even Kennedy and General Flood had been hit up.

"I'll take it all under advisement," said the president as

he looked at nothing in particular. Hayes listened for a few seconds and then said firmly, "I fully understand the gravity of the situation, Senator. Now if you'll excuse me, I have work to do." Hayes slammed the phone down in its cradle and shot Valerie Jones an extremely unhappy look.

Getting up from behind his desk he kept his eyes on his chief of staff and said, "That's the last one I'm taking. These people are more concerned about Israel than their own country."

"What did he say?" asked Jones.

"Pretty much that if I want to win New York next time around I'd better make sure this French resolution doesn't make it out of the Security Council." Hayes chose to stand rather than sit. "And if things weren't already bad enough, they went and sent tanks into Hebron. American-made tanks, I might add."

"Sir," started Jones, "I think we need to focus our efforts on getting the vote delayed."

Hayes ran a hand through his hair and then grabbed the back of his neck. "Bea?" He looked to his secretary of state for an answer.

"From what I'm hearing the French are hell-bent on putting this to a vote now. Especially since the tanks rolled in last night."

"Let's not forget about the suicide bombs," interjected Secretary of Defense Culbertson. "That's how this all got started. Israel has a right to defend herself and if the Palestinians are going to locate their bomb factories in residential neighborhoods, then no one should feel too bad for them when one of them blows up."

The secretary of state ignored her colleague and said, "Mr. President, I would never argue that Israel doesn't have the right to defend itself, but the reality is that the UN is fed up with this never-ending cycle of violence, and the assassination of one of their own has galvanized the entire assembly like nothing I've ever seen before."

Culbertson moved to the edge of the couch. "But there's no proof Israel had anything to do with the ambassador's death. In fact, it's preposterous to think they'd do such a thing."

The president turned his gaze on Kennedy. Now was the time to let the rest of the team in on what only a few knew. "Irene."

Kennedy closed the folder on her lap and looked at the secretaries of state and defense and General Flood. The president had been very specific about what he wanted her to say, or more precisely, what he didn't want her to say. There was to be no mention of the mysterious man who had met with Prince Omar. The Brits had quite an extensive file on the brother of the crown prince. While they felt that he was somewhat business savvy, or at least wise enough to surround himself with people who made good decisions, the Brits also felt that Omar was a bit dense. Their initial opinion was that they doubted Omar could be involved in something as complicated as the assassination of a UN ambassador. So for now, Kennedy was sticking with what they knew to be fact.

In a voice barely above a whisper she said, "There was no bomb factory in Hebron."

Secretary Berg stared at Kennedy. "Did the Israelis admit to this?"

"No. In fact they are standing by their story."

Culbertson asked suspiciously, "Then how do we know there was no factory?"

"We had satellite coverage of the attack. There were no secondary explosions."

"Then where did all the damage come from?" asked Berg.

"Sixteen Hellfire missiles fired by Apache helicopters."

"American-made Hellfire missiles," added the president, "fired by American-made Apache helicopters."

Secretary of State Berg made the connection first. "That's why they went back into Hebron last night. They wanted to clean up the mess."

"Or," said Kennedy, "knowing Ben Freidman, they'll plant the evidence to make it look like they were telling the truth the whole time and the Palestinians were lying."

"Or," contradicted Culbertson, "they simply went back into Hebron to clean out these martyr brigades."

"I'm sure it's a bit of both," agreed Kennedy, "but right now I'm inclined to believe one is a pretense for the other."

"The reality," said the president, taking control of the discussion, "is that we have an ally who is not being truthful with us."

"What is Freidman saying about the ambassador's assassination?" asked Berg.

Kennedy looked at the keen secretary of state. Berg was well aware of Israel's official denial of any involvement in Ambassador Ali's death. Her question by itself showed that she believed Mossad capable of conducting a brutal version of their own foreign policy.

"The director general is denying any involvement."

Culbertson grimaced. "Just because they lied about the bomb factory doesn't mean they had anything to do with the Palestinian ambassador's assassination."

"I'm not so sure," replied Hayes. "At a bare minimum, however, it proves that we can't take them at their word."

Culbertson turned to Kennedy and skeptically asked, "You don't really think they would have done something so brazen, do you?"

Kennedy took a moment to compose her thoughts. "I don't see the benefit of such an action . . . at least not here on American soil, but then again I don't have all the facts. For all I know this could be the start of an all-out offensive on Israel's part to clean out the West Bank once and for all."

"Why kill the ambassador then?" asked Berg. "All they've managed to do is galvanize the UN."

Until this moment, for several reasons, Kennedy had restrained herself from voicing her next comment. First and foremost was that she didn't want to believe Israel could be so reckless, but her strained relationship with Freidman and the assault of the suicide bombers on the Israeli psyche led her closer to the conclusion that they were indeed capable of such a brutal move.

"There is a school of thought"—Kennedy couched her words carefully—"that Israel no longer cares what the UN thinks."

The president had not heard this before and asked, "How so?"

"To be sure, there are elements within Israel that believe engagement is the only way to lasting peace and security, but there is a growing lobby that thinks every time Israel trusts her concerns and security to another country or organization, she gets burned."

Secretary of State Berg concurred. "They see the UN at a bare minimum as being unsympathetic and at worst, as blatantly anti-Semitic."

Kennedy agreed. "So by killing the Palestinian ambassador in New York, they're telling the UN what they really think of them, while at the same time sending a message to the Palestinians that they can be every bit as brutal as they are."

Culbertson started to see their point. "UN resolutions go unenforced all the time, so why bother trying to appease them."

"Exactly," replied Berg.

SIXTY-ONE

The armor-plated Mercedes limousine came to a stop in front of the north entrance to the West Wing. Two spit-polished marines stood at attention in their dress blues, one on each side of the door, like sentries to an ancient palace. Prince Abdul Bin Aziz stepped from the black limousine and buttoned his suit coat, while ignoring the reporters who were shouting questions at him from the lawn on the other side of the driveway. The cousin to the crown prince had left his keffiyeh back at the embassy. In fact, the only time he wore the traditional garb of his people was when he returned home or was forced to do so because of ceremony.

Over the last fifty-four years the ambassador had spent more time in America than Saudi Arabia, which was fitting, since he'd been born at the Mayo Clinic in Rochester, Minnesota. His early schooling had been handled by tutors and then at the age of fourteen he was shipped off to Philips Exeter Academy, the ultra-exclusive prep school in New Hampshire. After Philips Exeter it was on to Harvard for both his undergraduate and graduate degrees.

Abdul Bin Aziz had a great affinity for America. More

than anything, though, he admired his host country's secular approach to governance. He had seen the true evil that could be perpetrated by men with deep religious conviction and it scared him. This was why he owned three homes in America and rarely allowed his children to return to Saudi Arabia. Prince Abdul Bin Aziz believed that in his lifetime the House of Saud would fall. It would be trampled by the very fanatics his relatives had supported over the years.

The ultra-orthodox Wahhabi sect of Islam had spread like an unruly weed across his country and beyond, choking out all forward and rational thinking, silencing all dissenters within and without the faith, and damning millions of people to a belief system that had more in common with the Stone Age than the twenty-first century.

And now, in this dangerous time, he was once again sent to the White House by his cousin, the crown prince, to try to appease the fanatics without slitting their own throats.

SIXTY-TWO

The entire security team was tense. Twenty or so protestors stood on the other side of the heavy black steel gate, but that's not what concerned Uri Doran, the man charged with protecting Israel's Ambassador to the United States of America. It was the camera crews, two of them to be precise. Doran had been with Shin Bet, Israel's internal security service, for eighteen years. The organization was the rough equivalent of the Secret Service and the State Department's Bureau of Diplomatic Security. He'd learned over the years that cameras were far more dangerous than any bullhorn, sign or brick. Through simple editing, he and his people could be made to look like jackbooted thugs.

The Metropolitan Police had dispatched two squads to help deal with the crowd, but their presence did little to abate Doran's worries. He'd watched Washington's finest in action before, and with a record number of law suits for police brutality in the past few years, the men and women in blue were not about to forcibly subdue unruly protestors and put their careers in jeopardy. To make matters even worse, Washington was a town filled with professional protestors who knew exactly when and how to provoke a confrontation. When forced to move, they were prone to pratfalls and overly dramatic wails of pain as if their limbs were being twisted to the point of breaking. All of this was done, of course, right in front of the cameras to elicit maximum drama for the nightly news audience.

Doran clutched his tiny digital two-way in his hand and looked out across the embassy grounds at the protestors. For now they were acting somewhat civilly, but as soon as the ambassador's armored limousine began to move they would go nuts and rush the gate. For a moment he longed for his days in Argentina when the police would simply turn the water cannons on the crowd and be done with it. This was America, however, and he could hope all he wanted, but such a thing would never happen.

Sitting out the storm would be the best course of action, but the ambassador had told him this was not possible. His presence was requested at the White House, and given the current state of affairs, it was a request he could not ignore. One of Doran's men had suggested sneaking the ambassador out the back way, in one of the security sedans, but the head of the detail had dismissed it for two reasons. The first was that the ambassador was too vain to show up at the White House in a mere sedan, and the second was that none of the sedans were as safe as the ambassador's armor-plated gas guzzler. They would just have to gently inch their way through the crowd and fix the dents and scratches later.

Doran stepped back into the embassy to find Ambassador Eitan nervously pointing at his watch. The Shin Bet officer reluctantly nodded and brought his radio to his mouth. He alerted his team that the ambassador was coming out and then after waiting a moment he escorted the ambassador out the door and quickly into the backseat of the black Cadillac.

The random course to the White House had been chosen and the lead and chase sedans were in place. The heavy vehicle rolled slowly toward the gate. From his position in the front seat Doran could see the protestors begin their surge. Doran resisted the urge to grab the Uzi submachine gun from under the dash. *They were simple protestors and nothing more,* he told himself. He radioed his team, reminding them to stay calm. They'd been through it before.

The gates slowly started to open and the group immediately pressed past the four police officers trying to hold the line. Doran's orders were specific in one regard: if any protestor was foolish enough to try to run through the open gate they were to be immediately brought to the ground. Having witnessed the efficiency of Doran's men before, all of the protestors stopped short of the curb. The lead sedan nudged its way through the crowd, creating a path for the limousine, which stayed right on the sedan's bumper.

The protestors collapsed in around the limousine and began acting like berserk chimpanzees on some safari tour gone bad. They were hammering the limo with their signs, and although Doran couldn't see it, they would also be scratching the paint job with car keys. Out of nowhere came an object that caused Doran to freeze. He could do nothing but watch. It was against all standard security procedures to open the door. The metal cylinder was hoisted over the shoulder of one of the police officers and then a mist of bright orange paint began to coat the front windshield and the side of the car as the limousine kept moving.

As the three-car motorcade broke free, Doran swore to

himself and pressed the transmit button on his two-way, telling his people back at the gate to make sure the culprit was arrested. He would press charges this time and make sure the idiot received the maximum penalty allowed by the American courts.

The ambassador would want to stop now and clean the paint. Under no circumstance would he want to arrive at the White House with a freshly vandalized limousine. Doran would put his foot down this time, though. There was no way he was going to stop in a nonsecured area to clean the car. The Secret Service had a pressure washer available for just such a problem and it could be taken care of in mere minutes in a very secure environment.

The limousine's internal phone buzzed and Doran picked it up.

"Yes." He listened to the ambassador complain for a few seconds and then said, "No." The ambassador was used to getting his way. He began to demand that the car be cleaned. When the ambassador had run out of breath, Doran said, "Mr. Ambassador, we are not stopping, and that is final."

Doran hung up the phone and let out a frustrated sigh. He dreaded the confrontation that would take place later when they got back to the embassy, but he knew he was right. It was his job to worry about security, and the ambassador's to worry about diplomacy.

SIXTY-THREE

The president rose to his feet, and so did everyone else. He crossed the Oval Office and warmly greeted the Saudi ambassador. Clasping both hands around the prince's, Hayes said, "Mr. Ambassador, thank you for coming by."

Kennedy immediately noticed the forced smile on the Saudi ambassador's face. He was not looking forward to whatever it was that he'd been sent to say. She watched cautiously as the ambassador went around the room shaking hands. He was not his normal charming self. He barely made eye contact with Secretary of State Berg and Secretary of Defense Culbertson. He was slightly better with Valerie Jones and Michael Haik, but he only acknowledged General Flood and Kennedy with a slight nod from afar.

When the president and the ambassador were seated in the two chairs in front of the fireplace, everyone else took their place on the couches. Despite the president's warm welcome, a chill fell over the room almost immediately. Prince Abdul Bin Aziz was looking at the ground, waiting for someone else to speak.

Valerie Jones filled the void by announcing, "Mr.

Ambassador, we would like to assure you that we are taking the assassination of the Palestinian ambassador very seriously."

The Saudi ambassador kept his head down and looked up at Jones from under a pair of dark eyebrows. "And what are you doing about the recent attack on the civilian population of Hebron?"

Jones immediately retreated from the diplomatic arena. Such a blunt question could only be handled by the president or the secretary of state.

It was Secretary of State Berg who spoke first. "Mr. Ambassador, we are not happy with the recent developments in Hebron, and are putting as much pressure on the Israelis as we can."

The ambassador was careful to give Secretary Berg a skeptical but respectful look. "Madam Secretary, you either underestimate your influence over your allies or you have yet to exert the proper amount of pressure."

"Trust me, Mr. Ambassador." Berg glanced at the president for a second and said, "We are exerting a great deal of pressure on Israel."

"Then why may I ask is Hebron still under military occupation?"

Before Berg could respond, Secretary Culbertson said, "Because three suicide bombs killed thirty-one Israelis yesterday, bringing the twelve-month total to one hundred and seventy-eight dead and over five hundred injured." The secretary of defense let the cold statistic hang in the air.

Aziz clasped his hands and sat up a little straighter. "The violence is never ending. Somewhere, somehow, it must stop."

"I agree, Mr. Ambassador," replied President Hayes. "But you must agree that Israel is not acting without provocation."

"The other night when they bombed that neighborhood, killing hundreds . . ." Aziz shook his head. "They were not provoked."

No one in the room dared use the Israeli excuse that they were taking out a bomb factory, and it was a good thing they didn't because after a long moment of silence the Saudi ambassador added, "We have received intelligence reports that say there was no bomb factory as the Israelis have claimed." Ambassador Aziz turned his dark eyes from Secretary Culbertson to Kennedy and asked, "Director Kennedy, can you confirm or deny this?"

Kennedy was caught off guard by the ambassador but didn't let it show. Not wanting to appear a bald-faced liar she said, "We have heard the Palestinians' claims, but so far have been unable to verify them."

He kept his gaze locked on Kennedy. "And what of the Palestinian ambassador to the UN?"

Kennedy badly wanted to tell Aziz that his cousin Prince Omar was a suspect but that would be unwise. Besides, they had nowhere near enough evidence to make that connection. As recently as this morning Kennedy and Rapp had discussed the possibility of Freidman sending one of his agents to Omar and setting him up. Freidman had made a career of running very complex operations that looked like one thing and turned out to be something very different. If Omar was about to be the patsy for an Israeli operation they would know soon enough.

Answering the question put to her, Kennedy said, "We have absolutely no idea who killed Ambassador Ali, but are running down every possible lead."

"Including that the Israelis may have done it?"

"Including that the Israelis may have done it," answered Kennedy.

President Hayes cleared his throat. "Abdul, I value your

friendship, and I value the friendship of your country. We have made great strides as of late and I think we need to keep moving in the right direction."

"And what is that direction, Mr. President?"

Hayes looked momentarily miffed by the question. "Peace and prosperity. We need to continue to open up our markets to each other and work toward forging a long-lasting relationship."

"And what of the Palestinian crisis?"

"I've made myself very clear that this administration supports a Palestinian state."

Secretary of State Berg quickly added, "As long as Israel is recognized by the Arab states and her security is guaranteed."

Hayes nodded earnestly.

"Good," said Aziz. "Then we can count on you to vote for the French resolution this afternoon."

The silence was deafening, and after a long awkward moment the ambassador began to shake his head. "Must you always favor Israel?" He said this in a desperate voice that was barely loud enough for the room to hear.

"Mr. Ambassador," said Secretary Berg as gently as possible, "you know better than anyone how complicated this is."

"Yes, I do," he sighed, "and unfortunately it is about to get a great deal more complicated." Aziz turned to President Hayes. "My government is requesting that as a token of our friendship you vote for the French resolution for Palestinian statehood this afternoon."

President Hayes swallowed hard and began to sadly shake his head. "Abdul, I need time."

"For what, Mr. President? So you can try to convince the French to table their resolution?" It was now Aziz's turn to shake his head. "The time has come, Mr. President, to stop the bloodshed. The time has come for you to show that America can be evenhanded in this regard. I plead with you, Mr. President, the Arab people need to see that you will break with Israel when they are wrong."

Berg tried to draw Aziz away from the president. "Mr. Ambassador, I can assure you that the American people want peace in the Middle East, but it cannot be rushed."

"Madam Secretary, I can assure you, in turn, that the Arab people want a Palestinian state, and they are tired of waiting." Aziz turned back to Hayes and with genuine sorrow said, "Mr. President, I take no joy in telling you this, but I have been asked to inform you that if America vetoes the French resolution this afternoon, there will be severe repercussions."

"Such as?" asked Hayes.

Aziz took a deep breath and announced, "The crown prince will suspend all oil shipments to America immediately, and he has been given assurances by the other OPEC Gulf States that they will do the same."

SIXTY-FOUR

The ambassador's words hit home with an impact that rolled through the minds of the presidential advisors like a series of shock waves. No one spoke. There was nothing to say until the ambassador was gone. President Hayes had all but pleaded for the ambassador to give them more time, but the ambassador had been firm. It was time for an even hand and bold steps. Waiting a week or a month served no purpose other than to allow Israel to find a way to hold on to the land.

Kennedy watched as Valerie Jones escorted the ambassador from the room. The president's chief of staff followed him into the hallway in a desperate effort to get him to reconsider. Kennedy didn't need to be told what to do. Getting up from the couch, she walked over to the president's desk and picked up the handset of his bulky secure telephone unit. She punched in ten digits and waited for Charles Workman, her deputy director of intelligence, to answer. On the third ring she got him.

"Charlie, I need an immediate intel pull on everything we have over the last forty-eight hours between Saudi Arabia and the other Gulf States concerning a possible oil embargo against us if we veto the French resolution at the UN."

Kennedy listened for a moment and said, "No, it's first-hand. Ambassador Aziz just informed the president of their intentions." Again she listened to her DDI and then replied, "That's right. Use every asset we've got. I need some hard intel within the hour."

The director of the CIA returned to find a shell-shocked president and a very agitated secretary of defense. "Mr. President, this embargo could be construed as an act of war."

"That's interesting, Rick," chimed Secretary of State Berg. "That's what the Japanese said when we placed an oil and steel embargo on them back in forty-one."

The president looked to Berg, ignoring her historical comparison and asked, "Are they bluffing?"

Berg, who seemed to be taking the news better than anyone else, said, "I'm not sure, but the Gulf States do have a history of false bravado."

"Meaning?"

"Meaning . . . they might be unified at the moment, but who knows what next week will hold. Some of them are in the red . . . a few are barely in the black." Berg gestured with her hands that it was a toss-up. "I can't see a unified embargo holding for very long. We need the oil and they need our money."

"We can't allow this embargo to last a day," announced National Security Advisor Haik. "The mere mention of it could precipitate a worldwide recession. Markets would plunge overnight ten to twenty percent."

"But what about our reserves?" asked Culbertson. "We can increase our imports from Venezuela and Russia and the former republics . . . and if we have to we can drill in Alaska."

"Who says Venezuela and Russia won't go along with them," replied Haik. "And besides, all of that will take time. Two months from the onset of the embargo we could probably get back to near normal supply levels, but that's not what worries me. What worries me is the devastating effect it would have on an already strained economy." Haik turned his attention to the president. "The last time they really hit us with an embargo was in seventy-three, and it took us a decade to climb out of the hole."

Valerie Jones hurried back into the room catching the end of the national security advisor's comments. She quickly added, "And we ended up with interest rates at seventeen percent, runaway inflation and unemployment approaching double digits. Mr. President, we cannot let that happen again."

Her implication was clear. If the embargo was put into effect any chance he had at serving another four years would be dragged down with the floundering economy. Looking back at Jones, Hayes asked, "What did he say when you walked him out?"

"He says they are resolute in their decision. Now is the time for a Palestinian state."

Hayes sighed. "We have no choice."

The defense secretary wasn't quite ready to give in. "Sir, let's engage the French and see if we can get them to delay the vote . . . even a day or two. In exchange we could demand that Israel withdraw its forces from Hebron."

Hayes shook his head in desperation. The French would never go along with such a plan. They had center stage right now, and were not about to miss the opportunity to ram Palestinian statehood down Israel's throat.

"Sir, we can't do it this way," Culbertson stated with great conviction. "Israel will never honor the resolution

until a real cease-fire is in place and they have been given
assurances from all the Arab states. We need time to make
this work."

"Unfortunately," said Hayes, lifting his head, "we don't
have time."

"Let's at least try."

"I agree with Rick, Mr. President." Secretary of State
Berg looked at her watch. "The vote isn't scheduled to
take place for another five hours. We should see if we can
get a withdrawal in exchange for a cease-fire. Maybe even
propose a peace summit in Paris for next week."

"All right. See what you can do with the French."
Hayes motioned for them to get started and both cabinet
members got up. The president turned his attention to
Kennedy. "Is there a chance the Saudis are bluffing?"

"There's a chance, but I think there's a better chance
they're serious. I put a call in to Charlie to find out what
we've picked up in the last forty-eight hours. If they've
been talking we should have picked something up."

SIXTY-FIVE

David sat in front of his monitors and sipped a bottle of water. Everything was going according to plan. The traffic cameras were all on-line and working properly, his media source had confirmed the ambassador's appointment at the White House, and the world was watching. Washington D.C. was about to be rocked, and David couldn't have been more pleased with how things were playing out. As he'd predicted, the Israelis had sent their army into Hebron and the international community was busy filing protests. Palestinian suicide bombers were throwing themselves into the breach and making the Israelis pay the price. French Ambassador Joussard was playing his hand perfectly at the UN, and if Omar had been successful in convincing his brother the crown prince that now was the time for an embargo, the United States would be boxed in. All that was left to do was raise the level of violence one more notch, and his lifelong dream of a free Palestinian state would be a reality.

The black limousine came into view on the predetermined screen in the upper left corner. David put the bottle of water down and glanced at the remote firing device sitting in the heavy black case on his right. The bomb was already armed and ready to go. All he needed to do was pop the clear safety cover and press the red button.

The limousine made a turn and showed up on the next screen. David tracked it carefully through the city. It was close to the White House. The explosion would undoubtedly be heard by the president and the Secret Service would go into lockdown mode. David watched with great anticipation as the limousine neared the crucial intersection. At this point everything depended on its taking a right turn. David wiped his sweaty palms on his pants and counted the seconds.

The vehicle began to slow and then just as anticipated it turned onto Virginia Avenue midway between the State Department and the White House. David breathed a brief sigh of relief and looked to the next monitor, his fingers poised above the keyboard, prepared to manipulate the traffic light two intersections away. He could see the parked van now visible on two of the monitors. He entered the proper command and held the traffic light on red for another fifteen seconds. The limousine's brake lights came on almost immediately. David popped the plastic cover on the remote firing device and waited. The long black vehicle inched its way into position and then when it was a few feet short David reached over and pressed the red button.

SIXTY-SIX

Rapp appeared in the doorway of the Oval Office with Secret Service Special Agent Jack Warch. Rapp caught his boss's attention and motioned for her to join him in the hall. Aides and staffers were now coming and going, shuttling back and forth between other members of the president's staff and cabinet. The political machine was coming together for a unified assault on forestalling the UN vote.

Kennedy excused herself and joined Rapp and Warch. The Secret Service agent led them across the hall and opened the door to the Roosevelt Room. Rapp thanked the head of the Presidential Detail and promised to keep him informed.

Kennedy studied Rapp suspiciously and asked, "Keep him informed of what?"

"Our John Doe, who met with Omar and then flew to New York . . . Well, Olivia just found out that he left Penn Station at ten oh five the night Ambassador Ali was killed."

"And where was he—" Kennedy stopped short, knowing the answer before Rapp finished.

Rapp nodded. "He arrived at Union Station early Tuesday morning just before two."

The director of the CIA studied her top operative, wondering what to make of this unusual development. "Why would he come here?"

"That's a good question, and I'm not so sure I can answer it."

"I assume from what I heard you say to Jack, that you warned him of a potential threat to the president?"

"Yep. I just wanted to make sure the president wasn't making any scheduled public appearances today."

"So you think he's come here to kill again?"

It was obvious by the expression on his face that Rapp wasn't so sure. "I don't know, Irene. It could be something as simple as a preplanned escape route. Rather than try to leave the country and get caught, come to where you're least expected to go."

She could tell Rapp didn't buy his own line of thinking. "What do you really think? What does your gut tell you?"

Rapp struggled with it for a moment and then replied, "I think he's come here to do another job."

"Or," Kennedy added, "he lives here."

This was an entirely new line of thinking. There were plenty of former Special Forces guys living in the surrounding area, at least a few of whom were guns for hire. But there was something about him that was distinctly un-American. A certain look similar to his own. Most people would never notice it, but it was what gave Rapp the ability to blend in when he was operating in the Middle East and Southwest Asia. He thought about the guy being an American and said, "That's a possibility, but if the guy lived here, he would be more familiar with our capabilities, in which case I can't see why he'd risk being seen on camera."

"It's obvious."

"He doesn't know we're on to him," answered Rapp.

"Exactly."

"Or," said Rapp, "we're giving him more credit than he deserves."

"Either way have Olivia run a check through the DOD files."

"I'll do it, but what about bringing Mossad in on this?" asked Rapp.

Kennedy shook her head. "The president won't allow it, plus he still thinks the Israelis are behind this."

"That's nonsense."

"I'm not so sure," said Kennedy with a raised brow. "What if this entire thing is a complex sting launched by Mossad to implicate Prince Omar?" Kennedy could tell by Rapp's sour expression that he didn't buy it. "Just think about it for a minute. If John Doe is really Israeli and they sent him to con Prince Omar into playing the crown prince of Saudi Arabia, the one role he wanted more than anything in his life . . ."

"What's their endgame?" asked an unconvinced Rapp.

"Embarrass the Saudis and draw attention to their support of Palestinian extremists."

"I don't know, Irene," he said, frowning, "it sounds like a reach."

"I'm not saying it isn't, but it's one of several reasons why we can't go to Freidman and ask him who this guy is. I do, however, think it's time to bring the FBI in on this."

Rapp cringed. "I don't know about that."

"If this John Doe is in Washington we have no choice."

He instinctively recoiled against the idea, and it was not a reflection on the Bureau's competency as much as it was on the rule book that they'd bring along. If the FBI nabbed this guy they would have to play it straight up. Reluctantly, Rapp consented.

The two of them left the Roosevelt Room and walked across the hall to the Oval Office. At present there were too many people in the room to tell the president of the recent development. While Kennedy waited to have a private word with Hayes, Rapp called the CTC to tell Turbes to bring the FBI in on the investigation. Before his call could be completed there was a rumbling noise from outside the building. Rapp instantly tensed, knowing before anyone else in the presidential office that the noise was an explosion.

SIXTY-SEVEN

True to form, Marcus Dumond sat in his corner cubicle oblivious to the storm that was raging around him. The Bull Pen at the CIA's Counterterrorism Center was a labyrinth of five-foot-tall plastic and fabric dividers. Partly out of necessity, and partly out of humor, the aisles that cut through the area had been given names such as Abu Nidal Way and Osama Bin Lane. Dumond had been the chief planner and street namer of the ever expanding Bull Pen, and he had intentionally located himself on a dead street with limited access.

While his MP3 player cranked out the tunes, Dumond worked the keys of his computer with blazing efficiency, toggling back and forth between three screens, closing windows, opening new ones and shrinking or enlarging others. He was on to something. He wasn't sure what quite yet, but he was definitely on to something. Following Rapp's lead, he'd focused on recent transactions made by Omar's main assistant. The hardest nut to crack wasn't hacking into the secure networks of the institutions in question—that was easy. The real issue lay in the enormity of Omar's wealth. He used literally hundreds of banks to handle his vast fortune. That said, however, Dumond didn't waste his time surfing through the prince's transactions that were handled by Chase or the Deutsche Bank. In fact he immediately discarded all banks in the United States, England, Japan, Canada and Germany and focused on those nations known for their financial privacy laws.

Dumond had only to read the file on Devon LeClair once to know where to focus his attention. If given his choice, an anal retentive snob like LeClair would bank with only one group of people. The ever efficient Swiss were the perfect match. They thought of everything. They conducted themselves with a respectful, professional flair that properly schooled men like LeClair demanded.

Trying to run searches based on Omar's name or those of his various holding companies had proven to be too cumbersome. Dumond had two strategies he wanted to employ before he called in the money guys from Treasury and the FBI to pore over the accounts with a magnifying glass. He'd seen the men and women do it before, chasing down every check, wire transfer and charge to its final destination. It could easily take fifty agents six months to run a thorough examination of Omar's finances, and even then they might miss something. They had to do things the proper way, both politically and legally.

Even if they knew the tricks that Dumond employed, they would be too afraid to use them. The twenty-eight-year-old hacker from MIT could get results much quicker. None of the information he gathered would be admissible in a court of law, but Dumond had worked enough with Rapp in the past to know that he preferred to settle things in a less public forum.

Dumond had keyed in on three banks, two headquartered in Zurich and a third in Geneva. Each bank was among Switzerland's oldest and most austere, and LeClair was authorized access to each one. At first Dumond focused his attention on the larger transactions, five to ten million dollars. He came up blank, so he started over again looking for money that had been shuffled between the three banks he was focusing on. This also proved to be a dead end.

As a last resort he went through each account for the past month looking for smaller transactions from various banks on various days that all may have ended up in a single account. He paid special attention to the name of the banks the money was being transferred to. He was looking for an accumulation of funds in one account that would get him to the proper threshold.

Dumond was focusing on blocks of money and transaction dates. In his mind he was trying to piece together a down payment followed by a later payment for successful completion of contract. He couldn't find anything that was approaching five million dollars or even half of that number. Suddenly an amount and a bank caught his eye: $500,000 had been wired from one of the banks in Zurich on Monday to a financial institution on the island of Martinique in the French West Indies. He swore he'd already seen the same transaction. He began looking back through the transactions and sure enough, two weeks earlier LeClair had wired the same amount from another account to the same account in Martinique.

As Dumond looked at the name on the account in Martinique he couldn't help but think there was something familiar about it. His fingers remained poised just above the keyboard and his head began to tilt to one side. It was coming to him. The name was not that common. Like his own it was French, which would fit with the French West Indies, but there was some reason why it seemed familiar to him. Dumond pulled his arms back and crossed them in frustration. He had just seen the name somewhere and it was driving him nuts that he couldn't remember. He was about to give up and have the computer run a search when it hit him.

Dumond closed out one of his screens. His fingers flew across the keys in search of this morning's on-line edition of *The New York Times*. The home page popped up on his center screen and he scanned the sidebar for the story he was looking for. After a brief moment he found it and opened the article. In the first paragraph of the article Dumond hit upon the name he was looking for: Peter Joussard. He looked back and forth from one screen to the other, from the on-line edition of *The New York Times* to the balance of a bank account in the Caribbean containing one million dollars. Dumond attempted to calculate the odds that it was coincidence and quickly decided it wasn't, it couldn't be. Yanking off his headphones he grabbed the handset of his phone and dialed Rapp's mobile number.

SIXTY-EIGHT

I t had taken almost exactly an hour to figure out what had happened. The White House was under lockdown. No one was being allowed in or out. The president and the other principles had all been moved downstairs to the Situation Room. Jack Warch, the special agent in charge of the Presidential Detail, had originally ordered that everyone be taken to the bunker deep under the White House, but President Hayes had countermanded the order. He'd been in the bunker once before and had no desire to go back unless he absolutely had to.

When Warch saw how serious the president was, he relented. At a minimum he asked that they relocate to the Situation Room. Hayes agreed, and the National Security Team moved downstairs where they could monitor the crisis and stay in close contact with their various departments and agencies. The heavily armed and black-clad Secret Service Counter Assault Team had taken up defensive positions around the Executive Mansion and the West Wing. Stinger surface-to-air missiles had been unsheathed and readied on the rooftop and Stage Coach, the presidential limousine, was running and waiting on the South Grounds ready to evacuate the commander in chief from the premises if necessary.

The men and women under Warch's command had reacted with the precision and efficiency that he expected. They'd run the drills over and over until every agent and officer knew not only their own responsibilities, but those of the people who stood next to them. Now the one-hundred-plus-person force stood primed and poised, ready for whatever would happen next. As the minutes passed they began to realize that the White House was not a target. At least not today.

The initial reports that came into the Situation Room were that the State Department had been hit by a car bomb. Those reports were quickly proven inaccurate when Secretary of State Berg contacted her office and was told the point of the explosion was actually several blocks away on Virginia Avenue. The first real clues to the carnage were provided by a Fox TV crew that had been at the State Department doing a live shot. After recovering from the initial shock of the explosion they packed up their gear and hoofed it to the site of the detonation.

They were lucky enough to get to the scene before the Metropolitan Police could set up a perimeter. Fox broadcast live footage of fire crews trying to douse the flames of several twisted wrecks. The FBI and ATF arrived twenty minutes later and had the Fox TV crew moved to the other side of the barricades with the rest of the networks and cable outlets.

The bomb experts from the ATF and FBI quickly ascertained the exact point of detonation and found what little was left of the vehicle that had been used as the platform. After that everything was a little confusing. There were shattered windows on both sides of the street for at least a block in each direction. Injured people streamed out of office buildings, many of them with nothing more than paper towels to stem the blood that flowed from gashes caused by flying glass. The George Washington University Medical Center, just a few blocks to the north, was inundated with patients. Fortunately only a few of them had injuries that were life threatening.

The actual target of the bombing was not immediately obvious. Several cars were flipped, twisted and charred almost beyond recognition. Many of the buildings had received superficial damage, but none had collapsed. The true target of the attack came to light when someone from the Saudi embassy called to see if the ambassador was still at the White House. The answer was unfortunately no. It appeared the ambassador's staff, after seeing the footage, had tried to reach both the ambassador and his security detail. No one was answering their phones.

An FBI agent at the scene verified that one of the charred vehicles did in fact appear to be a limousine. It had taken the brunt of the explosion. Torn in half and flung across the street, it was now resting upside down in two pieces on the opposite sidewalk. The bodies inside the limousine were burned beyond recognition. The make of the vehicle was verified as a Mercedes with diplomatic plates. Prince Abdul Bin Aziz, the Royal Saudi ambassador to the United States of America, was dead.

President Hayes's range of emotions went from disbelief, to confusion, to outright anger. When Rapp entered the Situation Room for the second time the president was absolutely furious. He had been in the midst of trying to figure out what to say to the crown prince when CBS broke the story. The speculation began almost instantly. In the new twenty-four-hour news cycle it wasn't enough to just report the facts.

Talking heads were taking to the air on every station throwing the names of terrorist organizations around like they were corporations traded on the New York Stock Exchange. So-called experts were calling into question the effectiveness of the FBI and CIA and the new department of Homeland Security was being denounced by one particularly self-righteous pundit as a monumental failure.

During that initial media scramble to try to get ahold of the story, one lone voice caught the president's ear. A spokesman for the Palestinians wondered aloud if Israel could have been behind the assassination in an effort to delay the vote before the UN and drive a wedge between America and her greatest Arab ally. The story had struck such a chord that even Rapp paused to give it serious consideration. Both he and Kennedy shot each other quick, worried glances upon hearing the hypothesis.

If it wasn't for the fax that Rapp held in his hand he would have been more inclined to believe Israel was behind this entire operation. Prime Minister Goldberg was ruthless and daring enough to launch such a plan and Ben Freidman was the perfect person to carry it out. If this car bomb got pinned on any one of a dozen terrorist groups the crown prince and the rest of the House of Saud would put their wallets away and begin cracking down on fanatics like they had never done before. The Saudi ambassador and the crown prince were very close, having been raised together and schooled as if they were brothers. He was the perfect target, and what better place to do it than on U.S. soil.

Several things didn't fit, however. There was this mysterious John Doe seen meeting with Prince Omar twice in the last two weeks. There was the audio recording from the Brits that had them talking about war and money, and even more interesting was the sudden appearance of this John Doe in both New York City and Washington, D.C.

All of this could be explained away as some exotic operation by Mossad to put the Palestinians on the defensive, stick their finger in the eye of the UN and drive a wedge between the United States and Saudi Arabia. In a contorted complex way Rapp could see why Freidman might launch such an operation. The suicide bombs were not stopping and in the minds of men like Goldberg and Freidman action was always better than inaction. All of that fit with one exception.

Rapp held up the fax one more time and read it. This one piece of evidence unearthed by Dumond cast everything else they had in a different light. Rapp was about to tell Kennedy what the young hacker had discovered when a marine captain came up and told him he had an important phone call.

SIXTY-NINE

P resident Hayes was leaning forward in his leather chair with both elbows planted on the long shiny conference table that dominated the Situation Room. One hand clutched the white receiver of his secure telephone unit and the other was placed over his brow to shield his eyes from any distraction. He was talking to the crown prince of Saudi Arabia, a man he considered his friend. The prince was someone who Hayes felt truly wanted to see east and west merge peacefully, but was unfortunately saddled with a populace that for the most part preferred religious rhetoric and inflammatory speech over enlightenment and liberty.

Hayes knew Crown Prince Faisal and his cousin were close. That made the call difficult enough, but it was also difficult because Hayes was embarrassed; embarrassed that such an attack had occurred on American soil, just blocks from the White House, just minutes after the ambassador had sat in the Oval Office and delivered an ultimatum that if not heeded would put the tenuous American economy into a downward spiral. An ultimatum that certain hard-liners in Washington would deem an act of war.

The thought of that news alone becoming public caused the president to become momentarily nauseous. The conspiracy nuts and leftist anti-oil crowd would have a field day with that juicy connection. *Saudi ambassador comes to White House, threatens oil embargo and then is killed in explosion after leaving meeting with the president.* This would be next to impossible to contain. No matter how innocent he was there would always be those who would forever believe President Robert Hayes or someone in his administration had had a hand in the ambassador's death.

Hayes, in his attempt to console the crown prince, stated over and over how sorry he was and that he would make sure the perpetrators were caught and brought to justice. Something in the crown prince's voice told Hayes that the monarch did not believe him. As a final gesture, Hayes asked the crown prince if there was anything he could do to help ease the pain. Crown Prince Faisal made only one request, and it was one that given the current situation the president knew he could not refuse.

President Hayes slowly hung up the phone and with the expression of a beaten man said, "Inform Ambassador Brieseth at the UN that we will be voting for the French resolution this afternoon."

Secretary of State Berg and Chief of Staff Jones were alone with the president in the Situation Room. Both shifted in their chairs uncomfortably and exchanged nervous looks. It was Jones's job to speak first. She had known Hayes the longest and was his closest advisor.

In a soft voice Jones asked, "Robert, what did Faisal ask of you?"

"He does not want his cousin's death to be in vain. He wants me to help make a Palestinian state a reality."

Jones nodded thoughtfully. She did not want to face an oil embargo, but neither did she want to face the wrath of the Jewish lobby. "I'm not saying we shouldn't do that, but don't you think we should talk about it?"

Hayes simply shook his head. "There's nothing left to talk about. I don't trust the Palestinians any more than you do, but the truth is I don't trust the Israelis either. If we don't vote for this resolution we'll once again look like we're doing Israel's bidding, and we can't continue to look so one-sided in the eyes of the Arab world."

The secretary of state cleared her throat and said, "Excuse me, Mr. President, but Israel is the only democracy in a region dominated by dictators, corruption and a very dangerous strain of religious zealotry."

"I know all that, but it doesn't change the fact that we'll once again look like we're favoring Israel. Add to that the fact that the Saudi ambassador delivered us an ultimatum and then his limousine was blown up...." Hayes paused in frustration and through gritted teeth said, "The Arab street will think we killed him. They'll hit us with an oil embargo and consumer prices will skyrocket and our economy will go right into the tank. We are boxed in."

"Sir," cautioned Berg, "there are better ways to do this. I can guarantee you that Israel will defy the UN if the French march this resolution through the Security Council. This vote, sir, could very easily lead to open war." Berg leaned forward, stressing her next point. "We need to get a cease-fire in place first, and then come up with a well-thought-out plan and timetable, or all of this will be a disaster."

"How? The French have made it abundantly clear that they will not delay the vote."

"For starters, let's get Prime Minister Goldberg to pull his forces out of Hebron, and let's get him to do it immediately! The Israeli ambassador is in the building.

We can deliver a stern ultimatum and demand immediate action."

"And what about the vote?" asked a skeptical Hayes.

"We'll work on getting the French to delay it."

Hayes lowered his head and thought about it for a moment. The idea of getting the Israelis to pull out of Hebron was appealing, but he'd learned long ago that getting the French to do anything was never easy. Halfheartedly he nodded his approval. "Let's do what we can, but if nothing has changed by the time the vote comes up, we're going to support it. I see no other choice."

SEVENTY

Kennedy looked at the fax and like Dumond before her, she tried to calculate the odds of another Peter Joussard receiving one million dollars from one of Prince Omar's private Swiss bank accounts. It was Kennedy's nature to be suspicious, and thus she was inclined to lean away from coincidence and toward conspiracy. When she discovered that half of the money had been deposited in the Caribbean account the same day the Palestinian ambassador to the UN was killed, she all but ruled out coincidence.

Standing near the Duty Desk of the Situation Room, Kennedy looked up from the fax and asked, "Are we doing anything else to confirm that this account belongs to Ambassador Joussard?"

"Marcus is looking into his personal finances right now," answered Rapp.

Kennedy accepted the answer with a pensive nod and fought the urge to race into the conference room and tell the president. "And this John Doe"—Kennedy held up the photo taken from one of the surveillance cameras at Union Station—"anything else on him?"

Rapp shook his head in frustration.

"All right. Let's go tell the president."

Rapp reached out and grabbed her by the arm. "Hold on a second." He didn't like the idea of just dumping this stuff on the president without a game plan. Rapp knew what the president's reaction would be. He'd want to get the FBI and every other law enforcement agency involved and in the process they'd stir up so much shit, and cause so much unneeded confusion, this guy they were looking for would disappear. Rapp had an idea for a gambit that would allow them to see things as they really were.

After making sure no one could hear them, Rapp drew close to his boss and said, "This is what we should do."

KENNEDY ENTERED THE CONFERENCE ROOM first and announced to the various staffers who were present, "Principals only, please."

This was code for telling everyone who wasn't at least a cabinet member that something of a very delicate nature was about to be discussed. The handful of aides that were present immediately exited the room, leaving the secretary of state, the national security advisor, the chief of staff, the president and Rapp and Kennedy. Neither Kennedy nor Rapp bothered to sit.

Kennedy spoke directly to the president. "Sir, we have a couple of very interesting developments." Kennedy set the first piece of paper down. "This shot was taken from a surveillance camera at Penn Station in New York City the night that Ambassador Ali was assassinated and this shot"—Kennedy set down a second piece of paper—"was taken at Union Station approximately three hours later. The experts at Langley say this man is the same individual the British photographed meeting with Prince Omar. The same man who was picked up on surveillance cameras at JFK on Sunday."

Hayes stared at the two photographs for a few seconds and said, "So . . . if I'm hearing you right this man is in D.C."

"That photo is from early Tuesday morning, so we can't be sure he's still in town, but—"

"But we think he probably is," replied Hayes.

"Yes, sir."

"And are we thinking he might have had something to do with the explosion this morning?"

"As of right now, I would say yes."

"Do we have any idea who this guy is?"

Kennedy hesitated. "I'm afraid not, sir."

The president's jaw clenched in frustration. "What are we doing to catch him?"

"We've checked all of our databases on known or suspected terrorists, as well as everything the Brits have and Interpol. For reasons that are obvious we have yet to check with either the French or the Israelis."

"And we've come up blank," stated Hayes flatly.

"Yes, sir." Kennedy made no attempt to soften the truth.

Hayes looked away from Kennedy to his other advisors and asked, "Well then, what in the hell are we going to do?"

The national security advisor spoke first. "I think it's time we bring the FBI in on this thing. And if we think this guy is still in the country we should alert all local, state and federal law enforcement officers. We have to cast a big net and hope we catch him."

"Sir," said Rapp a bit too forcefully, "I think that's a bad idea."

Everyone in the room looked to Rapp. Even the unflappable Kennedy, who knew what they were up to, was a bit caught off guard.

Rapp glanced at Kennedy and said, "Show him the fax."

Kennedy set the last piece of paper down in front of Hayes and explained its significance.

Hayes studied the document and asked, "What are you trying to tell me?"

Rapp answered before Kennedy had the chance. "I think it's pretty obvious, sir. Ambassador Joussard was bought."

Hayes frowned. "Do we even know for sure if this account belongs to the ambassador?"

"We're working to confirm it, sir, but it's a pretty big coincidence."

Sitting to the president's right Secretary of State Berg was replaying in her mind a conversation she had had with her French counterpart. In an effort to get France to delay the vote, Berg had pleaded with the minister of foreign affairs to reconsider. As the conversation played out the minister had admitted something that was a bit unusual.

Berg decided it was time to share her thoughts. "Excuse me, Mr. President, but I'm inclined to agree with Mr. Rapp."

Surprised by his secretary of state's position, the president asked incredulously, "Why?"

"When I attempted to get the French to ease off of their position yesterday, the minister of foreign affairs admitted to me that even he was a bit caught off guard by what was going on in the UN. When I pressed him, all he would say was that Ambassador Joussard had acted without his approval. His excuse for this was that Joussard was a very eager politician and a close friend of the president. In addition to that, pushing for Palestinian statehood was nothing new. The entire country of France overwhelmingly supports the idea."

Hayes stabbed the fax with his index finger. "I need this verified, and I need it done fast. If we're going to get the vote delayed it will take some time."

Kennedy said, "We've got our best people on it."

"Now tell me why this"—Hayes waved the fax in the air—"should change my mind about alerting the FBI to this mystery man who seems to be in all the right places at the wrong time."

"Because once we do that, sir, he'll know we're on to him."

Hayes let out a heavy sigh. "I don't see how we can possibly keep this from the FBI."

"I agree." Always the political oracle, Jones looked to her boss and added, "There will be a congressional investigation into this and if" —she stopped and corrected herself—"when they find out you willingly withheld information from the FBI . . ." She didn't bother to finish the sentence. The painful expression on her face said it all.

Kennedy had coached Rapp that this would be the most influential argument for alerting the FBI. She'd also told him that it would come from Jones. Ignoring the chief of staff, Rapp focused on the president and said, "Sir, all I want is twenty-four hours." He spoke in a confident tone. "Give me a day, and I'll find out who this guy is and what he's up to."

The president believed him, but unfortunately they didn't have the luxury of a day to figure out what was going on. "We're out of time, Mitch. The UN is going to vote this afternoon. I'm sorry, but we're going to have to bring in the FBI."

Rapp had him right where he wanted him. "What if I can get the UN to delay the vote for a day?"

Hayes was cautiously intrigued. "How?"

SEVENTY-ONE

Ambassador Eitan had been sitting in the Oval Office for eleven minutes and thirty-eight seconds. The Israeli emissary to the United States knew this because he was a fastidious time checker. Having to wait to see the president of the United States was not an unusual occurrence, but waiting alone in the Oval Office was. Either intentionally or unintentionally it was very unsettling, and this morning had been unsettling enough. It had started with a frustrating conference call to his superiors back in Jerusalem. They told him to tell the Americans nothing, which was easy enough since he knew nothing, but incredibly irritating because his own government didn't trust him enough to let him know what was going on.

Then there had been the protestors and the bright orange spray paint. His security chief had refused to stop and clean the paint, and as he'd predicted, the camera crews stationed at the White House had descended on the graffiti-strewn limousine like a pack of rats on a garbage heap. And then the most unsettling thing of all occurred: the car bomb. Eitan and his assistant had been shoved into a corner table of the White House Mess and told to stay put. They were under lockdown. No one was to leave or enter the White House until the Secret Service said so.

While drinking his coffee, he had seen the news bulletins on TV reporting that the Saudi ambassador had been the target. Eitan was not embarrassed by the fact that he felt no sorrow for the man. He barely knew the ambassador, but that wasn't the reason for his lack of sadness. There were plenty of people who he'd never met that he regularly felt compassion for. Eitan was not an insensitive man; he just simply felt that it was about time others experienced the pain that he and his countrymen experienced on a weekly basis. Especially the Saudis, who through their so-called charities supported many of the groups who spilled Israeli blood in the most indiscriminate and inhumane of ways.

He had been at the White House for almost two hours and was growing more nervous by the minute. The UN vote for Palestinian statehood was creeping closer, and if Eitan didn't deliver his message soon it would be too late to do any good. His government was depending on him to move the Americans in the right direction. After almost two solid years of suicide bombs, the UN was about to reward the perpetrators of such violence with statehood. The United States had to stop such a precedent from being set.

PRESIDENT HAYES ENTERED HIS OFFICE with a determined stride and an angry expression on his face. That on its own should have warned the Israeli ambassador that something bad was about to happen, but at that moment someone other than the president had caught his attention. Actually two people had, but the second one of the two was far more unsettling. Eitan had expected to see

Secretary of State Berg, or Valerie Jones or maybe even Michael Haik. He was mildly surprised to see CIA director Kennedy, but it was the sight of her companion that literally made him slightly weak in the knees.

He had read stories about the man, but they were nothing compared to the things he'd heard. Eitan had been told he was capable of great violence. Even the formidable head of Mossad, Ben Freidman, feared him. The ambassador had never seen him in person, only in photographs. His hair seemed longer now, and he was very tan. If it wasn't for the fact that he'd followed Kennedy into the room he probably would have never known who it was. When the man turned and stared at Eitan with his dark brown eyes all doubt vanished. Eitan had seen eyes like that before and they didn't belong to diplomats. The ambassador quickly looked away and found the president standing before him.

"Mr. President," Eitan started, his voice a bit shaky, "I am very sorry about the attack on your country this morning."

Hayes stared back at the man, his suit coat unbuttoned and his hands on his hips, his eyes searching for the slightest sign of insincerity. "Mr. Ambassador, I'm short on time so I'm going to make this real simple. I want your country to pull its military forces out of Hebron immediately."

Eitan stood frozen before the president. He hadn't even been offered a seat and he'd been given an ultimatum that he knew would not be accepted. He licked his lips and tried to temper his reply. "Mr. President, I will gladly forward your request, but I of course can make no guarantees."

"First of all," replied Hayes, "it is not a request—it's a demand. And I want Prime Minister Goldberg to go on TV immediately to announce the withdrawal."

The Israeli ambassador was reeling. "But, Mr. President, I cannot make such a request without—"

Hayes held up his hand and stopped him from speaking further. "I know . . . you want a concession . . . and it is this: In exchange for an immediate withdrawal we will get the Security Council vote delayed until tomorrow."

Eitan felt himself begin to sweat. This was not an offer that he could take to the prime minister. He knew what his job was, and despite being caught off guard he gathered just enough confidence to hold his ground. "Mr. President, Prime Minister Goldberg will never agree to such a demand without assurances that you will veto the French resolution."

The president shook his head vigorously. "If the troops aren't pulled out immediately, we will make no effort to delay the vote. In fact, if the troops aren't pulled out immediately we will back the French resolution."

All Eitan could think to do was shake his head. "I'm afraid I will need more to work with . . . a concession of some sort."

What Hayes had to offer was the opposite of what the ambassador was looking for. "Here's something to work with. Tell the prime minister that I know what really happened in Hebron, and unless he wants his cabinet to collapse in scandal he'll announce an immediate withdrawal."

The president turned to his left and said, "Mr. Rapp, if you would please show the ambassador across the hall to the Roosevelt Room, we have it all set up for him to call Prime Minister Goldberg."

"I would like to go back to my embassy to make the call, sir."

The president testily replied, "I don't know if you've noticed, Mr. Ambassador, but we're running out of time.

If you want me to forestall a vote on Palestinian statehood I suggest you get the prime minister on the phone as soon as possible."

Rapp stood up with one arm pointing toward the door. The message he conveyed was simple. The president was done talking. With a sigh and a nod the ambassador reluctantly gave in. As Rapp escorted him from the room the Israeli's discomfort was obvious.

SEVENTY-TWO

The president was reluctant to give final approval to the next part of Kennedy and Rapp's plan. If the media ever found out they would eat him alive. Every leader of every country would scorn him and virtually every member of his own party would repudiate him. As Rapp had pointed out, though, there was no other option.

They were back downstairs in the Situation Room, just Kennedy and the president. Kennedy was resting the phone against her shoulder waiting for the president to answer her question.

She could tell he was having second thoughts. "Sir, this will not hurt you. This was my idea, and I gave the order. Mitch has already laid out plausible deniability. We have a source in place, and after what happened this morning no one will be able to criticize us for being overly cautious." Kennedy waited for a few seconds and then added, "Both our ambassador and the French ambassador are out of the building. Now is the time, sir."

There was no other option. The French were refusing to delay the vote, and Rapp insisted they not reveal what they knew about Ambassador Joussard until the time was right. That was ammunition they would use later. Ultimately the decision came down to trust. Hayes trusted Kennedy and Rapp, and in addition to that they were out of options.

Hayes looked at the director of the CIA and said, "Go ahead."

Kennedy punched in the number, and when the familiar voice of her counterterrorism director answered she said, "Jake, that phone call we talked about earlier . . . it's time to make it." Kennedy listened only long enough to receive confirmation and then hung up.

Kennedy had just ordered her director of counterterrorism to inform the UN of a suspected terrorist plot to attack the headquarters in New York City today. Turbes was instructed to say only that the suspected attack was linked to a larger plot including the car bombing in D.C. The media would be informed through leaks and United Nations World Headquarters would be evacuated within the hour.

RAPP WAS STANDING IN THE HALLWAY outside the Roosevelt Room, his back against the wall and his hands firmly clasped in front of him. Normally he enjoyed being as anonymous as possible but this morning he rather relished playing the role of intimidator. He'd even gone so far as to wait in the conference room alone with the ambassador until the Israeli had been forced to ask him to leave.

His injury was considerably better and despite not having slept much the night before he felt okay. This was because they were finally making some progress, taking action and forcing people to do things that would tell them more about where they stood. Sitting back and waiting for things to happen was contrary to Rapp's way

of life. He was about to open the door and rattle the ambassador again when his digital phone began to vibrate.
Rapp snatched it from his belt and checked the number
before answering the call. It was the CTC.

"Hello."

"Mitch, you're not going to believe what I'm looking
at." It was Olivia Bourne and her voice was elated. "I've
got our mystery boy on camera. He just checked in at the
United counter at BWI."

"Baltimore Washington International?" Rapp's voice
was eager. "You're sure it's him?"

"The computer picked him up first. It's been running
searches all morning at Reagan, Dulles, BWI, Union Station and Richmond." The facial recognition program that
Bourne was referring to was able to scan hundreds of images every second and instantaneously compare them
against a sample, which in this case was the earlier photograph of John Doe they had from his entry into the country. "It's him, Mitch, and if you hold on for a second I'll
give you a name and an itinerary."

Rapp's mind was already racing ahead. "Have you told
anyone?"

"Only Marcus. He's working on a name and flight
right now."

"Is he still at the counter?"

"No. He's just walked away, but we have him on camera. He's headed toward the security line. Hold on . . .
Marcus has a name. Don Marin. He's booked on a flight
that leaves for Paris at ten thirty-two, and from there it
looks like he's . . . connecting to Nice."

The frantic calculations and maneuvering came to an
abrupt halt. "Say that again," commanded Rapp. Even as
Bourne repeated herself Rapp barely paid attention. His
mind was already off, looking in a different direction, to-

ward Europe. He was no longer frantically trying to figure out how to get to the Baltimore airport in thirty
minutes. He was no longer trying to figure out how to
deal with the airport police and the FBI and everybody
else who would want to get their hands on the man who
had more than likely killed both the Palestinian and
Saudi ambassadors. He was suddenly seeing things with
great clarity.

"How are the cameras at BWI?" he finally asked.

"Good."

"Good enough to make sure he gets on that flight?"

There was a pause while Bourne did some checking.
"I've just pulled up his gate and they're already boarding
the plane. I don't think he has enough time to do anything other than go straight to the gate."

"But if he's got another ticket on another flight . . ."

"I'll keep an eye on him and make sure he gets on the
one to Paris."

Rapp stood calmly in the hallway clutching the tiny
phone to his left ear. If this went wrong, he would be severely criticized for not alerting the airport police and
having John Doe arrested. If he did that, however, there
would be a record, and a lot of witnesses. And even if he
did manage to get the guy away from the police and the
FBI he would have to try to interrogate him, which Rapp
detested. There was a better way, a little bit riskier, but in
the end, a way that was much more likely to give them
the truth.

Bourne's voice pulled him back to the moment. "What
do you want me to do?"

Rapp didn't speak at first and then he said, "Keep an
eye on him. Make sure he gets on that flight and get me
a surveillance team and a plane."

Bourne did not reply right away and then asked, "Are

you sure you don't want to alert the FBI and have him detained?"

No, he wasn't sure, but he was pretty sure, and if his luck held for another thirty minutes he'd be absolutely sure. "Let's keep the Feds out of this for now. Just don't lose him, and get me a plane."

Rapp stabbed the end button and then quickly dialed a number from memory. After several rings Scott Coleman answered and Rapp asked, "Can you and the boys be ready to leave within the hour?"

"May I ask where we're going?"

"South of France. Low intensity, mostly surveillance, but I might need you guys if I have to do any heavy lifting."

"Standard fee?" asked the retired SEAL.

"Of course."

"We're in."

Rapp was already on his way downstairs. "Good. I'll call with the specifics, in the meantime get ready to roll."

WITH HER FINGER POISED ABOVE THE KEYPAD of the secure phone Kennedy looked to the president and asked, "Are you ready?"

Hayes nodded and placed his hand near his own phone. Kennedy dialed the number from memory, and after she'd hit the last number she gestured for the president to pick up.

The voice that answered on the other end was not Ben Freidman's. It was one of his assistants, who politely informed Kennedy that Freidman was on the phone. Kennedy didn't doubt that. The director general of Mossad was undoubtedly talking to Prime Minister Goldberg about the phone call he'd just received from his ambassador in Washington. Kennedy told the assistant that it was very important that she talk to Freidman and that she would wait.

It didn't take more than a minute for Freidman to come on the line, and when he did his voice was cautious. "Irene, how are you?"

"Fine, Ben, and you?"

"I have been better. Much better."

"I would imagine so. Have you heard about our meeting with your ambassador?"

"Yes, the unfortunate development was just relayed to me."

"Ben, I'm calling you as a favor. One old friend to another. The president is very serious about this. He wants those tanks out of Hebron immediately."

"So I've heard," was all Freidman managed to say.

Kennedy knew he was not about to freely offer information. "That's not all the president wants, Ben."

With a tired sigh, Freidman asked, "What else does he want?"

"Your job," Kennedy replied flatly. "He wants you removed as head of Mossad immediately."

"That is ludicrous. Why would he demand such a thing, much less care who runs Mossad?"

"He knows you lied to us about Hebron, and allies don't lie to each other about things like that." Kennedy looked at Hayes while silence filled the line. She knew Freidman was trying to think of some excuse for deceiving them. "Ben, I'm sure you had your reasons, but now is the time to come clean. If you care about keeping your job, and keeping our alliance together, you'll tell me."

Freidman snorted. "David Goldberg is not about to start taking orders from anyone. Even the president of the United States."

"Really," replied Kennedy. Sensing Freidman's confidence was feigned, she said, "Even if it meant ending his career in political scandal? I'm not judging you for what happened in Hebron. God only knows how we'd react if we had suicide bombs going off every week, but you need to keep me in the loop, Ben."

"What do you know about Hebron?"

"No, Ben," Kennedy forcefully announced. "That's not the way we're going to do this. If you want to keep your job, and you want to avoid this scandal becoming public, you're going to answer the questions. The president is furious, Ben! Those were Apache helicopters and Hellfire missiles." She lowered her voice as if she didn't want to be overheard and said, "We have satellite footage of the attacks. The president wants to take the tapes to the UN and show the world that you and Goldberg are liars."

Seconds ticked by before anything was said and then finally Freidman spoke. He had no other choice than to admit the truth. "There was no bomb factory."

"Why didn't you tell me that from the start?"

"I'm sorry. I should have." The apology did not come easily.

"Why the cover story?" asked Kennedy.

"Because, I wasn't going to miss the chance to take every last one of those bastards out, but with them meeting in a neighborhood like that I knew they would claim a massacre."

"How did you find out about the meeting?"

"We had a source."

"Who?" asked Kennedy in a casual tone.

"Someone who was working for us."

Kennedy looked at the president for a second. "Who was the source?"

"I can't tell you that."

"Ben, we're on the same side on this. Trust me. I need you to tell me who your source was."

Freidman was reluctant and then said, "A Palestinian."

"Was he on your payroll?"

"No."

"Did you recruit him, or did he come to you?"

"A little bit of both, I suppose."

Kennedy had no idea whether or not this source of Freidman's was an important piece of the puzzle, but intuition and experience told her to dig deeper. "Ben, if you want me to convince the president to back off, I need you to send Jake Turbes everything you have on this Palestinian, and I need it immediately." For good measure she decided to add, "The president is meeting with the secretary of state right now. They are discussing how to bring the Hebron evidence in front of the UN."

Freidman tried to figure out what Kennedy was after. His Palestinian informant was dead along with all the other terrorists. He saw no harm in sending her the encrypted files on him, but instinct told him there was more going on here than he was aware of. One thing he did know, however, was that a great deal of damage would be done if the UN was told the truth about Hebron. After thinking about it for a good ten seconds, and seeing no better alternative, he agreed to send the information.

SEVENTY-THREE

It wasn't easy, but Rapp waited until their man had boarded the plane. He owed both Bourne and Dumond for not bolting on him and setting off the alarms that would have led to a three-ring circus at Baltimore Washington International. To stop the flight and detain their John Doe would have meant alerting the airline, the control tower, the airport police, the FBI and God only knew who else. The odds were very high that someone on that long list would call the media and alert them to something strange at BWI.

Any one of the twenty-four-hour news outlets or all of them were likely to show up and shoot footage of the inevitable FBI SWAT team in full gear hauling a man in a business suit off an international flight. It was no criticism of the FBI. They had their job and Rapp had his. It was just that Rapp's job was always done best when it was carried out as far away from the media as possible.

As he approached the soundproof door to the Situation Room he paused for just a second. The president and Kennedy did not need to know he'd been on the phone making arrangements. Rapp opened the door and found President Hayes, Kennedy, Secretary of State Berg, Chief of Staff Jones and NSA Haik all watching the bank of television sets and talking on various phones.

The news was out that there was a bomb threat at the UN. People were streaming out of the bland Orwellian building in droves as police cruisers set up makeshift roadblocks to keep any vehicle from getting within two blocks of the world headquarters. Rapp took a second to admire his handiwork. It had been his idea to phone in the threat.

He approached Kennedy and bent over to whisper in her ear. "Our John Doe just got on a flight bound for Paris."

Kennedy turned her chair so she could look Rapp in the eye. It was as if she had to make sure he wasn't kidding before she'd believe it. She told the person on the phone that she had to go and hung up the phone. Reaching over she grabbed the president's arm and in a voice loud enough so only he could hear she leaned in and repeated the news to Hayes. Rapp placed a hand on the back of Kennedy's chair and bent over to listen.

Before the president could react to the news Rapp took a knee and said, "Sir, this is what I propose we do. The flight is headed to Paris and then on to Nice, where I assume our guy will be meeting Omar . . . whose yacht is still docked in Cannes. I can have a team in the air in less than an hour. We can get there before he lands and have everything set up."

Hayes looked at Kennedy, who only shrugged her shoulders. "What about the French?"

"What about them?" asked Rapp.

The president had been thinking about how best to use the information to forestall the vote and now seemed like a good time. "I think we need to bring them in on this."

Rapp's expression turned from hopeful to hopeless.

Never one to sugarcoat things, he said, "I think that's a bad idea, sir."

"Listen," replied Hayes a bit testily, "the French are not going to roll over on this thing. As soon as the UN opens tomorrow morning they're going to convene the Security Council, and they're going to put this to a vote, and I'm not going to be able to veto it."

"Why not?" asked a defiant Rapp.

"For starters because I actually do think the Palestinians should have a state." Hayes firmly placed his forefinger in the palm of his hand. "And secondly because Crown Prince Faisal has asked me to." Hayes ticked off his point by adding a second finger. "And in light of what happened to his cousin just a short while ago, I'm inclined to grant his request."

Rapp began ticking off his counterpoints, every bit as determined as the president was. "We're talking about the same crown prince whose brother bribed the French ambassador with a million bucks. We're talking about the same crown prince whose brother has been meeting with some guy who just mysteriously shows up whenever someone is killed—"

The president interrupted, "I know Faisal personally, and I can guarantee that he had nothing to do with this."

"Can you?" asked a doubtful Rapp, and then in a more conciliatory tone added, "I happen to agree that Faisal doesn't have a hand in this, but I'd sure as hell like to make sure before we lay what little we know on the table."

"I would too, but we don't have time," the president said in frustration. "If we're going to get the French to change their minds we need to open a dialogue now. Secretary of State Berg wants to present the evidence of Ambassador Joussard's bribe to the foreign minister as soon as possible. She's confident that once they see the evidence they will recall the ambassador immediately."

Rapp's displeasure was obvious. "Sir, the moment we do that we've tipped our hand. People will be warned. Someone will alert Omar, and he'll fly the coop like that." Rapp snapped his fingers. "He'll go back to Saudi Arabia, and we'll never get our hands on him, and we'll never know how far-reaching this thing was."

"What if we have the French pick up this John Doe when he lands in Paris? We can have our people from the FBI present during the interrogation."

Rapp's eyes were closed and he was shaking his head vehemently. "Sir, if we do that we'll never learn the whole truth, and what little we do learn will take weeks if not months to extract from this guy. And that still doesn't solve Omar. I'm telling you the second we grab this guy, we risk tipping off Omar, and without more evidence no one is going to lay a hand on Omar."

Hayes sighed. "So what do you propose we do?"

"Give me twelve hours, sir. That's all I'm asking. I've got a team ready to go. We can get to Nice before John Doe arrives and shadow him every step of the way."

"And what if you come up empty?"

Rapp could tell the president was leaning in his favor. "We're no worse off than we are right now."

"Except that we're up against the clock with the French."

Rapp swore under his breath. "Sir, if I were you I wouldn't tell the French a thing. I'd wait until that smug bastard Joussard climbs up on his high horse tomorrow morning, and then I'd have Secretary Berg ask him what he thinks of bribery. After he gets done stammering, the secretary can clobber him over the head with the evidence. The resolution will never make it to a vote, and if it does by some off chance we can veto it in good conscience until a full investigation is made into Joussard's finances. And if the crown prince is upset, you can ask him what his brother is doing giving a million bucks to the French ambassador to the UN."

The president actually laughed. "That would be enjoyable, but the French are our allies, and I don't think we can blindside them like that."

Rapp was tempted to comment on the value of having allies like the French but he decided not to. He could tell the president was leaning in his favor. "Twelve hours, sir. That's all I'm asking. Have I ever disappointed you?"

The president was out of arguments. He looked to Kennedy for her opinion and she nodded. "All right," Hayes said, turning back to Rapp. "You have twelve hours."

SEVENTY-FOUR

David had found the long flight from America relaxing. He'd reclined in his first-class seat and ignored the in-flight movie. It was a drama, and he wasn't in the mood for it. Maybe a comedy would have grabbed his attention but definitely not a drama. What he needed was an escape from the harsh reality of what he'd been doing. David did not enjoy murdering, but he understood it as a necessary evil in a world where it was often the only way to get things done. Thousands upon thousands of lives had been ended in the quest for Palestinian independence. What would a few more matter? None of this was new to him. He'd known it from an early age. He had seen his path in life, knowing that someday he would have a hand in shaping the birth of his nation. And now that his dream was so close, the guilt disappeared in the hum of jet engines. At 45,000 feet somewhere over the vast Atlantic Ocean he tucked a thin blue blanket up under his chin and thought of Palestine, warm thoughts of a nation at peace, and then he fell asleep.

He'd landed in Paris and changed flights without incident. The first sign that something had gone wrong was when he landed in Nice and caught a news update on the television. He'd been incommunicado for the better part of seven hours and was starved for information.

The vote had not taken place. The UN had been shut down due to a bomb threat. David's eyes squinted at the television and instantly knew the bomb scare was a ruse. Angry but under control, he headed off in search of answers. Unfortunately, those answers would have to come from Omar. As promised, a limousine was waiting for him at the curb. David climbed into the backseat and settled in for the short ride down the coast. He was entirely oblivious to the fact that he was being watched.

RAPP STOOD AT THE WINDOW of his hotel room. The lights were off and he was careful to stand a few feet back from the glass. Before leaving the States he'd honored his new agreement with his wife and told her the destination and likely duration of his trip. She wanted to know if his sudden departure had anything to do with the car bomb, and after a slight hesitation, he told her that it did. All in all he was surprised how well the conversation had gone.

Rapp pressed a pair of high-powered binoculars to his face and looked down on the harbor of Cannes, in the South of France. The Albert Edouardo Pier stretched out before him. Some of the world's finest yachts were berthed for the night, crowded together with barely a foot to spare between each, all neatly tucked in. As grand and opulent as all the other vessels were one stood out above the rest. Actually, it towered above the rest. Rapp had seen wealth before. He'd traveled the world and visited many cities, most of them port cities, but he had never seen a noncommercial or military vessel as large as Omar's yacht. The massive ship was moored at the end of the pier, no individual slip was big enough to hold it. Omar's yacht was easily twice as large as the next biggest vessel, which was no small thing when one considered that it was parked in a harbor that was known as the ultimate playground for the world's wealthy.

Rapp had never met Omar, and until this week had only heard of him in passing. He suddenly had a great desire to meet this corpulent Saudi prince. The signs were easy enough to recognize; Rapp had seen them before. He knew how to analyze himself better than any shrink. He would like to put the prince on the other end of his gun and watch him squirm. Men like Omar were never humiliated. That was their biggest problem. They went through life with a very warped sense of reality. Their own lives took on an overexaggerated sense of importance while virtually everyone else around them became trivial . . . expendable . . . small. His yacht symbolized how Omar perceived himself. He was his ship, the biggest and thus most important. Everyone else was secondary. Only his desires were what mattered.

It was approaching midnight. Rapp and his team had arrived two hours ago and were in the process of calibrating all of their equipment to make sure it worked perfectly. They didn't need much. The British surveillance team that had been in place since Monday was on top of things. They briefed Rapp thoroughly, and as always their cooperation was excellent. Rapp had worked with the folks from MI6 before and had found them to be extremely good at their jobs.

In addition to what the Brits already had in place, and their own directional microphones, Scott Coleman had just finished placing listening devices on the hull of the yacht. Rapp looked through the binoculars at the small sailboat and watched as Coleman handed his scuba tank to one of his men and climbed aboard. The British sailboat was tied up two jetties over from Omar's yacht and was partially blocked by a sizable cabin cruiser. When Coleman was finally back on board the sailboat Rapp relaxed a bit. Everything was in place.

Their guy had landed. He was no longer John Doe. With the delivery of the encrypted file from Mossad, Kennedy had put a name with the face. He was Jabril Khatabi, the Palestinian who had given Mossad the intelligence boon that had turned into a massacre. The man who had started it all. A man who interested Rapp greatly. On the flight over, Rapp had read every scrap of Jabril's file, and the more he read the more interested he became. On the face of it, this Jabril did not seem like a pawn. Marcus Dumond had plunged into his financials and so far had discovered a personal fortune in excess of five million dollars, almost all of it in highly liquid assets. He had been educated at the very bosom of American agnostic liberalism, the University of California at Berkeley. He'd gone to work for a venture capital firm in Silicon Valley after college and had traveled the world, focusing mostly on investments from Arab oil people. Everything in his file pointed not to terrorism, but to capitalism.

If it weren't for the audio surveillance they had of his meetings with Omar, and the fact he'd been a Mossad informant, Rapp would have sworn the man was nothing more than one of Omar's abundant financial advisors. He found it hard to believe this wealthy man from a well-educated family was a terrorist, but the evidence was conclusive. Before the night was over Rapp was hoping to have a little chat with the Palestinian to see if he could clear a few things up.

They didn't have much time. The president's deadline was firm. Every time Rapp had talked to Kennedy she'd reminded him of that. Things in Washington had grown even more hectic since he'd left. Neither the French nor the Palestinians had been placated by Israel's withdrawal from Hebron. The Israelis now claimed incontrovertible evidence that there had been a bomb factory in Hebron, and they were prepared to present that evidence before an international board of inquiry. The evidence of course had been planted during the military occupation of the town, in order to save Prime Minister Goldberg from a controversy that would spell the end of his government.

The French ambassador to the UN had privately confronted the American ambassador and accused the CIA of doing exactly what they'd done; phoning in a bomb scare in order to delay the vote on Palestinian statehood. Ambassador Joussard was offended and indignant that the world's lone superpower would stoop so low. Even though he was right, it was rather amusing that the condemnation was coming from a man who'd been bribed into putting forth the resolution that was causing so much consternation in the first place.

Israel was offering to sit down and discuss peace with the Palestinians as soon as the Palestinians honored a cease-fire agreement. The Palestinians for their part refused to abide by a cease-fire agreement until they had it in writing that Prime Minister Goldberg would close and relocate every Jewish settlement in the West Bank. Prime Minister Goldberg flat-out refused such a request and the violence continued. Both the Russians and the Chinese were suspicious about the timing of the bomb scare that shut down the UN, and both were vowing to make sure the French resolution was voted on first thing in the morning.

The president was getting a great deal of pressure from

the secretary of state and his chief of staff to bring the French into the fold on the entire matter. Rapp had just spoken to Kennedy on the secure satellite phone and she had reassured him that although the president was tempted, he was going to honor his commitment of twelve hours.

SEVENTY-FIVE

David tipped the driver and declined the man's offer to carry his lone bag to the yacht. He stood for a long moment at the beginning of the pier and looked toward the hulking white ship. It seemed as if all of his strength and energy were being sucked from him. He did not look forward to seeing Omar. He desperately wanted information; he just wished there was a way to get it without having to sit down for a royal audience.

Reluctantly, he put one foot in front of the other and started for the white yacht. He was barely halfway there when he spotted Devon LeClair standing in the open gangway at the side of the ship. High above on the bridge David could see men in white uniforms moving about. He knew from previous visits that the ship was always more active at night. That was when Omar entertained, when he held his hedonistic parties after he'd returned from the discos and the casinos. The casinos in Cannes didn't even open until eight in the evening. The high rollers like Omar rarely showed up before midnight.

David secretly hoped Omar was gone and Devon could tell him what was going on, but he doubted he would be so lucky. Omar would want to hear all the details of his trip to America, especially the car bomb in Washington. That had been Omar's idea. At first David had said no. There were too many things that could go wrong, too many innocent bystanders who could be hurt. Omar persisted though. He'd badgered him for months and had thrown larger and larger amounts of money at him. He threatened to pull out of the entire operation, and send David packing. He pointed out that the brutal murder of the Saudi ambassador would put the crown prince in a position of sympathy. Omar explained that he had been preaching to his brother for years to stand up to the Americans and that when the time was right he would be there in his ear telling him what to ask of the Americans when they apologized for the shocking international incident that had taken place on their soil.

Everything hinged on the Americans. They had the veto power and they alone could stand in the way of the creation of a Palestinian state. Omar explained that international pressure wasn't enough. They needed economic pressure on their side and they needed the American president to feel guilty over the death of Crown Prince Faisal's favorite cousin. It wasn't enough to simply show the world once again that Israel was run by thugs. The world already knew that. Killing the Palestinian ambassador would rally the UN to their cause, but would it be enough pressure to forestall a veto by the United States? Possibly not.

David didn't like the idea of putting so much into his plan and coming up short. Omar was right and like everything else in his princely life he eventually got his way.

As he approached the gangplank he asked himself again what could have possibly gone wrong. They had thought of everything, but somehow the Americans had delayed the vote.

He forced himself to smile at Devon. "Good evening."

"You look tired," was all the Frenchman said in response.

"Thank you," replied David with feigned sincerity. "And you look marvelous as always."

Devon frowned at him from behind his glasses. "The prince is waiting for you in his private salon."

David nodded and stepped into the ship.

"Leave your bag, and I'll have someone put it in a stateroom. I assume you're staying the night."

"I suppose." David dropped his bag and headed down the passageway in search of his benefactor.

When he reached the lavishly decorated private salon he was pleasantly surprised to find only Omar and his ever present bodyguard Chung. This was where Omar usually entertained the call girls and prostitutes that he kept around for his perverse sexual pleasures. As with almost everything Omar commissioned, the room was overdone. Too many pillows, too many Persian rugs on the floor, too many silk panels on the walls and too much chiffon draped from the ceiling. The place looked like some kind of a cross between a desert harem and a whorehouse, which on second thought was probably exactly the look Omar was after.

Before David got far, Chung stepped forward, his eyes checking out the assassin from head to toe. David opened his suit coat and did a three-sixty so Chung could see that he was unarmed. It amused him slightly that Chung had stopped frisking him. It would have been very easy to hide a small-caliber pistol in the waistband of his underwear. There had been times lately where the thought had crossed David's mind. Omar disgusted him more and more. David knew what his own cause was, but with Omar it wasn't so clear.

At first the prince had espoused with great passion his belief that there was no more important Arab cause than Palestinian statehood. David had listened to Omar speak glowingly of his commitment to the Palestinian cause, and David had believed every word of it. That had been more than two years ago, and since then he had learned a great deal. First and foremost he'd learned that Omar didn't really care for anything other than his own pleasure. And sometimes his own pleasure involved watching other people suffer. Omar's feigned love of Palestine was the thin outer veneer of a sadistic hatred of Israel. Where David dreamt of a free Palestinian state as an end, Omar dreamt of a free Palestinian state as the beginning of an end . . . the end of Israel.

In an unusual gesture Omar stood. He not only stood but he smiled. He held out his arms like he was a father greeting his favorite son. Before David knew it he was being pulled in. It was part of the other side of Omar. His mood was infectious, whether he was up or down, he brought everybody with him like the tide. Right now he was up, and David couldn't help but grin.

"Come here," Omar's voice bellowed. "You have succeeded."

David allowed himself to be hugged even though he didn't feel like he'd succeeded.

"You have done marvelously," roared Omar as he patted David on the back. "Have you seen the tape?" asked Omar as he released him.

"No. I've been on a plane all day. I have no idea what's happened. What is this I hear about a bomb threat at the UN?"

Omar deflected the question with a flip of his wrist. "That is nothing. Only a delay tactic by the Americans. Come, you must see the videotape." Omar forced David

over to a chair in front of a large plasma TV. "Sit . . . sit . . .
I command you. When we are done we will go to the
casino and then the discothèque for some women."

David reluctantly dropped into the chair and watched
as Omar picked up a remote control. "What is going on
at the UN? Why didn't they vote?"

"There was some bomb scare, but do not worry. The
vote is going to take place first thing in the morning and
it is going to pass."

David eyed Omar suspiciously. "How do you know it
will pass?"

"I just talked with my brother. I've been talking to that
poor excuse for a man all day. I think he actually cried
when he found out Abdul had been blown up." Omar
stopped fiddling with the remote for a second and looked
at David with his most incredulous expression. "Can you
believe that a grown man would cry over such a thing?
My brother is a fool."

David was sure that somewhere, in some very thick
medical reference book, there was a term that described
Omar's personality, but he had yet to take the time to sit
down and look it up. Ignoring his obsession with his
brother the crown prince, David repeated his question.
"How can you be so sure it will pass tomorrow?"

"My brother, the weak fool, has been given assurances
by all of the permanent members that they will vote in
favor of the resolution."

"Even the United States."

"They have not given their word yet, but they have no
choice. As we discussed I convinced my brother that now
was the time for the threat of an all-out embargo." Omar
smiled and said, "After you killed Abdul, the president
asked my brother if there was anything he could do and
my brother told him to vote for the French resolution."

Omar began laughing so hard he actually began to shake. After he'd calmed a bit he added, "They are all such idiots."

All David could think to do was nod and smile.

When the tape was finally rewound, Omar hit PLAY and said, "You will not believe this. A film crew showed up just minutes after the explosion."

David watched as the screen went from black to black-and-gray and then finally a shot of people running down a sidewalk. In the distance was a cloud of smoke. Most of the people were running away from the smoke but the cameraman and several other people were running toward it. David began to feel himself sweat. He shifted uncomfortably in the chair. He had no desire to watch this, but he could feel Omar's eyes on him.

Suddenly there were people on the ground. The camera stopped at each one for a few seconds cataloging the tragedy and then the reporter began shouting instructions. The lens came up and the horizon was filled with smoke and the twisted burning wreckage of cars. David looked away and found Omar standing only a few feet away, watching him.

"You don't like this?" he asked with a gleam in his eye.

David managed to keep his voice calm. "I know what I did. I do not need to watch it."

"Oh, but you do." Omar walked closer to the TV. With one hand he gestured toward David and with the other toward the large screen. "This is your work. This is what you have accomplished . . . you should be proud of it."

Omar was smiling widely now and it occurred to David that he was probably taping this for his voyeuristic collection. "I am proud of what I did," David lied. He was proud of what he did in Jordan, he was proud of what he did with the attaché cases in Hebron, and he was even proud of what he did in New York, but this carnage that he was watching on TV, he was not proud of.

"Tell me," said Omar excitedly. "Do you think my cousin survived the initial blast?" The screen was now filled with images of a breached and burning limousine. "I hope he did, that American-loving bastard. Look closely, I think that is someone's leg!" Omar paused the tape and looked at his assassin for an answer.

David shook his head. He'd had enough. "My prince, I'm sorry, but I have no desire to watch this."

It took David only a split second to realize something was wrong, but by then it was too late. Omar was still smiling at him and watching him closely when suddenly he looked just beyond David and gave a signal. Before David could react something was around his neck and he was yanked backward. His hands immediately shot up, and his fingers desperately tried to get under the rope that was choking him. Omar was suddenly before him.

"I have enjoyed corrupting you." His gloating face was only several feet away. "Your intentions were so pure, and look at the great destruction you've caused." Omar turned and pointed to the TV.

David gave up on trying to get his fingers under the rope and reached back for Chung's head. He found a fistful of hair with one hand and began searching for an eye with the other.

Omar enjoyed the struggle. "You should have known better than to trust me. . . . You of all people." Omar shook his head like he was admonishing a child. "You always preached to me about security. You were the one who told me not to talk to anyone about our plans." The smile suddenly vanished from Omar's face and he leaned in close. "And you always kept asking for more money!"

David couldn't get ahold of an eye. Chung was too

strong. He began to realize that this was a fight he would not win. Specks of light started to appear on the periphery of his vision and his lungs began to ache. Suddenly Omar was very close to him saying something that he didn't bother to try to understand. His brain was too preoccupied with finding more oxygen. He could feel himself slipping away and his thoughts turned to the memories of his youth. To Jerusalem, and to his family. As his body began to relax into death he was comforted by the vision of his mother caring for the sick.

RAPP SLOWLY REMOVED HIS HEADPHONES and tossed them on the bed. He didn't leave the window at first. He just stood there like a hawk perched on a tall branch, looking down at the large white vessel. Some stubborn sense of fairness in him did not like what had just transpired, but there wasn't much he could have done about it. He tried his best to not let it bother him, but it did, and he could tell it bothered the other people in the room too. No one spoke for at least a minute.

Finally, Rapp turned to the others and said, "Pack everything up. I want to be out of here in fifteen minutes."

The team of technicians were already at work. One of them was in the process of sending the encrypted audio back to Langley, while a second had begun packing the equipment. The third had hacked into the hotel's network and was placing a worm to erase all security footage from the time they'd arrived until thirty minutes from now.

Before leaving, Rapp looked back out at the harbor one more time; at Omar's massive yacht and the limousine that was still parked at the entrance to the pier. The president would get all the evidence he needed and then some. Rapp had killed many times and could honestly say he'd never enjoyed it, or at the very least he'd never relished it. Yes, there'd been times where he'd felt just satisfaction in killing someone who deserved it, but that was about the extent of it.

Pensively, he turned away from the window with the expression of a man who was lost in thought. He put on his suit coat over his holstered 9mm Beretta and started for the door. He paused on the threshold and looked back at the three analysts. "Good job, I'll see you at the plane."

Rapp walked past the elevators to the stairs and started down. Raising his digitally encrypted radio to his mouth he said, "Scott, I'm coming down. Meet me by the east entrance of the hotel with the car."

SEVENTY-SIX

Omar was in a hurry to join in the revelry. He'd kicked everyone off the yacht so he could have his private meeting with David and with that little piece of business taken care of he was ready to enjoy the evening. His cousins had gone ahead to the Casino Club to try to procure some women for the trip to St. Tropez in the morning. He would much prefer it if they could find some young aspiring actress to join them, rather than the usual whores they had to pay for. The young ones were so much fun to corrupt.

Omar had lent large amounts of money to Italian, French and American producers over the years and the walls of the ship's upper gallery were adorned with autographed headshots of the silver screen's elite. The photos never failed to impress the naive teenagers. The size of the yacht, the opulence of the furnishings, the photographs, they overwhelmed the vulnerable young women. And if that wasn't enough, there was a full complement of drugs that could be used either overtly or surreptitiously to melt away their inhibitions.

Omar stepped from his yacht onto the pier. It was a clear night and the fresh air of the Mediterranean felt wonderful. Killing David had livened his senses. He couldn't wait for the rest of the evening's entertainment. His cousins would immensely enjoy watching the tape of Chung strangling the insolent Palestinian. None of them liked him. Omar had been very fond of David at first, but his impudent attitude had worn thin. His disapproving looks and his refusal to join in the sexual merriment became increasingly intolerable. He was only a Palestinian after all, and his place in the pecking order of the Arab tribes was at the very bottom. The fact that he didn't know his place in society and that he kept asking for more money was what had made the decision easy. Besides, Omar would sleep much easier knowing that David would not be telling or selling his secrets to the wrong party.

Rapp watched the portly Arab waddle down the pier in his shiny suit. His mountainous Chinese bodyguard walked in front of him, his head turning and his eyes deliberately sweeping the path before them like a spotlight atop a citadel searching for danger. Rapp had read the British surveillance reports, probing for a weakness. The boat would have been difficult, too many people and almost no set schedule. Someone was always up and moving about. There was the bathroom at the casino, and there was the party room at the hotel. There were all kinds of options that if Rapp absolutely had to, he could have made work, but he was short on time and forcing something often led to mistakes. In Rapp's line of work, mistakes could get someone other than the target killed or at a bare minimum cause an international crisis. Fortunately one very straightforward opportunity jumped off the page at him.

Rapp was not acting without orders. The president didn't know what he was about to do, but that had been intentional. In operations such as this it was best to insulate the president and the office from any blame. Rapp and Kennedy had decided it was time to send a message to the Saudis. No longer would they have free rein in financing terrorism as if it were some hobby to be enjoyed in one's spare time.

Through his earpiece he could hear the operational chatter of Scott Coleman receiving updates from the other men. It was nothing more than background noise for Rapp. He could clearly see Omar and Chung from where he was stationed. The others were there as backup to monitor the local police frequencies and finish the job if for some reason Rapp fell short, which he had absolutely no intention of doing.

CHUNG REACHED THE LIMOUSINE FIRST. Even though the casino was only a few short blocks away, Devon LeClair kept a limousine on twenty-four-hour standby. It was enough of an exertion for the prince to amble the length of the pier; he was not about to walk down the sidewalk to the casino. Before opening the door, Chung took one last look around, giving a group of youths across the street a long hard stare. Then when Prince Omar was ready Chung opened the door for his employer and helped him into the vehicle. Chung then somehow managed to fold his frame in half, and squeeze into the dark backseat, closing the door behind him.

The first bullet struck him in the face. So did the second. The silencer on the tip of the gun minimized the muzzle flash to barely a spark. Chung never moved other than the slight jerking motion his head made as each hollow point round penetrated his forehead. He sat motionless like some ancient stone statue, his posture upright and his hands open and resting on his knees. He never had even a fraction of a second to realize something was wrong. All in all it wasn't a bad way to die.

Omar would not be so fortunate. The door locks on the limo clicked simultaneously and the vehicle began to move. Omar reached for an overhead reading light and pressed it. A narrow beam of light shone down on him, and he looked around nervously. Something strange was happening. There had been several unusual noises, a few weak sparks, but the usually alert Chung was sitting still, unalarmed.

Somewhere near the front of the compartment there was movement and Omar suddenly realized someone else was in the car. The danger of the situation still had yet to register as he asked, "Who is there?"

Rapp, who was dressed in black, blended in perfectly with the dark interior and heavily smoked windows of the limousine. He leaned forward and in Arabic said, "I am a friend of your brother's." His words were carefully chosen.

Omar's eyes opened wide and his right arm reached for Chung. It was at that moment that he realized something was seriously wrong. He pushed Chung and the Asian man's lifeless body fell sideways into the door. Turning back to his assailant with panic in his voice he asked, "Who are you?"

"I am your executioner," Rapp answered, again in Arabic.

Omar, thinking the assailant in his car was a Saudi, said, "You cannot harm me. I am a member of the royal family."

Rapp smiled and changed to English. "I am an American, and as a favor to your brother I am going to kill you."

Omar's eyes grew even larger. He was shocked by the man's change of languages. "For what?" he croaked incredulously. "I have done nothing but honor my brother."

"You are a liar, and you have disgraced your family." Rapp again chose his words very carefully for every second of this was being recorded.

"I have done no such thing," stammered an unconvincing Omar.

Rapp looked back at him leaving no doubt that he didn't believe a single word the man uttered. "You had your own cousin, Abdul Bin Aziz, killed."

"I did no such thing."

"And I suppose you never called your brother a fool, and a poor excuse for a man?"

The quote struck a note of familiarity with Omar and his expression changed in a very subtle way. "I love my brother. I do not always agree with him, but I love him."

"Do you love him enough to admit that you had your own cousin killed?"

"I did no such thing!"

Rapp squeezed his left index finger and a 9mm round spat from the end of the silencer striking Omar in the knee. The Saudi prince lurched forward and screamed in agony. In all of his pampered life he had never felt anything so painful.

Rapp pointed the weapon at the prince's other knee and repeated the question. "Why did you kill your own cousin?"

Omar was now rocking back and forth, holding his shattered knee with both hands as blood oozed from between his fingers. "How much are you being paid? I will pay you millions," he pleaded.

Rapp squeezed off another round, this time striking the other knee.

Omar squealed and looked down in absolute horror at the fresh wound.

Rapp kept his voice under control. "Why did you kill your cousin?"

"Because I hated him!" hissed Omar. "Because he and my brother are leading my country in the wrong direction, and because I should be crown prince!"

Rapp didn't speak at first. Omar had said it all. As much as Rapp detested him he did not find this enjoyable. There was no thrill in watching him suffer. Even though he had no doubt the man deserved everything he was getting and then some, for Rapp it was just a job. He hesitated for only a second, and then raised his pistol and sent a single bullet into the Saudi prince's forehead.

EPILOGUE

The crown prince and his entourage had taken the top three floors of the Plaza Athenée in Paris. President Hayes by contrast had only taken the top two floors of the Bristol, but then again the president only had one wife. The Israeli and Palestinian delegations were spread around town at various hotels. The peace summit had caused quite a stir with the Parisian hotel community. Spring was fast approaching and, as always, rooms were scarce. With only two weeks to make arrangements, apologies and discounts were offered and schedules were changed. Parisians were proud to host a conference that might finally bring about a peace in the Middle East. Especially in light of the recent embarrassment they'd suffered due to the less than honorable actions of their country's ambassador to the United Nations.

The French intelligence agency, DST, had arrested Ambassador Joussard on charges of accepting a million-dollar bribe from a wealthy Saudi prince. To make matters worse, that same Saudi prince, along with his bodyguard, was found dead in Cannes the very same day of Joussard's arrest. And if that wasn't sensational enough, the strangled body of a known Palestinian terrorist had been discovered aboard the prince's yacht. The story was too juicy to resist and within days the press was all over it.

The details had been scarce at first, but slowly the picture of an international terror network funded by a spurned Saudi billionaire began to emerge. The group was being blamed for the assassinations of the Palestinian ambassador in New York, the Saudi ambassador in Washington and the increased suicide bombings in Israel and the West Bank, all in an effort to manipulate the UN and gain international sympathy for their cause.

The spokespeople for the Saudi royal family had been quick to disassociate Crown Prince Faisal from his estranged half brother Prince Omar. It was said that the two had not talked to each other in years, and that the Machiavellian Prince Omar had been all but banned from the royal court. He spent almost all of his time sailing the Mediterranean aboard his yacht, gambling and running his various enterprises. He was carefully profiled as a man without a country, and a man with little or no alliance to Saudi Arabia.

How Prince Omar had ended up dead was the cause of much speculation. One theory had it that Omar had gone back on a deal he'd made with the Palestinian terrorists, and had paid for it with his life. This leak was designed to send a message to wealthy Arabs who liked to dabble in bankrolling various terrorist groups. There was also the inevitable rumor that Omar had been eliminated by either the Israelis, the French or the Americans, for his hand in trying to manipulate the UN.

The truth about what had happened was slightly different. The French DST had arrested Ambassador Joussard only after President Hayes had made the French president a very gracious offer. Either the French could arrest their own ambassador, and save some face, or the

Americans would expel the ambassador and denounce him on the floor of the UN for accepting a bribe. For the French this was a no-brainer. President Hayes also suggested that in order to make amends for the upheaval at the United Nations it might be a good idea for the French to host a peace conference.

After the French agreed to host the conference it was fairly simple for President Hayes to get the other parties to show up. The Palestinians and Saudis were shamed into participating because of their unwitting role in recent events, and the Israelis were told they could either attend or face some very hard questions about what actually happened in Hebron. In the end, all the parties agreed it was mutually beneficial to at least sit down and talk.

Neither Rapp nor Kennedy were bothered that the credit for their hard work had been given to others. It was the way they preferred it. They had the gratitude of their president, and the personal knowledge that they had helped to avert an international crisis. Now they were about to ingratiate themselves to the crown prince of Saudi Arabia, and further cement the alliance between their two countries.

Rapp, Kennedy and the director's personal security detail were brought into the Plaza Athenée through a back door and escorted to a service elevator. From there they were taken to the top floor and met by a phalanx of bodyguards. Only Rapp and Kennedy were allowed to pass, but first Rapp had to hand his weapon over to one of the CIA security guys.

Rapp felt naked without his gun, but there was no choice in the matter. Even unarmed, the crown prince's bodyguards were less than thrilled about granting him an audience. They were escorted to a room where Rapp was simultaneously frisked by two men while a third stood guard with his pistol drawn. Kennedy stood off to one side, slightly amused by the stir that Rapp had caused. When the bodyguards were finally satisfied the two Americans were allowed admittance into a plush suite and left alone.

Neither bothered to sit, nor did they speak. Kennedy had asked for permission to have a team of technicians sweep the room, but the Saudis had declined. This either meant they were confident that their own people were up to the job, or they intended on recording the meeting for their own purposes. In reality it was probably both, which was why they would say as little as possible. Their mere presence, and the large manila envelope that Kennedy held to her chest, would say it all.

The envelope held a videotape, several audiotapes, and a thick file of financial transactions and phone records. The originals were all kept in a safe back at Langley. These were copies. The videotape had been lifted from Omar's yacht and contained the graphic footage of David being strangled, as well as Omar's personal thoughts on his brother's lack of manhood and intelligence. The audiotapes contained Omar's conversations with the crown prince leading up to and immediately following the assassination of their cousin. They revealed Omar's continued plea for an oil embargo, and finally, his confession in the back of the limousine before he was put out of his misery. All of it unassailable proof that Omar was in fact much closer to his brother than the press was led to believe.

There had been a debate as to whether or not they should erase Rapp's voice from the last tape. Surprisingly, Rapp had argued that it should remain. He was not ashamed of what he'd done, nor was he afraid of any reprisal from the House of Saud. He recognized that he had done the crown prince a great favor by ridding him of his errant brother. He had saved him the trouble of having to do it himself and risk a potential schism in the royal family. This way Crown Prince Faisal got exactly what he wanted and his hands and conscience were clean. He would be indebted to the man from the CIA.

They were not forced to wait long. An aide wearing a white keffiyeh and black robe entered the room through a side door and gestured for them to follow. Contrary to Arab custom Rapp allowed Kennedy to go ahead of him. If they had been in Saudi Arabia he may have reconsidered, but they were in Paris, and despite what Omar had thought, his brother was no fool. Crown Prince Faisal had been educated in America and this was a private meeting. There was no worry about offending someone's sensibilities or embarrassing the crown.

Crown Prince Faisal was sitting in a high-backed wing chair at the far end of the luxurious suite. He was dressed in traditional Arab garb as were the two large men who flanked him. He wore a white keffiyeh topped with a gold braid and a black robe trimmed in gold. The crown prince made no effort to rise and meet his guests nor did Rapp or Kennedy expect him to.

The representatives of the American government stopped next to the two chairs that had been placed approximately ten feet from Faisal. They both bowed and then waited to be told to sit. To Rapp, Faisal looked apprehensive and tired, as if he expected some trap to be sprung on him. His black mustache and beard accentuated the dark circles under his tired eyes. From all outward appearances the crown prince of Saudi Arabia had not been sleeping well.

Almost imperceptibly, Faisal gestured for them to sit.

They both did so, but neither settled in. Kennedy started by saying, "Thank you for taking the time to meet with us, Your Highness." Leaning forward, she set the envelope on the coffee table that sat midway between them. "President Hayes asked me to deliver this to you in private."

Faisal stared at the package, but didn't bother to pick it up or ask what was in it.

Motioning to the envelope with an open hand the director of the CIA said, "He wishes to keep this between our two countries."

To this, Faisal nodded his understanding. He had spoken to the American president on many occasions, and would be talking with him in the morning. The very fact that he had sent two of his top intelligence people to deliver this package spoke volumes.

"Your Highness," Rapp said, "I must warn you that you may find the contents of this envelope very disturbing. It is in no way our intent to upset you. We just thought it was best for you to know the truth."

This time the crown prince nodded more deeply, signaling that he clearly understood it would not be pleasant. He then looked directly into Rapp's eyes for a long uncomfortable moment. He stared at the man from the CIA as if he knew much more than he was letting on . . . maybe even who had killed his brother.

Finally, in a voice barely above a whisper, Faisal said, "Thank you." The crown prince then turned to his aide and nodded.

The man stepped forward, an unassuming smile on his face, and motioned for Rapp and Kennedy to follow. The meeting was over that quickly. They were escorted back through the suites and into the hallway without a further word. Kennedy's security detail was where they'd left them, by the service elevator. Rapp wasted no time retrieving his gun. He inspected the Heckler & Koch 9mm to make sure it was exactly as he'd left it and stowed it in the belt holster at the small of his back. He then buttoned his suit coat and everyone stepped into the elevator.

The group proceeded back to the hotel in a three-car caravan. Rapp and Kennedy made the short trip in silence. When they arrived at the Bristol they were taken to President Hayes's suite. Hayes was waiting for them in formal attire. He was scheduled to attend a dinner at the Elysée Palace, the official residence of the French president.

"How did it go?" asked Hayes.

Kennedy gave a noncommittal shrug while Rapp said, "I don't think you're going to be threatened with any oil embargoes for a while."

The president smiled in satisfaction and reached for a bottle of champagne that was chilling in a sterling silver bucket. He plucked it from the icy water and dried it with a nearby white towel. "I think a toast is in order," he announced as he began twisting the wire from atop the cork. When the wire was off, he draped the towel over the bottle and began gingerly working the cork free.

He completed the task without spilling a drop and then poured three flutes. When Hayes was done he handed a glass each to Kennedy and Rapp and then held up his own. "To a job well done, and a crisis avoided."

They all drank and then the president added, "These are truly momentous times, and the two of you have played a major role in getting these parties to sit down. Who knows," he added with a hopeful glint in his eye, "by the end of the week we could finally have peace in the Middle East." The president noticed Rapp's doubtful expression and asked, "You don't think that's possible?"

Rapp hesitated, and then said, "Sir, I think by the end of the week you'll probably have a document that *says* there's going to be peace in the Middle East, but I'm a skeptic as to whether or not that peace will ever become a reality."

The president frowned. He did not want his good mood spoiled. "Why do you think that?"

"Because there's an element within the Arab world that will settle for nothing short of the total destruction of Israel."

"That element hasn't been invited to the table. Israel and Palestine must coexist side by side. There is no other choice."

"I agree, sir, but that element doesn't want to be invited to the peace table. That's the problem. They only want the destruction of Israel."

"So what would you advise me to do?" asked a cautious Hayes.

"Exactly what you're doing, sir. Just make sure you hold no illusions about what it will take to really make peace. Those groups that don't want peace need to be dealt with, and there's only one thing they understand."

"What's that?"

Rapp reached behind his back with his left hand and drew his gun. He wanted to make his point with the president, bring him back down from the clouds. This part of the peace process was easy, with civilized men and women gathering in a magnificent city like Paris, talking about noble causes while the world press lauded them with accolades. At night they all went to bed secretly dreaming that one day soon they would win the Nobel Peace Prize, while several thousand miles away young Palestinian boys and girls were being trained to blow themselves up in the name of their god. Those so-called martyrs cared little about documents signed in fancy rooms by fancy men. It was not possible to reason with unreasonable people.

Rapp held his gun up in the palm of his hand for the president to see, and said, "This is the only thing the zealots understand, sir. If you want peace in the Middle East they need to be dealt with. Only then will Israelis and Palestinians be able to live side by side."

SIMON & SCHUSTER
PROUDLY PRESENTS

MEMORIAL DAY

by

VINCE FLYNN

**Available in paperback
from Simon & Schuster**

**Turn this page for a preview of
Memorial Day**

Mitch Rapp stared through the one-way mirror into the dank, cement, subterranean chamber. A man, clothed in nothing more than a pair of underwear, sat handcuffed to a small, ridiculously uncomfortable chair. A naked light bulb hung from the ceiling, stopping only a foot or so above him. The intense starkness of the light, and the man's state of near total exhaustion, caused his head to droop forward, leaving his chin resting on his chest. He was dangerously close to losing his balance and toppling over, which was exactly what they wanted.

Rapp checked his watch. He was running out of time and patience. He'd just as soon shoot this piece of human refuse and get it over with, but it was more complicated than that. He needed the man to talk, that was the point of this tediously orchestrated experiment. They all talked eventually, of course, that wasn't the problem. The trick was to get them to tell you the truth, and this one was no exception. So far he was sticking to his story, a story that Rapp knew to be an outright lie.

Adding to his sense of restlessness was the fact that the CIA counterterrorism operative hated coming to this place. It literally made his skin crawl. It had all the charm of a mental hospital without the barred windows and the beefy orderlies stuffed into their white uniforms. It was a place intentionally designed to starve the human mind of stimuli. It was so secret, it didn't even have a name. The handful of people who knew of its existence, referred to it only as *The Facility.*

It was off the books, not even listed in the black intelligence budget submitted in secret to Congress every year. The facility was a relic from the Cold War. It was located near Leesburg, Virginia, and looked just like all the other horse farms dotting the country side thereabouts. Situated on sixty-two beautiful rolling acres the place had been purchased by the Agency in the early fifties, at a time when the CIA was given far more latitude and discretion than it was today.

This was one of several sites where the CIA debriefed Eastern Block defectors, and even a few of the Agency's own who were snared in the net of James Angleton, the CIA's notoriously paranoid genius who was in charge of rooting out spies during the height of the Cold War. Very nasty things had been done to people in this crypt. This was where the CIA would have likely taken Aldrich Ames if they had caught him before the FBI did. The men and women who were charged with protecting Langley's secrets would have given almost anything for the chance to put the screws to that traitorous bastard, but they were unfortunately denied the opportunity.

The Facility was not a pleasant place, but it was a necessary evil in a world chock-full of sadistic deeds and misguided, brutal men. This was something Rapp was more than aware of, but that didn't mean he had to like it. He was neither delicate nor squeamish. Rapp had killed more men than he could even attempt to count, and he'd employed his craft in a variety of imaginative ways that spoke to the sheer depth of his skill.

He was a modern day *assassin* who lived in a civilized

country where such a term could never be used openly or even in private. His was a nation that loved to distinguish itself from the less refined countries of the world. A democracy that celebrated individual rights and freedom. A state that would never tolerate the open recruiting, training and use of one of its own citizens for the specific purpose of covertly killing the citizens of another. But that was exactly who Rapp was. He was a modern day assassin who was conveniently called an *operative* so as to not offend the sensibilities of the cultured people who occupied the centers of power in Washington.

If those very people knew of the existence of the Facility they would fly into an indignant rage that would result in the partial or complete destruction of the CIA. These haters of America's capitalistic might wanted to analyze what we had done to invoke such hatred from the terrorists, all the while missing the point that they were using the logic of a seedy attorney defending a rapist. The woman had on a short skirt, sexy top and high-heels—maybe she was asking for it? America was a rude and arrogant country run by selfish, colonialist men who were out to exploit the resources of lesser countries—maybe we were asking for it?

Under their narrow definition the Washington elite would call this place a torture chamber. Rapp, however, knew what real torture was, and it wasn't this. This was coercion, it was sensory deprivation, it was interrogation, but it wasn't real torture.

Real torture was causing a person so much unthinkable pain that he or she begged to be killed. It was hooking alligator clips to a man's testicles and sending jolts of searing electricity through his body, it was gang raping a woman day after day until she slipped into a coma, it was forcing a man to watch as his wife and children were sodomized by a bunch of thugs, it was making a man eat his own excrement. It was monstrous, it was barbaric and it could also be wildly ineffective. Time and time again such methods proved that most prisoners would say or do almost anything to stop the pain. Sign any confession, create terrorist plots that didn't exist, even turn on their own parents to stop the pain.

Rapp was a practical man, however, and the prisoner sitting cuffed to the chair on the other side of the glass knew first hand what real torture was. The organization he worked for was notorious for its treatment of political prisoners. If anyone was deserving of a good beating it was this vile bastard, but still there were other things to consider.

Rapp didn't like torture, not only for what it did to the person being brutalized, but for what it did to the person who sanctioned and carried it out. He had no desire to sink to those depths unless it was a last resort, but unfortunately they were quickly approaching that point. Lives were at stake. Two CIA operatives were already dead, thanks to the duplicitous scum in the other room, and many more lives were in the balance. Something was in the works, and if Rapp didn't find out what it was hundreds, maybe thousands, of innocent people would die.

The door to the observation room opened and a man approximately the same age as Rapp entered. He walked up to the window and with his deep set brown eyes he looked at the handcuffed man. There was a certain clinical detachment in the way the man carried himself. His substantial hair was well styled and his beard trimmed to perfection. He was dressed in a dark, well-tailored suit, white dress shirt with French cuffs, and an expensive red silk tie. He owned two identical sets of the outfit, and in an effort to keep his subject off balance, it was the only thing he had worn in front of the man since his arrival three days ago. The outfit was carefully chosen to convey a sense of superiority and importance.

Bobby Akram was one of the CIA's best interrogators. He was a Pakistani immigrant, and a Muslim, who was fluent in Urdu, Pashto, Arabic, Farsi, and of course, English. Akram had controlled every detail of every second of his prisoner's incarceration. Every noise, variation in temperature, morsel of food and drop of liquid had been carefully choreographed.

The goal with this specific subject, as with any subject, was to get him to talk. The first step was to isolate him and strip him of all sense of time and place. Immerse him in a world of sensory deprivation until he craved stimuli. Akram would then throw the man a lifeline; he would begin a dialogue. He would get the man to talk. Not even necessarily to divulge secrets, at least not at first. To do the job thoroughly and properly took a great deal of time and patience, but unfortunately time was a luxury they did not possess. Intelligence was time sensitive and that meant things had to be expedited.

Turning to Rapp he said, "It shouldn't be much longer."

"I sure as hell hope not," grumbled Rapp. Mitch Rapp was many things, but patient was not one of them.

Akram smiled. He had great respect for the legendary CIA operative. The two of them were on the front line of this war against terrorism. Allies with a mutual enemy. For Rapp it was about protecting innocent people against the aggressions of a growing threat. For Akram it was about saving the religion he loved from a group of fanatics who had twisted the words of the Great Prophet so they could perpetuate hatred and fear.

Akram checked his watch and asked, "Are you ready?"

Rapp nodded and looked into the depressing room at the exhausted, bound man. He mumbled a few curses to himself. If word got out about this, all of his accomplishments and connections wouldn't be able to save him. He was way off the reservation with this little hunt, but he needed answers and running things through the proper channels was sure to get him bogged down in a quagmire of politics and diplomacy.

There were too many varying interests at play, without even getting into the issue of leaks. The man bound and drugged in the other room was Colonel Masood Haq of the dreaded Pakistani Inter-Services Intelligence or ISI. Without telling anyone at Langley, Rapp had hired a team of freelancers to snatch the man and bring him here. The brutal murders of two CIA operatives, and a growing fear that al-Qaeda had reconstituted itself, had given Rapp the impetus to take action without authorisation.

Akram pointed at their prisoner as he began to nod off. "He's going to fall over any second. Are you sure you want to go forward with your plan right now?" Akram crossed his arms. "If we wait another day or two I'm very confident I can get him to talk."

Rapp shook his head and answered firmly. "My patience has run out. If you don't get him to talk, I will."

Akram nodded thoughtfully. He was not opposed to using the good-cop/bad-cop technique of interrogation. On the right person the results could be quite satisfactory. Akram himself, however, never resorted to violence, he was careful to leave that to others.

"All right. When I get up and leave that's your cue."

Rapp acknowledged the plan, and kept his eyes on the bound man as Akram left the room. The prisoner had no idea of how long he had been here, how long he had been in the hands of his captors or who his captors even were. He had no idea where he was, what country, let alone what continent. He had only heard one man speak, and that was Akram, a fellow Pakistani by birth.

He would of course assume that he was being held in his own country, probably by the ISI's chief competitor the IB, and because of that he would hold out as long as he could with hopes that the ISI would come to his rescue. He had been drugged and deprived of all sense of time and routine. He was exhausted and awash in a sea of sensory deprivation. He was a man who was ready to break, and when he saw Rapp enter the room, his hopes would crumble.

As Akram had predicted, the man finally dozed off long enough to lose his balance and topple over. He hit the floor fairly hard, but didn't bother attempting to get up. Having been in this hopeless position countless times during his incarceration he knew it was impossible.

Akram entered the room with several assistants. While the other two men righted the prisoner, Akram pulled up a chair and told his assistants to remove the man's restraints. When the prisoner was free to move his arms and legs, Akram handed the man a glass of water. The two assistants went and stood in the shadows by the door in case they were needed.

"Now, Masood," Akram said in the man's native language, "would you like to start telling me the truth?"

The man glared at his interrogator with blood shot eyes, "I'm telling you the truth. I am not a supporter of the Taliban or al-Qaeda. I deal with them only because it is my job to keep tabs on them."

"You know that General Musharraf has made it very

clear that we are to stop supporting the Taliban and al-Qaeda." Akram had maintained this persona that he was a fellow Pakistani from the moment he'd met Haq.

"I'm telling you," the man replied firmly, "the only reason I still meet with my contacts is to keep tabs on them."

Akram fired his questions rapidly, "And you're still sympathetic to their cause?"

"Yes I'm . . . I mean no! I'm not sympathetic to their cause."

Akram smiled. "I am a devout Muslim, and I am sympathetic to their cause." He tilted his head to the side. "Are you not a devout Muslim?"

The question was a slap in the intelligence officer's face. "Of course I am a devout Muslim," he blurted indignantly, "but I am . . . I am an officer in the ISI. I know where my allegiance lies."

"I'm sure you do," said a skeptical Akram. "The problem is I do not know where your allegiance lies, and I'm running out of patience." There was no malice in his voice as he said this, merely regret.

The man buried his face in hands and shook his head. "I don't know what to say. I am not the man you say I am." He lifted his head and stared past the bright light at his interrogator. His eyes were glassy and pleading. "Ask my superiors. Ask General Sharif. He will tell you I was following orders."

Akram shook his head. "Your superiors have forsaken you. You are nothing but a plague to them. They claim to know very little about what you've been up to."

"You are a liar," spat Haq.

This was exactly what Akram was after. Uncontrollable mood swings. Pleading and placid one second and then angry and antagonistic the next. Raising his hands in surrender, Akram's expression spoke of a sad resolve that he could do no more. "I have been very patient with you, and all you do is reward me with more lies, and insults."

"I have told you the truth!" Haq said far too quickly.

Akram gave him an almost paternal stare. "Would you say that I have been kind to you?"

The lack of sleep and drugs caused Haq to slip. He opened his arms and looked around the room. "Your hospitality leaves much to be desired." In a defiant tone he said, "I want to speak with General Sharif immediately!"

"Let me ask you, Massod, how do you treat your prisoners?"

The Pakistani intelligence officer lowered eyes to the floor deciding it was better to ignore the question.

"Have I laid a hand on you since you've been here?"

Haq shook his head reluctantly.

"Well . . . all of that is about to change." This was the first time Akram had threatened violence, either implicitly or explicitly. Their conversations up until now had consisted of Haq talking about his contacts, and going over and over the same well rehearsed story, Haq slipping up on a few details here and there, but for the most part holding his ground.

Akram studied his subject intently and said, "There is someone here who would like to see you."

Haq looked up, his eyes glimmering with hope.

"No." Akram shook his head and laughed ominously. "I don't think you want to see this man. In fact," Akram stood, "he is probably the last person on the planet you want to see right now. He is someone who I cannot control, and someone who knows for a fact that you are a liar."

"I am telling you the truth," he shrieked and reached out for his interrogators arm.

Akram caught his wrist and twisted it with just enough pressure to send the man a clear signal not to touch him. He looked down at the wide, pleading eyes and said, "You had ample opportunity to tell the truth, but chose not to. It is now out of my hands." With that Akram released the man's wrist and left the room.

Rapp did not enter right away. Akram told him it was best to let the tension build. They watched through the one-way mirror as Haq began nervously pacing back and forth along the far wall. He grew more agitated by the minute, until finally the bright overhead lights came on and Rapp entered the room.

The look on Haq's face was at first one of confusion and then disbelief. The arrival of the infamous American intelligence officer changed everything. Things began to click, to fall into place, and Haq instantly knew he was in much more trouble than he could ever have imagined.

Pointing at the uncomfortable chair Rapp barked, "Sit!"

Haq did so without hesitation. Rapp grabbed a small square table by the wall and dragged it over, placing it in front of the Pakistani. Looking up at the two guards he said in English, "I can handle him by myself."

As the guards left, Rapp laid a letter sized manila envelope on the table and then slowly took off his jacket revealing his holstered 9-mm Beretta. He draped the jacket over the back of the chair and began yanking at his tie.

"Do you know who I am?" Rapp placed the tie on top of his jacket.

Haq nodded and swallowed nervously.

Rapp retrieved two photos from the envelope and laid

them on the table. "Do these people look familiar to you?" He began rolling up his sleeves.

The Pakistani intelligence officer looked reluctantly at the photos. He knew exactly who the two people were, but also knew it was exceedingly dangerous to admit such a thing. Haq had been on the giving end of enough interrogations to know that he had to stay the course and stick with his story. Slowly he shook his head and said, "No."

Even though Rapp had anticipated the answer it did nothing to placate his rage. He placed his right hand on the table and brought his left hand around with blinding speed, slapping Haq so hard he knocked him out of his chair and sent him sprawling across the floor.

"Wrong answer!" Rapp screamed as he stepped around the table, his closed fist raised and ready to bash down on top of Haq like a sledgehammer.

Haq lay stunned on the floor. It was the first time one of his captors had touched him. Panic set in and he threw his hands up to block the blow. "All right! All right! I know who they are, but I had nothing to do with their deaths!"

Rapp grabbed him by the throat, and even though Haq was a good twenty pounds heavier, he yanked him off the floor and slammed him against the wall like he was a rag doll. "Do you want to live, or die?"

Haq looked at him with honest confusion on his face, so Rapp repeated the question this time screaming it directly into his ear. "Do you want to live, or die?"

Haq croaked his answer. *"Liiiive."*

"Then you'd better get smart fast." Rapp threw him back toward the desk and shouted, "Sit your ass back down, and look at those photos!"

Rapp circled around behind him, his fists clenched and his face flushed with anger. "Now, Masood!" he shouted the man's first name. "I'm only going to ask you this one time. I know more about you than you can possibly imagine." Rapp pointed at the two black and white photos. Did you have any hand, either directly or indirectly, in the murder of these two CIA employees?"

This time Haq brought his hands up before he answered. "No." His eyes were wide with terror as he scrambled to come up with an answer, any answer that would keep this animal at bay. "I don't think so."

I don't think so, was better than an outright denial. "You don't think so," mocked Rapp. "Masood, I think you can do a whole lot better than that."

"I don't know . . ." he said nervously. "This is a danger-ous part of the world. People disappear all the time."

"Yeah . . . like you. You stupid piece of crap." Rapp turned his neck toward the ceiling and yelled, "Play cut one." A second later Haq's voice came over the speaker system. Although Rapp was fluent in both Arabic and Farsi, he didn't know Urdu well enough to understand what was being said. He'd read the translation enough times, though, to know it by heart. The tape was of a phone call placed from Haq to an unknown person requesting a meeting. When the short recording was over, Rapp asked for the second cut to be played.

Rapp grabbed another photo from the envelope and let it fall into Haq's lap. "Recognize this?"

Haq looked at the photo of himself having coffee with Akhtar Jilani, a high ranking member of the Taliban. He remembered the meeting well, and as he listened to the audio of their conversation he suddenly felt nauseated.

As the voices played from the speakers Rapp announced, "Pretty sloppy work for a guy who's in the business of spying." Rapp placed three small photos on the table in a very deliberate fashion. One was of an infant and the other two were toddlers. "Any idea who they are?"

Haq shook his head nervously.

"They are the children of the two men you had killed." Rapp let his words hang in the air uncomfortably so the reality of what Haq had done could sink in. Then in the same manner as before he placed five more photographs on the table. They were black and white surveillance photos, the cute faces of Haq's five children framed perfectly in each one. Rapp stared down menacingly at the man and watched in silence as Haq began to weep.

Through sniffles and sobs Haq pleaded, "Please . . . I beg of you, don't do anything to my children. This is my fault . . . not theirs."

Rapp's face twisted into a disgusted frown. "I don't kill children, you piece of shit." Tapping the photos of the three American kids he said, "They will never see their fathers again." Rapp began circling the table. "Look at their faces!" he screamed. "Tell me why your kids should get to see you again?"

Haq fingered the photos of his children and began sobbing uncontrollably. While Haq continued to weep, Rapp drew his 9-mm Beretta and began screwing into place a thick black silencer. When the silencer was attached, he extended the weapon and grabbed the well oiled slide, pulling it back and letting it slam forward with a resounding metal-on-metal clank.

With a hollow tipped round in the chamber Rapp pointed the weapon at the Pakistani intelligence officer's head and said, "I am a man of my word, Masood. If you ever want to see those kids again you'd better give me a reason to let you live. You'd better start singing like a bird. I want to know everything you know about the Taliban and al-Qaeda. I want to know what this bold plan is that you and Jilani were discussing, and if at any point, I find out you're lying to me, the deal is off, and I'll blow your brains all over the floor. "

Rapp's thumb reached up, flicked off the safety, and pulled the hammer all the way back into the cocked position. "So what's it going to be, Masood? Do you want to go to work for me and see your children grow up, or do you want to die?"

Vince Flynn
AMERICAN ASSASSIN

**What type of man is willing to kill for his country
without putting on a uniform?**

Six months ago, Mitch Rapp was just an ordinary
college student.

Then the Pan Am Lockerbie terrorist attack stole the lives of two
hundred and seventy passengers, leaving thousands grieving. And
Mitch Rapp hungry for revenge.

Just the man CIA Director Irene Kennedy needs for her new
group of clandestine operatives.

Now, after months of intense training, Mitch finds himself in
Istanbul, where he tracks down the arms dealer who sold the
explosives used in the attack. Rapp then moves onto Europe,
leaving a trail of bodies in his wake. But his final destination is
Beirut where, unwittingly, he will walk into a trap – and straight
into his enemy's clutches.

The hunter is about to become the hunted, and Rapp will need
every ounce of skill and cunning if he is to survive . . .

'A cracking, uncompromising yarn that literally takes no
prisoners' *The Times*

ISBN 978-1-84983-034-8

Vince Flynn
TRANSFER OF POWER

What if America's most powerful leader was also its prime target?

On a busy Washington morning, the stately calm of the White House is shattered in a hail of gunfire. A group of terrorists has gained control of the executive mansion by means of a violent massacre, leaving dozens dead. Through luck and quick thinking, the president is evacuated to his underground bunker – but not before almost one hundred hostages are taken.

One man is sent to take control of the crisis. Mitch Rapp, the CIA's top counterterrorism operative, determines that the president is not as safe as Washington's power elite thinks. Moving stealthily among the corridors and secret passageways of the White House, Rapp makes a chilling discovery that could rock America to its core: someone within his own government wants his rescue attempt to fail.

'Vince Flynn is Tom Clancy on speed. He grabs you by the scruff of the neck on page one and doesn't let go' Stephen Leather

ISBN 978-1-84983-473-5